A novel

BETWEEN THE CLOUDS AND CLOUDS AND THE RIVER

Dave Mason

ALSO BY DAVE MASON

EO-N

Born in England and raised in Canada, Dave Mason is an internationally recognized graphic designer and cofounder of a number of software companies. His first novel, EO-N, *is the recipient of more than twenty literary awards including the Hemingway Award for 20th Century Wartime Fiction, and has been acquired for film and television. He divides his time between Chicago, Illinois, and Lunenburg, Nova Scotia.*

Design by Pamela Kim Lee / Multiple Inc.
www.davemasonwrites.com

Library of Congress Control Number: 2024911182

ISBN: 978-1-7357064-3-6 hardback
ISBN: 978-1-7357064-4-3 paperback
ISBN: 978-1-7357064-5-0 ebook

To family.
And to everyone who isn't, but is.

The truth has a million faces.
But there is only one truth.

Hermann Hesse

1

The trembling blade hovers above the radial artery, poised to release a warm flood that will pool on the grimy plywood floor. Once liberated, he knows that the crimson flow will carry with it every thought and memory, every instinct, hope, fear, conceit, uncertainty, and lie ever held within the gray mass it has nourished for so many years. The dull roar of the flames beyond the padded walls threatens to drown out the whimpering cries, and acrid fumes begin to overpower the combined stench of burlap and urine and fear. And though they are recited over and over and over, the choking pleas for mercy barely resonate, because deep down in his soul, he finally knows his own truth.

2

The lumbering machine lurched and swerved and dipped and rolled like a top-heavy boat on rough seas, the massive weight of it wholly unsuited to the sands of the shifting dunes. Huddled like newly-hatched baby birds in the halftrack's open-topped steel bathtub—and roasting like chickens in a pan—Leutnant Bernhardt Lang and, he guessed, all seven of his comrades, were all wishing like hell they were somewhere other than hell.

He'd ended up here, in a sweltering, waterless wasteland some thirty-five kilometers from Ben Gardane, Tunisia, by choice. Or at least, he'd tried to convince himself, by a sliver of a choice.

Nearly twenty-five years into what he still hoped against hope might become his own life, Bernhardt had not been able to remember being asked to weigh in on any significant decision that had shaped it. Mapped out, planned and designed—but almost never by him—he'd followed a prescribed path.

His six years in the custody of the Prinz-Eugen-Akademie had taught him many things in exchange for what he could only assume had been a considerable sum of his father's money. Driven as much by fear of failure as by natural curiosity, he'd excelled at the school's rigid academic aspects, but had still managed to disappoint his father by gravitating toward the imagined and created instead of the calculated and executed.

At first, he'd actually believed in the core concepts that the school drummed into its students over and over: duty, honor, justice, and the innate superiority of the Germanic people. But within months, it seemed, those supposedly fundamental beliefs had been tarnished by a reality so often and so perfectly articulated and demonstrated by his professors and classmates alike: that shit flows downhill.

In order to survive, Bernhardt had done as he'd seen others do. He'd kept his head down and his mouth mostly shut, and had simply not acknowledged the fact that when he had opened it, it had often been in pursuit of gaining altitude by raining shit down upon those who occupied the slopes below him.

When he'd been called to the Wehrmacht, he'd once again found himself looking up, as another brown deluge had poured down upon him.

Still, he'd done well under pure military rule. He'd emerged as somewhat of a sharpshooter during his training, despite his recurring headaches and slightly off vision, a lingering and probably lifelong aftereffect, the various experts had guessed, of the serious head injury he'd sustained at age fourteen. The soft snow had become as unforgiving as a brick wall and as harsh as a paved road when impacted at full race speed, and the elite team of Austrian doctors, he'd later been told, had worked feverishly to save his life, even drilling a hole into his skull to relieve the pressure.

The seriousness of his injuries had been confirmed for him when he'd surfaced to discover that even his father had made the journey to Vienna. His mother had apparently prayed as hard as she could, especially when he'd died a little. Bernhardt hadn't known he'd died at all, of course, until he'd been informed when he'd eventually become alive again, his mother asking expectantly and excitedly if he'd "seen the bright light" or "reached out and touched the hand." From beneath his bandages, he'd not been able to see her disappointment in his answer, but he'd felt it just the same.

As the brutally inelegant Hanomag struggled to skirt another of the million or so identical dunes it had managed to navigate during its torturous life, the monotony of its maddening yet comforting symphony of grinding vibrations, rumbles, creaks, and groans suddenly shattered into a thousand violent hammer strikes.

"Raus! Raus! Raus! Raus!"

Barely audible even to himself, Bernhardt detected his own voice. In a slow motion dream, he turned to see the recently promoted idiot, Hauptmann Bauer, frantically searching for his weapon on the metal deck as the rear hatch slammed down and the two soldiers closest to it dropped out. Bernhardt flinched instinctively as one of the men vaporized, a large portion of his upper torso transformed into a bright pink mist in the blinding desert sunlight, his helmet spinning crazily through the air to clatter to a final resting place on the vehicle's scalding gridplate.

As soon as the next pair of men tumbled and stumbled from the vehicle, Bernhardt and two others followed them like lemmings over a cliff.

First boots, then knees, then elbows and torso sinking into the scorching sand, he rolled to his right in an attempt to find cover behind the desert turtle's steel track, just as a projectile of some sort punched a clangorous hole through the vehicle's pathetically thin shell. Oddly, the subsequent detonation was both crushing and weirdly soundless as the high explosive instantly ignited every nonmetallic item still inside the disabled machine. He looked up just as Bauer—at least he thought it was Bauer—flew heels over head from the inferno to land a couple of meters beyond him, screaming his final breaths into the sand as the fire consumed him.

Squinting into the glaring landscape, unable to locate the unseen attackers, Bernhardt struggled to breathe away his fear, and to assess the situation. Around him, most of his comrades lay dying or dead in the sand, the vehicle's driver, he figured, likely roasted in his seat. To his left were two seemingly untouched survivors, the last of the six replacements who'd arrived a week or so back. Ears still filled with a smothering, high-pitched roar, he could only see the silent screams in their wild eyes.

A pair of fast-moving vehicles suddenly emerged from behind a dune about fifty meters to the south. Bernhardt could see they were fitted with the kinds of heavy weapons usually found on aeroplanes, and they were driven by bearded wild men who wore leather gauntlets, aviator goggles, and Bedouin-style head coverings. Like wolves circling mortally wounded prey, the two vehicles easily flanked the shattered halftrack, their crews relentlessly pouring machine gun rounds into its burning hulk.

One of the terrified young soldiers had apparently had enough. Throwing his rifle into the sand and his hands into the air, he rose to his knees, shouting something unintelligible. Almost immediately, his companion echoed his initiative. Bernhardt shouted to warn them, but detected no voice when he opened his mouth. When a bullet passed through the outside of the closest soldier's thigh, however, Bernhardt's brain paused to take note of the fact that he could suddenly hear the boy's screams.

Ignoring the impact puffs, Bernhardt scrambled over the sand and put his full weight on the terrified soldier's stomach, then he jammed his knuckles deep into the wound, yelling above the boy's shrieking and the roaring flames and the jarring metallic bullet strikes for the other young soldier to remove his tunic belt and tie off his wounded comrade's leg.

In the chaos, none of them saw the four khaki-clad, keffiyeh-wearing Tommies who materialized from the dunes right behind them, screaming at the tops of their lungs for them to put their "fuckin' 'ands in the fuckin' air!" But when the world went suddenly, terribly silent, Bernhardt heard them loud and clear.

It was over.

3

Miraculously, against any and all odds, Frank Gardner managed to detect a faint whiff of woodsmoke through his own personal fumes. Perhaps more incredibly, he got himself out of his front porch chair and around to the west side of his house in only a few seconds.

Without stopping to think, he kicked in the partially open shed door to find a kid—a boy—laid out among the assorted cartons and tools and junk on the grimy plank floor, faceup, eyes squeezed shut, arms outstretched. Holding his breath against the smoke, he snatched the kid up and got him the hell out of there just as the bottom edge of the rickety old structure's ancient boards began to flicker and crackle, then shuffled him around to his porch while simultaneously checking him for damage as best he could. To Frank's amazement, the kid didn't make a goddamn sound as he set him down against the wall and barked at him to stay put.

As fast as he could, he rambled back around the house to unspool his wall-mounted garden hose and turn its stingy flow on the now ambitious flames. A few minutes later, the pint-sized blaze effectively put down, Frank lit up a cigarette and watched with some satisfaction as a plume of white vapor snaked its way up through a few raindrops and disappeared into the gray clouds beyond the towering black firs and cedars.

He'd shut off the faucet and was looping the hose back onto its holder when the sound of crunching gravel got his attention. One eyebrow arched, he watched the squad car's familiar passenger-side occupant jump out and strut across his muddy driveway toward the gently steaming shed. By the time Frank had made his way to his front steps, the vehicle had also disgorged its less enthusiastic driver, who commenced smartassing the moment he got himself vertical and laid eyes on Frank.

"Hey, Frank," he said, "what's going on? Someone said they saw smoke. We figured it was just you lighting up another coffin nail, but we thought we better come check it out just the same."

"Just letting off a little steam, Whitmore," said Frank. "Sorry to ruin your nap."

The cop scanned the scene, quickly zeroing in on the life-sized statue sitting on the porch. Shaking his head as he walked toward the house, he fished a small black notebook and a stubby yellow pencil from his breast pocket. In the shelter of the top porch step, he stuck his tongue out to wet the lead and began scribbling.

"Well," he said, "look who we've got here. Wouldn't wanna be this kid when he gets home. Sure as shit gonna face some music."

"Music?" said Frank through a cloud. "The hell does that mean?"

Kusyk—the passenger-side cop—suddenly reappeared, speed walking around the corner and nodding a silent okay at Whitmore before delivering his succinct report. "Fire's out, Bob." He knocked the rain from his hat as he stepped up onto Frank's porch, and stopped dead in his tracks at the sight of the boy. "Oh, boy," he said. "Sorry, Frank, but it seems like this kid's just trouble, you know? Third time we've had to collect him from someplace or other in the last few months. Never done anything like this though. I mean, really. Arson?"

Frank took a slow pull on his cigarette and glanced over at the boy. *This kid,* he thought, *wasn't interested in arson.*

"Trouble?" said Whitmore. "Trouble's putting it mildly. My guess is his parents did their damnedest—well, his father, anyhow, since the deadbeat mother just up and took off—but I got no doubt this one's eventually headed to the pen. Him and a few others around here. But we try to look on the bright side," he said, chuckling at his own joke before he'd even told it. "They're the ones keeping us cops in the cop business, eh?"

Frank looked the kid over. He sat on the porch exactly where he'd left him, as motionless as a stack of firewood, but for the occasional suppressed cough or sniffle. Tear and rain streaks on his grimy face revealed smooth, pale skin, and his dark eyes were intense as they stared, barely blinking, at the worn sole of one of Frank's old boots, tipped over near the porch railing.

Whitmore worked at tucking his notebook back into his pocket. "You wanna press charges, Frank?"

Frank arched an eyebrow. "Goddamn good thing you Mounties always get your man. Hell, no, I'm not gonna press charges."

Head shaking side to side, Frank thumped across his porch and through his front door, returning a moment later. He flicked the last inch of his cigarette onto the wet gravel and turned his back to the cops. It took longer than it should have, but after convincing his reluctant lower limbs to do the almost impossible, he managed to sit cross-legged on the porch decking directly in front of the cross-legged boy. *That's a reflection,* Frank thought, *you probably don't wanna see.* He took a deep breath.

"I'm Frank Gardner," he said. "What's your name?"

Nothing.

The kid remained as inert as the grim remains of the small book he'd been clutching when Frank had found him. Now it lay like a dead thing on the planks between them, its black cover bent back to reveal shredded edges where the fire-starter pages had once lived.

"Don't care much for books?" said Frank.

Nothing.

Frank glanced over his left shoulder at the two cops, both of them variously pointing at the kid and gesturing in the general direction of the shed and jabbering at each other, pretending to do cop things, but most likely, Frank thought, talking hockey.

He turned back to the kid.

"Listen," he said, voice low. "Those guys don't know the whole deal, and it's okay with me if they never do. How about we keep what almost happened here today between us?"

An almost imperceptible something stirred somewhere behind the kid's thousand-yard eyes.

Releasing an involuntary groan, Frank reached forward, grabbed the kid's black book, and pulled it into the shadow of his aching knees, between his mud-caked boots.

"How about a trade?" he said. "I keep that, and you take this?" He extracted a small object from his jacket pocket and placed it on the deck between them, right where the book had been, its yellow wrapper and big black and red letters the exact opposite of the tiny gold leaf letters stamped into the rippled ebony of the small volume's austere exterior.

"Hey, Frank?" Kusyk called out. "We gotta get the kid home. Someone'll be calling you later to talk to you about your shed."

"Okay, okay!" said Frank. "Just give me one goddamn minute more, would you?"

Turning back to the boy, voice low and soft again, Frank nodded at the brightly colored object.

"Yours if you want it," he said. "Consider it a present. From me to you. A thank you, really, for reminding me that I've been thinkin' about fixing up that shed."

Nothing.

Frank nodded toward the yellow-wrapped object.

"That's named after a real good friend of mine," said Frank, "but with an exclamation point, which means you gotta say it loud. Like you really mean it, even if you're just saying it inside your head. Anyway, you hang on to it. For later, maybe, when you wanna feel some good."

A long moment passed before the boy, without glancing up, reached out and tucked Frank's offering into the pocket of his wet and smoke-stinking jacket.

Frank nodded as he picked up the black book and dropped it into his own jacket pocket, then held out his gnarly right hand, the thumb—seemingly attached to the rest of his hand by a thick wedge of scar tissue—dead vertical. Eyes back to their semi-focus on the old boot, the kid slowly extended a grime- and snot-smeared hand, and Frank gave it a firm but gentle shake.

"Frank," he said. "Thanks for stopping by."

Squinting through another cloud of white smoke, Frank could barely make out the top of the kid's black-mopped head through the rivulets of rain on the police cruiser's rear window as it spit gravel and pulled away.

4

They were a sorry lot. More than two hundred of them crowded the barbed wire compound, hot, filthy, stinking, and perpetually thirsty.

Two and a half hours after their surrender, Bernhardt and the two surviving replacements had been delivered here by four of the jeep-riding Long Range Desert Patrol wild men who'd so efficiently wiped out the rest of their comrades. Bernhardt had been impressed by their daring, and by their demeanor. The Tommies were tough, most certainly, and good at desert killing, but they'd treated their captives with surprising respect, and given them food and water and cigarettes. And the British had provided excellent field first aid to the boy with the gaping wound in his thigh. He'd since disappeared, presumably—hopefully—to a hospital tent somewhere.

"Don't you worry, mate," one of the Tommies had said as he'd lit Bernhardt's cigarette and thumped him hard on the shoulder. "Your friend there may be in the fuckin' desert, but 'e'll be right as fuckin' rain in no time!"

The bearded soldier and his friends had all laughed uproariously at the joke, Bernhardt thought, obviously meant for their own benefit. He'd never let on that, thanks in large part to his grandmother, and to

Cary Grant, and to some extent his hated schooling, he'd understood almost half of their words.

A few hours later, in a very polite conversation with a couple of German-speaking British officers sitting at a table inside a sweltering canvas tent, Bernhardt had shared the minimum—enough fragments of the truth—to convince them that what he'd told them was all he knew. After all, he'd explained, in German, he was just a freshly minted leutnant. No one, he'd said, had ever told him much more than where to go and which direction to shoot in when he got there. And, he'd pointed out, no one had ever taken the time to tell him why any of this had ever been necessary in the first place.

For nearly four days inside the wire, they'd waited. And wondered. And they'd slept rough, with grossly insufficient numbers of only the thinnest of blankets, forcing angry, unhappy, thirsty, hungry, injured, exhausted, and quarrelsome men into close quarters to try to keep the frigid night air at bay.

Today, Bernhardt had guessed by the level of activity outside the perimeter, would be the day they'd move.

Like dust-covered sheepdogs with tin helmets and bayonets, about two dozen loudly barking British soldiers had eventually rounded up Bernhardt and the others and pointed them in the same direction, and within an hour's plodding march roughly eastward under a blistering sun, they'd been joined by what had looked to Bernhardt to be a few hundred more battered and downcast German and Italian prisoners.

Within another four hours, their ranks had been swollen by what Bernhardt guessed had to be another seven hundred or so grimy new faces. It was only near sundown, when their heavily armed escort— now multiplied, he estimated, to fifty or sixty Tommy and Indian guards—had delivered them to a much larger and more densely populated barbed wire compound, that he began to guess at the true scale of their defeat.

Eight miserable days later, following another shivering predawn chow line that had ended with a mug of reasonably hot tea and a bowl of not quite cold porridge, Bernhardt found himself included in one of the first cohorts of bedraggled and exhausted prisoners to be jammed into a khaki-colored, canvas-backed truck.

Over the next five and a half hours, they traveled east, to a port, where Bernhardt and his new companions had been surprised to be well fed and then guided, to their growing alarm and consternation, aboard an American freighter.

They were the cargo, the rumor mill quickly divulged, to be carried by a flotilla of recently unloaded merchant vessels as it attempted to return to North America, where it would no doubt take on yet another load of weapons and materiel destined to contribute to the annihilation of German forces in North Africa, and then, Bernhardt assumed, in Sicily, and Italy, and beyond.

The prisoners all knew full well the risks involved in ocean travel, but, as Bernhardt heard them repeatedly remind each other, none of them really had much choice in the matter.

As for Bernhardt himself, personally he was more than happy to be in one piece, out of the line of fire and out of the desert—for the time being at least—and in the hands of the British and Americans. The alternatives, he knew, were so much less pleasant to contemplate.

On the deck of the dull gray American liberty ship, he actually felt liberated, rather than imprisoned, and under the watchful eyes of his heavily armed but strangely tranquil new hosts, he slowly but surely wiggled his way to the ship's rail, where the soft ocean breeze cooled the midafternoon Mediterranean air and the crowded calm allowed him to smoke. And to think. Perhaps the Americans were placid, he thought, because they knew things he didn't? Perhaps their almost casual confidence was rooted in ideas or realities of which Germany simply had no concept?

At any rate, he'd noted, the food his new keepers had provided down on the docks had filled his belly most pleasantly, proof enough for him that Germany, with its meager and virtually tasteless rations, was doomed. After all, an army—he'd learned from either Napoleon, or Frederick the Great, or maybe from Schneider, the asshole feldwebel he'd endured back in Munich—marches on its stomach.

Long before the ship's horn sounded three long blasts later that evening, Bernhardt had fully resigned himself—as, he was sure, had the majority of the other three hundred and forty-two POWs onboard the SS *Sea Owl*—to a new fate. Whatever that fate might ultimately entail, none of them could know.

But, Bernhardt had decided, at this point at least, this new war was a hell of a lot better than the one he'd been in two weeks ago.

5

For four consecutive days, the warm sun and the Atlantic's gentle roll had lent a deceptively peaceful calm to the journey, and Bernhardt had decided to relish the sensation as long as he could. On land, in the transit camps, he'd had room to move, space in which to keep his head down and his mouth shut and to keep to himself as much as possible. But now, on the densely packed ship, the conversations were practically unavoidable.

"Their camps are fucking brutal."

A gap-toothed airman who claimed he'd been unlucky enough to parachute into British hands somewhere near Tobruk was spouting off. "You know they're just fucking with us now," he said, "treating us with a little kindness so they can hammer us when they have us where they want us."

"Horse shit," came the succinct reply.

A one-armed tank gunner apparently captured in a battle near Benghazi, the speaker had introduced himself to Bernhardt as simply "Krumpf" on the second day out. They'd shared a few silent cigarettes since. "They've had us where they wanted us for weeks…" he said. "Some of us for months. And they have us where they want us right now. Why the fuck would they treat us better in a combat area compound or on a prison ship than they would in a camp in the middle of America?" As he turned, he blew cigarette smoke toward Bernhardt, but the wind whipped the white cloud away. "What do you think?"

"I think you guys think too damn much," said Bernhardt, his half cigarette bobbing in unison with his chapped and cracked lips, his eyes narrowed to the glaring sun. "We're on this boat, in calm seas, under a warm sun, eating decent food, and heading away from a lot of people and places that tried to kill us. You're worried about what's ahead? I say just enjoy the ride and figure out the future when we get to it."

Bernhardt turned to the railing and squinted into the brilliant starbursts glinting off the swells. He had no idea how many days it might take to get them where they were actually going, he only knew that every second of every minute of every hour took him further away from the parched hell of North Africa.

When the torpedo hit nine hours later, Bernhardt was in his bunk belowdecks, hovering, as he'd trained himself to be, somewhere between unrelenting vigilance and blissful oblivion. The initial crump and violent shudder of the impact had been followed by deeply resonating grinding and piercing creaking sounds that were quickly joined by shrill alarm bells, shouts of panic, and the escalating roar of frantic men hammering desperately on locked bulkhead doors as the ship's dim interior lights suddenly flickered and went dark.

Fully dressed, boots on, Bernhardt leaped to his feet, heart and adrenaline pumping.

Every day since they'd set sail, and eventually with his eyes closed, he'd traced the steps from his bunk to the bulkhead door, from the bulkhead door up to the next deck, and from the next deck up to the world. Now that preparation took control. Gripping the rails and stanchions he'd mapped out in his head, he counted his footsteps off out loud as he fought his way through the panicked bedlam of men colliding and cursing and clambering every which way in the blackness.

Within seconds, he bumped up against a loud throng of frantic prisoners pushing and shoving each other, their combined weight no doubt threatening to crush those unlucky enough to be jammed against the steel bulkhead and door. The deck tilting beneath his feet sent a wave of barely suppressed panic through his gut. Suddenly, two beams of bright light swept over the melee. A couple of American sailors with flashlights and pistols yelled something unintelligible, and immediately the trapped prisoners surged forward to try to propel themselves through the opening. A single shot rang out as one of the Americans stumbled backward, the bullet going God knows where.

Desperate to keep his feet beneath him, Bernhardt fought to surf the flow of humanity through the hatchway and up the two ladders that led to the ship's main deck. A massive wave of relief temporarily washed away his claustrophobic dread as the bowels of the ship ejected him into a fresh terror of shivering blackness, driving rain, and absolute chaos.

To his left, some of the American sailors were firing the ship's stern-mounted deck gun, shooting, Bernhardt could only assume, at what they must have thought was the shadow of their enemy. Unseen others above and behind him were squirting what he guessed were smaller caliber antiaircraft shells across the waves, the arcs of their white phosphorous tracers burning multiple afterimages into his retinas, the intermittent muzzle flashes periodically illuminating the pandemonium all around him. In the stroboscopic confusion, he saw a couple of Amis struggling to lower a lifeboat. When one of them clubbed a prisoner who tried to push past him, the violent downward sweep of his pistol crumpled the man to the deck, and others immediately stepped onto and over him.

Bernhardt felt a sudden hard pull on his sleeve and coiled himself to strike at its source.

"Hey! Hey!" A burst of machine gun lightning revealed the tank gunner, Krumpf, tugging at him with his one hand. "This way. Come on!" He turned and shouldered himself through the mob, Bernhardt tight on his tail, and they fought to make their way toward the back of the ship.

"Going down by the stern," the gunner yelled, "probably holed near the engine room! If we're going to get off it's got to be from back here. We can just step into the water and swim for it, hopefully find a lifeboat or something to float us when we get clear. If we go the other way we're fucked. We'll get pulled under. You ready, man?!"

Bernhardt felt his chest heaving, his pulse hammering. *Hell no,* he thought, *but what choice do I have?*

The ship was, in fact, tilting them steadily toward the black water at its stern, and it had started an increasingly disconcerting roll to starboard, escalating the disorientation and fear. The roar of indecipherable voices rose as the horde of panic-stricken men around them began to scramble for higher places, toward the bow. Fighting hard to control his breathing, Bernhardt turned as Krumpf yelled.

"This is it, man! Time to go!"

They moved quickly sternward along the starboard railing.

Almost unable to think, his mind and his body struggling for any sense of equilibrium, Bernhardt practically resigned himself to the role of observer as he followed Krumpf's lead. Thirty seconds later, heart pounding, hands shaking, he climbed the railing and paused with one leg over each side, momentarily straddling the known and the unknown.

For a long, strange second, Bernhardt marveled at the perfectly ironic, insane beauty of it all.

Just weeks ago he'd been in a sun-bleached, waterless wasteland, in danger of being killed by his enemies, and now he was on the verge of plunging into the sunless depths of a watery grave, propelled there by his own countrymen.

He swung his inboard leg over to the ocean side of the railing, and held himself above the surging, swirling blackness. As he glanced up to see Krumpf's asymmetrical form backlit by the sporadic flashes of tracer rounds still emanating from somewhere above them, the two men's terror-widened eyes met in the flashbulb madness and they nodded to each other.

Then, almost simultaneously, they launched themselves into the Atlantic ocean.

6

For a time, the quiet room had been anything but.

The boy felt like he'd cried forever, but, he knew from bitter experience, forever only feels like a long time. It doesn't last forever.

Through the night, his rage and his thirst and his hunger and the glare of the naked light bulb had prevented him from actually sleeping, but he hadn't been able to prevent himself from wetting his pants, and now his own stench mingled with the dry burlap stink of the room. With his free hand, he reached through the hole in his jacket pocket and closed his fingers around the bright yellow paper-wrapped object tucked between the shell and liner.

Earlier, in the house, his father had simply been too busy to discover it, too busy slapping the back of his head over and over in order to punctuate his low-toned but pointed admonishments, that he—slap—"will not tolerate insolence." That he—slap—"will not tolerate disobedience."

The physical assault had temporarily ceased as they'd made the walk. Once outside, Joseph had known better than to do anything that might exacerbate things in the barn. He'd made that mistake once. Of course, when they'd reached the muffled confines of the quiet room, the auditory violence had resumed, abating only as the restraints had been placed around his ankle and wrist. Then the barrage of demands for repentance had quickly escalated, punctuated by excruciating and paralyzing jolts that threatened to smash his teeth and jaws as they crushed against each other.

He'd made barely a sound, said not a single word, during any of the torment. He'd decided long ago that he'd never give his father that satisfaction again. He was never sure if that made things go easier or harder, but he'd decided that would be his way.

Only when the handleless door had been left ajar and he'd been left alone in the stinking silence had he allowed his heaving cries to accompany the liquid rage and frustration and despair and loneliness that flowed down his cheeks.

After a time, drained of his tears, almost emptied of his defiance, his thoughts drifted, his mind desperate to take him someplace good. When a sharp pain, possibly real, possibly imagined, jolted him back to reality, he suddenly remembered the hidden object. Free of his shackles and hearing nothing but his own breathing, he took a chance and fished the thing out. Its shiny yellow and red and black delivered an instant shock of color to the monochrome room.

Oh Henry!

He mouthed the words, being sure to yell them in his mind, as he'd been instructed, and he wondered what other kinds of friends the old man might have if one of them had had an actual chocolate bar named after him.

Suddenly conscious of the passage of time, he turned the beautiful thing over in his hand once more before carefully stuffing it back into its hiding place.

This time, he'd been able to endure.

He'd save the feel-good, he thought, for when he really needed it.

7

The old girl was barely cutting it, her worn out gears, Frank thought, grinding about as badly as his knees did on cold October mornings. And he'd noticed that while the mostly downhill going-to-town runs were hard enough on what was left of the truck's brakes, the heading-back-home opposites were a serious challenge for its over-the-hill engine.

At the main road, he swung left and felt the pickup surge and practically sigh with relief to be on pavement once again, the machine suddenly seeming almost confident in its ability to negotiate the rain-slicked but less demanding contours of the pitted two lane blacktop that ran alongside the river. A few minutes later, he steered to a stop, cranked the ignition key counterclockwise, and waited patiently for the aging blue beast to hammer and knock itself into silence. Beyond its cracked and wiper-scarred windshield, a small, manicured patch of wet greenness lay in deference to an imposing limestone facade, designed, Frank fully understood, to project power to those who were on the wrong side of it.

Flipping his collar up against the drizzling chill, he cut across the grass, climbed the granite steps, and swung open one of the heavy, oversized doors. The institutional smell hit him like an old, wet blanket, an unpleasant olfactory combination, he guessed, of the building's age, layer after layer of yellowed floor wax, endless gallons of disinfectant, and the sour demeanors of generations of its occupants.

Black and gold leaf lettering on rippled, wire-gridded glass told him where to go next.

"Morning, ma'am," he said. "My name's Frank Gardner. I'm here to see, uh…"—he squinted at the letter in his hand—"…Principal Holliman."

"Oh, yes, good morning, Mr. Gardner. Mr. Holliman is expecting you." The smile-free woman behind the desk stood as she spoke, and Frank took her next words more as a command than an invitation.

"Follow me."

She led him down a short, wood-paneled hallway, past a gallery of black-framed photographs of dour, gray people, their discouraging faces, Frank thought, clearly designed by nature to have the exact same effect on the powerless as the building itself.

Frank heard a baritone voice mumble something as the woman announced him, and in seconds an impeccably dressed, Brylcreemed man was at the door, smiling and gripping Frank's hand with both of his and pulling him extra close as the woman beat a hasty retreat.

"Mr. Gardner," said the man. "I'm Principal Holliman. So good of you to come on this terribly dreary day." He put a hand on Frank's back and applied a gentle but insistent pressure to guide him. "Please, please," he said. "Come in, and make yourself comfortable."

As Frank nodded and maneuvered himself into one of the office's two oak visitor chairs, Principal Holliman made his way around his substantial desk, its polished surface geometrically populated with an engraved gold plastic nameplate, a black bordered green blotter, a black telephone, and a wooden tray holding a white teapot, white cups and saucers, two silver spoons, and white containers of milk and sugar.

It took Frank a second or three to register it, but soon after his meticulous host had assumed his position, he concluded that the rock hard seat of his own chair seemed to be set at least a couple of inches lower than the padded one on the other side of the wide wooden expanse, the net result being that for a few moments at least, he and Lionel J. Holliman saw almost eye to eye.

Hands tightly clasped, smiling a deeply concerned smile, Holliman jumped right in. "I'm so very sorry about the damage to your garden shed, Mr. Gardner. And by a malicious act of arson. Tremendously upsetting, I'm sure. Can I offer you some tea?"

"Thanks, Mr. Holliman," said Frank, "but no, not really all that upsetting. Not for me at least. And I'll pass on the tea."

The principal nodded as he spooned two perfectly flat teaspoons of sugar into a cup, then stirred the liquid counterclockwise, exactly three times.

"Well I'm certainly relieved to hear that, Mr. Gardner. It's kind of you to be so understanding, given the circumstances."

"Yeah, well," said Frank, "that shed was mostly full of old junk that hadn't seen the light of day for a while. And it probably would've fallen down all by itself before long, anyway. I just wanted to be sure everything was okay. You know, no real harm done?"

"Mmmm," said Holliman, pausing for a sip. "No one seems to have suffered any injuries, if that's what you mean. But as for the structure, Mr. Gardner… I assume you'd like to at least repair it? I'm happy to offer you some small compensatory amount for your troubles. Say, three hundred dollars? To cover your materials? And of course, in cases of student vandalism, I insist on a degree of personal responsibility in rectifying any damage caused."

Frank had guessed some kind of cash offer might be coming. He hadn't figured on the second part of the deal. Neither of them was the reason he'd come here today, but then again, he wasn't really sure why he'd agreed to come.

"Yeah," said Frank, "I guess I might consider that. But just so I'm straight, how does a young kid get held personally responsible for something like that? How's he supposed to come up with three hundred dollars?"

Holliman cleared his throat and shifted in his chair. He placed his cup in its saucer. "Oh, I'm sorry," he said. "Please excuse my lack of clarity. Because the, ah, incident occurred while the child was under the jurisdiction of the school, during school hours, the school will cover the cash compensation. The child himself is twelve, almost thirteen, quite old enough to be responsible for his penance. As I said, it's our policy that wherever possible, vandals and…and other ne'er-do-wells must pay in some way. They must work to atone."

"Well, I don't know about that," said Frank. "I'm not interested in babysitting. And I can't be responsible if a kid gets hurt."

The principal smiled. "Please, Mr. Gardner. As you'll see here, a parental agreement has been signed, and all liabilities have been waived. And the physical work will no doubt do the boy some good."

Holliman slid a sheaf of typewritten papers and a black fountain pen across the desk. "In this case," he said, "the proposal is at least seven hours per Saturday for eight weeks. You can pick the boy up right here, in front of the school. He'll be here at 7:00 a.m. sharp. I'll personally guarantee it."

As Frank made the turn off the relatively smooth paved road and onto the lumpy gravel, he glanced down at the envelope concealing its fifteen crisp twenties and the agreement he'd signed, legal absolution, he knew, intended more to protect the school and the offender's parents from any further repercussions than to protect him. Bouncing gently in the notch between the pickup's bench seat and its back, the envelope's pristine whiteness looked about as out of place in his world as a twelve year old kid.

But beyond all of that, Frank couldn't stop thinking about the fact that until he'd seen it typed out in black and white—until he'd brought it up himself—Principal Lionel J. Holliman had never once mentioned that he and the boy he'd just sentenced to hard labor actually shared the same last name.

8

He'd gotten airborne a couple of times, but he'd never made a peep. When the weather-beaten truck finally clunked and clattered itself into silence, its equally timeworn driver climbed out and walked around to its passenger side. Then the old man—anyone with gray hair just had to be old—yanked the rusted door open. As he turned to walk away, he barked something almost unintelligible.

"Pitter-patter," he said, "let's get at 'er!"

The boy swung his legs around and slid himself down off the vinyl seat, boots landing with a crunchy thud on muddy gravel. He raised his eyes just in time to see the broad back of a red and black checked shirt disappearing behind the unfortunately familiar house.

"Well?" he heard the man yell into the trees. "You comin' or not, kid?!"

Joseph stood rooted like a tree for what felt like at least an hour before plucking up enough courage to inch his way toward the corner of the porch, the sounds of snapping, cracking, banging, and creaking getting louder as he got closer. Five steps further revealed the spectacle of weathered and charred boards flying through the air to clatter themselves into a rapidly growing jumble. Three more steps revealed the old man hunched over, cigarette dangling, ankle deep in wreckage, knocking one of the still-vertical boards loose with a hammer.

"You know," said the man, "I never liked this shed."

Joseph had no idea if that was something he was actually supposed to know. Thankfully, before he could even begin to try to figure it out, the man continued. "Full of worn out stuff and used up junk," he said. "Reminded me of myself every goddamn time I looked at it."

Joseph stood stock-still, unsure what to do. The old man nodded to his left.

"There's gloves on that stump there," he said. "You gotta protect yourself. Always. That's job one in this nasty goddamn world. And there's another hammer in that bucket. Soon as you're ready, you jump in here and help me."

Joseph couldn't remember the last time he'd been asked to "help" an adult do anything. He'd been told what to do plenty of times. Told to dig the vegetable patch. Told to mow the lawn and trim the hedges and rake the leaves and sweep the barn. Told to wash the windows. Told to make his bed and to get down on his knees and scrub the floors and toilets with soap that burned his hands and eyes and left his skin cracked and dry and red. And he'd been told to do lots of other things that he hadn't wanted to do. But asked to "help" an adult? Not in a long, long time.

The well-used gloves were way too big for him, the cuffs extending almost halfway to his elbows, but somehow their pre-bent fingers felt oddly right, the dirty brown leather almost caressing the backs of his hands, a little hard and crusty on his palms. He clenched his fists and felt the pleasant resistance of the shiny, sweat- and grime-tanned surfaces as they surrendered. Cautiously, he shuffled nearer to the old man and gripped the wooden handle protruding from the faded red pail. As another board clattered onto the growing pile, the source of its airborne journey stretched with a loud groan and arched a slightly graying eyebrow his way. The old man flared up a fresh cigarette and nodded toward the partially skinned shed.

"Well, kid," he said, "this is why you're here. I guess your father figures you got a personal debt to pay. I figure what the hell. Wood right there," he said, "and yank any nails you see like this."

Joseph watched carefully as the man showed him how to tap the pointy end of a nail, flip the board over, slide the curved, V-shaped part of the hammer under the slightly protruding nub, and lever the corroded brown metal from its place. The man held the result up for inspection before dropping it into a battered coffee can.

"Don't worry," he said. "You'll get the hang pretty quick. We can reuse the good ones. Save a buck or three, right? And don't go hurting yourself. Or me."

Within a couple of virtually wordless and sweaty hours, they'd made themselves a pretty good pile of boards and had collected what looked to Joseph to be about a half of a tin of nails. And once he had gotten the hang of things, he'd surprised himself by feeling strangely okay about it all.

Abruptly, the old man let loose an especially loud groan and tossed his hammer into the red bucket, the volume of the human-generated sound more startling than the clatter the tool had created.

"Okay, kid," he said, "when a man's done a good job of work, he's earned himself a sit down and something good to eat. Come on."

They sat in the shade of the porch and ate. Cheese, dry sausage, bread, some bright red tomatoes the man said he'd grown himself, and a couple of glasses of cold lemonade to drink. Joseph sat cross-legged on the boards, arms like heavy rubber bands, but feeling weirdly, achingly good. He watched the man stab at chunks of food with a beat up old knife, intermittently sticking it into the porch decking.

When the stabbing and eating were done, the man slipped his knife into the leather sheath on his belt, pulled his sweat-rimed, dirt colored hat down over his eyes, and with a freshly lit cigarette dangling from his lips, tipped himself back against the wall of the house, one foot propped up on an upside down tin bucket, his bulk audibly taxing the old wooden chair. Via peripheral vision, Joseph watched him open one eye and take his cigarette out of his mouth.

"So, uh, you ever talk at all?" the man asked through a white cloud. "Ever, you know, put a couple of words together, in a row, and kinda let 'em come out of your mouth so other people can hear 'em? It's good to do that sometimes. Reminds us we're different from other animals."

The old man paused for another deep drag and sent the resulting plume of white smoke skyward before continuing.

"Well," he said, "that's what somebody tried to tell me once. But I've been around people who were just like animals, and animals I'd swear were people. You know what I mean?"

Eyes down, mind full of words that would never be heard, Joseph took another silent sip of lemonade.

"Well, maybe you don't know what I mean," said the old man. "I hope you don't anyway. You're too damn young to have to know about any of that stuff."

With another thundering suddenness that startled Joseph enough to make him jump, the man dropped his foot from the bucket and slammed the two front legs of his chair onto the porch decking. Then, seemingly propelled by another alarming groan, he lurched to his feet.

"You remind me a little," he said, "of another guy I knew once. Real hard worker. Never said much. Funny though, when he did talk, he always had something to say. You did real good today, Joseph…" He reached up and patted the cigarette pack in his shirt pocket.

"Joseph. Is that what I should call you? Or you got somethin' else? Like Joe? Joey? Maybe one day when you feel like putting a couple of words together you can tell me if it's something otherwise. 'Til then, it is what it is."

Unsure what to make of anything that had happened over the previous six hours, but through much more curious eyes than he'd owned when he'd opened them that morning, Joseph Holliman watched Frank Gardner lumber down his porch steps, simultaneously extracting his pack of smokes and yelling into the trees.

"Come on, kid!" he called out. "Another hour, then I gotta get you back before you turn into a pumpkin."

9

In the six long days since they'd last met, the old man had done some shopping.

Still nervous—but not quite as nervous—Joseph reached a hand down to fish the designated pair of worn leather gloves from the red bucket, simultaneously eyeing the stacks of new lumber and shingles sitting near the cinder block and concrete foundation of the old shed.

"Oh, hey," said the man, flaming another cigarette as he walked toward him. "Almost forgot. That bag right there? On top of those new boards? That's for you."

Joseph's eyes flitted to the lumber pile, then back to Frank, then back to the lumber pile. His stomach climbed up a few rungs. He wasn't sure if he was really supposed to, wasn't quite sure if a trick was being played on him, but after the old man nodded and blew smoke in the bag's direction, Joseph shuffled over and opened it.

Heart pumping a little faster, he peered inside.

Light brown and shine free, the gloves were pristine, brand new, and still connected to each other by a string. He wriggled into one of them and its delicious texture hugged him. Instinctively, he raised his hand to his face and breathed deeply, the rich aromas of flawless leather and fresh lumber and dry pine forest wrapping around him like a blanket.

"Well, whaddya know," said Frank, suddenly and somewhat scarily looming over him. "Fits you like a glove! Get it?" That got the man grinning and coughing as he reached to his belt and extracted his old knife.

"Here," he said, offering the leather wrapped, beaded handle to Joseph. "Cut that tie, there. They kinda work a little better if you put one on each hand."

Joseph cut the string, then held the knife blade out to Frank.

"Uh-uh," said Frank, hands at his sides. "First, this knife is sacred, so you gotta say a little thank you in your head every time you use it. And second, so are my fingers. Whenever you pass someone something sharp, unless you're actually plannin' to do some damage, you offer 'em the handle first. What they do after that isn't your problem."

Chagrined, Joseph spun the knife around and carefully gripped its blade. Then he held it out, handle toward Frank, and this time Frank took it.

"Attaboy," said Frank as he tucked the blade back into its leather home. "So here's what we're gonna do this fine Saturday. We're gonna burn, and we're gonna build."

He reached into his red and black checked shirt pocket and flipped a small box high into the air. Joseph reacted instantly, snagging it like a hawk with leather-clad claws.

"Well, big guy," said Frank. "Wanna finish what you started?"

An icy hand gripped him deep inside, and Joseph directed a nervous glance at the matchbox. These were the very things that had gotten him into so much trouble, although, he'd thought many times since, if he'd finished what he'd set out to do that day, he wouldn't have been around for any of the pain that had followed.

"Go ahead. There's starter paper right under there. See it?"

Joseph followed Frank's gaze to the jumble of charred and broken boards.

"Found it on the shed floor after I hauled you out of there that day. Kinda caught my eye. Saved it, you know, in case I needed it." Frank pointed with his cigarette.

Joseph stood motionless, running it all through his baffled head.

"What?" said the old man. "You want me to do it?"

Sweat beginning to form in his armpits and behind his knees, Joseph looked sideways at Frank and almost imperceptibly shook his head. Hands moistening inside his new gloves, he stepped toward the pile of wood and crouched, pulling off and carefully stuffing the perfect deerskin into his jacket pockets before sliding the tiny cardboard tray out of its white goose-adorned bright red sleeve.

He fished out one of the matches and held it to the rough strike patch.

"Whoa!" said Frank, stepping forward. "Hold on! Make sure you close the goddamn box up before you strike that thing. Wouldn't want to accidentally burn anything now, would we?" He arched an eyebrow at that. "Especially you."

Sheepishly, Joseph slid the matchbox shut and kneeled in the dirt. He inched forward, but froze just as he was about to drag the match along the sandpaper. He needed to be sure his eyes weren't deceiving him. He could see the words clearly, although they ran crooked and partly obscured across the wrinkled and water stained paper. They were the kind of words he'd been forced to read almost every day, the kind of words he'd been forced to try to memorize and recite out loud, knees weak, stomach in knots, voice almost unable to escape him.

When the match flared, he stared into its awesome brilliance for a few seconds before touching it to the edge of the nearest piece of thin white vellum, the helter-skelter sentences it held underlined in pencil, at some point, he knew, by his own hand.

He that covereth his sins shall not prosper:
but whoso confesseth and forsaketh them shall have mercy.

o o o

Frank had impaled another hotdog—the fifth—on the end of the twisted coat hanger roasting fork, and he watched with something akin to amazement as the kid eagerly held it out over the glowing coals.

"This is living, huh?" he said, swigging root beer. "Another good day's work and another fine meal."

No answer, came the reply.

They'd gotten off to another solid start, and for the third straight Saturday, Frank had been impressed with the kid's work ethic. To his continued surprise, the boy had given him nothing but energy, carrying lumber that seemed like it should've been too much for him, and hammering nails like a natural once he'd been shown how to hold the knockometer—as Frank had called it—at the end of its handle, not in the middle. Although Joseph had bent a fair number, and it had typically taken him more than a few attempts to successfully sink one nail, Frank had been sure to let him know that he'd improve with time and practice.

"Well, kid," he said. "Whaddya think? From where I sit, we got ourselves the beginning of something. Something to build on. That's always a good thing."

Knowing no response would be forthcoming, Frank let loose a deep sigh and flicked his cigarette butt into the hot embers, then, with a suitably loud grunt, he picked himself up off his lawn chair, gathered up an armful of hotdog buns and ketchup and mustard, and walked toward the house. As he reappeared and dropped himself back into his seat, Joseph swallowed his final bite and wiped his face on his sleeve. Frank lit up another smoke and studied the late afternoon sky for a couple of seconds, a scattering of pink-tinged clouds visible against the azure through the tall evergreens.

"Well," he said. "Looks like it's getting to be about that time. I guess we, uh, better be getting ready to get you back. But I want you to think about something for me." He paused for a long drag. "Seems we met because, well, because maybe…well, I don't know. Because maybe you wanted to be someplace other than wherever it was you had to be. Maybe one day you can tell me about that, huh?"

Joseph said nothing, and Frank saw his furtive glance quickly drop to the ground. There was something, Frank thought, like shame or guilt or sadness in the boy's eyes. He let a minute or two pass, and looked back up into the trees as he spoke the next words.

"Mr. Holliman," said Frank. "Your father. I don't know him, but he seems like the kind of man who might have a lot of rules."

The boy remained silent, but Frank saw his jaw set hard.

"Can't be easy for you at school, I bet, principal's kid and all. But I guess it's one of those, how do they say it, play the hand you got dealt kind of things?"

He sensed Joseph glancing up at him.

"Look," said Frank, expelling a long cloud, "sometimes you gotta be where you don't wanna be, but that doesn't mean you can't leave whenever you want."

Out of the corner of his eye, Frank saw it. A thought—maybe even a question—had flashed across the boy's face. Elbows on his knees as he stretched his fingers out over the coals, Frank tossed his cigarette butt into the red heat, then pushed himself to his feet.

"Well, whadda you say we call it a day?" he said. "Just set your gloves up on top of the lumber pile. I'll take care of 'em for you."

While Frank tossed a couple of shovelfuls of dirt onto the hot coals, the kid shuffled over to the stack of new boards and carefully aligned his barely broken-in gloves perfectly parallel to the old, worn out pair already there.

10

He'd heard the men calling out, heard the roaring and creaking death sounds of the ship as the seawater had rushed and gushed and foamed into the places it was never meant to go, the violence and pressure and weight of it rending the heavy steel as if it were tissue paper.

Low eastern skies beginning a slow transition from impenetrable blackness to feathery gray, apart from the odd moan or muffled voice calling out, the ocean had gone silent. On rolling swells littered with bits of paper and clothing and cigarette packages and all manner of indeterminate odds and ends, men floated here and there, dead and alive and halfway between, no longer captors or prisoners, no longer Americans or Germans, just pathetic human specks bobbing on a vast nothingness, the sea their only enemy now.

They'd managed to stay together, Bernhardt struggling to help Krumpf keep his head mostly above the oily water, until they'd bumped into a lifeless Ami sailor. Now Krumpf wore the Ami's life jacket and Bernhardt only had to do his best to keep himself afloat.

In a dream, Bernhardt turned toward bubbling, hissing sounds. He watched open-mouthed as a black shape surfaced about a hundred meters or so away to the west, the dripping angles and contours of it reflecting the dim dawn light. As the same sight obviously met other eyes, a rising chorus of mostly German voices called out.

"Help! Help us!"

A blinding searchlight beam suddenly snapped on, tracking left and right across the water in a quick sweep, then just as suddenly snapped off. Bernhardt thought he could make out a handful of men desperately trying to swim toward its source, but he was simply too exhausted to try. As the chorus of pleas once again escalated in intensity, the submarine continued south and vanished.

By the time the first low sun rays peeked over the horizon, the cold had transformed Bernhardt's fingers into unbendable steel. He lost his grip on the life jacket. Seconds later, choking seawater tried to end him, but adrenaline jolted him back to life. Flailing his arms and legs to get himself back to air, gasping and terrified and confused, he regained the surface to discover that Krumpf had drifted some twenty or thirty meters away, his head lolling with the motion of the swells. Summoning what he feared might be the last of his strength, Bernhardt struggled to close the distance.

"Hey," he croaked as he finally got two clawed fingers hooked into the gunner's floating, empty shirtsleeve. "You've got to stay awake. Hey. You okay?"

Something was wrong.

Bernhardt pulled hard and spun Krumpf around. With his free hand, he reached for the man's remaining arm and tried to shake it, but it was like trying to shake a wet sack full of raw meat. There was simply no life there. Bernhardt knew that Krumpf could have succumbed to the cold, or to the oil and seawater he'd ingested, or to a hundred other things that had finally added up to his end, but he also knew that the gunner no longer needed the Ami life vest. Loosening its ties, and without so much as another thought, he let Krumpf's body slip away. His one and only focus was to wrestle himself into the flotation device before the last glimmers of his strength and will left him for good. Long seconds later, exhausted, numbed by cold and shock, he laid his head back on the life vest's kapok-stuffed collar and wondered, just for a moment, if the nothing he felt now was the last thing he'd ever feel.

The voice was weak, barely there.

"Anyone there? Jesus H. Christ. Anyone?"

Bernhardt thought he understood the words. He couldn't ignore them. Willing his slowly kicking feet to propel him in what he thought might be the general direction of the voice, he eventually saw a man clinging to a piece of lumber, eyes closed, head barely above the water. Bernhardt tried to call out, but his voice was barely audible even in his own ears.

"Ich bin hier. Hier drüben."

The man struggled to raise his head, then began to look around energetically, erratically, as if in complete darkness.

"Hey! Hey!" he called out. "Here! I'm over here!"

Seconds later, Bernhardt reached the man, clearly an American. His windpipe on fire from retching saltwater, Bernhardt struggled to speak.

"Bist du in Ordnung?" He forced his exhausted brain to switch to English. "You okay?"

The man wasn't okay.

In the rosy dawn rays, his blistered face was bright red and raw, his eyebrows completely gone. His puffy, inflamed eyelids were closed tight, and Bernhardt assumed he was unable to open them. He reached out and grabbed one of the man's arms. "Warten Sie mal. Ich habe dich," he said, before switching to English again. "I…have you."

At Bernhardt's touch, the man suddenly began to babble loudly, frantically, his panic and dread and relief ejected through chattering teeth, while he flailed one hand in the direction of Bernhardt's face.

"Jesus Christ, buddy, I'm fucked here! Can't see a goddamn thing. Fuck! You gotta help me! You gotta get me outta here!"

Weakly, Bernhardt tried to calm the man, but fear and exhaustion soon did the job for him. The sailor's head slumped, and Bernhardt twisted a shriveled white hand under the collar of his shirt to try to hold him fast to the wooden beam barely keeping him above the water.

"Festhalten…Hang on."

Bernhardt couldn't be sure how much time might have passed, but he was pretty sure he'd dreamed that a low-slung ship had appeared on the southern horizon, and that it had slowed some distance out. He was almost sure that he'd imagined massive black letters—K-231—painted on the angular gray-on-gray camouflage of its rust-bleeding hull. But he was absolutely sure that he'd hallucinated some of its crew lowering a small boat and eventually hauling him over its gunwale and wrapping him in a dark blanket.

11

Forty-three men.

Forty-three of the SS *Sea Owl*'s original complement of three hundred and ninety-six officers and crew and guards and prisoners now huddled in practically every nook and cranny of HMCS *Calgary*'s deck. Those who'd been most seriously injured—the fractured, the burnt, the crushed and torn, the half-drowned and the oil-choked— had been tended to by what passed for the warship's first aid personnel, but their capacity to deal with the scale of the situation they'd sailed into was as limited as their medical facilities and equipment.

On the corvette's foredeck, Bernhardt shivered uncontrollably beneath a blanket, the shock and relief of the last six hours setting in as his limbs slowly and excruciatingly regained some blood flow. To his left, under a foul weather coat, the blistered and red-faced American slumped lifelessly against him, grotesquely misshapen eyelids clamped shut. It took a few moments to be sure, but Bernhardt finally decided that the man was asleep, rather than dead, as he probably should have been. Black-clad legs and a pair of rubber boots suddenly appeared, and Bernhardt looked up to see a baby-faced sailor extending a wooden tray on which remained a few mugs and biscuits.

"Hey, buddy," said the man. "Here you go."

Gratefully, Bernhardt nodded and took one of each.

"Danke vielmals," he said.

By crumbling and dissolving the biscuit in the tea, Bernhardt managed to get the lukewarm slurry down in almost one excruciating gulp, but the massive effort took the last of his energy, and his body made it abundantly clear to him that it had had enough. Seconds later, he surrendered to the unbearable weight of fatigue, closed his eyes, and with his last conscious thoughts, willed himself to be elsewhere.

Kicking up a small blizzard as he slid to a smooth stop on a crest, he turned to look up at his tracks, visible evidence of the sequence of decisions and actions he'd taken in order to arrive at this specific place, at this specific moment.

The brilliance of the winter sun.

The smell of the pines.

The cold wind in his face as he'd cut graceful arcs through the pristine powder.

He'd long sensed that perhaps he'd discovered his true self here, in these mountains, running through their towering forests, wading in their ice water streams, hiking their steep trails, skiing their sun-bright declines. He loved the physicality of it, no question, but he loved the freedom of it the most. Freedom. No one could touch him here, no one could tell him what to do, what to think, which direction to go. Only nature ruled this place, and this, he'd come to believe, was where he belonged. This was the thing to which he belonged.

But the official notification had arrived at the school a few days before, the smirking schoolmaster handing it to him with undisguised glee.

"Compulsory military service for your country," it had said.

He'd read it over and over on the train ride, and he'd concluded one thing: he hated that word—"compulsory." He hated absolutely everything it represented. No choice. No options. And what exactly, he'd asked himself more than once, is a country?

He'd thought through the question enough to feel confident in confronting his father with his logic.

"A country is not a thing, father," he'd reasoned. "Borders do not physically exist. A country is only an idea—a construct. How can anyone be compelled to do anything—how can anyone be owned—by an idea?"

But both his dismissive father and the weight of the consequences behind the symbol engraved in black on the top of the bright white letterhead had said otherwise. They'd both stated forcefully—and unequivocally—that Bernhardt didn't belong to himself. They'd both made it abundantly clear that he had always belonged to the faceless old men who operated the machinery that he knew would propel him, against his will, toward a future, he'd suddenly come to understand, that he had simply never owned in the first place.

Hours or days later, disoriented and far beyond uncomfortable, Bernhardt surfaced to discover that salt had dried to a white crust on his rubbery, chafing clothing, that bunker oil had clotted in his hair and swollen his eyelids and split his lips wide open, and that seawater had scoured his throat and wrinkled and blanched every centimeter of the skin that held his aching body together. In short, he'd awakened to find out that he was still alive, and that he wasn't entirely sure how he felt about that.

To add to the fact that he was not dead, Bernhardt soon learned that he was now in the custody of the Royal Canadian Navy.

After a time, the Canadians brought a man from their engine room up to the deck to speak—in terrible, broken German—with a man some of the prisoners must have brought forward to speak—in terrible, broken English.

And so eventually Bernhard had learned one other thing.

Through the Canadian interpreter, Bernhardt had been asked to formally introduce himself by the now fully reanimated, eyebrow-less, red-faced, and apparently now partially sighted American.

"My name," the man said, waving a right hand outward, as if for a shake, "is Ethan T. Walsh."

Again, Bernhardt thought it best to conceal any understanding of English whatsoever, so in German he asked the young sailor to translate. The Ami rambled on about how he was from someplace called Colorado Springs, and he thanked Bernhardt profusely for saving his ass out there, and said that for sure he'd be dead if it wasn't for him, and that he'd only joined the navy for a change of scenery, you know, and that if he ever made it back to the mountains he'd stay put for goddamn sure and goddammit what a crazy fucking idea going to sea was, huh? He talked so fast that there was no way either Bernhardt or the struggling interpreter could keep up, but when he stopped jabbering, he paused for a breath and a few thoughts, and then he asked the young Canadian sailor to be sure to tell Bernhardt one thing.

"He said I should tell you, but exactly like he said it," the kid finally spit out. "He said that, uh, if you're ever in a fucking spot, to get ahold of Ethan T. fucking Walsh. No shit. He said you may be a fucking Kraut, but you're okay with him."

Lacking the energy to even try to generate a verbal response, unable to reconcile his uncertainty and gratitude and amazement, Bernhardt nodded and clamped a hand on the American's forearm. A few minutes later, he watched through slitted eyes as a couple of more able-bodied, blanket-cloaked Americans helped the babbling sailor from Colorado Springs move to another part of the deck.

Suddenly terribly alone, Bernhardt's exhausted body failed him. Barely breathing, he slumped into the space where his new American friend had been. For a second, he imagined some semblance of heat, some ghostly remnant of the fleeting humanity that had been Ethan T. fucking Walsh, but a more practical part of his brain told him that was idiotic. At war with his overactive mind, unable to control his shivering or unclench his fists, powerless to quell the gutworm of trepidation that had taken up residence inside him, Bernhardt closed his burning eyes to cold reality and looked for oblivion.

o o o

Five and a half days later, Bernhardt and his fellow POWs found themselves, once again, behind wire.

He'd seen pictures, of course, and films, and he'd read about it many times in his grandmother's treasured *Life* magazines, but glimpsed through a steady drizzle in the half-light of a drab daybreak, Bernhardt had been absolutely dumbstruck by the skyline of what he recognized as New York City. He wondered if the farm boys, gaping in silent awe around him—who'd likely never left their small towns and villages in Silesia or Schleswig-Holstein or Bavaria before finding themselves in the infinite emptiness of the sands of North Africa—were now, like him, struggling to comprehend the massive implications embedded in Manhattan's skyscraping power.

An hour or two later, they debarked from the ship.

Re-processed and re-rubber stamped and re-tagged, the prisoners were medically inspected and fed and allowed to shower, and best of all, they were each given rations of American cigarettes and chocolate bars. By day's end, they'd been confined in warehouses outfitted with individual cots and blankets and even pillows, where—Bernhardt included—they'd all slept the sleep of the dead.

A German-speaking American officer addressed them at the first morning roll call. This was a temporary holding facility, he said, and they'd be moving again soon enough.

It's a strange thing, Bernhardt thought, to live under clouds of uncertainty while floating on waves of relief, and stranger still to be completely disconnected from the things that had been drummed into you as being essential to your life.

In this no-man's land, there seemed to be no real enforcement of rank, no military structure. But there was most definitely an order. For reasons he couldn't quite pinpoint, his fellow prisoners exuded something cold and distant, virtually every face projecting distrust bordering on menace, so among hundreds—possibly thousands—of his own countrymen, Bernhardt kept mostly to himself, conversations limited to clipped requests for lights for cigarettes, or comments about the "chow," as the Amis referred to it.

Three days later, along with twenty-one sullen and anxious others, Bernhardt was ushered into an olive drab, canvas-backed truck and transported to a new location in a journey, he estimated, that took him and his cargo mates approximately three hours northward.

The new destination itself, Bernhardt was surprised to discover, after overhearing one of its apparently longer-term tenants, was another transit camp, quite large, housing almost fifteen hundred German and Italian prisoners.

"Guys leave all the time," the man had said. "And more arrive. The ones with suntans and cracked lips, they're the new meat."

Over the next eight weeks, Bernhardt would learn a lot.

First, he'd learn that living conditions in American prisoner of war camps were nothing like he'd been told they might be. The prisoners were treated well by the guards, fed good food, and provided with books and playing cards and footballs. Strangest of all, they were encouraged to write home to tell their parents and sweethearts how good life was for them, on its face a well-meaning gesture, but in reality a no doubt effective way, Bernhardt surmised, for the Americans to promote the good treatment of Allied soldiers and sailors and airmen who might fall into German hands. They were also—the able-bodied and seemingly able-minded among them—assigned to work parties, but the tasks involved mostly tending the camp's vegetable gardens and performing assorted menial tasks such as pushing brooms and cleaning latrines.

Second, he'd learn that although he'd been mostly disinterested during the droning formal English lessons forced upon him at school, thanks mostly to his grandmother he had a natural ear for the language. The American guards were a talkative lot, most likely more than happy, Bernhardt figured, to be spending their army lives guarding disarmed enemy soldiers, rather than trying to avoid being killed by fully armed versions of them. As the weeks stretched on and on, Bernhardt took every opportunity to work on his English skills, repeating every line uttered by Gable and Bogart and The Duke during movie nights, and doing his best to replicate every expletive-laden epithet and command and off-hand comment spit out by the guards.

He continued to keep his head down around his fellow prisoners, careful not to get caught fraternizing with the Amis. But fraternize he did. In exchange for a few packs of cigarettes, he managed to get himself reassigned from kitchen detail to the camp's tiny library, and there he was able to take advantage of almost unfettered access to its assortment of English books, enabling him to move one giant step closer to his newly established goal: mastering the subtleties of speaking American.

It was then that he'd learn the hardest lesson of all.

On a brilliant autumn afternoon his boots crunched the gravel path that led away from the library steps, the rich scents of fallen leaves and rain almost as intoxicating as the old book smells that had embraced him for the past four hours. When he stepped into the narrow passage between the library and auditorium, his unconscious defenses detected movement in the shadows to his right, but, too relaxed, too lost in his own little America, he was unable to fully process the information before something heavy and hard and violent came down. From the ground, he looked up through blurry eyes to see three blurry men, strangers who nonetheless claimed to know him well.

"You traitorous fuck."

A boot collided with his ribcage, the pain as sharp and pointed as the voice that leaned in close.

"We know you've been reading. Hugo. Hemingway. Conrad. All shit. All illegal, as you well know."

Another boot, this one producing a sickening muffled crack, came down on his left leg just above the ankle.

"This is a warning. There won't be a next time."

The last thing Bernhardt was vaguely aware of—before a third boot impacted the side of his face—was the sensation of something being wrapped tightly around his neck.

The doctor who'd eventually patched him up had told him that when he'd been found by a night patrol, the guards had immediately assumed they had another murder on their hands. But the wire garotte twisted around his throat had only been "decorative," the doctor had said. "You got yourself a couple of cracked ribs, a broken leg, and a bad headache, but basically, someone let you off easy, fella."

For almost a week, whenever Bernhardt had not been reading or rereading a handful of old American magazines, he'd either slept or seethed or stared at the ceiling above his infirmary cot. He'd had time to think.

He fully understood the hard line, and had learned to navigate it, because he'd lived it. His father had embodied it for as long as he'd been able to remember. And of course, at school the pecking order had been well established.

There, from day one, he'd instinctively toed the line, gaining small measures of safety by displaying the unquestioning like-mindedness and compliance that pecking orders value. Any deviation from the prescribed way was despised and punished, because deviation from the prescribed way was simply un-German. And so he'd conformed. Beyond that, he'd learned that his own physicality had clearly contributed to his status. At twelve, as new meat, he'd been less than nothing to his much larger and more brutal older schoolmates. By thirteen or fourteen years of age, he'd almost managed to become…something, his ski team accomplishments and unquestioning obedience to the dictates of his superiors gaining him a modicum of tolerance, if not respect. By seventeen, he'd taken on a completely new form. Nearing two meters in height and closing in on eighty-five kilos, he'd come to understand that in all of the eyes that mattered he'd become one of the physically, intellectually, and morally elite, and he'd wielded his status with the confidence afforded those lucky enough to find themselves in possession of such attributes. He'd almost come to believe that he actually was special, but in his heart of hearts he'd known that was simply a lie he'd told himself.

More than once he'd found himself staring into the darkness of the dormitory, simultaneously ashamed of the pain and humiliation he'd inflicted on some pathetic inferior, and terrified that the others might find out what he really was.

A few days before his Wehrmacht-dictated departure from the academy, he'd almost revealed himself.

The kid—as so many others before him—had fit the profile.

Undersized.

Understrength.

Underenthusiastic.

Underpatriotic.

Underfriended.

Undereverything.

They'd cornered him behind the gymnasium, a favored spot for "training." But for some reason, on that day, in that moment, Bernhardt had suddenly felt this one boy's despair and fear and loneliness as if they were his own. And so he'd made a rash decision: he'd stepped between the worm and the pecking order. To his relief, no one had dared to challenge him, his size and strength and his reputation for toughness likely preventing any pushback. Of course he'd known that he'd had virtually nothing to lose, that he'd soon be gone from that place, and that the hapless kid would ultimately be resubmerged in the bucket of shit from which he'd been temporarily extracted. But lying wide awake in his bunk that night, Bernhardt had once again questioned his own place in the order. He wanted to be superior. To be elite. But what kind of superior man would be so willing to go along, to surrender his soul to the whims of others, and to force others to submit to his? By morning, although he hadn't known it, something inside him had changed.

The Wehrmacht, of course, commanded subservience at gunpoint, every demand for conformity he'd experienced at the academy codified and amplified at the highest level. But by the time he'd finished basic training, the rumors about massive losses in the east had been flying, cracks and fissures in the invincibility of the new Germany, to which he belonged, laid bare. More and more, he found himself silently chafing under its hypocrisy and bluster and self-delusional demands. When the service branch posting option had been posed to him—the illusion of an actual option at least, no doubt precipitated by his father's influence—he'd taken it.

Once in North Africa, through setback after setback and retreat after retreat, the last shreds of Bernhardt's belief in the underpinnings of the innate superiority of the Reich had quickly evaporated, like a water droplet in the desert sun. Yet even here, in America—in the clutches of the very enemy he'd been told over and over again had been inferior—there were those who still believed the lies, and who still adhered to the brutal practices required to keep them semi-alive.

The camp police had conducted a brief investigation, but it was well known that the Amis pretty much left the prisoners to their own devices when it came to order and discipline. They policed the German officers and NCOs, but they left the German officers and NCOs to police their own rank and file. The prisoners knew that the Americans tolerated the periodic Nazi salute, and even allowed the odd article proclaiming Germany's natural superiority and predicting the Führer's ultimate victory to grace the camp newspaper from time. But as long as hardline Nazi activities inside the wire didn't involve escape attempts, theft or destruction, the murder of fellow prisoners, or the harming in any way of guards or other service personnel, the Americans basically looked the other way.

Two weeks from the day that Bernhardt had received his warning, during a quick check up, a camp doctor fed him the news. A former U-boat crewman had been found, gagged with an oily cloth and hanging by the neck from a thin wire in the prison gymnasium.

"Sounds like another of your buddies got a little visit," the Ami doctor declared as he poked an ice cold finger between Bernhardt's still tender ribs, "from the Holy Ghost."

Two days later, a crutch under one arm and a canvas personal bag slung over his shoulder, Bernhardt limped from his barracks. A couple of rifle-toting, cigarette-smoking guards pointed the way, and he made his way across the muddy compound to join a line of about two hundred and fifty others who were being loaded into a parade of dark green buses, the crisp white stars inside perfect white circles practically glowing on their sides.

They'd all had their preconceived notions, of course, formed by whatever they'd been told, and by whatever they might have been able to determine for themselves. As a boy, Bernhardt's initial perception of America had certainly been shaped by that of his father—that as a nation it was soft, weak, decadent, hedonistic, and mongrel, at best a second-rate society essentially composed of the world's castoffs and misfits. But that view had been countered by the glamorous and exciting Hollywood films and American magazines and music his grandmother had loved, much to his father's consternation. As a soldier, he'd not personally faced the Amis in combat, but he'd met enough men who had to have begun to question what he thought he knew. As far as he could tell, those men certainly didn't seem to think the enemy to whom they'd surrendered were anywhere near as undisciplined, sloppy, ill-equipped, or reluctant to fight as his father and his superiors had so often claimed.

Now, as a prisoner of war under the jurisdiction of these strangely benevolent captors, he'd come to see Americans in a much different light. His most recent experiences, with the Ami doctors and nurses who'd put him back together after his own countrymen had come close to taking him apart, had at first angered, then confused, then deeply disappointed him. And it had dawned on him that almost nothing Germany had told him about America—or indeed about Germany—appeared to be true.

Though armed guards watched them like hawks from the platform and the surrounding rooftops as they boarded, the train cars into which they climbed weren't the industrial boxcars in which they'd traveled across Germany as newly minted soldiers of the vaunted Reich. Pullman cars, they were called, and they were absolutely luxurious. An hour or so after departure, when black porters offered the prisoners sandwiches and water and coffee, Bernhardt's jaw practically hit the floor.

As the train rolled on and on and on, each and every German face was pressed, at one time or another, to the various slits and cracks in its window coverings. By the time it had passed through a full day of seemingly endless, factory-rich cities, Bernhardt had only been able to assume that each and every American citizen must have owned at least one, if not two automobiles. And hundreds and hundreds of corn- and wheat-covered but cowboy-free kilometers before he'd reached his next destination—where once again he'd been processed and rubber-stamped and medically inspected and well fed and assigned to a clean barracks—he'd concluded that neither his father's nor Hollywood's versions of this vast country were factual.

But he'd also arrived at a much deeper realization: that there was absolutely no way that Germany's lies could prevail against America's truth.

He'd crossed a continent, and crossed a line.

12

The big saw cut deep and fast, throwing off a fragrant shower of sawdust and chips that covered the ground like snow.

To be paid eighty American cents per day—"the exact same as a goddamn private in the US Army!" he'd been reminded numerous times—to spend his time outdoors in such beautiful surroundings was beyond crazy, and Bernhardt still couldn't believe his luck.

His first American winter and the night sweat bitterness and pain of his library injuries mostly behind him, he felt himself growing stronger and stronger every day, the food, the spring air, and the physicality of the work all contributing to his overall well-being. He'd come to like his new existence. Most all of them had.

When they weren't within the confines of the camp, they were in the employ of a rotund, bald, fifty-five-year old American of few words who had, they'd all immediately noted, something decidedly German about him.

His name was Herman Eisenhut, and his business was wood.

Each morning, Bernhardt and about sixty of his fellow prisoners boarded white camp buses that drove them the five or so miles to the steep mountainsides. There, various teams would survey and carefully select the trees, while others would put their backs into felling and limbing and dragging. Down at Eisenhut's mill, more prisoners would feed the raw logs into the whining saws, while others would haul and grade and stack the resulting lumber, all of it bound for the American people—and for the American war effort. Each evening, the prisoners would be returned to the camp and its good food, warm showers, and comfortable bunks.

"When I was young, I lived in a place like this," said Bernhardt one morning, as Smithson—Smitty to the other Ami guards—flared a match. "Mountains are home to me."

"Jesus H. Christ, Fritz," said Smitty. "You sure you're a goddamn Kraut? You talk like some movie star, like you're from New York fuckin' City or someplace."

"I was there only one time," said Bernhardt. "My bad English comes from some other place. A place with mountains."

Smitty shook his head.

"Oh, yeah?" he said. "I don't know where that is, but just thinking about uphill walking makes me fuckin' tired, and I been in this state my whole goddamn life. The flat part. I got no interest in giant goddamn trees that'll kill ya when they come down."

Bernhardt laughed. Over the course of almost nine months in captivity, his English had improved to the point where he felt he could understand around fifty, maybe sixty percent of a conversation with an American, unless, he'd deduced, the American happened to be from one of the southern states like Alabama or Mississippi. Smitty, Bernhardt knew because he'd been told about twenty-five times, was from the eastern side of Montana, and like almost every other guard, he called almost every German Fritz. Or Hans. Or Adolph. But no German ever took offence to that. The Americans were good to them.

"Hey, Fritz," said Smitty, squinting into the midmorning sun. "I got another piece of important knowledge you can add to your personal encyclopedia of America. You see that little bit of snow over there?" he said, pointing into the shadows on the north side of a stand of scrubby firs with his cigarette between his index and middle fingers. "And that one? And that one over there? You know what the Indians call that kind of snow?"

Bernhardt smiled as he looked around, and shook his head. "Nein. Uh, no."

"Apache snow!" said Smitty. He raised his rifle and pointed it into the trees, moving it from side to side, sighting on each snow patch to emphasize his words.

"Apache here. Apache there. Apaches everywhere!"

Smitty and another guard burst out laughing. Bernhardt struggled to make sense of the wisecrack, but laughed anyway. These Americans, he thought, are jokers, most certainly, but they're jokers with loaded weapons.

"Okay, kids," Smitty shouted as he glanced at his watch. "Recess is over! Time to get your pathetic, surrendered asses back to fuckin' work!"

Twenty-eight prisoners got to their feet and picked up their various axes and saws and shovels. As he walked to the battered truck that would take him and his team back to their cut, Bernhardt saw her. Dark hair flowing in the warming breeze as she dropped an armload of rope and tarpaulins into the bed of a dark blue pickup truck, the girl glanced at the prisoners as they marched by. She wore the clothes of woodsmen— boots and dungarees and a heavy shirt—but in a way that Bernhardt could never have imagined. And to Bernhardt, her sunglasses added a distinct air of Hollywood glamor.

Smitty more than tapped Bernhardt's left shoulder with the butt of his rifle.

"Hey!" he growled. "Don't you go gettin' any fuckin' ideas there, Fritzy! I got full dibs on that sweet little piece."

Bernhardt turned to see Smitty's unsmiling smile, and the business end of the guard's weapon pointed at his crotch.

"You wouldn't wanna be the one dumb bastard," said Smitty, "who survived the war in North Africa, only to get his fuckin' balls shot off in Bridger Falls, Montana, now, would you?"

"No," said Bernhardt as he shook his head, turned, and stole a last, furtive glance.

"My, ah, fuckinballs are going to survive the whole war."

13

A few flakes of late spring snow drifted through the pines as Bernhardt and Fischer—one of only three survivors of a U-boat that, he'd claimed, had been sunk by an RAF flying boat somewhere off Nova Scotia—got themselves ready to take down the last tree of the day.

"Pretty ironic, huh?" said Bernhardt as he dribbled a thin stream of oil onto the chain on the huge two-man saw. "Best in the world. Invented by a German. Why didn't we just figure out how to sell the Americans a whole lot more of these things? Maybe sell the British a whole lot more cars, instead of challenging each country to an idiotic national duel to the death?"

"You think too much," said Fischer. He was small, and wiry-strong, and to Bernhardt he seemed life-smart, but his almost beardless face betrayed his youth. "That stuff's not up to guys like you and me. We're only cogs in the machine. The machine sent me to the North Atlantic and you to North Africa. And now the machine has sent us here. Could have been a whole lot worse. Maybe one day you can ask some of those poor fuckers the machine sent to Russia. If any of them survive."

Smoke-laden breath clouding around him, Bernhardt picked up his end of the chainsaw and gave it a final once-over.

"Okay, Fish," he said. "I'll take the heavy this time. Let's get this one down and get back to some warm chow."

He used American words now even when he spoke German. They all did.

The tree was a monster—Bernhardt figured almost a hundred feet tall and bigger around than most—but the submariner and the desert soldier had learned their new forest trade well. The chain's teeth bit into its massive trunk as if it was butter. They hammered steel wedges into the felling cut with the flat backs of their axes, then worked the cumbersome machine some more, notching the tree—as they'd been taught, and had learned from hard experience—so that it would fall in the right direction. But even the most expert cutters can run into the unknown. The tree's tip began to lean toward its intended destination, but its trunk suddenly split vertically, violently kicking Bernhardt's end of the chainsaw back toward him, twisting him hard to his right, and jerking the wet metal handle out of his hands.

As the two men dived away in an effort to get themselves clear, the massive pine toppled with a thunderous crack, fortunately falling essentially downhill the way they'd planned. But as Bernhardt reached out to try to break his fall, a long splinter sheared off and sliced through the air, crushing his right palm onto a jagged, broken branch before bouncing itself away into the scrub. A frantic Fischer reached Bernhardt just as he got to his feet.

"Jesus fucking Christ, Bern! You okay? Still in one piece?"

Bernhardt grimaced and held up his shaking, streaming hand.

"Yeah, basically," he groaned through gritted teeth, "but I think I'm going to need a medic."

"Son, you're fuckin' lucky I learned a few things over in that god-damned French mud."

Herman Eisenhut tossed a bloody curved needle and a pair of scissors into a stainless steel bowl, then turned and thumped Bernhardt on the back with a heavy paw.

"I sure hope," he said, "you wipe your ass with your left hand."

With foghorn resonance, the old man bellowed through the open kitchen door.

"Goddammit, Helen," he yelled. "Get in here and finish this up! I got plenty other things, you know?!"

A couple of rolls of white gauze in her hand, the young woman Bernhardt had caught a glimpse of a week or so back appeared in the doorway. Surreptitiously, he watched her rummage around in a drawer, unable to take his poorly averted eyes off her. As before, she was dressed like a logger, but she carried herself with the kind of grace, Bernhardt found himself imagining, that implied some deep, underlying strength.

"My father's pretty good with a needle and thread," she said. "But it looks like your violin-playing career might be over."

With a mix of semi-comprehension and awe, Bernhardt smiled and nodded mutely as she gently lifted and inspected his mangled hand. Her touch almost paralyzed him, and when she smiled a slightly crooked and brilliantly white smile, then puffed a strand of hair away from her face and simultaneously flipped her head back, the softness of her swept over him like rain in the desert.

"What's your name, soldier?"

"Ah, Ich heiße…" he stammered, unable to muster the English words for some reason. "Ah, Bernhardt."

"Well, Mr. Bernhardt," she said, "sorry we had to meet under such painful circumstances. My name's Helen. Eisenhut."

Despite the intense, throbbing pain, Bernhardt enjoyed every second of the next few minutes. As Helen Eisenhut daubed her father's needlework with more disinfectant, then spun gauze around his hand

and secured it with a couple of strips of tape, Bernhardt pretended not to watch her every move, but he was especially spellbound by a tiny mole on her forehead. When she suddenly glanced up, he immediately looked away, afraid her eyes might have actually met his.

"Okay," she said, too soon. "All set. Guess you were pretty unlucky and pretty lucky, all in the same day."

He kept his eyes on his bandaged hand as she tidied up.

"You're going to need to lay low for a week or six," she said, "and let that heal up. On my way out, I'll tell my father you're gonna be out of action for a while, and I'll make sure he tells the camp to get a doctor to check you out. They should change that dressing every couple of days, but in the meantime, if you smell Muenster cheese, well"—she smiled—"it won't be crackers you'll be needing."

Bernhard had less than half of an idea what she'd meant, but he'd liked the sound of one hundred percent of it. He plucked up the courage to look her in the eyes.

"Danke. Uh, thank you, Miss Eisenhut. You're most kind."

She turned and walked to the door, pausing to puff-flip another strand of hair from her face.

"Helen," she said with a soft smile. "My name's Helen. And you're welcome. See you around, soldier."

14

Letters from home. In the middle of a war.

While a prematurely old and clearly exasperated Unteroffizier had shouted out each lucky man's name into the smoke and commotion, Bernhardt had once again marveled at the absurdity. Two countries each trying to murder the other into surrendering to their will still thought that allowing and enabling the transmission of personal messages between their captured and free citizens should be allowed.

In some ways, Bernhardt understood what he'd been told about the Soviet approach to war and prisoners much more clearly: Yesterday you belonged to a country that wants to kill me, my family, my friends, and my countrymen. Today you belong to me. But tomorrow you will belong to no one, because you will no longer exist.

The simplicity of that all made perfect sense to him.

In so many, many ways, America still did not.

Regardless, he knew there would be no letters for him. His father had not spoken to him—and had apparently forbidden his mother to do so—since late 1941, when Bernhardt had confronted him about his newest factory workers, two hundred or so stubble-haired and funereal women his father had trucked in from some nearby facility to assemble engine components for fighter aircraft.

"How dare you insinuate?!" his father had bellowed. "How dare you?! I'm helping to keep those people alive! I give them purpose! If not for that work they'd be… unnecessary!"

"No one is unnecessary, Father, only unfortunate," Bernhardt had declared, stone faced and sure and emboldened by the knowledge that his time under his father's thumb was running short. Through it all, his voiceless mother had focused on her almost untouched dinner while his father had glared open-mouthed in stunned, neck-bulging ire.

Bernhardt had shipped out to North Africa a few days later.

That his father had been too busy to see him off that day had been a blessing he'd cherished, for it had allowed him a last moment alone with his mother. When the shouting and whistle-blowing had begun, they'd embraced, and she'd put a soft, warm hand on his cheek, but even then, in perhaps one of the most uncertain and disquieting moments of his life, she'd been unwilling, or perhaps unable, to say the words, and in the end, he'd simply left her sobbing in stoic silence in the fumes and the grime and the rumbling, mechanized chaos of the transport depot.

The mail call stretched on and on, a result of the steadily increasing camp population. They'd seen more and more new arrivals in the last few months, sailors and airmen from time to time, but most notably Wehrmacht and SS soldiers who'd been captured in Italy. It was the firsthand news they brought with them that the prisoners craved most. The actual progress of the war was mostly kept from them by their captors, or they assumed that what they were being told was false or exaggerated, so any information they could get straight from a reliable German source was like gold.

It troubled Bernhardt to know that British and American bombers were apparently over Germany day and night, and that the Allies were moving steadily north through Italy. To some extent, it also troubled him that while some part of him feared the future, he couldn't help the rest of himself from relishing the present. Sure, he'd listened dutifully to the new boys and their grim stories of what mostly sounded to him to be the slow but steady defeat of a crumbling Reich, but during his time in the crisp air of the Montana mountains, working for actual pay under the supervision of strangely generous and almost benevolent captors, surrounded by massive trees in forests so thick that there seemed to be no end to them, Bernhardt had rarely thought about Germany or his parents. Maybe not at all.

And then the Unteroffizier called his name.

The envelope was small, and in spite of his efforts, his bandaged right hand trembled as he struggled to hold it against his thigh so his left hand could tear it open. The document inside was typed, rather than handwritten. Businesslike, to the point, dated some three months earlier, it offered no sentiment. No love. Only pain.

My father being my father, he thought.

January 17, 1944
Son,
Your mother has passed.
I am carrying on and doing my duty.
Assume you are doing the same.
Father

o o o

During a sunny Thursday lunch break a couple of months later, Smitty let the news slip. But, the prisoners all knew, there was nothing inadvertent about his words. Bernhardt simultaneously doubted them and hoped for them to be both true and not true.

Allied forces—"fuckin' millions of 'em," Smitty said—had landed on the beaches of France. And of course, he said, "the gutless Kraut shitbirds hunkered down anywhere in the vicinity immediately crapped themselves, turned tail, and started hauling their sad sack asses back to Germany."

Bernhardt looked over at Fischer, and Fischer looked back.

"The machine is breaking down," said Fischer.

From that revelation forward, the prisoners clearly understood the progress of the war simply by tracking in detail the various locations of capture reported by incoming POWs: Normandy, Paris, Arnhem, the Ardennes.

They all sensed what was coming.

They all guessed what was inevitable.

What they couldn't have guessed was what that inevitability might mean to them.

15

Although it loudly proclaimed the opposite every time he tried to pick anything up, almost five months after he'd nearly lost it, Bernhardt's V-scarred hand had been declared sufficiently healed. He'd worked the mess hall for the past eight weeks, chafing at the indoor duty despite the sub-zero Montana winter. Finally, Christmas had come and gone, and in the cold, early spring, they'd assigned him to the skidder crew, where his new job was to spur and cajole the poor horses as they struggled to drag massive logs out of the bush toward the trucks that would haul them down to the mill.

Bernhardt had never really been around animals, had never even had a dog as a child, as his father had angrily dismissed his initial timid pleadings months prior to his seventh birthday. "Don't be ridiculous," his father had sneered. "Animals exist solely to serve man. What possible service could a dog ever provide to you?"

He'd quietly expressed his ongoing hopes to his mother countless times after that, but doubted that the subject had ever been brought up with his father again. For a time he'd actually suspected he'd been shipped off to boarding school just to shut him up. Now, years distant from that painful and definitive denial, Bernhardt found himself viewing the

Eisenhut draw horses as the flesh and blood equivalent of machines, there to serve a purpose and nothing more. When he needed them to move, he snapped his whip. When he needed them to stop moving, he heaved on the reins that jammed the choking bits against their jaws and forced their tongues back into their throats. Day in and day out, he barked at them incessantly, commanding them to do his bidding, to bend to his will, exactly as his father and his older classmates and his teachers and his Wehrmacht and US Army overseers had done with him.

The lunch whistle sounded as the sun cracked the clouds wide open.

Under the semi-watchful eyes of Smitty and two other guards, Bernhardt and his eleven coworkers had just set the horses to water and laid their various tools and themselves down when a guard they didn't recognize stepped out of a jeep and stormed toward them, both hands on his carbine. "Get your worthless Kraut asses back to work!" the man shouted. "The fuck are you Nazis doing sitting down?!"

A few prisoners—Bernhardt included—got to their feet. Curious but not quite alarmed, Bernhardt lit up a smoke as Smitty and the two other guards shuffled over to hear whatever the angry guard had to say. Inexplicably, a lanky prisoner named Schlemmer walked toward the gathered Americans, and Bernhardt heard him ask—loud and clear and in almost perfect English—"You guys just fucking with us?" A rifle butt to the stomach dropped him to the dirt.

"Come get this fucking fool!" shouted Smitty.

Bernhardt and another prisoner hustled over and helped the gasping Schlemmer to his feet, while the rest of the Germans gaped in wide-eyed shock. Smitty and the other guards turned their attention and their weapons toward the now clearly startled prisoners, and the unknown guard barked again. "I said get your sorry asses back to work! There's no fucking lunch break today."

That evening, while the prisoners consumed what they all judged to be somewhat less than standard food, the rumors started to make themselves known.

"Heard it from a new guy," someone said. "He said the Americans overran some kind of camp. Near Ohrdruf."

Another man chimed in. "I heard that, too. There were hundreds, maybe thousands of dead prisoners there."

"Here it comes," a third voice growled. "They tell lies to justify what they're going to do. Open your fucking eyes! There are too many of us now. They need an excuse to get rid of us."

Bernhardt took it all in, his mind unwilling to believe, but his gut telling him otherwise.

o o o

For weeks, the tension and anxiety in the camp had ramped up. Head down, saying almost nothing, Bernhardt had simply tried to do his assigned job as the demands for more and more productivity had escalated.

Something had changed.

Over a few cigarettes, he'd shared his observations with Fish and Schlemmer and they'd both agreed: the once almost benign guards had definitely begun to take a more malignant and frequently more violent tone, the food had continued to decline in both volume and quality, and the showers had gone lukewarm at best. They all felt the effects of the something. But they wouldn't fully understand its origins until a Saturday evening in early July.

Under sternly barked orders, Bernhardt, Fischer, Schlemmer, and a few hundred other silent and bewildered prisoners had shuffled into the camp's gymnasium. They'd been told to "sit the fuck down" and "shut the fuck up."

Cross-legged on the hardwood floor, Bernhardt stared at the screen until the lights dimmed.

The newsreel absolutely stunned him.

The white bodies, naked and emaciated, had been thrown into piles like cast-off limbs bucked from harvested trees. Gaunt, pajama-clad ghost-people stared into the cameras from behind hollow, haunting eyes, silently pleading for humanity to help them. American soldiers questioned a few obviously frightened German guards—men and women alike—while others in various states of dress lay dead on the ground around them, the clear signs of savage beatings and summary executions there for all to see.

Bernhardt watched in clench-jawed horror. Then suddenly, near the end of the film, his horror multiplied a thousandfold.

A small group of grim-faced GIs, some with broken cigarettes protruding from their nostrils, others with their eyes barely visible above their handkerchief-covered noses, stood by in barely contained disgust as a column of equally grim-faced German civilians filed through the gates of the camp, eyes averted from the cameras, heads lowered. As the film continued to reveal its horrendous scenes, Bernhardt, too, instinctively averted his eyes, but something inside him decided against it. He glanced back toward the flickering screen just in time to see what he could never unsee.

Two older men in shirts and ties stood up to their knees in a jumble of pale and shrunken and cadavers. Obviously tasked with moving the skin-covered skeletons one by one, they swung an emaciated corpse by its oversized hands and feet, the momentum carrying the gangly body up and onto a heavy cart already laden with fifteen or twenty specters.

One man's angry, hateful eyes met the camera lens, just for a second. Mouth open, breath caught in his chest, Bernhardt couldn't be absolutely sure of what he thought he'd seen, but the sinking feeling in his gut insisted he'd looked into those eyes thousands and thousands of times. Never once had he seen them project shame or guilt, and they had not appeared to do so even then. Clammy hands clenched into fists as he swallowed desperately hard to suppress the urge to vomit, Bernhardt heard his father's word echoing in his head.

Unnecessary.

To a man, the stunned and silent POWs looked nowhere but down as they shuffled out of the gymnasium fifteen minutes later, the Amis noticeably more physical and vocal than ever before, shoving the prisoners with their rifles, bellowing demands for the "fucking Krauts" to "get a fucking move on," and to "straighten up the fucking lines." Bernhardt barely heard the taunts and commands. He felt as if he was trapped in a tomb.

In the overheated confines of his bunk a half hour later, the gut wrenching scene played over and over, and he struggled to make sense of what he was feeling. In the blink of a familiar eye, two worlds had collided. He sought to nurture disbelief in an effort to diffuse his shame, but he knew in his heart that what he'd seen—what he knew he'd never, ever share with anyone else as long as he lived—was a cold, hard truth. When the sun's rays broke over the mountains some seven hours later, he was still staring into nothingness, wishing he, too, could be nothing.

From that terrible moment on, as the guards had steadily ratcheted up the abuse, Bernhardt had simply swallowed himself, unwilling or unable to be fully alive in a world he could no longer even pretend to understand. But today, under a relentless sun, under relentless pressure, Bernhardt could feel himself burning inside and out.

"Hey, Cap'n Hook!" Smitty's voice boomed right behind him. Listless, sullen, Bernhardt turned.

"Yeah, Fritz," said Smitty. "I'm talkin' to you! That fuckin' claw you got for a hand's no excuse. You don't get that hillside cleared out by six, there's no fucking chow for you or your crew tonight. You got that?"

One of the horses, an old dun-colored mare named Betty Grable, had once again proven to be especially troublesome, still stubbornly unwilling, despite years of relentless human cruelty, to submit to the grinding drudgery of her life.

Sweating and swearing and hating every second of his own miserable existence, Bernhardt chained Betty to a pine almost a meter in diameter. Exhausted, defeated, fighting against his own desperation, he barked the commands and brought the whip down. But as Betty grudgingly attempted to shift the massive trunk in the dense bush, Bernhardt heard the fifteen-minute whistle sound, and he erupted.

As if in a dream, he watched his whip come down hard, over, and over, and over. He heard himself screaming, furiously exhorting Betty to get her lazy ass moving or he'd make fucking sure she was the dinner his crew would eat. And he watched as she suddenly faltered, dropping first to her knees, then buckling completely and collapsing to the ground. Boiling frustration now blind rage, Bernhardt grabbed her foamed bit harness and screamed. "Get up and get back to fucking work!"

In that moment of crazed fury, Bernhardt accidentally looked into Betty Grable's eyes, and he suddenly understood that she was looking back at him. Instantly, he felt as if he'd stepped outside of his own body, as if he'd become an observer instead of an active participant in the events unfolding in the mountain scrub. Through tears of rage, the reflection of his own insanity overwhelmed him, and he slumped to his knees, soul-deep anguish and sorrow and regret brought powerfully and unavoidably to the surface by Betty's confused, pleading gaze.

Why? he imagined her asking. *Why are you doing this to me? Because you can?*

Betty struggled mightily for a brief moment, trying desperately to raise her head from the ground, to will herself into the living world once more, but Bernhardt had seen countless men do the same, guts ripped out by shrapnel, legs and arms destroyed by mines and bullets, despairing as all the promises of their unlived futures had drained into the hot desert sands.

As he'd done for a few of them, he reached out a hand. He stroked the white blaze on her scarred nose, a pathetically inadequate attempt to redeem himself as her unblinking eyes passed silent judgment on him. And as those eyes began to focus on nothing, he watched his own tears mingling with hers as she drew her final breaths.

"I'm sorry, Betty," he whispered. "I'm so very, very sorry."

That night, as he tossed and turned, wide-eyed and sweating in his bunk, Bernhardt was simply unable to force his mind elsewhere, unable to shake the accusing look of despair and bewilderment and imploring, agonizing sadness in Betty's eyes. Why? he asked himself. Why had she lived such a horrible life, and died such a horrible death? Simply because creatures more powerful had chosen that for her? And why, he asked, had he been so willing to not only take up, but escalate the infliction of her pain and suffering to such a point that it had eventually killed her? Because more powerful men had chosen that for him? No, he answered, ashamed and enraged by his own cowardice.

Because I allowed it.

Bernhardt's sleepless, burning eyes were just able to detect the dim glow of the mountain dawn on the scratched plank underside of the bunk above him when the notion struck him.

In many ways, he thought, they were the same, Betty and him. Neither of them would have chosen the lives they'd been given. But,

Bernhardt had realized, in one huge way they were simply worlds apart. He had options that Betty Grable had never had. Because unlike poor Betty, unlike so many others less fortunate than him, Bernhardt had finally come to understand.

He still had the ability to choose his own end.

16

The rumors had been flying.

"Hitler killed himself."

"Hitler made a deal with the Allies to attack Russia."

"Hitler escaped to Argentina."

"Goebbels killed Hitler and assumed power."

"Goebbels killed Hitler and escaped to Argentina."

Whatever the unknown truths, one thing was certain. The Amis had been sure to let them all know that Germany had surrendered unconditionally, Smitty in particular lording that fact over them as if he'd personally defeated the vaunted enemy. He was at it again today.

"I guess we kicked your sorry fucking Kraut asses," he sneered. "I'm thinkin' we should turn you all over to the goddamn Russians and let 'em finish the job."

A member of Bernhardt's newly formed work crew—a Panzer driver from Essen who also spoke almost perfect English—straightened up. "Oh, fuck you, Smitty," he said with a derisive sneer. "You think you had something to do with that? You never even left this camp. The only battles you ever fought were against your belly and your fucking bald spot. And you lost both of those."

The burst of laughter was immediate, with even Smitty's fellow guards unable to contain themselves. Smitty's eyes widened and his sweat-streaked face boiled bright red, his neck bulging like an over-inflated inner tube as it strained to escape the confines of his damp shirt collar. Enraged, charging, he pointed his weapon directly at the Panzer driver's face. The driver stood firm, calm and unmoving, which, Bernhardt guessed, infuriated Smitty even more.

"You sad sack fucking Nazi losers won't be laughing when you get back to that bombed-out shitpile you used to call a country!" he bellowed. "If you make it back, that is!"

It took two guards to talk Smitty down.

° ° °

With Fischer and Schlemmer and the Panzer driver and five other men, Bernhardt had been assigned to a mill cleanup detail, their make-work tasks barely keeping them from falling asleep in the warm sun.

Midafternoon, a dark blue pickup truck skidded to a stop in the loose gravel in front of the log house that served as the mill office, and from the open doors of the workshop a few meters away, Bernhardt watched in awe as its driver slammed its door and took the porch steps two at a time, clearly on a mission.

Like a magnet, his broom pulled him toward the office porch. Obediently, he followed, hoping to catch another glimpse. He detected muffled, indecipherable voices through the wooden walls, their volume and intensity rising by the second as he swept his way closer to a window. Through his reflection on the glass, he saw it, as he'd first seen it as a five- or six-year old through the polished oak balustrades across from his Rheinstrasse bedroom—his red-faced, clench-fisted father standing over his sobbing, fallen mother, her left hand clutching her cheek and her right raised in a feeble attempt at self-defense. It wasn't the only time he'd swallowed his helpless rage.

His jaw unconsciously clenched and his pulse quickened at the sight, but his urge to boldly crash through the window and intervene was immediately suppressed by uncertainty and fear. Afraid to act on his first instinct, but compelled to do something—anything—he dropped his broom handle on the porch boards and made his presence known. Through the glass, he saw a startled Herman Eisenhut spin around at the sound. Seconds later, Helen Eisenhut appeared on the porch a few meters from him, wet and angry eyes turned his way for a split second before she jumped into the still-running pickup and sprayed gravel.

"The fuck you lookin' at?"

Mr. Eisenhut was suddenly on the porch, stubby left thumb steadily rubbing the palm of his right hand. To no one in particular, he spoke quietly, ominously. "Sometimes people don't wanna listen," he said. "So you gotta make 'em." As he turned to walk back inside, he looked directly at Bernhardt. "You hear me, boy?"

Bernhardt nodded, his jaw clenching once again as his broom and his impotence pulled him back around the corner of the porch.

o o o

The days ran longer, and Bernhardt knew his time was running short. They'd all heard the chatter about their immediate and long-term futures, and the tension in the camp ramped up even more, seemingly in diametric proportion to the diminishing volume of letters from home.

"They're getting ready to send all of us back to wherever we came from. Any day now. Back to wherever home was," said Fischer. "But I'm from Cologne. Not sure what's left there…" His voice trailed off as he sucked in a lungful of smoke.

Schlemmer chimed in. "Well fuck," he said, "if that's true and the Amis send me back to Lübeck, they could be sending me right into the hands of the Russians. I hear they shoot most of their prisoners, and work the rest to death, just for fun."

Bernhardt's blood ran cold at the thought.

An artillery officer from Görlitz who'd been captured at Arnhem had told him that he'd been told—by someone who'd been told—that the Soviets had overrun Silesia in February or March, and that no one expected them to be leaving anytime soon. It appeared, Bernhardt feared, that for all intents and purposes, the little slice of what used to be Germany he'd once called home might now be forever under the crushing boot heel of the Red Army.

That evening, bone-weary on the rumbling bus making its way back toward the camp, Bernhardt exhaled another long pull from his cigarette. He watched absentmindedly as the open window slipstream whipped his smoke away, its ghostly vapor instantly scattered to the breeze to vanish into the towering forests blanketing the snow-capped mountains that seemed to prop up the sky. Then more intently, slightly more energized, he repeated the action. Following a third exhalation, he closed his eyes, breathed in a deep lungful of cooling air, and savored the intoxicating scents of burning tobacco and exhaust fumes and pine needles and dust. And he made a decision.

Germany, he thought, *is history.*

America, he thought, as he opened his eyes, *is the future.*

He would live in the future.

17

They'd worked the plan out quickly, because time was simply not on their side.

As predicted, the Amis had started processing batches of prisoners out of the camp—with a few exceptions, those with the longest tenure typically the first to depart—and empty bunks now dotted virtually every barracks.

From what Bernhardt had been able to deduce, when it came to attitudes about repatriation, the prisoners basically broke down into three groups. The more ardent Nazis in the camp, though relatively few in number, were still vocal in their disgust for the gutless weaklings who'd surrendered, and who had clearly betrayed the Führer by living instead of dying.

"Fucking delusional," said Fish softly, through smoke-laden breath. "Still talking about resurgence and counterattacks and reclaiming the greatness of the Reich. Now?"

Bernhardt nodded. Schlemmer spit into the scrub. "Assholes," he said. "They think no one knows they raised their hands, too."

Their once mighty power to terrify and intimidate evaporating, the true believers were increasingly ignored, if not outright scorned, by the much more populous second group of prisoners, those who felt a massive sense of relief that their war was finally drawing to a conclusion, and who felt no urge to pursue the lost cause in which they may or may not have once believed. The vast majority of those men simply wanted to get back to their homes and their surviving loved ones, to get on with trying to rebuild their lives and their shattered country.

The group in which Bernhardt and Fischer and Schlemmer found themselves tended to hold another point of view. Many of them hailed from the eastern reaches of prewar Germany. And many had received the devastating, crushing news at one time or another: that their wives and children, their mothers and fathers and brothers and sisters, their aunts and uncles and cousins, had vanished from the face of the earth. Others had heard nothing of their loved ones for years, and so they'd long since assumed the worst while faintly hoping for the best.

For some, there was simply no home to go home to. Where once they might have been hoping to return to their civilian occupations or studies, they now understood that they faced the very real prospect of imprisonment and forced labor, or hardscrabble lives of poverty and sickness as their damaged bodies and minds ultimately succumbed to the war after all. And many of the members of this group—Bernhardt among them—for the most part viewed their time in America with fondness. They'd learned the language and gained an appreciation for their former adversaries—at least those with whom they'd had the most contact— as tough but predominantly fair and generous and honorable people The Amis were far from friends, but Bernhardt had long since stopped thinking of them as enemies. And he, for one, completely understood the animosity they'd displayed following the grim revelations in the newsreels. Although he'd explained it to absolutely no one, unlike some of the remaining hardcore devotees, he needed no convincing that the horrors depicted in the films were true. He knew it in his soul.

He and Fischer and Schlemmer had just sparked up their Camels as they waited for the morning bus that would take them to the mill. And in that moment, alone together, Bernhardt decided to confide in the two men he'd come closest to thinking of as friends.

"I'm not going back, boys."

"Back?" said Fischer. "Back to what? To your broom?"

"No, dummy," said Bernhardt, voice low. "I mean to Germany. To Chemnitz. There's nothing there for me now, and the only reason I volunteered to go to Africa in the first place was to keep myself away from the Russians. I'll be goddamned if I'll walk right into their hands now. Not after everything I've been through. What about you?"

Fischer toed at a piece of loose gravel for a long moment. When he looked up, his eyes were hard. "I don't know where my parents or sister are," he said. "I don't even know if they're alive. I hear Cologne is in ruins, and my little brother vanished in Ukraine."

Bernhard glanced over to see Schlemmer take a long drag on his cigarette, then look up to follow the white smoke curling away into the gentle morning breeze.

"Goddamn," said Schlemmer. "I sure like these American smokes. What are you thinking?"

Bernhardt looked around furtively. "You both rode the train," he whispered. "This is a great big country. If we can get ourselves out of this camp, we've got a chance. The worst thing that can happen is they catch us and send us where they were gonna send us anyway."

"Uh, the actual worst thing that can happen," said Fischer, "is that someone shoots us."

"No different than letting them ship us home to get killed there," said Bernhardt. "But minus the long, boring trip."

They stood silent for a moment, but more like half a moment.

"Okay, Bern," said Fischer. "I'm ready to live again."

"Ah, what the hell," said Schlemmer.

Then they all grinned, and they all took long, deep puffs on their American cigarettes. And so it was decided.

◦ ◦ ◦

Under a too-bright moon, they made their way to the mill.

It really hadn't been that difficult to get through the wire, stolen shop pliers unnoticed and the guards most likely asleep in their tower huts, as they'd been so many times lately. They covered the distance in less than ninety minutes, the ruts and puddles of the familiar dirt road beneath their feet, the rich smells of the forest all around them, their lungs and legs fully accustomed to exertion at altitude.

On reaching the mill yard, lit only by a few over-door downlights here and there, they split up, Fischer heading toward the canteen to rifle through the cupboards, Schlemmer moving to the machine shop to root around as quietly as he could.

Bernhardt tried the office door, unsurprised to find it locked. Skirting the building to its shadowed western facade, he peered through a window into blackness. With as gentle a tap as he could manage, he popped a small, shirttail-wrapped rock through a single pane, the sound still louder than a thunderclap to him. Carefully, he snaked an arm inside to flip the latch and free the lower sash, then climbed in, trying to coax an impossible silence from his boots as he stepped down, first onto a toilet seat, then onto a glass-littered floor.

He eased the bathroom's door open and stepped into a narrow hallway. And then, almost definitely, he heard something. His heart jumped into his throat and he froze, goosebumps crawling up his arms and legs and into his scalp as his mind raced to process what it had just taken in. Not half a second later he heard it again, the muffled but distinct sound of a woman's voice, cut short mid-word by some means or another.

Fear threatened to seize him, but experience assured him that despite this unforeseen wrinkle, at this moment he was still in control. *Just breathe,* he thought. *Think.* He remained still as various courses of action played out in his mind like a movie.

The next words, fearful and fierce and emphatic, were almost as clear as if their source was standing right next to him.

"Stop it! I said no!"

The voice was clearly emanating, Bernhardt decided, from behind the office door some five feet ahead and slightly to the right of him. As he crept forward, he heard and felt rumbling footsteps, and he knew instinctively that they weren't created by a woman. He took another half step forward and rapped a knuckle once on the door, then took two steps back and coiled himself. Then he sucked in a deep breath and watched as the doorknob directly opposite him twisted. When he heard a deep voice mumble something and the door began to swing inward, he sprung forward with his eighty-nine kilogram mass, hammering it open with all of his strength. He felt the impact, heard the thud of solid wood hitting equally solid skull. And somewhere beyond that, he heard a high-pitched scream.

Regaining his balance and his bearings in the open doorway, Bernhardt saw the prone form of a man, smelled the whiskey and cigarettes. Beyond the moonlight panels on the floor, a girl was huddled on the office's old sofa, arms clasped around herself.

"Who is it?!" she said. "Oh my God! Who is it?!"

Bernhardt recognized the voice immediately. After all, it was virtually the only female voice he'd heard in years. He stepped forward, his feet catching for a second in a piece of blue cloth. A blouse. He reached down to pick it up, took another half step forward, and held it out, eyes downcast as a lightning-quick hand snatched it from him. Then he stepped backward, and flinched ever so slightly at the sharp sound as his boot heel inadvertently propelled a loose button across the floorboards like a bullet.

"Please," Bernhardt said softly. "I, uh….Are you okay, miss?"

She'd been crying, and her breath was still coming hard, her words halting but defiant.

"Who…what are you doing here?"

Bernhardt's voice caught in his throat as the full implications of his new circumstances began to crystallize. Of course he had no business being here, no way to explain his presence away. By his own foolish, unthinking actions, he'd been discovered, and he'd put them all at risk. Heart beginning to race, growing panic barely suppressed, he struggled for answers to a hundred rapid-fire internal questions. Why hadn't he just turned around? Why hadn't he just run? Why hadn't he…? The lump on the floor emitted a soft moan, and he stepped closer to it in case it decided to attempt movement. And to hide in the shadows.

"I didn't think he'd get like that…like he couldn't hear me…like he couldn't care less what I said. We were just…out, you know? Goofing around. He had a bottle. Drank a little too much I guess. But how could I…how could I be so damn stupid?"

Her self-doubting questions echoed Bernhardt's own. Afraid of what silence might bring, he forced the English words out.

"I…I need to be on my way. I didn't mean to disturb."

"Disturb?"

Bernhardt kept his eyes focused on the bright squares on the floor as Helen Eisenhut slipped on her blouse. He almost gasped when she took a half step toward him, into the moonlight.

"I know you," she said, almost softly.

"Uh, not really, miss." What to say? What to do?

"You're from the camp. What are you…? Are you… escaping? But why would you do that now? I mean, isn't the war over? Aren't you going home soon?"

Bernhardt's gut churned, his every instinct telling him to do now what he should have done in the first place. To not be here. And then he looked up, and he saw her eyes. And in that instant, an inexplicable sense of calm came over him. He hoped he'd heard correctly, hoped he'd understood, but he'd almost felt sure that something in the tone of her voice—the tone of her questions—had conveyed the opposite of accusation, the opposite of fear. And that hope carried fear and uncertainty and self-doubt away from him.

He stepped into the light.

"I…I can't do what other people tell me to do anymore."

A long pause told Bernhardt that he wasn't the only one who didn't know what to say next, what to do.

The lump on the floor moaned again.

"You'd better get what you need," she said, "and get out of here before he wakes up. He's a guard. Maybe you already knew that?"

The moment gone, Bernhardt moved to the desk and rifled through a drawer until he found it. He'd been in the office a few times, sent to fetch or deliver various things, and he'd seen where Mr. Eisenhut kept it one day when the drawer had been left open.

He picked it up, relishing the familiar heft in his hand. She shrank back from him at the sight of it.

"What do you want me to do, miss?"

"Oh my God, no," she said. "I mean…what do you mean?"

Bernhardt looked down at the revolver, then snapped his head around as another groan made itself heard. "Oh, no, miss," he said, "I didn't mean… I mean what do you want me to do? For you?"

"Oh, God," she said, "I…I don't know. I only know I don't want to be anywhere near him ever again. In fact, I…" She paused for a short eternity. "Actually," she said, "I just damn well decided." She took a full step forward. "I don't want to be anywhere near this place ever again either."

"Miss?"

"It's Helen."

Head down, gaze focused almost completely on the prone man, Bernhardt watched from the corner of his eye as she turned her back to him, ran her fingers through her hair, and wiped her face with her sleeve. Composed, she spun to face him.

"Take me with you."

"Miss?"

A hundred new questions formed as Bernhardt sensed her rising to the possibility of her newly formed idea.

"You heard me," she said, voice stronger now, almost commanding. "Take me with you. I'm almost as much a prisoner here as you are. My father's…well, he is what he is. He's just no good since…" She nodded toward the lump on the floor. "Turns out this guy's sure as hell no good. This whole damn place is no good. There's nothing here for me, and I… Well, I just decided. I want out."

Bernhardt stood stock still for a few seconds, synapses once again firing through endless scenarios in another attempt to make sense of the unforeseen. Abruptly, he straddled the moaning, crumpled form, reached down, and rolled it onto its back.

"I know this man."

Bernhardt tucked the pistol into his belt and patted the unconscious guard down, recoiling as a loud belch escaped from somewhere in the man's rancid depths and the already overwhelming stench of booze and tobacco and sweat intensified. In one of the guard's shirt pockets he found a silver flask, shook it, and twisted its top. With his left hand, he pinched the man's nostrils tight, and almost instantly the Ami's mouth gaped open in an unconscious act of self-preservation. For a brief second, Bernhardt thought he saw the guard's eyes open, thought he saw them struggling to focus on him, but they closed again, and the man choked and gurgled and spluttered as Bernhardt drained the last of the flask's remaining contents into his open maw.

Bernhardt tossed the empty flask to the floor, then he stood and looked at the jagged triangular scar between his thumb and fingers, his hand steady in the moonlight.

"My name is Bernhardt," he said, extending his hand, palm up.

"You helped me once," he said. "I'm happy to repay that kindness."

"Where the fuck were you?!"

Fischer and Schlemmer were more than a little agitated.

"Sorry," said Bernhardt. "I, uh, ran into something unexpected."

Helen Eisenhut stepped out of the shadows and into the cone of light cast by the hooded bulb above the machine shop door.

"This is Miss Eisenhut."

Bernhardt grinned sheepishly as Fischer's jaw dropped. Schlemmer's words audibly confirmed the disbelief his utterly stunned expression conveyed. "Jesus Christus!" he said. "Wo kommt sie her? Und wovon zum Teufel redest du?! Wir müssen hier weg!"

"English," said Bernhardt. "Remember, only English." He needed them cool-headed. He needed everyone—most of all himself—to believe he had a plan. "I'll explain later," he said, "but Miss Eisenhut is coming with us. There's a car parked behind the shop. And a pickup truck. We can take them."

"Let's go!" implored Fischer. "We need to be away from this place.

It will be light in less than three hours and we need to disappear."

"Don't worry," said Bernhardt. "We will. But first we need to take care of something. And make a couple of stops."

Bernhardt turned to Helen. "You know how to drive, yes?"

"I grew up in a logging camp, soldier," came the quietly indignant reply. "I bet I know a whole lot of things you probably think I don't."

18

Head pounding relentlessly and unbearably to the beat as a tinny Johnny Mercer urged him to ac-cent-tchu-ate the positive, teeth and lips and swollen tongue fouled with God only knew what, the man willed open a sticky eye and tried his best to figure out where the hell he might be and what, exactly, he might be doing there. One thing he figured out within seconds: he'd puked at some point—or more likely at a few points—and a repulsive, cold paste had coagulated on his face and in his hair, gluing him to what he eventually determined was the front bench seat of his car.

Clammy left hand gripping the cold steering wheel, eyes squeezed tight, Private First Class Eugene K. Smithson struggled to pull himself into a half-seated position, pain and regret radiating through his head and body as he fought unsuccessfully to get his lifeless right arm to help tip his bulk over against the driver's side door. The exertion immediately prompted another uncontainable wave of nausea, and pushed out another surge of the putrid pore-stink that had soaked his clothing almost enough to mask the fact that he'd pissed himself.

Nothing could mask the fact that he wasn't wearing any pants.

When the Buick's door suddenly burst open, Smitty spilled out face first onto the gravel, the completely numb right arm he'd slept on for the last four or five hours flopping like a raw pork tenderloin, useless. Groaning as if he'd been shot, he managed to roll over just in time to get a one-eyed view of a policeman placing his hat on the car's roof, holding his breath, and leaning in to shut off its idling engine and headlights and radio. When the cop's upper body reappeared, he replaced his cap with his left hand as he spun on his heel and took a long look down his outstretched right arm at the puke-slimed object pinched unenthusiastically between his thumb and index finger.

"Well, whadda we got here?"

Holding the befouled envelope up to catch the early morning rays, the policeman twisted his head and squinted to read the address engraved on its top left corner.

"Eisenhut Logging. Bridger Falls, Montana."

The cop tilted his head a little more in order to tackle the beautiful cursive fountain pen handwriting, smeared and partially obscured by a disgusting yellow-brown slick.

"Petty cash."

Powerless to stop the incessant pounding in his head, Smitty fought to shake the grit from his face, to force words past his swollen tongue, but the herculean effort triggered another spew of acidic liquid that pooled in the gravel around the policeman's right shoe. The cop wiped his sole on the prone guard's puke-wet shirt, then reached back into the car. With a pencil through its trigger guard, he lifted a shiny silver revolver from the driver's side floorboards. Leaning down to get a better look at Smitty's equally shiny but ashen and green-tinged face, the cop spoke through gritted teeth.

"Welcome to Helena, son," he said. "Now I suppose you better be showin' me some ID."

o o o

"This is it."

They'd changed into the ill-fitting dungarees and work shirts and heavy jackets taken from the mill's machine shop, and they'd buried their camp clothes in the woods somewhere off the side of a pitch black highway. Each man's canvas bag contained his share of the food pilfered from the canteen, a couple of packs of cigarettes, and the few dollars and personal effects they'd managed to retrieve from their prison camp hiding places.

Bernhardt distributed the bottom pieces of the map he'd taken from Smitty's glove box, torn precisely so that their present location essentially occupied one corner of each man's segment. The plan, Bernhardt knew, wasn't really a plan, so much as a rudimentary shred of an idea. Each of them would simply move away from the marked corner of his piece of map.

"Okay, Fish," said Bernhardt. "Southwest is you. Schlemmer, you go southeast. We've made it this far"—he stabbed a finger at the dot at the center of the very bottom of his piece of the map—"but maybe this was the easy part."

"Butt," said Fischer. "What the hell kind of a name is that for a place to start from?"

"Fish, you big jerk," Bernhardt said. "I'm pretty sure it's pronounced 'beaut,' which makes it about as good a place as any, don't you think? If you're right, it sounds like a place none of us want to end up in."

They grinned and nodded and shook hands in silence, then Bernhardt stood for a moment and watched as Fischer headed toward the bus terminal. Schlemmer moved off toward the train station a few blocks over.

When his two friends—well, the closest things he'd ever really had to friends—had disappeared, Bernhardt turned and climbed into the pickup truck's passenger seat, then he smiled and nodded as its driver spun the vehicle's wheels in the gravel, the anxiety-induced expenditure of energy getting them virtually nowhere until the rubber found the pavement and propelled them west.

19

The desks were connected to each other, their black cast iron frames bolted to parallel flat wooden rails at their bases. Uncomfortable seats and slanted worktops evenly spaced, it was as if the physical properties of the children who were fated to occupy them for endless hours five days per week were simply expected to conform to certain predetermined specifications. Each writing surface had been uniquely decorated by the hands of countless amateur artists over the years. Joseph's particular desk—3B—second from the front in the third row from the classroom's front entrance door, featured an impressive gallery of assorted doodles and initials and mostly incomprehensible but presumably swear-ish words so dense that it had been virtually impossible for him to glean any real meaning from them, no matter how much intense effort he'd put in.

Behind him, her dark hair cut in a style that Joseph could only assume matched her mother's, sat Audrey Kindrachuck. That Audrey had taken so much pleasure in being the first to reveal and speculate on the sad or sinister or tragic reasons for the sudden departure of Joseph's mother two years prior had cut him to the bone. What kind of a kid wants to make someone small? He'd wondered ever since.

In front of Joseph sat the one kid whose arrival had made him feel tall.

They'd met on day one of sixth grade. On that day, and really, ever since, Simon Charleyboy had been the new kid: the worst thing a kid can be. Well, almost the worst. They all knew there are some things that kids who want to be like all the other kids can hide, but the way you look on the outside isn't one of them.

That first day, Joseph had watched the new boy's back heaving as he'd been sharply and publicly admonished by the diminutive and universally hated Mr. Atkinson to "Buck up, lad!" while being pierced, Joseph knew, by the same needles of collective cruelty and disdain for otherness he'd felt directed his way so many times.

Joseph had decided right then.

At that very first recess, he'd made his way over to the spot by the wall where the lonely figure had stood, head down. Joseph had said nothing, just leaned against the bricks until the bell had rung and the stampede back into hell had commenced.

The next day, words.

"Asskisson."

"What?"

"Ass. Kiss. Son."

When the grin had finally split Simon's face, it had lit him up, and that had lit Joseph up, and from that point forward, the two of them had still been alone, but they'd been alone together. By the end of that September, they'd become inseparable, or at least, they were whenever they could be.

They were walking home, about twelve minutes from the school to the corner of Joseph's street near the edge of town, Simon facing a slightly longer stretch alone on the road north.

Simon had become a new kid, he'd explained to Joseph, because his father had gotten a job at the Atlas. His mom didn't like it much here, he'd said, all alone in the tiny house all day with his little sister, and he'd often heard his parents arguing through the thin walls at night. Most times, he'd said, about money, and other times about missing family, and about whatever else it was grownups argued about.

Parents, they both agreed, talked about a lot of strange things.

"Yeah," said Joseph. "My father says that some people were made different, so God would know who to let into heaven."

"Huh?" said Simon. "I thought God just let all good people into heaven. He needs other clues?"

"Yeah, that kinda doesn't make sense, huh?"

"Well, my dad," said Simon, "says everyone's the same down a mine. Everyone's coal color."

The two of them talked about all kinds of things, but the subject of Joseph's mother never really came up. Simon knew, of course, that Joseph's father was the school principal. He'd already met Mr. Holliman on more than one occasion, ordered to the feared and hated office for infractions as minor as not having his pencils sharpened before Mr. Atkinson's class, and as major as being unable to control the churning of his anxious, new kid stomach.

During that first week, Joseph had sat across from Simon as he'd struggled to choke down a few mouthfuls of whatever his mom had thought might least offend his senses. But on that day, it had been tuna with celery and mayonnaise, and Simon had immediately lost his battle, spraying a regurgitated whitish mess onto the table and the floor and his clothes.

The uproar from the kids, including Joseph, who'd instinctively leaped away from Simon's vicinity as if they'd been blasted from cannons, was instant.

As was Simon's punishment.

Principal Holliman had, unfortunately, been passing by the lunch-room and had witnessed the commotion through the doorway. Joseph had watched in petrified horror as his father had descended on his new friend like a hawk, and in the terrible vacuum of the suddenly soundless room, his father's words had been as cold as the lumpy wet slime that coated Simon's new shirt.

"Do you think the good Lord wants you to waste the bounty He has provided? Eat, boy."

The kids, Joseph included, had looked on in horror as Simon, now terrified as well as humiliated, had choked on another repulsive sandwich bite and instantly vomited again. And they'd been unable to look away as Simon had been shoved facedown into his mess, then dragged out of the dining hall by his collar. Naturally, all eyes had then been turned on Joseph, and another burning avalanche of guilt and shame had threatened to crush him back into oblivion.

When Simon had finally crept back into class an hour later, he'd still been wearing his washroom-rinsed shirt, and his red-rimmed eyes had sunken into the murky hollows in his ashen face. For the rest of the afternoon, he hadn't made eye contact with anyone, and he hadn't made a sound.

And at the ringing of the dismissal bell, instead of making a left out of the exit doors with Joseph, Simon had grimaced at him and turned in the opposite direction, back toward the hated office.

With a cold, heavy stone in his gut, Joseph had made the walk home alone.

20

The palms of his gloves, Joseph noted proudly, had begun to sport a rich, dark brown sheen, mounting evidence of the five consecutive Saturdays he'd spent hauling and sawing and nailing and sweating. Surrounded by a cool forest of lush black-green, now punctuated by periodic explosions of vibrant reds and oranges and yellows, he and the old man hammered away, each in his own mind, almost in rhythm.

Joseph had quickly come to cherish Saturdays.

He'd wake long before first light, unable to control eyelids that simply insisted on being wide open, and he'd stare into the slowly waning gloom, waiting—forever, it seemed—for the thump of his father's fist on his door. At that always jarring alert, he'd leap from the relative warmth of his covers to run-walk into the chill of the bathroom, to pee, and to wash his face and hands and to brush his teeth. Then he'd retrace his steps, make his bed, and get himself dressed in what he'd come to think of as his work clothes. Eyes on the kitchen clock as it ticked painfully toward seven, he'd make sure to be extra double sure to earnestly proclaim his heartfelt thanks for the bounty before him, then he'd methodically choke down the bland, unadorned oatmeal that his father always claimed would sustain him and give him strength. And of course he'd clean his bowl and spoon perfectly before returning them to their storage places and standing for inspection and dismissal. There was absolutely no way he was getting himself into any sort of trouble on a Saturday morning.

About the third or fourth week in, once released from his father's clutches, Joseph had begun to run, rather than walk, the five blocks to the school. Each and every Saturday morning since week one he'd arrived to find Frank Gardner already waiting out front, rain or shine, cigarette dangling, leaning against his pickup's front right fender with his arms folded across his chest, an exaggerated scowl of disdain on his face. And each and every Saturday morning, Frank had pretended to look at a watch he didn't wear and had said the exact same thing: "What'd you do? Sleep in?"

It had taken a couple of Saturdays for Joseph to understand that Frank, an adult, was joking with him, and that the joke was that, of course, Frank knew what Joseph knew—that Joseph had absolutely no control over any aspect of events in his own life. After five weeks of it, Joseph had begun to look forward to that same dumb joke as much as he'd ever looked forward to anything he could remember in his long twelve years of life.

Early afternoon, the two of them were sitting in the October sun, wordlessly and voraciously consuming the peanut butter and jam on white bread sandwiches Frank had made. And it just happened.

"Thank you."

Midchew, the old man suddenly froze like a statue, then arched an exaggerated eyebrow and squinted hard into the trees. "Whoa," he said. "You hear something? Coulda swore I heard something."

Gut churning with uncertainty and anxious anticipation, Joseph stared at his sandwich, retreating back into the safety of silence as Frank swallowed and turned toward him.

"Listen, kid," said Frank, "you don't have to thank me for a goddamn thing. I should be thanking you. I've got myself about three-quarters of a fine new outbuilding here, and if it wasn't for you, I'd have four-quarters of a rundown old piece of crap shed instead."

This time, Joseph couldn't help himself. The smile just…emerged. He chanced a quick sideways glance up at Frank, and something in the way the old man had taken another pull from his cigarette told Joseph that he'd witnessed it.

"Remember the first day you came here?" Frank asked, Joseph unsure if his involuntary flinch at the question had been seen. "Well, okay," he said. "I don't mean the actual first day. I mean the first day you came to work. You were pretty goddamn scared, I bet. But you know what, you impressed the hell out of me. I mean, you're just a kid, and you're forced to come and work all by yourself with some scary old bastard? The scary old bastard is me, just in case you weren't following along too good."

Joseph smiled inside at that. Not outside.

"So, I've been thinking," said Frank. "We're getting close to done with this project, but for my liking, it's uh, well, it's going a little too fast." Joseph glanced up at him, stomach letting him know it wasn't too sure where this conversation was going. "Doesn't seem like you've paid your debt," said Frank. "I think maybe you, uh…you need to spend a few more Saturdays here. I mean if you want to, that is."

Joseph's eyes narrowed as he tried to be sure he was understanding what Frank was saying. Then he forgot to be scared, and another word fell out.

"More?"

"Well, yeah," said Frank. "If you want to."

Joseph couldn't believe what he was hearing. No one had asked him what he wanted to do since he couldn't remember when, and he wanted what Frank Gardner had asked him so badly that he felt like screaming "Yes!" at the absolute top of his lungs. Instead, he simply nodded and half smiled and tried to keep the water from his eyes.

"Well, okay then," said Frank. "I'll work it out with your father. Tell him I've got a few more things I need you to do. I'm afraid you're gonna be busy for a few extra Saturdays, for sure."

The hush of waving treetops had descended on them by the time Frank spoke again.

"Remember what I said a while back? About having to be someplace, but being able to leave whenever you want? You remember that?"

"Yes, sir."

"Hey," said Frank, "I'm not sir. I'm Frank. Okay?"

Joseph nodded mutely. The old man downed the last of his pop in one long pull, then lit up another smoke. "Look," he said. "The actual day we first met, the day this whole thing really started…"

Joseph stared hard into the fire as something small and unwanted stirred in his gut.

"…There was a book involved, if I recall."

Joseph stole another fleeting glance at Frank. The old man pulled a worn paperback from his jacket pocket and held it out. Joseph sat motionless, but his thoughts forced themselves to be heard.

"I…I'm not allowed."

"Not allowed what?"

"Books like that."

"That so?" said Frank. "Even if it's part of your job?"

Joseph shot him another quizzical look.

"See, from now on," said Frank, "your job, if you want it, that is, for some of the time you're here on Saturdays, is to read. To me. And I get to choose the book, 'cause I'm the boss. Like this one. Go on, take it if you want."

Joseph reached out an uncertain hand and took the small volume. In his lap, he turned its cover toward the sun, captivated by the rich browns and blues and greens of its soft watercolor illustration, and its yellow and white letters.

"I just figured maybe," said Frank, "that might be someplace you'd wanna visit."

Joseph dropped the book to his lap and his chin to his chest.

Inside him, something he couldn't remember feeling for a long, long time grabbed hold and squeezed tight. No matter how hard he tried, he simply couldn't stop his eyes from welling up, couldn't swallow away the lump that filled his throat.

A long moment passed before he understood.

Those terrible, uncontrollable things weren't happening because he felt pain or fear or anger or loneliness or sadness. They were happening because someone actually wanted him around.

21

For days, he avoided opening the book. Books made him afraid.

His father had made it clear, over and over and over again, that the sinfulness of man could only be assuaged by one book, and that virtually all others, including the vast majority of those assigned to him by his various teachers over the years, were not only pointless drivel, but also dangerous drivel. How they could be both pointless and dangerous at the same time had been a question Joseph had known better than to ask.

In the flashlit dome beneath the tenuous protection of his sheets and blanket, he stared at the paperback's cover: two men on a raft, both barefoot and wearing straw-colored hats, one standing and leaning against a long, straight pole that angled into the water, the other sitting on a box or a barrel or something, a pipe in his mouth, a curved fishing pole in his hands arcing toward the water.

He'd been on a boat once.

His mother had taken him to visit his aunt and uncle. He was pretty sure he'd laughed and run and played and gorged himself on all kinds of delicious food. He'd even had a pop, in exchange for the easy promise to never, ever mention it to his father.

He was pretty sure he remembered that.

But he couldn't be sure of much else about that time now. He'd been maybe five or six, and his father had solemnly informed him that his aunt and uncle had been killed soon after, and that was most of what he remembered now—the gut-punch suddenness of it, his mother crying mutely into the kitchen sink as his father had spelled out the sad and terrible facts. His uncle, his father had explained, must have been drunk out of his mind, no doubt coming back too late at night from one of those despicable movie theaters, or maybe someplace worse. Their car had been crushed like a tin can. The Mounties had done whatever the Mounties did in such cases, but in the end, his father had said, the truck driver who'd hit them had a family to feed and he was a good, churchgoing man, and maybe he'd had a few drinks, but he was really sorry, and it really wasn't his fault, and so that had been the end of that.

Cautiously and carefully, Joseph bent the worn front cover back and leafed through the first few pages.

By the time his heavy eyelids asserted their irresistible will some ninety-five minutes later, he'd been in a world he'd never dreamed might exist, where they spoke in a way he'd never heard. He'd met a boy named Tom, and another named Huck, and they'd played a prank on a man named Jim. And right up to the very moment that his thoughts had been consumed by the dark, Joseph had still been with them.

22

To say Joseph was nervous would be like saying water was wet.

Miss Hamer, their still-brand-new-to-them grade seven teacher, had handed out the dreaded assignment the week prior: an oral presentation on a science-related topic of their choice. As zero hour had approached, the energy in the classroom had become palpable, some kids eager for the event, others obviously terrified, most somewhere between.

The first kid had made a poster about photosynthesis, and had haltingly pointed to various bits and pieces of it as he'd explained how plants somehow managed to turn sunlight into oxygen. The next kid had stumbled through six painful minutes of electricity and magnets. Next, Audrey Kindrachuck had delivered an incredibly confident but actually incomprehensible talk about something that had involved baking soda and vinegar. Joseph had been too gut-sick to pay attention to any of them.

When the door suddenly opened and he turned to see his father enter the room, his gut-sickness threatened to make itself visible. He clenched everything he had, and squeezed his eyes tight as he quickly looked away.

The low enormity of his father's voice pierced the room.

"Carry on, carry on," it said. "Please, Miss Hamer. Children. Don't mind me. Just thought I'd stop by to see how things are going."

All eyes suddenly on her, Miss Hamer—who Joseph and Simon had unanimously agreed was not only the youngest but also the nicest and prettiest and best teacher either of them had ever had, ever—smiled weakly and nodded almost imperceptibly.

"Well, of course," she said. "Welcome, Mr. Holliman. We're just getting started with our science presentations. Let's see, who's next?"

She glanced down at her desktop, and called Simon's name.

Simon rummaged in his desk, then turned his head and nodded at Joseph. Joseph managed to unclench himself just enough to nod back. Moments later, a weighted and wrinkled brown paper lunch bag dangling from one hand, and seemingly buoyant despite the combined pressure of the twenty-six pairs of eyes now one hundred percent trained on him, Simon took a breath, cleared his throat, and began.

"I'm Simon," he said, to snickers that verged on barely suppressed laughter. As she was prone to do from time to time, Miss Hamer glared at the various offenders and snapped her fingers exactly three times, drawing the momentary attention of almost everyone. Joseph's eyes never left Simon, and Simon's surprisingly confident gaze never strayed from his taunting audience. With a growing sense of awe, Joseph watched his friend stand strangely firm, back straight, chin high, almost defiant. He'd never seen anything like that from Simon. Ever. Yet here he was, practically staring the stupid smirks off the faces of the classmates who held him in such low regard. When the room finally fell silent, Simon spoke again, his voice clear and steady and strong. Maybe, Joseph thought, even proud.

"And this," said Simon as he reached into his brown paper bag, "is my topic."

The object he held aloft was a little bit longer and quite a bit fatter than the thumb that held it firmly against the tip of his outstretched index finger. Essentially flat where it met his thumb and tapered to a point at the other end, it looked like a curved and polished chocolate brown and black rock, and every kid in the room was suddenly sitting forward in rapt, open-mouthed attention.

"Before we moved here," said Simon, "my dad worked in a mine in Alberta. In a place called Drumheller. Drumheller's famous for all kinds of things, like coal, but it's mostly famous for dinosaur fossils. My dad says they find them all the time between the seams—coal is actually fossilized plants buried way down in the ground—so he knows what to look for. But we found this in a weird rock formation called hoodoos, in a place called the Badlands. We looked it up in a book at the library, and the book said it might be an Albertosaurus tooth, and if it is, it's probably about sixty-five or seventy million years old. Scientists say fossils like this are evidence that Earth is always evolving—"

"Thank you."

Quiet but incredibly loud, the sudden interjection of the all too familiar baritone voice sucked the air out of the room, and left Simon standing open-mouthed, as rock solid as the thing he held aloft.

"I think we've heard enough," said Principal Holliman. "Thank you, young man."

"Oh, but Mr. Holliman," said Miss Hamer, clearly unsure what was transpiring, "I think Simon has more to share with the class. He certainly knows his subject…"

"Yes, well," said Mr. Holliman, "be that as it may, Miss Hamer, I think the other students have heard quite enough conjecture, don't you? Why don't you move on with the rest of the class?"

Joseph wished he could disappear. Trapped, he watched in horror as his father once again turned his icy attention directly to Simon, his thin smile an obvious and glaringly ineffective attempt to warm the now unmistakably frigid atmosphere.

"Simon, I'd like you to join me in my office," said Mr. Holliman. "I'd like you to tell me more about your…about this object. I'll expect you momentarily." He nodded at the clearly bewildered and flustered Miss Hamer, and Joseph saw his father's disingenuous smile drop away as he spun on his heel. Seconds later, Principal Holliman slipped out of the room the same way he'd come in, leaving an enormous stunned silence in his wake. All eyes turned to Simon. Mouth still hanging open, hand still in the air, Simon turned to Miss Hamer.

"Am I…am I in trouble, miss?"

Before she could muster an answer, Simon turned to Joseph. The burn of humiliation once again reddening his face, Joseph looked at the speckled green linoleum, hoping against hope but knowing full well what likely awaited his friend. Through it all, he felt Simon's fear as strongly as if it were his own.

Miss Hamer's heels clicked loudly as she walked to Simon and put a gentle hand on his shoulder. Her voice soft as the general buzz in the room began to escalate, she smiled warmly, tried to reassure him.

"Oh, no, no, no," she said, "that was very interesting, Simon. Very interesting. I just think Mr. Holliman wants to get a closer look at your science exhibit." Gently, she extracted the fossil from Simon's hand and dropped it into his brown bag. "Run along now, and do as he asked. You can rejoin us when you're done. Okay?"

Jaw tight, eyes intense in his stone face, Simon nodded and began the long shuffle from the front of the classroom to its rear door. As he passed Joseph's desk, he managed to catch Joseph's eye and mouth the words: "It's okay."

Joseph knew full well it wasn't okay.

His instincts and his own experiences had already hinted at the kinds of words he feared—in fact he knew—his father would use.

He'd used words like them to justify "enlightening" Joseph just a few weeks prior, after Joseph had made the mistake of wondering aloud where every other person on Earth had come from, if, as Reverend Ainsley had reminded them all earlier that Sunday morning, Eve was the only woman God had ever created, and she'd only had sons.

Insolence.

Blasphemy.

Temerity.

Sacrilege.

Joseph had heard such words countless times, but he still didn't understand exactly what they meant. He only knew that they invariably summoned the wrath of God, and that for him, the instrument of that wrath was his own father.

When the third period bell rang a few minutes later and Simon had still not returned to his place in class, Joseph made a decision. Or maybe the decision had been made for him. His hand shot up.

"May I go to the washroom, miss?"

Permission granted, Joseph casually strolled to the rear door of the classroom, but once in the hallway, he practically sprinted to the nearest exit. Bursting through the fire door, he took an immediate hard left, ducking low to keep his head and torso below the row of classroom windows that ran almost to the end of that wing of the building. At the small stretch of solid wall between the last classroom and the school offices, he paused, adrenaline pumping to the drumbeat in his sternum and ears. And then he steeled himself, and stood tall.

It's pretty hard to stand tall when you're only twelve or thirteen years old. Even harder when you're only six, or seven, or eight. But he'd tried for his mother. As his mother had tried for him.

The first time he could remember, the dinner fork in his hand had been enough.

Screaming at his father to leave his cowering, sobbing, and pleading mother be, he'd tried to plunge its tines into the soft flesh of his father's calf with all of the force his small body had been able to muster. The piercing howl of rage that had filled his ears had been only temporary, as something had almost immediately extinguished all sound and light and sensation for him. When he'd struggled back toward the surface, in a strange room, in a strange bed, he'd only been able to detect faraway snippets of his mother's voice.

"...always climbing..."

"...that darned barn..."

"...matter of time before he fell..."

Stranger still, he'd imagined that just above the water, his father had been holding his hand.

Back hard against the school wall, Joseph sucked in four or five deep inhalations, looked down to confirm that the fire extinguisher was actually in his hands, and then coiled himself and swung it with everything he had.

The weird silence that followed the cacophony of shattering glass and clattering venetian blinds was prominent but fleeting, and almost immediately filled with the loud exclamations of shocked and panicked adult voices. For that split second, time came to a standstill. Then, as if he'd been snapped back the way he'd come by a giant rubber band, Joseph crouch-sprinted back to the fire door vestibule, where his wildly hammering heart caught in his throat, the enormity of his stupidity only outweighed by the mass of the stone in his stomach that confirmed his desperate situation.

Exit only.

Handleless rust red doors had trapped him, taunted him, defeated him, and so he simply stood in the cold and waited for the inevitable.

It was Ass Kiss Son who burst forth in a froth, and who angrily and loudly marched Joseph down the hallway toward the wreckage of his father's office, his shoes barely even contacting the linoleum tiles as he hung virtually suspended from his own choking shirt collar.

Hours later, manacles once again chafing his left wrist and right ankle, his back and buttocks and thighs once again screaming in silent agony, Joseph struggled to make sense of what else he was feeling.

He hated the things his father did to him. He hated his father for doing them. And he hated his mother for leaving and for allowing them to happen, almost as much as he loved her for everything else. But most of all, he hated that because of all of it, both at home and at school, he lived in almost constant fear. And shame.

As he stared into the rough weave of the burlap inches from his face, a truth revealed itself.

In the midst of the earlier chaos, in the final seconds before his inevitable descent into his father's wrath, he'd glimpsed Simon's face in the crowd of gawking hallway onlookers. His friend's watery-eyed smile and grateful nod had clarified something that had confused him for as long as he could remember—something about the difference between his two parents that he'd never been able to understand.

In the foul, sound-dead, burlap-padded cell, he suddenly realized that he was proud of what he'd done to invoke his father's wrath.

Because when you care about someone, you take the pain.

You don't give it.

23

"You're crazy, you know?"

The sun warm on their cold faces, they'd been leaning against the wall in their usual morning recess spot away from the kinetic hullabaloo of the schoolyard when Simon finally brought up the day a week prior that they'd both tried to put behind them.

"When that stupid fire extinguisher came through the window, I mean, I didn't know what the heck was happening. All I know is that Mr. Holliman...well, your dad...he forgot all about me pretty quick."

Joseph grinned and nodded but said nothing, just continued to pretend to be focused on the swarm of kids running and jumping and tagging each other and trying not to fall on the gravel that passed for the school's playing field.

"He didn't like that word."

"What word?" said Joseph.

"Evolution," said Simon. "He didn't like the word evolution. He said it was a fairy tale word bad people made up to try to make the world a worse place. He said he didn't want to, but, well, he had to... you know?"

His grin long gone, Joseph was afraid to ask, but he did it anyway.

"Had to do what?"

"He said he had to educate me. He had to help me feel truth."

A long twenty seconds passed before the next words bubbled up.

"I didn't know what that meant," said Simon. "He…had a stick. He told me to put my hand on the edge of the desk. But then you did what you did, and he yelled at me to get out. Everyone was yelling. I was so scared, I cried like crazy."

Joseph's gut churned, as it always did whenever the topic of his father came up, whenever he thought about the things his father did out of love. He'd lived with it for all of his life. He'd never known any different, yet he'd always known, deep in his heart, that it was wrong.

"You know what was worse?"

Simon took a breath or two. Joseph said nothing.

"He took my fossil. He put it on the floor, and he stomped on it until it broke. I couldn't help it. My mom knew something was wrong when I got home, and she made me tell her. Then she made me show my dad and explain what happened when he got home. He went crazy. My mom had to calm him down. I never knew 'til after, but the next day, my dad went to the school. That night he asked me if I lied, if I made up a story because…well…because your dad said I dropped my fossil and broke it."

Mercifully, the bell jolted them back to the present, and Joseph escaped the pain in his best friend's eyes by leading him into the loudly babbling, jostling, shuffling queue that would get them both back into the warmth of the place that so often chilled his soul.

24

"Pitter-patter, let's get at 'er!"

Progress on the shed had slowed to a crawl. Over four weeks, Frank had installed an old pot-belly stove and some secondhand windows he'd worked a deal on, and each Saturday, as Frank had insisted, up until lunch they'd hammered and sawed and painted and whatever. But right after they'd eaten, Joseph had settled into his new job, diligently working his way through the books Frank had picked out. Except it wasn't work. Joseph had loved every second of it. In fact, he'd discovered that out loud to Frank, or silently to himself under the protection of his covers, he simply loved reading.

He'd become best friends with Huckleberry Finn. He'd faced the flames with Guy Montag, felt Joe Bonham's loneliness and bitterness and pain deep in his own gut, and he'd revered Isaac Edward Leibowitz. But more than anything, he'd done as Frank had said he would. He'd traveled. To Narnia. To Chicago. To Fresno and Anopopei and Monterey and London. He'd begun to understand that some books held powers he'd never imagined: the power to provoke thought, and to connect him to people who inhabited worlds and faced challenges beyond his own. Whenever he'd asked questions about Hawkeye, or Willy Loman, or

Snowball or Napoleon, Frank had done his best to answer them. But today Frank had come up with a question of his own.

"What'd you do to your arm, there?"

Joseph knew Frank had seen them the week prior, when they'd both reached for the nail tin at the same time. Just visible between his shirt sleeve and his glove, the red marks encircling his left wrist had been obvious in the bright sunlight. But Frank had let it slide. Until now.

"Oh, that?" said Joseph. "I…uh…I got that fooling around at school. Kids call it Indian burns."

"Yeah?" said Frank.

Joseph squirmed a little too visibly. "Yeah, it's okay. Really. It's just kids doing kid stuff."

As Joseph knew he did whenever he needed to contemplate his next move, Frank took a long drag. He directed another nod at Joseph's extra long-sleeved shirt. "Any of those kids ever take things too far," he said, "you let me know."

Joseph nodded.

Frank reached down beside his chair and retrieved a crumpled Granger's bag he'd brought out from the house. From its depths, he fished out a small, rubber band-wrapped notebook and set it on the floor between them.

"Happy birthday."

A smile cracked Joseph's face. "It's not my birthday, Frank."

"Well, happy last Saturday in November. I got you something."

"A notebook?" said Joseph.

"Yeah, a notebook."

"I've got lots of school notebooks already."

"Sure," said Frank. "But this one's got nothing to do with school."

Joseph shot Frank a quizzical look.

"What does that mean?"

"I figured maybe," said Frank, "you might wanna write your own story. Or stories, if you're so inclined. For fun."

"What, like a school assignment? But for fun?" Eyebrows arched, Joseph smiled. "Thanks, I guess."

"A lot of things in life," said Frank, "depend on how you look at 'em."

They wrapped up a little early. On the short drive back toward the school, windshield wipers struggling to smear away raindrops and the odd wet snowflake, the silence was loud.

"You okay, kid?"

Joseph looked up.

"Yeah," he said. "I've just been thinking. About stories."

"Oh, yeah?" said Frank.

"Yeah," said Joseph, boldness rising. "Can I ask you something? About you? I want to know your story."

Cigarette bouncing between his lips as he negotiated the last quarter mile of the main road, Frank said nothing. For a second or two, Joseph wondered if he'd made a mistake, somehow crossed a line, but when Frank nodded and smiled a little smile, he guessed that maybe there really had been no harm in asking. It wasn't until the pickup's right front tire bumped up against the curb in front of the school and Joseph swung one leg out of his open door that Frank broke the silence.

"Hey."

Joseph turned.

"You can ask me anything," said Frank, "anything. If I know the answer, I'll tell you. If I don't, I'll tell you that, too. But some answers, well…they need time. Okay?"

Joseph nodded and planted both feet on the wet pavement.

"Okay."

"Y'ever notice," said Frank, "how some of the best stories don't make much sense when you're in the middle of 'em? They make sense at the end? I'm still working on that part, okay? See you next time?"

Joseph smiled and nodded. "Yeah."

Joseph slammed the pickup's door, and although he definitely heard its low rumble change slightly as it clunked into reverse, he knew without looking back that it hadn't moved an inch before he'd walked out of earshot.

25

The good weeks ticked by with a monotonous rhythm.

Each Sunday morning, Joseph suffered through Reverend Ainsley's interminable—some of the more daring kids sometimes said, in hushed tones, "fucking boring"—service, then spent the rest of the day laboring at whatever menial task his father had assigned, and trying his absolute best to avoid drawing any attention to himself whatsoever. On Monday mornings, he prepared himself for five days of mostly boredom: rote memorization, dry mathematical repetition, dull stories about men discovering places, Simon had pointed out, where other people already lived. It was only Simon, well, and English class, and the fact that Miss Hamer had really started to seem like the opposite of a teacher, that made school seem almost half okay. But now, an hour or so of each evening—and almost half of one whole day—had become magical. During those times, he'd come to realize, he lived another life.

He set the book down. "Geez, 1984 sure sounds like fun."

Frank laughed. "Take it from me, kid," he said. "1944 wasn't all that goddamn great, either."

"I barely knew 1964," said Joseph. "1984 sounds way worse."

"I think it's supposed to. But the future depends on history."

Joseph looked at Frank, questions forming.

"What does that mean? Can't do nothing about what already happened, right?"

"Can't do anything, Joseph. Not nothing. Besides, you sure can do something with what's already happened. You can try to understand it, so if you see something start to happen again you might have a half a clue what to do. Trouble is, some history's what happened, and some's just somebody's version of what happened. Usually somebody who needs somebody else to believe something."

"So how can you know?"

Frank leaned back and huffed a column of smoke into the rafters. "Well, I don't know. I guess you gotta find a way to be smart enough to not get told what's what. You gotta look at everything from every which way, get as smart about a thing as you can, then think it all out for yourself. Whenever anyone's telling you something, figure out what they might have to gain by having you believe it."

"So is history real or not?"

"Well, sure," said Frank, "but from where I'm sitting, there's what happened, and there's what people are willing to say happened. Plus people's memories get all messed up, for a lot of reasons, so even their best versions of the truth get fuzzy. Course, some people try to bury it deep. Trouble is, the goddamn thing's still alive down there. Trust me."

Joseph laughed. "Jeez," he said, "how's anyone supposed to make sense of that?"

Frank paused for a moment, eyes on the wet snowflakes beyond the glass.

"Yeah, that's a bit of a tough one," he said.

"Not sure I follow," said Joseph, "but now I really gotta ask you. Why are you telling me stuff? Why do you care about my future? About what happens to me?"

Frank opened the little door on the stove and peered into the flames.

"Damn good questions, kid," he said. "I've been around, I guess. Seen a few things. You showed up in my shed one day, and I know for goddamn sure that when anyone tries to do what you tried to do… well, especially a kid, a person's gotta wonder about the history behind that. I only agreed to meet with your father out of curiosity. I wanted to find out if you were okay and all, but I must have wanted you to come work with me too, 'cause here we are. I don't know… Doesn't really make sense to me either, but there it is."

Frank turned his attention to the wood basket, searching for a few seconds before extracting a perfect piece. With a satisfied nod, he placed it among the flames and watched as it began its transformation.

"You never had to be here, you know. Far as I'm concerned, you never owed me a goddamn thing."

Joseph looked down and thumbed at the book's pages, afraid to look up. "No, no. I—"

"Look," said Frank, "people don't get to choose much in life. We don't get a say in where we get born, what color our hair or eyes are, how tall or short we are. We don't get to decide who our parents are. We get what we get."

He took a long drag on his cigarette, blew the smoke toward the rafters.

"Can't choose your friends either."

"Huh?" Joseph looked up.

"I don't know about you," said Frank, "but I never figured it was up to me. From time to time, someone showed up in my life and something just, I don't really know, something just clicked. And that was that. We were friends. Or more than friends. Hasn't happened too often, but when it has, it has."

Frank winked, and closed the stove door with a bang.

"When you think you've figured out what the hell that means," he said, "you let me know."

26

The cop car's high beams swept through Frank's kitchen window around eight. A kid, Whitmore said, had been reported missing about an hour before, and they were checking "the usual spots." Frank's blood ran cold at that, warming only a little when Kusyk announced that it was a ten year old named Robbie Marsh they were looking for, and there were already groups of volunteers fanning out from the boy's house in town.

"Jesus," said Frank. "My place is a usual spot to look for runaway kids? You guys sure seem to get a lot of those around here." Kusyk offered a grim half smile. Whitmore arched one eyebrow. Neither said a word.

A light dusting of snow earlier in the afternoon had added a new layer to what had already been there, and a quick flashlight survey of Frank's yard revealed no evidence that feet of any size had disturbed it since.

"Okay," said Frank, huffing out a cloud and dropping his cigarette butt in the snow. "I know why you're really here."

Calling the boy's name over and over, the three of them checked the school, then moved on to the playground and the baseball dugouts in the park next to the hockey rink. Forty minutes on, Whitmore was losing patience, maybe agitated, Frank guessed, at getting pulled away from his TV dinner.

Their next guess was a place, Kusyk said, they'd visited more than a few times before. Just north of town, Whitmore pulled the cruiser to the side of the road that skirted the river.

"Back in there," he said, pointing into the snow-kissed trees. "Way back. There's an abandoned pickup truck and a whole lot of empty beer bottles. Kids like to hang out there and whatnot. They call it going to see Rusty."

Crazily gyrating flashlight beams contrasting the snow against the trees, they spread out, about ten feet or so between each man. In a small clearing where the trees gave way to a small patch of bush-covered flatness, Frank spotted them.

He immediately called out his find.

"Gotta be fresh," said Whitmore. "The new white stuff only got here a couple hours ago."

While Whitmore sent Kusyk back to the cruiser to radio it in, Frank followed the trail into the brush and trees. About thirty yards on, near the ice-veneered riverbank boulders, he found what he feared he might, but hoped he wouldn't. A few seconds later, a hard-breathing Whitmore stumbled up and trained a second bright white flashlight beam on the tiny face.

"Goddammit," said Whitmore, pulling out his notepad. "The hell was this stupid kid thinking? Now we got paperwork."

Frank was on Whitmore in a second, fists bunching up the front of his jacket, the sudden impact sending the cop stumbling backward and shocking the aggravated smirk from his face.

"How about you shut the fuck up, Witless?!" Frank yelled. "Show some goddamn respect for this boy! The fuck is wrong with you?!"

A panting Kusyk suddenly stepped between them.

"Okay, okay, you two!" he said. "We sure as heck don't need any of that right now."

Straightening his jacket, Whitmore glared at Frank.

Abruptly, Kusyk dropped to one knee and reached down into the snow at Whitmore's feet. As he stood, he shook a few crystals from the object he'd retrieved. He turned it over in the beam of his flashlight.

"Look at this," he said. "Leather wrap, a few beads. Kinda looks like an Indian knife." He held the knife up for Whitmore's inspection. "Think the kid was carrying it?"

"No, idiot!" barked Frank. "Gimme that goddamn thing."

He snatched the knife from Kusyk's hand and slid it back into the empty sheath on his belt. "That's worth more," he growled, "than the both of you combined."

Leaning against the parked cruiser just over half an hour later, a third cigarette burned down to its last, Frank quietly seethed as he watched the attendants load the gurney into the back of the ambulance. It had been the sight that had met Frank when his flashlight beam had first illuminated the huddled boy that had taken hold of him, and wouldn't let go.

He'd found the kid in the almost snowless hollow beneath a dense pine bough, curled up on his right side, his frail arms wrapped around his knees in an obviously futile attempt to protect himself from the cold. In the flashlight glow, the small space between the boy's pajama top and his pants had revealed bright white skin, flawless except for a couple of small round marks on the otherwise perfect surface. Frank had inched a little closer and trained his beam on them, one dark pink and the other deep red and scabbed over. But it had been the raw marks that ringed the boy's left wrist that had dropped an icy stone into his gut.

He'd waited and watched in grim silence as the two cops had inspected the scene and made their notes. Finally, as the ambulance's rotating lights had flashed through the blackness of the trees, Whitmore had tucked away his notebook and made the official declaration.

"Seems pretty cut and dry," he'd said. "There's nothing more to be done here."

As the cops had waved their flashlights to signal the ambulance attendants coming toward them through the brush, without a word, Frank had pushed past them. Chest heaving, eyes burning, he'd knelt in the snow and draped his own jacket over the boy, a feeble attempt to do something—anything—to protect him.

Too late.

∘ ∘ ∘

Robbie Marsh's funeral, of course, had been beyond awful.

Frank hadn't ventured into the church, and at the windchilled gravesite, he'd hung back near the trees, twenty or thirty feet away, not wanting to be part of it, but needing to be just the same. Whitmore's surprising hand on his shoulder jolted him from his thoughts.

"Sorry, Frank."

"For what?"

"That things, you know, worked out like they did," said Whitmore, "and…well, for what I said."

They watched in silence until the grim gathering of family and friends began to make its way to the parking lot. Frank sensed Whitmore turning to leave.

"You looking into it?"

"What?"

"This," said Frank, nodding toward the gravesite.

Whitmore shook his head.

"No," he said. "There's nothing to look into. Coroner confirmed the kid died of exposure. Tragic, I know. But that's really all there is."

"Look," said Frank. "You saw the marks, right? On his back? On his wrist?"

"Can't comment on that, Frank," said Whitmore, voice low. "Let's just say we're, uh, looking into some things. Principal at the elementary school reported some suspicions a while back. Said he thought maybe the kid's father was, well…he made some allegations."

Whitmore headed off toward the path, his boot prints trailing him through the thin layer of white. Puffing a last lungful of smoke and condensed breath into the frigid air, Frank dropped his cigarette butt into the slush and mud and pine needles and ground it into invisibility with his boot. When he looked back up, his eyes settled on two people standing terribly alone at the gravesite.

Dark, red-rimmed eyes staring from the bottom of cavernous wet hollows, stringy strands of coal black hair hanging slick across his forehead, a tall, thin, bearded man stood with an arm tight around the heaving shoulders of a petite woman as she sobbed uncontrollably.

Before Frank could look away, before he could find a way to undo his inadvertent intrusion into the most personal of moments, Robbie Marsh's father raised his head from his son's grave. He nodded once. And Frank nodded back.

Frank pulled his collar tight against the chill as he hurried to catch up to Whitmore. Neither man said a word as they covered the last fifty feet to the parking lot. When the cop put his hand on his cruiser's driver's side door handle, Frank called out to him.

"Hey, Whitmore," he said. "I know I'm not telling you anything you don't already know, but the things people die from aren't necessarily the things that kill 'em."

Stone faced, the cop said nothing. He simply nodded, climbed into his car, and drove off.

Moments later, Frank settled into his truck and coaxed it to life. Hands shaking with anger or grief or fatigue or only God knew what, he put the vehicle into gear and drove the hell away from the pain he knew Robbie Marsh's parents would never, ever leave behind.

27

The adults passed it off as a foolish adventure gone horribly wrong.

Assembled in the school gymnasium, the kids had all solemnly bowed their heads as Principal Holliman had spouted some words about "suffer the little children" and about young Robbie Marsh having "gone to a much better place," but Joseph hadn't really heard any of that. His mind had been filled with a thousand other things.

Earlier that morning, while mindlessly fulfilling his duties as a hall monitor, he'd mopped the school foyer after the stampede of the opening bell. Through the windows in the small alcove beside the big front doors, he'd seen it—a diminutive woman almost collapsing to her knees in the slush of the school's front pathway, and a tall, thin, black-haired and bearded man's obvious anguish and pain and anger as he'd tried to support her. And he'd seen his own father, and the feigned look of concern on his face that had immediately vanished when he'd turned his back on their suffering to climb the wet stone steps. As he'd strutted past him in the loudly echoing entrance hall, his father hadn't even acknowledged Joseph's presence. He'd simply brushed a few rapidly melting white crystals from his perfect black suit and walked purposefully toward his office.

28

They'd made the chains themselves, looping together the hundreds of alternating strips of green and red construction paper. They'd coaxed endless globs of smelly yellow-brown LePage's glue from their white-crusted, rose-rubber-topped bottles. They'd sprinkled the glitter. And they'd folded the pieces of white paper over and over before tracing the patterns on in pencil and—with tiny, dull, round-tipped scissors—cutting away the little wedges that had magically turned them into snowflakes. As they'd pinned and Scotch-taped the decorations to the walls and door frames and blackboards and tables, the kids had all relished the anticipation.

Well, most of them.

For most of the children, the weeks leading up to the Christmas break were filled with the promise of good things to come: of time away from the drudgery of school, of chasing hockey pucks across frozen ponds and sledding down snow-covered hills, of hot chocolate and tiny marshmallows and warm living rooms filled with pine tree scents and decorations and presents and love.

For Joseph, the anticipation was always more like dread.

His mother had left them one December morning, unwilling or

unable to face another day—not even that most holy of days—and, to Joseph's everlasting pain and anger and sadness, unwilling or unable to take him with her. He'd tried his hardest to believe it had been the latter, for what mother would abandon their child to the fate that his had surely known would befall him?

Not his beautiful and loving and thoughtful mother.

Not Angela Holliman.

Never.

In the weeks, months, and now years that had followed, his father had continued to punish the person he'd obviously held responsible for her departure, the person whose personal inadequacy and lack of moral character had tested his temper from the day he'd been born. Perhaps even before he'd been born. That his mother had tried, time after time, to defend her son before both Lionel Holliman and God had been, his father had declared, inexcusable.

And so Angela Holliman, too, had taken the pain.

On a beautifully crisp, mid-December Tuesday evening, his father had arrived home in one of his moods. There'd been nothing unusual about that.

What had been unusual had been the forever that had followed.

Joseph had been hunkered down at the kitchen table, his mother's familiar humming to the music on their tiny radio, the warmth and delicious aroma that spilled into the room whenever she opened the creaky oven door to check on her chicken stew, and the amber-blue-black sky beyond the ice-crusted window above him filling his senses with momentary, transient good. But they'd lost track of time, and as soon as the front door had slammed extra shut, they'd both known it was too late.

"Joseph," his mother had said, softly, urgently. "Why don't you run along upstairs and clean up for dinner now? Take your homework with you. Go on."

The first tactic in his mother's standard operating procedure was to always, always keep him out of his father's sight, but as he'd slipped his partially finished map of postwar Europe into his social studies textbook and hurried to snatch up the colored pencils strewn about the table, one of them had left a one inch streak—cerulean blue—on the otherwise pristine white tablecloth.

"Mom, I…"

Thinking quickly, his mother had hustled over to try to obscure the tiny disaster with a dinner plate, but before she'd been able to fully achieve her subterfuge, a hand had reached from behind her and snatched the ceramic disc away. Joseph's mouth was still open—his breath still held prisoner in his lungs—when his father's hand had swung around with such force that it had knocked him to the floor.

Joseph's last, incomplete memories of Angela Holliman were her silent scream as she'd reached for him, and his father's emotionless face as he'd reached for her. As if viewed through a long tunnel, or maybe from underwater, Joseph had watched—or maybe he'd imagined—his mother being dragged backward out of the kitchen by her hair, hands clawing ineffectively at the source of her pain and terror.

He'd never seen her again.

He'd been terrified to ask, but three horrible days later he'd finally mustered up enough courage.

"Your mother has revealed her true self," his father had stated, quietly but absolutely definitively. "You won't be subjected to that any longer." And nothing more.

That evening, from the relative safety of his darkened bedroom window, Joseph had seen his father carrying assorted cardboard boxes to his car.

The next morning, a Saturday, their neighbor, Mrs. Roselle, had stayed with him while his father had gone off, he'd said, "to an important meeting."

Midafternoon, as he'd known he might, Joseph had found Mrs. Roselle softly snoring under a blanket on the living room couch. Breath held, he'd tiptoed up the stairs and into his parents' bedroom.

At first, everything had seemed almost normal.

Two single beds with crisp white sheets beneath perfectly flat gray blankets. One night table between them, a bible centered below its simple lamp. A small oval rug. In three out of a chest of six drawers, he'd found his fathers socks and T-shirts and underwear, his carefully rolled collection of black ties, a small box with an assortment of collar stays and cufflinks. But Joseph had felt the emptiness of the other three drawers as if it were a vacuum consuming him, and his eyes had watered as he'd worked to slide the last of them silently home. When it had wedged itself slightly sideways, he'd carefully retracted it to straighten it out and try again. But the movement had shifted the drawer's floral printed parchment lining, and as he'd reached in to return the thin paper to its original position, he'd seen it.

With laughing faces partially obscured by the spiraling pink roses lithographed on the faded, semi-translucent sheet, the small piece of rectangular white-framed paper had dared him to reach for it. And so he had.

The two of them looked as if they'd been having the time of their lives. In floppy summer hats and sunglasses, bare feet and cropped pants, they were stretched back in striped, low-slung beach chairs, half-filled glasses with ice cubes and straws and what looked to be tiny umbrellas held out boldly toward the camera. They were smiling—laughing, even—as if they'd shared something special and fun and absolutely fantastic, or maybe just ordinary, for people like them, people who loved life. Or who were loved by life.

Joseph's jaw had dropped when he'd realized that one of them was, or maybe at some future point would become, Mrs. Angela Holliman. He turned the picture over. A single word, scrawled in pencil. Graffton. Panic rising as he'd suddenly realized he'd lost all track of time, he'd quickly tucked the snapshot into his back pocket, smoothed out the floral liner, and silently returned the drawer to its place.

There'd been no tree that Christmas, and there'd be no tree this Christmas. No stockings. No presents. No lights. No love.

"You know it's not about any of that, Joseph," his father would say, once again.

Since that brilliant and terrible and ever-fading December day, Joseph's only connection to the life that had offered him more than chilling emptiness and almost constant pain had been a small piece of paper coated with a shiny film of light-sensitive emulsion. Fragile. Precious.

He'd never blamed his mother, or at least he'd tried not to blame her. But of course he had. Unable to make sense of so many conflicting feelings, he'd tried his very best to block all thoughts of her from his mind, and had almost managed to achieve a sort of numb existence, punctuated only by the often excruciating penance for either his or his mother's sins—he knew not which—that his father extracted from him from time to time. Afraid to reach for any sliver of happiness because he knew it would only serve as fleeting contrast to his almost overwhelming sadness, he'd resolved himself to an unfeeling, middleground life. But cruelly, inevitably, the holiday-induced joy of others never failed to tear away his microscopically thin defenses.

Facing rigidly to the stage in the school's gymnasium as his father's distant voice droned on and on about the wonderful pageant Mrs.

Mallory and the younger children had just put on—as always, centered on the miracle of the blessed Virgin Mary and the manger and the wise men bearing gifts—Joseph's mind swam. Why was he expected to love this one baby so much, to celebrate its birthday with joy, when his father wouldn't even celebrate his own son's? In the absence of his mother, his birthday had once again come and gone without a word, and he wondered if his father had even known. He looked down at his hands and squeezed his eyes tight. He blocked out his father's words, blocked out the world. And finally, mercifully, it was over.

Pent up energy suddenly palpable, the children stood almost as one, and a loud buzz of excited voices flooded the gymnasium as they crowded the doors and eventually made their way down the glittered and paper-chained and snowflaked hallway. Joseph shuffled, shoulders slumped and head down, slightly behind an animated Simon. Back at their homeroom, the two of them wrestled themselves into their jackets and mumbled their goodbyes and Merry Christmases to Miss Hamer, then headed for the school's front door.

As the two of them emerged into the chill of the afternoon, they were met by the overlapping voices of the handful of moms and little brothers and sisters who'd come to walk their loved ones home for the holidays—as Joseph's mother had done when he was younger. Joseph watched his shoes shuffle across the granite until he heard a warm voice call Simon's name, and he looked up just in time to see a smiling Mrs. Charleyboy reach out as Simon practically jumped into her embrace.

Joseph stifled his tears and tried hard not to be jealous of his friend, because he so badly wanted to be him. For a second or two, as he watched them, he allowed himself to imagine—maybe even hope— that he heard his mother call out his name one more time, but the hard reality before him only honed the sharp edges of envy.

And then suddenly, like a foghorn cutting through the excited babble of voices he knew were not for him, he heard it.

"What'd you do? Quit school?!"

Under his old jacket, Frank Gardner had worn his newest red and black checkered shirt, which, Joseph guessed, meant it was probably less than five years old. It looked like he'd shaved, and maybe even tried semi-successfully to slick down his stubbly, mostly salt and some pepper hair. He almost looked nice, and Joseph's heart jumped a beat or two as a combination of elation and fear immediately gripped him.

"What...what are you doing here?" said Joseph.

"Well," said Frank, "I actually came to see your father. Just wanted to drop something off, since I guess I won't be seeing you for a couple of weeks."

Joseph's grin lit up his face from ear to ear, until a familiar voice from behind him extinguished the glow.

"Mr. Gardner," said Lionel Holliman, "it's certainly a surprise to see you here."

"Actually," said Frank with a soft smile, "I was on my way in to see you."

"Well," said Holliman, "I suppose we could meet in my office for a few minutes if you like. But as you can see, school is now officially out for the holidays and I must be leaving soon, so that Joseph isn't left at home alone too long."

"Yeah," said Frank, "I see that now. Sorry. Guess I didn't realize today was the day for that." He shot a wink and a quick smile Joseph's way. "Anyway," he said, "we really don't have to make it a big deal. Just wanted to give you this."

Frank held out a terribly wrapped object.

"Just a little something," he said, "for under your tree."

Lionel Holliman stood unmoving.

Joseph Holliman stood petrified.

"Thank you, Mr. Gardner," said Holliman, "but unfortunately we can't accept. We keep our own holiday traditions. It's a…family thing. Perhaps you wouldn't understand."

"Well," said Frank, "nobody's ever accused me of being a wise man, but I figured I could still bear a gift."

His father's silence roared as Joseph glanced up at Frank. Frank bowed his head and contemplated the package in his two rough hands for a long, long second before he looked back up.

"Have a good holiday, kid," said Frank, eyes momentarily locked onto Joseph's. Joseph couldn't miss the change in Frank's eyes as they moved to focus on his father.

"As for you, Mr. Holliman," said Frank quietly, firmly. "You don't know the first goddamn thing about what I understand about family."

Joseph's breath caught in his chest, and he froze, stunned by the events unfolding right before his eyes. He'd never heard anyone speak to his father in that way, and his blood ran cold as his father turned his icy glare on him.

"Joseph," said his father, his voice low but loud, "you will make your way home immediately, is that clear? I will deal with you later."

Some of the other eyes around them began to turn their way, and Joseph felt their prickly heat as Frank Gardner's deep voice cut through the crowd noise.

"You're gonna do what, now?" he said. "Deal with him? What's that supposed to mean?"

Holliman's thin smile preceded his next words.

"Goodbye, Mr. Gardner."

"This has nothing to do with Joseph," said Frank. "He didn't ask me to be here."

Lionel Holliman, smug condescension dripping from his lips,

drove his next words home like a sword.

"This boy is none of your concern," he said, "and as his father, I will deal with him as I see fit. You'll only make it more difficult for him the longer you insist on pursuing this conversation."

A roaring silence suddenly gripped the crowd, as if an icy north wind had whipped away the last remnants of its joy. Frank glanced over at Joseph and nodded, then moved up onto the same step on which Joseph and his father both stood, positioning himself solidly between the two of them.

With his face just inches from Holliman's, his bulk towering over the smaller man, Frank spoke in a voice so low it was almost a whisper, although to Joseph it rang out like a thunderclap.

"So, that's how it is, huh?" said Frank, something dark—almost menacing—below the surface of his words. "I'll leave," he said, "but understand this. If I find out anyone's laid a hand on this boy, or has mistreated him in any way because of something he didn't do, they better ask real hard for God to save 'em."

Frank turned to Joseph and put a scarred hand on his trembling shoulder. "Merry Christmas, Joseph," he said. "I'll see you soon."

Joseph hoped against hope that it would all be over, but as Frank turned and walked down the steps, his father just had to get the last word in, and they spun Frank back around.

"One final thing, Mr. Gardner," said Holliman. "You will not be seeing Joseph soon. It's become abundantly clear to me that letting the boy extend his time working off his debt to you was a mistake. That arrangement is now terminated."

Joseph felt his blood turn to ice and his rage ignite, and despite his almost crippling fear, he simply couldn't prevent the words from making themselves heard.

"No!" he pleaded. "You can't do that!"

Quick as a viper strike, Lionel Holliman seized his son's jacket collar and yanked him forcefully backward.

As he began to march Joseph into the school through the crowd of silent, gobsmacked parents and wide-eyed children, Frank called after him, quietly but clearly.

"Start prayin'."

29

Raindrops the size of peas drummed on the metal and the glass. When Helen pulled the pickup up to the pumps under the gas station awning, the silence woke him immediately.

"Hungry, soldier?"

Bernhardt sat forward and rubbed the sleep from his burning eyes with his knuckles.

"Ja, miss."

He caught her arched eyebrow.

"Ja?" she said. "Did I just hear ja? You're not gonna get far in this neck of the woods if you use words like that. It's yeah. Yeah. Come on now, say it."

He smiled sheepishly. "Yeah."

"And it's not miss," she said, "it's Helen."

She unzipped the canvas duffel lying on the seat between them and pulled out a brown envelope, then flipped it open and withdrew a crisp ten dollar bill. Bernhardt arched his own eyebrows as she stuffed the envelope back into the bag. She turned to him as she reached for the truck's chrome door handle.

"Don't worry," she said, "that's all mine. Earned fair and square.

But even if it wasn't, my father's got plenty more where it came from. Trust me, war's good for business. Just not good for people, right?"

Bernhardt waited—a little anxiously, he had to admit—as an elderly gas jockey topped them up. Helen returned a few minutes later, materializing at the rain-streaked passenger side window with a greasy white paper bag in one hand and two Cokes in the other. He popped the door.

"Slide over," she said. "Your turn at the wheel. I'm so hungry I'm going to need two hands to shovel this in."

She insisted he repeat the words a few times before she let him have any of the cheeseburger and fries and Coke that were the most delicious things he'd ever tasted, and for a few minutes they drove in relative silence, the droning of the tires and engine, the patter of the increasingly sporadic raindrops, the rhythmic flip-flop-flip-flop of the windshield wipers struggling to cope with them, and the smacking of lips the only sounds.

Wiping his hand on his trouser leg, Bernhardt turned his head in time to see Miss Helen Eisenhut, eyelids squeezed tight, cramming an oversized cluster of fried potatoes into her mouth. Mission accomplished, she opened her eyes just in time to catch the tail end of his sideways look, triggering an involuntary burst of laughter that sprayed some or all of the unchewed fries onto the dashboard and floor. That got them both laughing.

Nervous laughter, Bernhardt thought, but good laughter.

A few minutes later, she'd tidied things up and gotten serious.

"Okay," she said, "what's the plan, Stan?"

"Planstan?"

She laughed. "Where are we going? What do we do? Now that we're...free?"

Free.

Bernhardt hadn't been free since the last time he'd strapped on his skis and felt the cold mountain air on his face. He hadn't been free in a long, long time.

"Well," he said, his attention now on more than the black road stretching out beyond the headlight beams, "I, uh, I had not really thought so far as that. I, uh, thought I would be walking. Alone. What… what do you suggest?"

"Well" she said, " I haven't exactly had time to think any of this through either. I'm not sure how they do things where you come from, but round these parts, unattached young men and women don't just show up in some town and go quietly about their business. 'Cause you can be double damn sure that whatever their business is, the busybodies in that town are going to make it their business to make it everybody's business. You following me?"

I'm sitting right beside you, he thought. *How could I be following you?*

"No," he said. "I mean yes. I think so. Of course, I…I had not thought of that. Maybe I…should get out. Go my own way."

If Bernhardt had dared to glance over at her, he'd have seen her purse her lips and focus her gaze on the truck's radio until the tiny lines across her forehead vanished and her freckle returned to its resting place. Instead he'd held his breath, and his focus on the road, in silent anticipation of her reply.

"Look," she said, "it's practically raining cats and dogs. It's almost dark. I barely know where we are. You sure as heck don't. And sure, I don't know you and you're an enemy soldier and all, but for some reason, my instincts are telling me you were raised to be a gentleman. So how about we just pull over someplace and get some shut-eye in the truck, and you prove me right? And then we figure out a real plan come daylight?"

Bernhardt rolled the window down an inch or two and sucked in a deep lungful of cool air. He wasn't always sure he understood what she was saying, but she talked a lot, and he kind of liked it.

"Pull off the next good chance you get."

Seems she also liked to tell people what to do, so as instructed, a few minutes further on, he made a right turn that took them onto a muddy side road. He brought the truck to a stop in the shelter of some trees. When the engine and windshield wipers and headlights clicked off, the almost silent blue-blackness of the dying day closed in on them like an enormous curtain.

"Okay," said Helen, "I'll stay on my side, and you stay on yours, and we'll be just fine."

Bernhardt tugged on the chrome handle and levered the driver's side door open with his left elbow. When he stepped out and closed it behind him, the world outside the truck completely enveloped him. The rain had, but for a few stray drops, it seemed, passed them by, leaving a most beautiful scent in the air. He looked up to see a handful of stars pinpricking an inky sky above an almost motionless evergreen canopy. The ticking of the cooling engine and the sporadic pock-pock-pock of heavy drops falling randomly from the branches were the only sounds, and when he turned back and reopened the door, the truck's interior light instantly brought him back into the intimate closeness of glass and vinyl and steel, the lingering aroma of long gone fried potatoes, and the magnetic field that seemed to surround Miss Helen Eisenhut.

Incredulous, he tried to drink it in, and he glanced up instinctively when a frigid droplet ran through his hair and shivered its way down the back of his neck. He couldn't help but let out an audible gasp.

"I, uh, think maybe I see some stars up there," he said. "If it's all the same to you, miss, I'd like to sleep under the, uh, under the canvas. Back there. I...well, I just think I need fresh air."

He wrestled off his jacket and held it out to her.

She hesitated for a brief second—wheels clearly turning behind those dark eyes—before reaching out and taking it. When he clicked the door shut, he couldn't help but notice that the warmth of her soft smile stayed with him long after the glow of the truck's tiny interior light had vanished into the blackness.

30

"**B**oy," she shouted, "I could sure use a cup of coffee!"

Bernhardt folded his torn half map and glanced up as Helen Eisenhut walked from the trees, hair tied back, face damp with stream water, radiant in the early glow.

"You sleep okay back there, mister?"

"Oh, yes, miss," he said. "I've, uh, slept in wurst places than this."

"Your English is pretty good," she laughed, "but it's worse, not wurst. I guess that means you need breakfast, huh?"

She tossed her canvas bag into the back of the truck, then clambered up onto its passenger side seat and slammed the door.

"Well," she said, "which way is the right way for the first real day of our brand new lives?"

Bernhardt slammed the driver's side door and gripped the truck's black steering wheel hard, its smooth surface cool and comforting, the impossible promise it held even more so.

"The direction we go now is good, I think. But miss? I mean, Helen. I, uh, I don't know where I'm going…don't know what's ahead for me, no matter which way. You understand what I am saying?"

She twisted in her seat, her left knee at least a meter away but suddenly perilously close, he noticed, to his right thigh.

"I do understand," she said, "but whatever each of us left behind got us to be right here, in this pickup truck, in the middle of I don't even know where. What I do know is I haven't felt this good in a long, long time. Since Mama…well, practically since I was a little girl in pigtails, I guess. And it was you who got me here."

Her last sentence made Bernhardt's eyebrows arch up, and she noticed.

"No, no," she said, "not against my will, silly. Because you helped me. I guess we've…well, I guess we've helped each other now, and I'm thinking maybe we should keep doing that, at least until each of us figures out what's next. You okay with that?"

Eyes focused somewhere down the narrow dirt road that stretched out ahead of them, Bernhardt nodded.

"Ja," he said.

And before she could correct him, he turned and grinned.

"Yeah."

○ ○ ○

"Welcome to the Lakeshore Diner. What'll it be?"

Helen ordered them bacon and eggs and toast and orange juice and coffee as Bernhardt kept his eyes on the brilliant blue-green expanse of the lake sparkling just beyond their window.

Of course Helen had done all of the talking.

Bernhardt had needed no reminder, but after she'd finally convinced him that actually going into the diner might be okay, she'd cautioned him at least three times against engaging in chit chat. He'd agreed without fully understanding the terminology, but when the waitress—who, Bernhardt deduced from the look Helen shot him, clearly liked to both chit and chat—asked, "You folks just passin' through or plannin' to stick around?" Helen casually ventured enough of the essential truth to sound convincing.

"Well," she said, "John here's back from the war, so we're just… looking for what's next, I guess."

"Well, that's wonderful," said the waitress. "My boy's still over fightin' the Japs someplace or another. On those itty bitty islands. Where were you at, John?" It took Bernhardt a second or two to realize that he was John, and the waitress's smiling eyes and expectant attention fell on him like a small avalanche.

His pulse quickened. *Come on,* he thought. *Say something!*

"Africa."

He hoped his tightlipped smile said enough to end his portion of the conversation.

"Well," the waitress replied, "your mama must be real glad to have you home. Where is home anyway?"

Bernhardt directed a quick, panicked glance Helen's way, but she jumped in as if she did this kind of thing every day.

"Oh," she said, "John's from, ah, way out east. His mama passed some years back and she was all he had left, and vice versa, you know? And my family's down in Florida. We're out west here looking to make ourselves a brand new start."

The waitress lit up as if she'd just had an epiphany.

"Well, you two just sit tight," she said. "I'll be right back."

Thirty seconds later she reappeared with a fresh pot of coffee. She topped up their cups, then, with a satisfied grin, slapped a white business card down in front of Bernhardt.

"I'm Darlene," she said. "My husband runs a little outfit just south of here. Don't know if you got any interest in the idea, or in stickin' around here for a while, but if you do, he's always complaining about trying to find some help worth a damn, pardon my French. Got a real good Flathead boy, but seems like the war's got most young men like yourself busy doing other things right now."

"Flathead?" said Helen.

"Honey," said Darlene, "you're sitting in Flathead Indian territory right now. At least that's what they say. To my mind they lost this place fair and square a hundred years ago, but what do I know? Anyway, you think about it."

She gestured beyond the window.

"As you can see, Flathead Lake sure is a pretty sight, and Rollins here is a handsome little place. But to my mind, we could use a couple of pretty and handsome new faces like yours. Food at the diner's first rate, though!"

She winked, then walked over to talk with an elderly couple who'd just sat down.

Voice almost a whisper, Helen flipped the card over and over in her fingers.

"Crosby and Lennox Logging," she said, "Big Arm, Montana. Logging? Geez, what else would it be?" Darlene had written her name on the back in perfect cursive.

"What do you think?"

"Think?" whispered Bernhardt. "What do you think I think? They must be looking for me by now, and we're not so far from the camp. A few hundred kilometers."

"Well, yeah," said Helen, voice low, "except you mean miles, mister. And all that may be true, but here's the thing. They might be looking for you, but they're not looking for us."

Bernhardt's confused look spurred her on.

"First," she said, "they've got more than just you to worry about. Like your two friends, for example? And remember, they've also got themselves a camp guard who was dumb enough to rob my father's company and go AWOL trying to make a run for it. On top of all that, my father probably thinks I took the pickup truck and headed for my aunt Tillie's place in Florida like I did when I was sixteen. I left him a note when I went back to grab my things. Said I'd let him know. Maybe."

She's smart, Bernhardt thought. *Smarter than most of the officers in the Afrika Korps.*

"So my guess is," she said, "no one's even going to think twice about a nice young married couple, him just back from the war and all, who might be looking to make a quiet new life in a beautiful place like this."

She looked across the sunlit road to the sparkling water and the deep blue green mountains beyond, then dropped a few dollar bills onto the table. Bernhardt sat eyes down, mind racing through possibilities while trying the name John on for size over and over.

But when he looked up, Helen Eisenhut's optimistic eyes locked on his in a way that made thinking unnecessary.

31

"What can I do you for?" said the man in the chair.

More than a little confused by the man's question, Bernhardt said nothing. He handed the man the business card and glanced around the gloomy, junk-filled shed, its grimy, oil-stained workbench almost completely hidden beneath scattered tools and assorted gas cans, and behind piles of tires, toolboxes, coils of cables and chains, and a blue oil drum, against which leaned what appeared to be the door from a once-red truck of some kind.

"Yep," said the man as he looked at the card. "Buck Lennox. That's me. Who the hell are you?"

Butterflies swarming, Bernhardt put on his very best American voice, just as Helen had coached him in the diner parking lot.

"Sir, on the back. Your, uh, wife. Darlene said I should see you. About a job."

"Oh, she did, huh?"

Olive drab sleeves rolled to reveal thick, oil-streaked forearms, gray-blond hair cropped army short, deep lines around eyes the color of the lake, half-smoked cigarette bouncing above a white-stubbled chin, the man sounded like he looked.

"That woman pretty much gets herself in everyone's business," he laughed. "Specially mine. You know anything about trees, son?"

"Yes sir."

"I mean you know anything about cuttin' 'em down?"

"Yes, sir."

Buck Lennox got up from his chair and walked over to an open wooden crate sitting on the floor near the workbench. He returned with a gunmetal object and tossed it to Bernhardt.

"What's that?"

"Uh, wedge, sir."

"Well I know that, son," said Buck. "I wanna know if you know what it's for."

Bernhardt smiled sheepishly.

"Felling cut, sir."

"Well, damn, son. Sir on every sentence? You been in the service a little too long? Lemme see your hands."

Bernhardt set the weighty chunk of metal on the top of a tire and held out his hands. Buck grabbed his wrists firmly and rolled his hands back to front.

"Smooth calluses and a real big-boy scar, but still got five on each," he said. "In my experience that indicates a reasonably lucky man who probably knows how to work. War or woods?"

It took a moment for Bernhard to process the man's question. To him, the triangular scar that connected his thumb to his hand was a tangible reminder of two things: the constant dangers of logging and the critical importance of luck.

"Oh," said Bernhardt. "I cut trees. A big one cut me."

"Okay," said Buck, nodding. "Seven to six. Six days a week. Forty cents an hour. Cash envelope every Saturday evening. And Sundays we don't do nothin'. Start tomorrow if you like."

Bernhardt looked around the jumbled shed one more time, the soft light diffused by its hazy and cracked windows barely illuminating the place. Clearly, Crosby and Lennox Logging was nowhere close to the kind of operation he'd gotten used to, but, he figured, a job's a job, and it's not forever.

"Thank you, sir," he said. "I'll be here. Just, uh, questions."

"Shoot."

"Well," Bernhardt said, rethinking Helen's enthusiasm for "hiding in plain sight" while searching for the words she'd instructed him to say. "My, uh, wife is with me. Your wife, Darlene, said something about a place to stay." And, wanting a better sense of his tactical situation, he boldly, perhaps recklessly, chanced a question of his own. "Should I, uh, meet Mister Crosby?

Buck Lennox chuckled.

"Well," he said, "lemme see. I got easy answers for you. One, my darlin' wife's question is actually her way of telling me she wants to set you up in our little cabin over by the lake. Fine by me. It ain't much but it'll hold you for a while if you like. And two, there ain't no Mister Crosby. I made that guy up when I first got started so a few folks around here would take me more seriously. But keep that to yourself, you hear? I told everyone he's off in Washington making big deals with the war department. You go let Darlene know you're on the payroll and she'll square y'away. I'll have coffee goin' tomorrow, bright and early."

Buck Lennox stretched out a grease-blackened paw.

"I still got one question for you, son," he said.

"What's your name?"

32

The aroma set his stomach into motion the second he stepped through the front door.

An hour or so earlier, he'd left Helen at the little cabin with Mrs. Lennox and made the drive to the shed and back, to get familiar with the route, Helen had told Darlene, but mostly, Bernhardt knew, to spare him from the chitting and the chatting.

The two women had been busy.

"I paid the first month's rent," said Helen, "so don't you worry about that. Darlene said she'd normally get thirty dollars but she cut us a break, you being just back from the war and all, and took twenty-five. She loaned me some sheets and towels and whatnot and she even left supper for us. A housewarming gift, she called it. It's in the little stove right there. There's an icebox, and a fireplace, and right out there's the lake, which isn't too hard to look at either. Well? What do you think?"

He moved toward the back screen door, pulled by the image of the porch and the lake and the mountains and the pinking evening sky beyond, perfectly framed, like a painting in a gallery.

He sensed her shuffling around in the room behind him and was suddenly afraid to move, afraid he might wake up in a different place.

"I…I don't know what to say, miss. Helen. Don't know the words."

He felt the air shift when she moved, and he strained to see her lean a shoulder against the doorframe without actually looking at her.

"Well, John," she said, emphasis on the second word, "I sure hope you like your new first name, because it's the same as my grandfather's. But Steele? How the heck'd you come up with that anyway?"

"Oh," he replied, "Mr. Lennox, he asked my name and… Well, I just said the first thing that came into my head. Stihl. It was right there in front of me. On a chainsaw."

She laughed. "Well, I kind of like it," she said. "It sounds strong, and names should mean something, you know? We can work on those words a little, that's for sure, but you could say you liked it here. That'd be a good start."

Bernhardt grinned. "Oh, I like it very much," he said. "More than that. I…"

"That's good enough for me, soldier," she said. "Kinda feels like we landed on our feet, huh? Two runaways without a plan? Now we've got ourselves a little breathing room, a little space to move around in. To think."

"Leere Seite," he said.

"What?"

He grasped for the English. "A…blank page."

She turned to him.

"Yeah," she said, "like a blank page. You know, my mama used to read to me when I was little, and she always told me to make sure my life was a good story, 'cause at the end, that's all I'd ever be. I guess I kinda forgot about that after she went away. Well, I'm remembering now, and I've got an enemy soldier to thank."

She smiled. He cringed inside, but said nothing.

"Quite a start to my new chapter," said Helen. "And to yours."

She walked to the icebox and returned with a bottle in each hand.

"Almost forgot," said Helen. "Darlene dropped these off, too. I think I heard you German boys like your beer, so I reckon we should mark this occasion with a toast of some kind."

They sat on the porch chairs and said nothing for a few moments, each immersed in the strangeness of the new, and in the majesty of the purple sky slowly painting itself black over the lake. When they finally readied to clink their Budweisers together, Bernhardt struggled to find any words at all, so Helen said them for him.

"To stories."

33

Burning eyes wide open, his mind seeing only what he hoped he was about to do, Joseph Holliman lay motionless in the moonlit darkness.

A muffled thump—or maybe an imagined muffled thump—jolted him into focused consciousness, and he immediately dispatched a hand to reconnoiter under his covers, unable or unwilling to take in any new oxygen until his fingers encountered the chisel, its sharp steel blade now warmed almost to body temperature.

In the wake of the incident on the school steps, the walk home had been agonizing, his father's cruel words like a chain around his neck, anxiety like a fist around his heart, fear and hatred and despair like razor blades in his gut.

He'd thought about running a thousand times, had even done it once or twice. But each time, he'd been hunted down, dutiful officers of the law only happy to drag him back to hell, where he'd been made to suffer the terrible consequences. His latest failure to escape—for what he'd foolishly hoped would be forever—had only brought fresh agonies. His father's insistence on personal atonement for his vandalism of Frank Gardner's shed had inadvertently and unknowingly taunted him with fleeting glimpses into another world—a world of brand new work gloves and laughter and perfectly hammered nails and stupid sayings and hotdogs and Coca-Cola and so many, many other wonderful things—that he was now certain he would never be allowed to inhabit.

He hated himself for that failure more than he hated his father. After all, it was his own inadequacy—his weakness and stupidity and inability to see his plan through to its intended conclusion—that had, once again, caused the pain of history to repeat itself.

Earlier this evening, as he had countless times before, his father had asked for forgiveness as he'd meted out the punishment for his son's sins. Voice deadened by the smothering burlap, emphasis on certain words, he'd brought the heavy leather strap down repeatedly, forcing the air from Joseph's lungs as its weight had bruised him to his bones and its hard edges had threatened to cut his flesh like a dull knife.

When the restraints had finally been removed from his wrist and ankle, Joseph had not had the strength to move, and so his father had simply left him there, the small door slightly ajar. Eventually, his thirst had dragged him back from wherever his delirium had taken him, and he'd gathered enough will to stumble through the gloom of the barn and across the shadowy yard toward the almost lightless house.

But this time, the beginning of a new end had accompanied him. He'd taken the cold steel tool from its designated spot on the perforated wall above his father's workbench and carried it with him to his room, unseen.

An hour later, as he'd struggled to choke down one more forkful of God's tasteless bounty, from across the brutally silent kitchen table, his father had casually unleashed another flood of misery.

"By the way," his father had said coldly, without even glancing up, "I've been informed that Mr. Charleyboy has elected to uproot his family again. Immediately, as of the new year, your troublesome little friend will be attending school in Kimberley."

That gut punch had been more powerful than anything ever delivered by his father's hand, but Joseph had managed to retreat to his room before his tears could betray his despair. Staring into the blackness, pillow soaked, inescapable sorrow and hopelessness had threatened to drown him, but hatred had reached for him with warm hands.

Outside his bedroom door, Joseph gripped the chisel in both hands, its weight somehow increasing as he took his first halting steps toward the terrifying.

Even in the gloom at the end of the short hallway, illuminated by the scant rays that had somehow managed to escape from Mrs. Roselle's bug-encrusted front porch light and make their way through the diamond-shaped glass in the Holliman front door, he could tell that his father's bedroom door wasn't shut tight.

Odd.

Instantly frozen, he strained his ears in an effort to detect a rustle or a bump or an exhalation.

Nothing.

From somewhere, Joseph summoned the courage to approach the abyss. Closer now, the black void between his father's door and frame doused him in a new wave of dread. Pulse pounding, airless lungs screaming, he pushed gingerly and the door angled slowly inward, its soft creaking almost deafening as it revealed more of the now otherworldly but still familiar room.

It took a few seconds for his pupils to adjust.

Normally immaculate, his father's bedroom was a jumbled mess. The black metal bed was empty save for a single crumpled pillow near its middle, and its woolen blanket and pristine white top sheet lay in careless twists on the floor. The small bedside table had been tipped over. Beside it, the bible that had occupied the table's surface for time immemorial now lay splayed open, facedown on the floor, a few of its sacred pages folded and creased by its own weight. When Joseph took one more tentative half step, a sliver of moonlight glinted off a puddle of water beside a glass lying on its side on the oak boards.

Something had happened here. Something beyond him.

Breath shallow, he crouched and saw what he instantly recognized as the shine of wet footprints on the hardwood—one strangely in the shape of a boot, others more like those he'd left on the bathroom floor on countless Saturday evenings.

He jerked bolt upright.

His plan in complete disarray, panic beginning to overwhelm his skin-deep determination, Joseph spun on his heel. Open mouthed but almost unable to inhale, he followed the shining path that led to the stairs, the liquid trail alien and threatening in the eerie glow from Mrs. Roselle's lightbulb.

Careful to place his weight at the extremity of each tread, a stealth trick he'd learned from a Hardy Boys book, he slowly made his way to the ground floor. In the stillness of the house's tiny entrance hall, a breath of icy air across the bone cold tiles numbed his soles. Instinctively, he traced the chill to its source: the open kitchen door, its short floral curtain moving ever so gently in the breeze.

Breath now coming impossibly hard, he struggled to decide if the smears of water shining dimly on the kitchen's linoleum were inbound or outbound, and in that moment, all resolve left him.

Hands frozen and clammy and trembling, his clearly foolhardy plan shattered by something he could never have foreseen, the massive weight of the chisel and the unexplainable trail of wet footprints on the dull floor suddenly and emphatically reminded him of his impotence and his smallness.

Shaking with fear and frustration more than with cold, he left the kitchen door wide open to the freezing night and, careful not to leave any footprints of his own, he turned and quickly retraced his steps back to his room, where he burrowed as far into the imaginary safety of his covers as he possibly could.

Eyes wide, struggling hard but failing to restrain his runaway mind, he gripped the lifeless chisel as if it were his mother's own hand, his anger and disappointment at his pathetic inability to do what he so badly wanted to do threatening to destroy him. Shivering, hating himself and his father and his mother and the very life he'd been given, he rolled over and screamed his pain and frustration and anguish into his damp pillow.

When something jolted him back to reality less than half an hour later, Joseph practically leaped out of bed in confusion, three-quarters convinced he'd only dreamed his earlier excursion. But this time, the heavy steel chisel really had fallen to the floor with a terrifyingly loud clunk. Panicked, he scooped it up and stashed it back inside its mattress hole hiding place. Only then did his overtaxed senses alert him to the soft fumes.

He threw off his covers and tiptoed to his door.

Silence.

He crossed the room to the window side. Sniffing in hard, he thought he detected a whiff of smoke where the night's cold air found its way between the window and its frame.

With his pajama-sleeved forearm, he worked to rub away a patch of the frost that had staked a solid claim on one of the bottom panes. He scanned the scene beyond the glass. As far as he could tell, the world outside seemed normal, the blues and whites of the snow-bright yard between the house and the blackness of the barn no different than any other night.

And then he saw it.

A flickering yellow-orange glow illuminated the tops of the fir trees at the back end of the barn, and for a few brief seconds, Joseph Holliman almost believed in God.

34

Buck Lennox had earned his name. A seemingly tireless worker, his specialty, it had soon become clear, was bucking—sawing felled trees into logs—and even two of them were finding it a little hard to keep up. As soon as Bernhardt and Paul, his partner on the heavy two-man saw, had taken one big tree down, Buck was barking for another.

"Doesn't slow down, huh?" said Bernhardt.

Paul just shook his head. Almost three days into their acquaintance, the big man hadn't uttered much more than an occasional "okay" from time to time. Seemed he wasn't much for words, which was a shame, Bernhardt thought, because more than anything, John Steele needed to hear a lot more words.

They'd talked it all out that first night, as they'd sat on the back porch with their beers and plates of Darlene's venison stew. They were to be a married couple in public. In private, Mrs. Helen Steele had gently but firmly reminded him, "we're just roommates." She'd had to explain that word a few times, and they'd both agreed for about the hundredth time that words would have to be the most important things in their lives for the foreseeable future.

When that first Saturday evening at six o'clock rolled around,

Bernhardt and Paul stowed their tools and gas cans and gloves, done for the week. Buck unlocked a workbench drawer and fished out two white envelopes. He handed one to each member of his new team, grinning past his smoke.

"Three's a whole lot better'n two, boys," he said. "Well it's one better, that's for goddamn sure!" He laughed at his own joke. "That was a good week of work," he said, "and you boys sure as hell earned a pay package and a day of rest. John, me and Darlene go to church up in Kalispell, since that's where she's from. You and the missus are welcome to ride with us if you want. Seven fifteen a.m., we'll pick you up at the cabin. Paul, we'll see you Monday."

Paul nodded once, and Bernhardt worked to process the flood of confusion and anxiety-inducing thoughts in his head. Day of rest? Church? A crowd of people?

That evening after supper, he pulled out the map and located the cabin, then ran a finger up the long road to Kalispell.

"Look," said Helen, "I know it's a little risky going anyplace with a lot of people, but if we don't go, it might seem a little bit suspicious. Besides"—she grinned—"in church it's one man doing all the talking, and it sure as heck isn't gonna be you. I'll bet you a week's pay it'll be Darlene's voice you hear the most on the ride there and back. And I'll make sure it's mine second. You can be last on the list, okay?"

Anxiety subdued only a notch, Bernhardt smiled weakly.

"Now let's work on some words a little. Tell me about your books, Mister John Steele."

At the last second, he'd stuffed them into his canvas bag along with a few clothes, his razor, a comb, a toothbrush, a couple of packs of smokes, and the tiny roll of dollar bills he'd managed to squirrel away. Tucked beneath his prison camp bunk, library books had proven to be one of the things he'd treasured most about his new life in America and, thanks to his own countrymen, one of the things that had caused him the most pain. But the good had far outweighed the bad, and he'd figured the US Army probably wouldn't miss them.

"I…well, I liked to read, as a boy. My grandparents loved books, magazines, movies, stories. My mother, too, a little. But I think my father only loved…money. In the camp I found I could get English pretty good. Came easy to my ear, maybe. I thought I could get more English if I read more books."

Helen walked over to the low table beside the couch where he spent his nights.

"*For Whom the Bell Tolls*," she said. "*Drums Along the Mohawk. Northwest Passage.*"

"Just stories," said Bernhardt. "But I think more. When I read them I left the camp. Became someone else. Does that make sense?"

She smiled.

"Well, look at us now," she said. "We're both someone else."

She opened the cover of Hemingway's novel and flipped through the first few pages.

"Feels a little chilly tonight. I'm thinking we need a fire," she said. "And I'm thinking we need to start it with this."

He cringed at the ripping sound. Helen held up the book's title page and turned it toward him. He'd seen the same purple rubber stamp so many times it had become invisible to him.

"Property of US Government," she said. "Camp Ashland. Bridger Falls. Montana."

Sheepishly, he took the page from her hand, crumpling it into a ball and tossing it into the fireplace as she searched each volume for any more unwanted evidence. When the flames had finally begun to flicker nicely, Helen flopped down on the couch.

"When I was little," she said, "my father made fun of me for saying a word wrong. I don't remember what word, exactly, 'cause apparently I used to do that a lot. But I do remember it was a ten dollar word." She glanced over at him. "That's a real big word," she said. "Anyway, my mama came down on him like a ton of bricks, told him the only way I even knew that word was because I was smart enough to read it in a book. She said I just didn't know how to say it right because I never heard anyone else say it right."

She picked up the three novels from the side table.

"So I'll tell you what," she said. "I like stories. And you like stories. And your English is pretty darn good, but you need to hear a whole lot of words spoken correctly. How about you pick a book, and I'll do the reading tonight?"

An hour later, just as Gilbert and Lana Martin arrived at Gilbert's rundown swampland cabin to find Mrs. Weaver stoking the fire, the teacher quietly got to her feet, put down the worn copy of *Drums Along the Mohawk*, and smiled softly as she draped a heavy woolen blanket over her motionless student.

35

White clapboard brilliant against cloudless blue skies, the Westside Methodist Church was chock full of people, just another Sunday-usual, as Darlene had proclaimed on their first visit.

Wearing what would still have to pass for church clothes, John walked in, arm in arm with Helen, still sweating more than he should be for a July morning. But with three Sundays under his belt, he'd gotten a little more comfortable with the routine. The horn on Buck's old Chevy would honk twice, and he and Helen would climb in, her in the back with Darlene, him up front. Then Helen would work her magic for the forty or so minute drive up to Kalispell. Same on the way back.

"If y'ever want to avoid talking," Helen had explained right before their first churchgoing expedition, "ask someone about themselves. Most people'll be more than happy to take it from there."

Helen's information gathering and withholding skills had impressed John.

They'd learned about Darlene's family, and how, way back when, her grandfather had built the little cabin they were now living in with his own two hands, and how she'd met Buck out on the beach one day, and hadn't he just been so darned handsome, and how her father hadn't really approved of Buck on account of his Baptist ways, but that they'd come to be okay with him after Buck came to Westside and then they'd gotten married and Jesse had been born almost exactly nine months later, oh, and they were just so proud of Jesse since he up and joined the Marines at seventeen, and she and Buck had had to sign special papers and everything. He'd been gone almost two years now, she'd said, and they were pretty sure he was still okay, since they hadn't heard otherwise like some other folks they knew from around.

At least a couple of times, Darlene had asked questions directly of John, but Helen had masterfully butted in with her own answers after only a few halting words from "the horse's mouth." She'd been unable to explain that phrase to him.

Buck, on the other hand, pretty much just drove, window down to let some breeze into the car and to let at least some of his and John's cigarette smoke out.

On this particular Sunday, Westside Methodist's large and loud preacher, the Reverend Edward G. Smythe, had announced that he wanted to "remind us all of our rightful places within the great plan."

"Right here in the book of Genesis," he proclaimed, "it's spelled out for us. Let us make man in our image, after our likeness. And let him have dominion over the fish of the sea and over the birds of the heavens and over the livestock and over all the earth and over every creeping thing that creeps on the earth."

He paused for effect, and held a black bible aloft.

"Dominion," he said, "over the fish of the sea and over the birds of the heavens and over the livestock and over all the earth and over every creeping thing that creeps on the earth. That means you." He pointed at a man in the second row. "It means you, sir." He pointed at another man near the front. "It means you." Then he pointed directly at John, immediately inducing in him a very strong desire to be someplace else. "It means that as long as you serve the good Lord, and abide by His ways, until you get to heaven, you are the king of your own kingdom right here on Earth. You rule over what you see.

"As for you gentle lady folk out there," the reverend continued, "well, don't you worry, because the good Lord has a plan for you, too, right here in Genesis."

At that, he paused again, this time to look deeply and intently into the eyes of each woman in the front rows of the congregation.

"Your desire shall be for your husband," he said, "and he shall rule over you. Seems so perfectly natural, doesn't it?"

Later, in the safety of the cabin, they'd breathed another collective sigh of relief, grabbed themselves something to eat, and, as they'd begun to do after their very first church day, sat themselves down on the porch to run through whatever John hadn't been able to understand.

"Dominion?" said Helen. "Let me think. I guess that's a fancy word for 'control.' It's like if you have a dog, the dog has to obey you. You have dominion over it. Same if you catch a fish, you can kill it if you want to, because it's not a man. Does that make sense?"

"So, dominion means man is ruler? Man rules all the animals?"

"Something like that, yes."

"But also man is the ruler of woman. A woman has to obey. Does that make sense?"

Helen laughed out loud.

"Not to me, mister! But the world's full of stuff that doesn't add up. Most people just look past those parts and only remember the parts that make their own lives better."

36

Two days after it had been printed, a copy of the *Independent-Record*, dated Helena, Montana, Monday, August 6, 1945, lay on the table in the workshop of Crosby and Lennox Logging. Squinting hard, third cigarette of the morning already dangling from his lip, Buck read the headline aloud.

"Would you get a load of this?" he said. "New destructive atomic bomb dropped on Japan. Jesus H. boys…"

He refolded the newspaper and tossed it across the grimy table toward John.

"Here, Army," he said, "you read the small stuff. With my eyes, it'll take me all goddamn day."

Eyebrows arched, stomach knotted, John flitted his focus from Buck to the newspaper, then to Paul, and then back to the newspaper as he worked to suppress a flood of panic that almost made him choke on his extra long sip of coffee. He scooped up the paper and tipped back in his chair to buy a little more time.

Keep calm, he thought. *They don't even know if you can read.*

He sounded out each word carefully, slowly, as American as he could—as Helen as he could.

"Missile using pent-up power of universe is answer to peace bid refusal. Each bomb equals twenty…thousand tons of TNT. This awful bomb is the answer, President Truman said, to Japan's failure to heed the Potsdam demand that she surrender uncon…unconditionally at once or face utter destruction."

He paused to sip a little more lukewarm black-brown liquid, and to assess. To his immense relief, Buck and Paul were both leaned back in their chairs, Buck lighting up another cigarette and Paul with his nose in his cup. Neither seemed suspicious of his stumbling, or what he feared, despite Helen's insistence otherwise, might still have been a too Germanic delivery.

"Well, keep goin'," Buck growled through a cloud. "Give us the goddamn details."

"The…the atomic bomb has been one of the most closely guarded secrets of the war. It is…harnessing of the basic power of the universe. The force from which the sun draws its power has been loosed against those who brought war to the far east. The raid on Hiro…Hirosh… on Hiroshima, located on Hon…shu Island, had not been disclosed previously. The enemy base that was hit was a major…quartermaster depot and has large ordnance, machine tool, and aircraft plants. We are now prepared to ob…to obliterate more rapidly and completely every productive enterprise the Japanese have above ground in any city. We shall completely destroy Japan's power to make war."

The implications of the next sentence caught John completely off guard.

"Mister Truman said the Germans worked f…feverishly, but failed to solve the problem. We have spent two billion on the greatest scientific gamble in history, and won."

John looked up, almost afraid to breathe, knowing full well he'd likely mispronounced or stumbled over at least ten percent of the words.

Neither member of his audience seemed to have noticed.

"Well, damn," said Buck. "Goddamn!"

He puffed smoke with each word, and the clouds hung in the air. "Looks like the goddamn Japs are fucked!" he announced loudly. Then, a little quieter, a lot more pensively, "I sure as hell hope that's good news for my boy."

In the silence that followed, John looked into the swirling dregs in his cup, almost relieved, but focused on two new thoughts. *The war will be over very soon. And Germany had been trying to make the same kind of terrible weapon.*

With a sudden jerk, Buck tipped his chair forward onto all four of it legs.

"Ain't nothin' to do after that news but go cut down some more trees," he said. "I gotta make a run down to Polson this morning. You boys head back to that stretch we were workin' yesterday."

For the very lucky, thought John, as he got to his feet, *life goes on.*

37

When the breeze shifted the branches above him, he loved the way the dappled sunlight turned the insides of his eyelids bright pink. They'd had a productive morning, felling far more than the number of trees Buck had requested of them, and the old man had run another load down to the mill.

"War's gonna be over soon," said John into a stream of smoke. "If he made it through, Buck's son will probably be coming home. And a whole lot of other boys. Maybe time for me to move on."

"Too bad."

Stunned, John laughed as he turned to face Paul.

"You okay? That's two whole words."

A glimmer of a smile worked its way onto Paul's face.

"Listen," said John, "we've been working together for a whole lot of weeks now, and that's a first. Now I've got you talking, I...I don't even know your last name. Don't know how old you are, where you're from, or if you got a wife or whatever."

Paul leaned back against a stump, draped an arm across his eyes. For a moment, John thought he'd fallen asleep under the warm sun.

"Born near here. Seventeen."

Seventeen?! thought John. He'd been betting on twenty-five at least. "Well," he said, "that explains why you're not in the army."

John had time to take two long drags before Paul spoke again.

"Cousin went."

"Went where?"

"Army," said Paul.

"Where?"

"Dunno," said Paul. "Uncle said they wanted his words."

"His words?"

"Yeah. Words they tried to kill."

"What does that mean?"

"Means they only care," said Paul, "'bout what they can own."

The increasingly loud and squeaky roar of Buck's truck rumbling and bouncing back up the trail put an end to things, and they both scrambled to their feet and got to work acting busy. As he screwed the gas cap back onto the big Stihl, John glanced over at Paul.

"I'm gonna need more words out of you now," he said, "now I know you've got them."

The big kid simply smiled, then walked over to the truck to see if Buck needed a hand.

o o o

"It's one bomb that can destroy a whole city. That's what they said in the newspaper."

Helen had brought out a pie, and the rich aroma of apples and cinnamon and perfect brown crust surrounded him like a warm hug in the cool evening air.

"Well, that's good, right?" said Helen. "I mean, we've got it, so we should use it. Better us than them."

"I don't know," said John. "I've seen… I know what small bombs do. A lot of Germany is gone now. But the paper said they only used this new bomb on a military base, so—"

"Well, there you go," said Helen. "They just wanted to show 'em what we had. Bring the Japs to their senses."

"I guess," he replied. "Buck says it's a blessing, that their son was probably going to have to fight on Japan if this didn't happen. And that really would not have been so good. I…I learned something else though…"

He took his time scraping up the last few smears of apple and crumbs, savoring the final forkful.

"Germany tried to make this weapon. I'm just real glad it didn't."

"Look at you," she said with a smile. "Real glad. See? You're talking like a real American!"

He grinned and set his plate and fork on the low table between their chairs. Out on the beach, a couple of shore birds accomplished whatever tasks they'd set themselves to and flittered away, their melodic back-and-forth chirping audible even after they'd disappeared into the darkening sky.

"Speaking of talking like a real American," said John, "Paul spoke today."

"Go on!" she said. "What'd he say?"

"Not much really. But he's just seventeen years old. Said his cousin went in the army, because they needed his words. I don't understand. What does that mean?"

"I'm sure I don't know," she said, "but I know this. Your words are getting pretty darned good, and that's what matters to me. Now I'm turning in."

Forty-five minutes later, he slid a piece of paper between pages 164 and 165 and set the book on the couch-side table. He turned off the light, lay back, and pulled his blanket up under his chin. And as his eyes stared wide open into the night, five real American words repeated themselves over and over in his mind.

That's what matters to me.

38

On August the ninth, Buck said he'd heard on the kitchen radio, they'd dropped another atom bomb, "just to seal the goddamn deal," and about a week later, Japan had surrendered. Three and half weeks after that, the letter had arrived. Jesse Lennox was coming home.

"Well son of a bitch, boys!" exclaimed Buck. "We did it! Guess we gave those goddamned Nips what they gave us a hundred times over."

"I guess we did, huh?" said John, not exactly sure who we were.

"Jesse'll be stateside in six or seven weeks," said Buck, "home two, maybe three weeks after that. Gonna be a real big Thanksgiving this year, I can tell you. Darlene's over the goddamn moon."

The day had been a good one, trees falling like dominoes, Buck bucking like the bull of the woods, and by evening they'd hauled three full truckloads down to Polson. Pay envelopes in hand, John and Paul walked to Paul's rusted-out pickup.

"Appreciate the ride," said John. "Helen had to run to town for supplies today. Third time this week. I think she's feeling locked up."

"Yeah?" came the reply.

"Yeah," said John, "she kinda lives for Sundays, I think."

"Me too," said Paul.

"Not me," said John. "Pretty busy for a day of rest."

"Your choice."

Not exactly, thought John. "Listen," he said, "I'm meaning to ask you something about Sundays."

"So ask."

"You go to some other church someplace?"

Paul bounced the truck through the wide puddle at the turnoff. A miniature flood of brown water surged up through the makeshift wooden floorboards that covered the hole beneath John's boots. He leaned down and dipped his cigarette butt in the murky liquid before it drained away, then flicked the soggy result out of his window and onto the mud skirting the side of the road.

"You got a leak in your boat," said John. "I was on a leaky boat once, and once was enough."

Wet inside and out, the truck crunched to a stop in the cabin's gravel driveway. Paul shut off the ignition and sat like a stone.

"Got one of those cigarettes?"

First time, John thought, *he ever asked.* "Yeah, yeah…"

John lit them both up. Paul focused straight ahead.

"I was a kid," said Paul, "maybe seven, eight. They took me."

John fought the urge to open his mouth.

"Law said. For my own good. For the best." Paul took a deep drag, and exhaled his next words. "Was for the worst."

"What do you mean?" said John. "Who took you? Where?"

"Down Saint Mary's. Government agents."

"What, they made you go to school?" said John. "Every kid goes to school."

"Not like that."

"Like what?"

"Grandfather came and got me when I was eleven or twelve and that was that," said Paul. "Said there must be bad reasons to keep me there if I kept runnin' away."

"They…kept you there?" said John, his own memories rising. "Like a…like a boarding school?"

Paul nodded.

"What's that got to do with Sundays?" said John. "With church?"

"Don't wanna be anyplace," said Paul, "where there's white collars."

o o o

He heard the pickup truck door slam, then the soft clunk of her boots as she ran across the front porch. She'd made another trip over to Polson, and Buck had sent Paul and him home a little early for a Wednesday. "Not a good idea," Buck had declared, "to be slicing into tall trees with metal saws when a lightnin' storm's coming at you. See you fellas bright and early."

At the front door, John took the grocery bag from her arm.

"Wow," said Helen, "am I in the right house?"

"Mrs. Steele," said John, "would you care to follow me?"

He led her out to the little table on the tiny back porch, where a stubby candle flickered and a cold beer waited. He couldn't tell if the look on her face was pleasantly quizzical or seriously suspicious. He decided to go with the former.

"Please," he said with exaggerated grandiosity, in his best American accent. He'd rehearsed. "Enjoy the shelter of our elegant outdoor dining room, and take in our unmatched waterfront view, while I attend to the kitchen. I'll be right back."

Although he was afraid he might have overcooked it a tiny bit, he'd figured a couple of slices of Buck's best venison—pounded mercilessly into submission and then breaded into schnitzel—would taste just like his mother's. He was horribly wrong, but Helen was wonderfully diplomatic.

"Oh my gosh, John," she said. "This is amazing. I'm amazed!"

He grinned sheepishly. Amazed, he'd come to understand, doesn't necessarily mean impressed.

"I thought," he said, "maybe you're feeling, what do they say? A little bit copped up here?"

"Cooped up, you mean?"

"Yes, cooped," he said. "Cooped up. I thought maybe you might like a little change. Like maybe someone else to do some cooking. You probably wish it wasn't me, huh?"

Fully laden fork suspended just shy of her lips, she laughed.

"Oh, I've had a lot worse than this, I can promise you. My father couldn't fry an egg."

They both chewed hard in awkward silence for a moment or two before looking each other in the eye and simultaneously bursting into laughter. Knives and forks quickly met plates, and the eating part of dinner was mercifully over. They walked their dishes into the cabin and, as usual, Helen vehemently insisted on washing while he dried.

"Drying is easier," she said. "I'm doing you a favor."

He looked at her sideways.

"If you say so."

They worked in silence for a couple of minutes, until John decided to break the news.

"Buck and Darlene's son is coming home. A month, maybe two. That makes me…a little nervous."

"Why," said Helen, "because he's in the army? He might—"

"Marines," said John. "Paul said it's like the army of the navy, but I don't know what that means. He was on the other side of the world from me, but, well, maybe it's time to go, huh?"

Helen wiped the sink and counter down and hung the dishrag over the water spout.

"Maybe," she said, "but on the other hand, it might look pretty strange if we just up and take off out of here now, you know what I mean? Anyway, I got something to show you if you wanna grab us a couple more beers."

He thought he could sense something more beneath her words, but whatever it was stayed put. Rather than dig deeper, he decided to do as she'd asked, taking two bottles from the icebox and heading for the back porch while she disappeared out the front door for a few minutes, only to reappear with shopping bags swinging from both hands. She plunked herself down and took a swig of Budweiser.

"I picked up a couple of things besides groceries down in Polson," she said. She reached for one of the bags, hair flopping forward and prompting her to flip it back with one of the protruding lower lip puffs he'd come to know so well. Proudly, she held up her trophies.

"Got myself some new things," she said, "and I got you a few new shirts. And a jacket. Hope they fit, 'cause right now, your Sunday clothes look just like your Monday clothes."

John smiled. "I'll be a daper Dan!"

She laughed. "Well, I was shooting for Dapper Dan, mister, but daper'll do, I guess."

He watched her rummage in the bags again. *I hope,* he thought, *she flips her hair again.*

"I got you something else."

She placed a book on the table in front of him.

On its dustcover, a barefoot man in worn denim overalls and a stained brown hat stood between a seated woman and a barefoot boy, their gazes seemingly fixed on a crawling parade of old cars, each laden with all manner of furniture and tools and pails and spare tires, their drivers following each other across a barren yellow landscape toward distant purple hills. He realized his mouth was hanging open.

"*The Grapes of Wrath*," she said.

He picked the book up and turned it over in his hands.

"Steinbeck," he said. "A good German name."

"John Steinbeck," she said. "That's a real good American name. You read that one? Or maybe you saw the movie?"

"No, no," he said. "We uh, didn't get a whole lot of new movies where I was living, and the books were pretty old."

"Well," said Helen, "I figured it would be a good way to celebrate the other thing I got in town. I got a job. At the library. Darlene said she saw a sign down there a while back and thought maybe I might be interested. I start Monday, so there'll be plenty of these coming your way."

She was beaming, energized, her candle-lit face luminous against her dark curls in the gently falling evening light. *How*, he asked himself for about the millionth time, *did I get here?*

Of course he'd been asking himself that question his entire life, in good times and in bad, and he'd ultimately concluded that there was simply no rhyme or reason to anything that happened to him. His father had hammered him over and over with his own belief: that there was some grand plan, some divine force propelling people to do the things they did and to become the men and women they were. But his experiences had all catalyzed the hardening of his own beliefs: that the kinds of people who can make choices do so, and the kinds of people who are powerless to make choices are forever at the mercy of those who can. He'd come to the conclusion that where most people go and what they do is rarely up to them, and given where he'd been and what he'd seen and done, he'd had a hard time believing any of it was the doings of any divine hand.

He held up his beer bottle in salute, grinning ear to ear.

"Now," he said, "I have an easy German word for you to learn. Wunderbar."

Before he could translate, she reached over and squeezed his free hand. The word sounded absolutely perfect coming from her.

"Wonderful."

39

Permanently fingerprinted coffee mug in hand, about an inch of cigarette ash hanging on for all it was worth, Buck was animated.

"Well, boys," he said, "about seven thirty last night, that big, old, beautiful Greyhound pulled into Kalispell. Darlene was bawlin' like a baby to see her own baby, an' I don't mind tellin' you fellas, I sprung a little leak myself."

As he and Darlene had driven United States Marine Corps Private Jesse Lennox home, Darlene had, Buck said, "asked about a thousand questions without waitin' for a single goddamn answer."

When they'd got to the house, he said, Jesse had gone right to his room to stow his gear, then Darlene had sat him down on the front porch so she could bring him out a tray, Buck said with a laugh, "with enough sandwiches and cookies and cake and lemonade for a damn platoon." Darlene, he said, had taken the whole day off work from the diner so she could prepare "more goddamn food than I ever seen in one house in my entire life."

John grinned.

"Well, that's Darlene," he said. He only partly meant what came next. "I'm real happy for the both of you," he said. "Glad he's home."

"I know I don't have to tell you this, John," said Buck, "but I'm guessin' he's pretty tired an' all. From everything, you know. Plus that long boat ride, and whatever they had him do in California, then the bus trip up home. He's gonna rest up for a few days, I reckon, maybe a week, and Darlene'll try to put a little more meat on his bones. Then he'll come work with us. Be good to have another set of hands around Crosby and Lennox. Yeah?"

Hidden wheels turning, John smiled and nodded.

Paul looked at his boots.

40

By the second week of October, the Montana mornings had begun to dawn a little later, and in blue-white, but the afternoons still managed to fade into night over brilliant oranges and yellows and greens. On this notably brisk morning, the so-called heater in Paul's truck had struggled to make a difference, and they'd both been surprised to arrive at the shop to find the coffeepot cold. John had just begun to wonder about things out loud when the sound of a truck crunching gravel reached them. They heard Buck's deep voice calling out to someone, and as the big sliding door jerked open, they understood why he was a little late.

Buck was fired up.

"John," he said, "this is my son, Jesse. Jesse, this is John. Course you remember Paul."

John jumped up and stuck out a hand. He'd practiced.

"John Steele," he declared. "Welcome back."

A little shorter than Buck and a whole lot less muscular, Jesse Lennox, John immediately decided, also looked a whole lot less than happy to be standing there. Without a word, without even a hint of a smile, he reached out and shook John's hand.

Paul stayed put in his seat, and no hand was extended to him, just a barely perceptible nod.

Half a Camel already burned away, Buck got busy being Buck.

"Me and Jesse got breakfast at the house already so we're all set. You guys finish up your coffees, then we got the last of that northwest stand to clear. Jesse'll swamp, you guys cut, I'll buck, and together we'll choke and skid 'em out of there."

Buck capped off the morning's orders with the same confusing phrase John had heard him say on countless occasions, whenever his enthusiasm for his backbreaking work became too much to contain.

"Pitter-patter," he said, "let's get at 'er."

o o o

"You know Jesse from before? Before he went away?"

Index finger knuckle on his right hand bleeding through a layer of oily grime, all of his fingers chilled against the cold metal, John was swapping out a chain. Something much harder than lodgepole pine had sheared off a whole lot of its teeth with a violent screech and a jerk that had almost sent the two of them flying.

"Yeah."

"He always that quiet?"

"Nope."

"Never thought I'd meet anyone could say less than you do in a whole week of working with him," said John. "Compared to him you're a—a Schwätzer."

"A what?"

From time to time it was inevitable, John knew, that a word from his past life would find its way into his present. But Paul never seemed to notice. *Maybe he just chalks it up,* John always assumed, *to me being from someplace way out east.*

"Like a… like a guy who talks too much, you know. Compared to him you're a—"

Paul cut him off. "Blabbermouth."

They both grinned as John wiped the oil away from the machine's identity plate with a greasy rag.

"Stihl Type A," said John. "Made in 1929. I'm older than that. You know Jesse awhile? You friends when you were young?"

Paul looked down as John slipped the new links over the drive sprocket.

"Just from work," said Paul, "but Jesse's not the friendly type. Just Buck and Darlene."

Together they snapped the bar back in place, and stood up and stretched to ease the creak out of their knees.

"Grandfather knew Buck from way back," said Paul, "not Jesse."

John watched Paul wrestle his massive fingers into his gloves and pick up the heavy end of the saw as if it was a bucket full of dry leaves. They headed over toward a big lodgepole and Paul craned his neck to size it up.

"Grandfather said every seed grows its own tree."

Two hours later, they'd made their way back down the muddy road and had offloaded their assorted gear at the Crosby and Lennox world headquarters, as Buck liked to call it from time to time. Paul and John were at the table, two mostly empty Coke bottles on the table in front of them, when Buck and Jesse walked in through the big doors. Buck handed out the white Saturday envelopes.

"Hell of a week boys," said Buck, "hell of a week. I swear we give 'em enough logs to build a thousand houses."

"You mean sold 'em, don't you?" snapped Jesse. "Don't go givin' any more fuckin' dollars away."

Jesse's clipped words shocked John for a couple of reasons. In a week of acquaintance, they were close to the first he'd heard out of him, and their tone was harsh. Disrespectful. Buck laughed it off. Jesse looked directly at Paul.

"Got a habit of givin' money to people who don't deserve it, don't he chief?"

Paul downed the last of his Coke as Buck interjected. "Ease up there, boy. Paul's a damn good worker."

"Better'n me?" said Jesse.

Buck shut it down before it could escalate.

"Like I said, hell of a week. Let's get on home."

As soon as he'd climbed in and slammed the passenger door on Paul's truck, John leaned an elbow out of the window and puffed out a long stream.

"What was that about? Back there?"

Paul cranked the ignition key and the vehicle eventually rumbled to life. He glanced down at the envelope on the bench seat beside him. "One time," he said, "right after I started, there's too much money in my pay package. Couple bills stuck together. I went back in the shop and showed Buck. He said 'cause I told him, it was mine. Jesse heard him and went crazy. Said Indians are already thieves, no sense giving them money for free."

"What did Buck do?"

"Don't know," said Paul as he put the truck into gear. "But since then, Jesse and me ain't right."

41

The Reverend Edward G. Smythe was really on his game.

"From Corinthians," he said, before raising his voice almost to a shout. "The weapons we fight with are not the weapons of the world."

He held up a newspaper with a giant black headline for all to see, then, voice reaching a whole new decibel level, he repeated the passage to hammer home his point.

"I said the weapons we fight with are not the weapons of the world! What does that mean? It means that God has surely blessed us with the tools we need in order to vanquish our enemies. The faith, moral clarity, superior intellect, and indomitable fighting spirit needed to prevail over lesser men, over those who would seek to drag us down to their level, over those who might seek to enslave or even annihilate us if we refuse to bow to their will."

He thrust the newspaper even higher.

"I think you'll all agree it's mighty clear just exactly who has the power and might of the Lord at their backs."

Immediately following the words "lesser men," it had happened. Without turning her head, Helen had reached over and squeezed John's hand, her thumb gently rubbing the vee of scar tissue, before quickly returning her hand to her lap. For John, the echo of that warm, gentle pressure had completely wiped away any and all further thoughts, replacing them with nothing but feelings, and the rest of the service had been a blur.

Forty minutes later, outside the church, Darlene had dragged Buck and Jesse around to chit and chat with a few people, the usual rounds, Helen pointed out, made clearly less usual by the presence of her Marine Corps son. They eventually made their way back over to Helen and John, and Darlene gathered them together.

"Wasn't that just wonderful?" she said. "I think him talking about the end of the war like that was a nice reminder for us all." She looked from Jesse, to John, and back to Jesse. "A reminder of the brave things you wonderful boys did, with God's help. And I want to celebrate. How about coffee back at the house? Might even have some biscuits. What do you say?"

Helen, also as usual, jumped in.

"Well, that's awfully generous of you, Darlene," she said, "and normally we'd be more than glad to take you up on your hospitality…" She paused as she looked over her shoulder at John. "But John kind of promised Paul he'd help him out with something right after church."

"Well, how about when they're done, Paul's invited, too!" said Darlene. "He's practically a Lennox, anyway."

Helen's casual lie had caught John a little off guard, but it was Jesse's reaction to Darlene's response that stunned him.

"The fuck he is!" said Jesse. "I just spent a whole year killin' sneaky little yellow-brown bastards, and watchin' 'em killin' my buddies. I'm not breakin' bread with anyone looks like him, acts like him."

The long moment of silence that followed was palpable, almost painful.

"Oh, come on now, Jesse," said Darlene, trying to soften things.

She reached out a hand for Jesse's elbow. "Paul's not the enemy."

Jesse jerked his arm away. His voice was low. Mean.

"Well, he sure as shit ain't one of us," he snarled. "You heard the preacher. Lesser men. Who the hell you think he's talkin' about, huh? Can't tell me that son of a bitch and his kind wouldn't take everything from us if they could. Our money. Our land. Our lives. Our whole goddamn country. Just like the fuckin' Japs tried to."

Buck took a half step forward. "Hey! You watch your goddamn mouth, boy," he growled. "You're not in the Marines now."

"The hell I'm not," Jesse shot back, turning to get in a final volley before he marched off toward Darlene's car. "Once a Marine, always a Marine," he said. "And once an enemy, always a fuckin' enemy!"

Eyes focused on the gravel, John listened in wonder as Helen immediately worked her magic, filling the rough silence with smooth words.

"Maybe Jesse's a little tired today, huh," she said, "or maybe the sermon got him remembering some things a little too much?"

"I'm so sorry," said Darlene. "He just, well, I…I just don't know what's gotten into him. Please, excuse me…" Hand to her lips, she headed off down the path that led to the parking lot.

"Oh, Darlene," Helen called after her, "it's okay."

"It sure as hell isn't okay," growled Buck, "but maybe we all better take a rain check, huh?"

They drove home in virtual silence, John unable to speak. In fact, he could barely even think beyond his own memories. Jesse's outburst had shocked him, not only for its unvarnished hostility, but also for its familiarity.

The farewell dinner his mother had insisted on holding on the eve of his departure for Tripoli had predictably degenerated into a tirade in which his father had declared his son's Afrika Korps posting to be an almost holy mission. It was to be a new beginning, his father had ranted, "a modern-day crusade to reclaim Germany's rightful place on the dark continent," a campaign that would allow Germany to "finish the job" that his older brother Wilhelm, an honored member of the Schutztruppe, had begun on Shark Island, he'd said, "against the sub-human Herero baboons."

Simultaneously, part of John's mind simply couldn't shake the warm memory of Helen's hand on his.

He'd felt a sudden, stabbing coldness in his gut when the preacher had said the words "lesser men." He'd heard that term, or terms that implied the same thing, countless times. From the older boys at school. From his teachers and superior officers. He'd been told over and over that the qualities inborn in true German men would naturally ensure triumph over the treacherous and malignant and inferior enemies of the Reich, and would guarantee the prosperity and safety of all they and it held dear.

Hell, he'd not only believed those words, he'd repeated them.

And yet he'd achieved none of those things.

He'd spent years imprisoned with thousands of other German men, all of whom had failed. According to every measure inferred by their leaders, each and every one of them had proven to be inferior to their country's enemies. And like him, he'd figured that each and every one of them had to know—whether they acknowledged it or not—that by its own definition, a defeated and destroyed Germany was now the embodiment of the weakness it had so despised in others.

So of course he'd known without a doubt that those two small words—spoken by a man of God within a country that had helped to destroy Germany while it was also almost single-handedly crushing Japan—were absolutely describing him.

By her touch, by her unspoken words, he'd known that Helen had understood what he'd felt. But when Jesse Lennox had spit his own version of self-aggrandizing hatred into the Sunday morning air, he'd finally begun to understand that he had no idea what it was like to be the true target of such words, simply for being alive.

42

"Jesse's gonna be taking a little time off," Buck had declared. "Got a little personal business to see about. It's just gonna be us Three Stooges again for a little while."

A brief Monday morning rain had brought the forest to life, its brilliance bouncing sunlight upward into the trees, the tip tops of their towering darkness crisp against the already stunning sky. They were out near Forrey Creek, working the last stretch of a gentle slope dotted with lodgepole, an easy-peasy day by Buck's hard-charging standards. Wax paper-wrapped sandwiches long gone, John lit up another smoke and held the pack out to Paul.

"Nah."

"Nah?" said John. "Nah? You mean no thank you, John? Where'd you learn your manners?"

"From people look a lot like you."

John laughed out loud.

They sat in silence for a while, feeling good, but John had been thinking, and the question just popped out.

"Why doesn't Jesse like you?"

"Never has," said Paul.

"Okay, but why?"

Paul took his time.

"Buck gave me this job."

"So what?"

"Buck looked out for my grandfather, when he got back."

"Got back?" said John. "Back from where?"

"From the war."

"Buck was in the war?" said John. "The first war?"

"Yeah," said Paul. "With my grandfather."

John's mouth dropped open.

"My father up and died while I was in that school. So when I got out, and got big, Buck gave me this job. Grandfather said Buck's a good man. He is. But Jesse's not like Buck. He's got hate for me."

"No kidding," said John. "Hates you because you're an Indian."

"That's what he doesn't like," said Paul. "Hates me for something else."

"Why?" said John. "For what? You were, what? Maybe fourteen when he left?"

"Fifteen. Almost sixteen. Jesse had a girl."

"Had? What do you mean, had?"

"Norma Jean Ellison," said Paul. "Said he was gonna marry her. She left."

"What's that got to do with you?" said John.

"She's always nice to me when she come by the shed to visit Jesse. Too nice, maybe. She saw me with a book one time. We talked a little. She said she read it, too."

"So what?" said John.

"She gave me a book," said Paul. "Jesse found out. Went crazy. Said people like me were too stupid to read, and she had no business

trying to teach me, and was she sweet on me, a dumb savage? He…
he hurt her. So I hurt him. Bad. I took him down hard."

John nodded and crushed his cigarette butt with a heel. When he
glanced up, it was obvious that Paul's eyes were looking a long way off.

"Where'd she go?"

"College down Bozeman. Jesse signed up right after."

43

"What'd you do over there?"

He'd always figured that one day he'd have to answer. He'd even prepared what he thought were a few credible responses. But he'd never dreamed the first real inquiry would come from Paul.

They were walking a new stretch, climbing really. Buck had driven them as far up the rough track as he could get before leaving them to figure out the best way to turn this new mountain of trees into the next molehill of money.

"Like a puzzle, right?"

"Sure," said Paul.

"Start over there, north of the road?"

"Sure," said Paul.

"What do you think?" said John, waving in the general direction of his proposed targets with one hand while digging out his pack of Camels with the other. "We take out those five or six right there first? Good slope down and a pretty decent spot for a landing so Buck can get turnarounds done quick?"

"Sure," said Paul. "Gonna answer my question?"

"Sure," said John, his sheepish grin visible through his personal smokescreen. "Uh, mostly I was bored, or getting shot at by people I couldn't see. The desert is…nothing but sand and rocks and thirst," he answered truthfully. "That's why I like it here. Green and blue and a little wet now and then. Nicer people, too. Well, mostly."

Paul grinned at that one.

"Feels…" said John. "I don't know. Free. You know what I mean?"

"Nope."

"No? You don't love it up here?"

"I love it fine," said Paul, "but it's not free. Me neither."

"Well, everyone needs a job to make a living, if that's what you mean."

"Not that," said Paul. "I like working for Buck. I just don't like I gotta work for Buck."

John puffed another white cloud skyward, a puzzled look right behind it. "Okay. Now you gotta tell me what that means." His eyes followed Paul's gaze into the treetops.

"Means all this used to be free," said Paul, "before there was white men here to own it."

John had read some of the books, seen a few of the old films: Henry Fonda and Errol Flynn and John Wayne and a whole host of brave soldiers and cowboys and plucky pioneers fighting for their very lives against relentless hordes of vicious savages.

"Didn't your people own it all before that?"

"Didn't own it," said Paul, "lived on it. From it. But it got taken. Hellgate, they called it. Treaty. Grandfather said that was the right name for it."

John ground his smoke out on a rock, and they began the descent back to the trail head.

"Tell me," said Paul. "How's this Flathead territory, but white men own practically everything in it?"

"But doesn't your family own its land, and its house?"

"Made to own it," said Paul. "Law said grandfather had to take his little plot. Plant it. Tend it like a white man. Government sold off everything else to homesteaders. First guns, then words. The laws they made up, that's how they took it all."

o o o

Paul's question had lit a fuse that had burned right through their almost silent dinner that evening, John's mental efforts to extinguish it clearly impacting his ability to hold any kind of conversation.

"Okay," said Helen from the far end of the couch. "What's eating you?"

John smiled weakly, a little confused by her words at first. "Eating me?"

"Bothering you, silly," she said. "You've got a terrible poker face."

"Poker face?"

She smiled. "Come on," she said, "out with it."

"Paul asked me…about the war."

She sat back, eyes on the fire, but looking at something far away. "I'm surprised it took this long," she said. "What'd you tell him?"

"My mother said tell the truth because it's easier to remember," said John, "so that's what I told him. Or at least part of it."

"Well tell your truth to me," she said. "I should know it too, since we're married and all."

The flutter in his stomach appeared on his face in the form of a smile. He shrugged. "I just told him I was… getting shot at in a desert. That's it."

"Well that might work on some people," she said, "but it's sure as heck not gonna work on anyone who might know something about that stuff. You need details, like what, uh…like what outfit were you with, and where you went. That kind of thing."

"Outfit?" he said. "You mean like, a…regiment or division? I…I don't know…"

She scrunched her face into thinking mode, the little mole on her forehead moving inward as it did whenever her focus turned the same direction.

"Okay," she said, "how about this for an out? If anyone ever drills you, you tell 'em the North Africa part, but the rest of it you're not allowed to say. Sworn to secrecy or whatever. At least until we can figure out some credible details."

She stood and headed toward her bedroom.

At the door, she turned to him and smiled. "One day, when you're ready," she said, "maybe you can tell me what you really did over there. Until then, let's both go with 'if I told you, I'd have to kill you.'"

One day.

John had come to realize that his entire being practically froze solid inside every time he heard her say things like that. He knew she had no idea how much he'd come to want "one day" to actually exist, for them to be safe, and together, in a future without worry, without the constant fear of losing their pretend life gnawing at his gut.

He smiled as he watched her lean against the doorjamb. With a single motion, she pulled the ribbon from her hair and shook her curls out into the dim cabin light. Then the smile left her face, and he felt her next words as much as he heard them.

"Listen," she said, "I feel it, too, most days. The two of us, doing what we're doing after…after doing what we did. We've got secrets together now, don't we? My mother told me something about the truth once, too. She said… Well, she told me a person should tell just enough of it not to hurt someone unnecessarily. She said if a little bit of fiction makes someone we care about feel better or be safer, then the good Lord's perfectly okay with that. So, good night Mr. John Steele, who spent some time getting shot at in the desert. Your secrets are safe with me. Sleep tight."

He had no idea how long he lay staring into blackness, his mind swimming circles around a single question for which he had no answer.

How can something that feels so right be born from something that feels so wrong?

44

On the fourth Thursday in October, she brought the thing home.

"Okay," said Helen. "Open your eyes. Happy birthday!"

"It's not my birthday."

"Well, it's not Christmas," she laughed, "so it must be."

Paws like a bear cub, the little black and brown furball was pretty much half tail.

"Mrs. Connors down at the library had a litter." She grinned at John's open mouth and arched eyebrows. "Well, not her, silly. Her dog, Belle. This one doesn't have a name yet. I figured if we weren't going to keep it we shouldn't get too attached, but what do you think? Might be good to have a little extra company."

The energized creature scrambled its way up onto the couch and eventually onto John's lap, all puppy smells and soft warmth against his still-cold hands.

"How are we going to take care of a dog," he said, "while no one's here? You're gone four days a week. I'm gone six. Church on Sundays."

"I figure he can stay in the cabin," she said, "or we can build him a little dog house right outside, or maybe he can go up in the woods with you? You know, keep the wolves and bears away?"

John flopped back on the couch and laughed out loud as the clumsy animal clambered onto his chest and sniffed and licked and nuzzled at his face.

Over and over, before countless birthdays and Christmases, he'd quietly but insistently begged his mother, hoping against hope that she might secure his father's consent. And on every single occasion, he'd been silently but firmly denied by the people who'd supposedly loved him. Now, for no particular reason, without knowing anything at all about his years of sad disappointment, someone he'd only known for a handful of months had brought him the very thing he'd so wanted for so long.

He buried his nose in the wriggling puppy scent to hide the flood rising in his eyes, but his throat closed up so tight his next words could barely escape.

"October 25, 1945," he whispered.

"Greatest birthday I never had."

45

"What was the book?"

"Huh?"

"The book," said John. "The one that started the trouble with Jesse and his girl."

They were slinging the choker around a big pine when the question popped into his head. Helen had brought him another pile from the library the night before, and he'd charged right into narrating *The Call of the Wild* to her, both of them laughing at the name of the book's main character, a man-sized dog named Buck.

"*Ransom of Red Chief.*"

"Why'd she give you that?" said John. "It's about Indians?"

"Nope."

John laughed. "You big jerk," he said. "Do I really have to ask you each question individually? You know what the next one is, right?"

Paul paused for maximum effect. "Yep."

"Come on!"

"Okay," said Paul. "'Cause of my name."

"What? Paul? The book's about a guy named Paul? Written by a guy named Paul?"

"Nope. Written by a guy name of O. Henry."

"So what?" said John. "Your name's Paul."

"Paul's my last name. My real name's Henry. Henry Paul."

John's jaw dropped, then he shook his head and laughed.

"Nah," he said, "you don't look like a Henry to me. So where's the O?"

"My middle name," said Paul.

"Yeah...?" said John. "And...?"

"And nothin'," said Paul.

"What do you mean? O is your middle name? Just O?"

"Yeah," said Paul.

"Come on," said John. "O?!"

Paul brushed some debris from his jacket. He reached down to his belt, and when his right hand reappeared, he held a knife out toward John, his grimy fingers on its blade. John took it and turned it over and over in his hands, its leather thong handle wrap and a few tiny glass beads dotted here and there shiny with time and use. He said nothing.

"Mother said October's a month to remember. My grandfather— her father—got murdered by a government warden up Swan Valley one October, way back. My grandmother killed that man. I made that when I was a kid, to honor her."

"Well goddamn!" *More than one guy here,* thought John, *going by another name.* He passed the knife back to Paul.

"So why not Henry? Why Paul?"

"Maybe," said Paul, "'cause I couldn't say Henry when I was little. Don't know how Norma Jean knew—maybe Jesse found out from Buck and told her to try to make fun of me—but she wrote inside the book she gave me. Said, 'to the real O. Henry.'"

He smiled into the trees.

"She's always nice to me."

204 | *Dave Mason*

Together, they winched the big log out of the scrub and laid it alongside the others, the next load for when Buck got back from Polson. John lit up a smoke.

"So what was the book about?"

"Huh?"

"The book," said John. "The one by the guy with almost the same name as you."

"Wasn't a book, really," said Paul, "just a story. Two guys kidnap some rich guy's kid, calls himself Red Chief. Kid's such a jerk, they end up payin' the rich guy to take him back."

"Ha!" said John. "I'm gonna have to read that one."

"Heard you try to read a newspaper once," said Paul, deadpan. "You read books?"

John grinned. "Don't tell anyone," he said. "That's a secret."

They wrestled the choker cable into a coil. When Paul finally stood up tall, he wiped his face with his jacket sleeve.

"Okay," he said, stuffing his gloves into his jacket pockets. "I got one more secret for you."

"Oh, yeah?" said John.

"Yeah," said Paul. "Buck's name isn't Buck. It's Francis. He's been Buck long as I've known him, but Darlene told me people used to call him Frank."

46

Helen popped up from the cave beneath the sink and puffed a strand of hair away from her eyes. At that, John popped up from behind *Twenty Thousand Leagues Under the Sea*. The puppy, who'd acquired the name Zeus, stayed right where he was, curled up on the couch at John's feet.

"You sure you don't want me to do that?"

"Listen, buddy," said Helen, "I've been fixing things my whole life. It's what I do. You really think you can do it better?"

"Probably not," said John, "but I thought I should ask."

She laughed a little laugh. "Right!"

Helen clattered a wrench into a bucket and stood, wiping her wet hands on her dungarees. "Done," she said. "Now let's get outside and enjoy the rest of this beautiful Sunday. It's not going to stay this warm for long."

John slid back down behind his book.

"Come on, mister. A little fresh air'll do you good."

He dropped the book to his chest. "A little fresh air? You know I spend six days a week outside?"

"Well, yeah," she said, "but I don't. And besides, you're sure not spending those days the way you're gonna spend this one. Now let's go."

Three and a half wonderful hours later, Zeus had learned that he already knew how to swim, and John had learned all about the magic of drinking cold beer on a crisp, sunny, late autumn lake shore, and of hoping a few fish are dumb enough to bite down on hooks with feathers and tinfoil tied to them.

More than anything, he'd come to know the glorious feeling of releasing all but the one fish you've decided is perfectly suited to occupy your one and only frying pan.

47

"People do it all the time."

At John's insistence, they'd skipped Sunday services and made the drive to the home of the Hell-Roaring Ski Club. He'd read an article in a copy of the Kalispell newspaper he'd found in the church, a story about a local man who'd founded the club back in the thirties and had lost an arm in Italy, it said, while fighting as a member of an American army division that wore skis.

The visceral memories had surged through him.

On the road up, secondhand skis and boots and poles bouncing in the back of the pickup, Helen had been more than a little nervous.

"Well, I think it's absolutely crazy," she said, "strapping boards to your feet and trying to ride them down a mountain without killing yourself. Do you have any idea what you're talking about?"

"I've seen it done," said John. "It'll be fun. Trust me."

"Trust you?" she laughed. "You forgetting who Mr. John Steele really is?"

He knew she was kidding, knew she was as much a part of their make believe as he was, but still the subtle pangs of something close to guilt were never far away. For a second, he thought about saying nothing, but the words just found their own way into the air.

"I...I never forget," he said. "Ever. But when I'm with you, when we're Mr. and Mrs. Steele, it feels, well, it feels...real. And I, well, I like how that feels."

Afraid to look, eyes pointed dead ahead, he strained his peripheral vision in a futile attempt to gauge the tiniest inkling of Helen's response. Instead he felt the bench seat depress slightly as she slid over right next to him. His heart almost stopped when her leg touched his and he heard her next words.

"Well, Mr. Steele," she said, "I like it, too."

Ten exhausting but exhilarating hours later, they celebrated the day with plates of significantly improved schnitzel and potatoes, washed down with a couple of perfect beers.

"To skiing," Helen laughed, "and to survival!"

"Come on," said John, "how about to a great first day on the slopes? You did great, really."

"Well," she said, "I don't know about that, but now you've got to tell me something real. That wasn't your first time, was it?"

John dangled a third piece of venison just below the tabletop, setting the plates and bottles and silverware and candle shuddering when a clumsy furball bumped a wooden leg in its excitement. He made an exaggerated "oops" face in response to Helen's phony scowl, then leaned forward on his elbows.

"Truth?" he said. "No. Not my first time. I grew up there. Not there like Whitefish...I mean...in mountains. Switzerland sometimes in winter. And in summer and winter at my grandparents' house in Germany. They died when I was away..."

He took another sip of Budweiser and focused his gaze on the tiny flame between them.

"That was where I felt…where I felt like I could be anybody or anything I wanted to be. My grandparents wanted that for me, I think. Grandmother always tried to teach me English. She learned as a girl in Zurich, and she made me practice, over and over, so I could sound like, uh, Cary Grant, she said. She liked him."

"Well," said Helen, "a girl could do a whole lot worse than Cary Grant. I don't know who you sound like, but if we're talking movie stars, well…" She paused to think for a second, her chin in her hand. "I think you look a little more like…Gregory Peck."

He smiled.

"Is he a singer? Because Grandmother loved phonograph records, too. We would both sing along, to uh…'Winter Wonderland' with Guy Lombardo and His Royal Canadians. Or 'These Foolish Things'… by Benny Goodman, I think. And she loved Ray Noble…"

Helen smiled. "I've got my love to keep me warm," she said. "Oh, my mother loved that one, too."

The cabin fell quiet. They were together, but each of them was clearly somewhere else, until John broke the silence.

"My, uh, my grandfather didn't sing," he said softly, "but he had all sorts of books, about talking birds and pirates and jungle explorers. He was curious about everything. My grandparents were just so… They knew my mother was too weak to stop my father from making me be what he wanted me to be. I…I know she loved me, but she wasn't strong enough to protect me from him. Anyway, the war took me away from all of that. Now my parents are dead, too," he lied, just a little. *Dead,* he thought, *to me, anyway.*

"It's not easy to be someone's kid sometimes," said Helen.

He looked past the flame.

"Sounds like you were pretty lucky," he said, "to have a mother like you had."

"She was my rock," said Helen. "She was tough and smart and she made me who I am. After she died I kind of realized it was her who made my father who he was, too. I don't think he ever really showed her how much he needed her or loved her when she was alive, and he was just so damn angry with the world—and probably with himself—after she passed that he never got over losing her. I just couldn't be around that anger anymore."

Helen leaned toward the candle, radiant in its warmth, dark eyes on his.

"I don't know," she said. "Seems to me life's just too damn short not to tell the people you care about how you feel about them." She dropped her gaze to the flame. "Funny, though," she said, "sometimes you don't know how you really feel about someone. You just go along, living life, and then one day… Well, you think about what life might be like if they weren't around."

She stood and walked to the fireplace, its warm flickers reflecting off the silver tinsel and bells she'd hung from the tiny fir tree in the corner. His eyes never left her as she tossed a blanket and a couple of cushions onto the rug, dropped to one knee, and leaned over to nestle another piece of firewood among the glowing embers. Her next words were gentle, but they squeezed his heart like a vise.

"Well, Mr. John Steele," she said, "how about you and I cozy up right here for a while and tell each other some more truths?"

48

They were on their way to Buck's. On practically every other morning since he'd come to work at Crosby and Lennox, John had walked into the shop to find Buck a minimum of two smokes and at least one coffee into his day. A bitterly cold March 25, 1946, had broken that streak.

At the house, Darlene was strangely quiet.

"Everything okay, Mrs. Lennox?" John asked. "Buck wouldn't give me a straight answer on the phone."

"Come on in," she said. "I've got the coffee on. He said you'd be stopping by."

John and Paul shucked their grimy, snow-caked boots on the porch and Darlene ushered them inside in their socked feet, waving in the general direction of the kitchen table as she headed down a hallway.

"You boys take a load off. I'll fetch him."

They sat in the warmth of the Lennox kitchen, surrounded by flower prints and white see-through curtains and the delicious blended aromas of coffee and bacon and cigarettes.

On the lace-covered table, a folded newspaper sat atop a small pile of books, *Cannery Row* the only one with its spine facing away from the wall. *Kind of odd*, thought John, *for a guy like Buck to be in a place like this. Everybody's got more than one version of themselves.*

The coughing reached them before Buck did, and Buck looked like he shouldn't have even tried.

He stopped in the doorway.

"Sorry, guys. Darlene's got me in lockup. Be back tomorrow…"

Darlene jumped in as she placed two flowery china cups of black coffee on the table.

"The heck you will," she said. "You'll do exactly what the doctor told you."

Chagrined, Buck rolled his eyes and hacked a couple of times.

"Okay, okay," he growled, "maybe a couple of days. But I'll be back soon. Meantime, the new chains are out on the porch. Think the two of you can finish up at the flats'n get the last of those logs down to Somers? Told him I'd load him up by end of the week."

John shot a quick glance at Paul and got an instant nod back. "No problem," he said. "Doctor might have told you to stay home, but you should know who's the boss by now, huh?"

Buck's eyes flitted to Darlene and she smiled a little smile.

"Oh, he knows," she said, "and he knows he's gotta stay off his feet for a while. Doctor said no exertion…"

"And no goddamn cigarettes," said Buck. "Can you believe that?"

John shook his head, and smiled one of those "what are you gonna do" smiles.

"Jesse be back soon?"

"Don't think so," said Buck. "He's, uh, gonna be tied up down in Bozeman for a spell. Taking care of that business."

"Okay," said John, glancing at Paul, "don't you worry about a thing. Just enjoy your little holiday and let Darlene take care of you. We'll take care of this business."

Paul and John finished up their coffees and said their goodbyes, and Darlene handed each of them a bright yellow-wrapped candy bar as they stood to leave.

"Here you go, boys," she said. "Take these with you. They make everything just a little bit better."

49

Ten days had gone by in a blink.

Darlene had laid out coffee and biscuits before heading off to the diner, and John laid the fingerprint-grimed white envelope on the lace tablecloth between them.

"Somers said to tell you he doesn't miss you one bit."

Buck grinned.

"Can't thank you and Paul enough for what you guys've done for me and Darlene. Last time I spent this long on my ass I'm pretty sure I was wearin' a goddamn diaper."

John smiled and nodded. "I think we're getting the hang of it. Old man Somers seems like a…well, like he'd rather be doing just about anything but running a sawmill. But he seems almost okay as long as Paul isn't around. Not too keen on him for some reason."

Buck coughed a little as he nodded and swirled the coffee in the bottom of his cup.

"Yeah, I know," he said. "Lot of people don't treat Paul or his folks the way they should. Just as soon have 'em gone from here altogether. It ain't right, but it's how it is." He leaned back in his chair. "I'm dyin' for a goddamn smoke."

John picked up the white envelope and tossed it six inches closer to Buck.

"Open it."

Buck's eyes widened at the sight of its contents.

"What'd you guys do? Rob a bank?"

"Might've been easier," said John. "Let's just say me and Paul had a little help the last few days. You know, so we could both keep cutting while the logs got to the mill."

"Jesse come back? If he did, he sure hasn't been around here."

"No, Buck," said John. "It was Helen…"

"Helen?"

"Yeah. She knows a thing or two. Like how to run a skidder and load a truck and drive it to the mill. She worked a couple of days with us. That's how we got so much extra footage down to Somers."

"Where the hell'd she learn about stuff like that?"

They'd worked out the story details beforehand, just enough truth in them to make it all sound plausible.

"She spent time in the woods growing up," said John. "Relatives. Said it was the best summer camp in the world for a tomboy." Another word she'd had to explain to him a few times.

"Wouldn'a pegged Helen for a tomboy, John. We talking about the same girl?"

"Same Helen," said John, with a grin. "And, uh, one other thing. I, uh… Well, we sort of hired Paul's nephew, Albert. His oldest sister's oldest boy. He's a good, strong kid, and he worked real hard. Me and Paul paid him a little out of each of our pay. We'd…well, we'd kinda like to keep him."

With one deeply lined but strikingly clean hand, Buck scratched at the white stubble on his chin while the other one thumbed the white envelope open again.

"Well, I'll be goddamned," said Buck. "Looks to me like there's a pantload of dollars in here. So whatever you guys have been doing, well, seems to me you should keep on doing it. That goes for the new help, 'cept from now on they'll be getting a pay package from Crosby and Lennox. Fair?"

John grinned as he stood.

"Fair."

John had already stepped out onto the porch and was wrestling his boots back on when the thought popped into his head. He turned, tapped on the glass, and cracked the door about six inches. When Buck looked up, he gave it his best shot.

Buck's laugh-coughing reaction to the dead-on impersonation echoed in John's ears all the way home.

"Pitter-patter," he'd growled. "Let's get at 'er."

50

The clack clack clack clunk had become an almost nightly lullaby.

When the library had gotten its new typewriters in, Helen had immediately claimed two of its castoffs. The good one had gone to the Crosby and Lennox shed, recently cleared of derelict gear and junk by young Albert, and rearranged almost to the point of orderliness by Helen. The one with the missing 'E' had come to the cabin.

"My mama taught me," she'd said. "She told me being good with words makes people good with the world." John had taken to it immediately, hunting and pecking with three fingers and a thumb to copy pages from the books Helen brought home from the library.

He worked the keys for a few more minutes before yanking the crisp white sheet from the rubber roller with a satisfied grin. He'd come to love the sound of that low, whirring buzz.

"Done. Another page of *A Tr Grows in Brooklyn*."

Helen looked up and smiled as he laid the paper, words side down, on the pile on the table. Then he spun his chair around, laced his fingers behind his head, and stretched his feet out in her direction. He watched her yawn and rub her eyes.

"Tired?" he said. "Trouble keeping up the pace?"

"Why, Mister John Steele," she proclaimed, jumping to her feet, hands on hips in his favorite feisty pose, "I am keeping up the pace just fine…"

He nodded with a grin.

"Now, I appreciate your concern and all," she said, "but you know, if I was the kind that took things like that the wrong way, I might be the kind to have half a mind to make you sleep back out here on this couch tonight."

He smiled and jumped to his feet, and in two steps he was inches from her.

"Only half a mind?" he said. "What's the other half thinking?"

"If you play your cards right," she said, "you just might find out."

"We're gonna play cards?"

She laughed. "Do I have to explain everything to you?"

He smiled and pulled her close.

"Nope," he said. "Not everything."

51

"Well," said Darlene, "I've got a little bad news, I'm afraid."

Helen had called to ask about Buck, and had immediately sensed the stress in Darlene's voice.

"I drove him up to Kalispell last night. Doctor said they want to keep a little closer eye on him for a few days. Worried about fluid in his lungs…"

"Oh, Darlene," said Helen. "I'm so sorry. Can we see him?"

"Well," said Darlene, "he's at Sisters of Mercy. I think it'd just be wonderful if you all could swing by. It'd raise his spirits, I'm sure."

Just after four forty-five, Helen tapped on the window of Buck's room, and she and John spent the next half hour hugging Darlene and joking with Buck. Of course, despite the slightly disconcerting pallor in his cheeks, Buck was basically Buck, growling about having to be lying in bed on a beautiful afternoon, and unfavorably comparing the hospital food to Darlene's cooking. When he asked about Paul, Helen glanced over at John and told a good lie, explaining to Buck and Darlene that unfortunately Paul had some kind of family commitment that evening and couldn't make it.

"He sends his very best, though," she said.

Helen didn't mention what Paul had really said when she'd told him where Buck was: that Paul had said he thought of Buck Lennox like a favorite uncle—more than that, even—and that he knew everything would be okay.

But there was just no way he was ever going to set foot in a hospital run by nuns.

52

The day it happened started like so many others.

John had thought about it almost every single day of his life since: how you never know which day is going to be the one, how we all go through life thinking each day's going to be better than the last, until we live one that's a hundred, or a thousand, or a hundred thousand, or a million times worse than all the others.

"Okay, me and Paul…"

"Paul and I," Helen corrected him with a smile.

"Okay, okay. Paul and I will take Albert and Zeus with us. Albert can clear out the pecker poles and help get us set up. Speed things up. Zeus can keep the bears away, or nap like he usually does."

"Sounds like a plan," said Helen. "Buck's convinced that since I tidied up the shop, I'm his business manager now. He's got me digging into some paperwork for him today, so once I finish that up, I'll swing by and run the new load to Somers. I can meet you back here tonight with the rig and we can ride home together in the truck."

They'd had a good week.

The weather had smiled on them, and with young Albert's help, they'd made more than their anticipated quota of cuts. And like Zeus, John had loved to see Helen show up at the work site. It always seemed just a little bit sunnier whenever she came around.

At about two thirty, she'd ruffled the dog's giant head, hugged John, shouted and waved to Paul and Albert, put the big rig in gear, and pulled out, bound for the mill down in Polson with the makings of another solid payday. An hour or so later, Paul and Albert and John had loaded the saws and axes and gas cans and toolboxes and buckets and Zeus into John's pickup.

Done for the day, Paul and Albert nodded their see-you-laters and rolled out for home in Paul's truck, while John and Zeus headed back to the headquarters of Crosby and Lennox to meet up with Helen.

It was impossible not to notice the strange car in the yard.

The big dog clearly noticed it, too, standing at attention on the passenger side of the wide bench seat as John pulled the truck to a stop.

"Don't normally get visitors around here, huh, boy?"

Seeing no other signs of life, John called out, thinking maybe Darlene had gotten herself something new to drive. It wasn't until he'd hauled the heavy saw from the truck bed and humped it to the shed door that he noticed it was already unlocked and cracked open a couple of inches.

He pulled it wide and Zeus ran in.

"Hello?" John yelled. "Someone in here?" As his eyes adjusted to the late afternoon gloom, a familiar face emerged from the shadows by the workbench. Not familiar to Zeus.

"Hey, Jesse," said John, "how you doing?"

"Been better," said Jesse.

He was sitting in Buck's usual chair, a bottle and a glass and an ashtray with a smoking cigarette in it on the table in front of him. John wrestled the big Stihl over to the workbench.

Zeus hung back.

"Come on, boy," said John. "It's okay."

Without taking his eyes off the man in the chair, the dog slowly trotted over and lay down at John's feet. John pulled off his gloves and tossed them onto the bench.

"When'd you get back?"

"Always wear your gloves, right?" said Jesse. "That's what Buck says. Always protect yourself first."

"Sure, Jesse," said John. "That's good advice, no matter what."

"Sure," said Jesse. "I'm thinkin' maybe I been a little too lax in that department."

"Not sure I understand," said John.

Jesse got to his feet and looked around the dimly lit shed.

"Been a few changes round here, huh? I been gone, what, a couple weeks? And you clear the place out and move right in?"

"No one's moved in, Jesse," said John. "Just trying to help your folks through a tough stretch. And it's been months."

"I don't give a shit how long it's been," said Jesse. "All I know is you and that big fuckin' Injun been actin' like you own the goddamn place. Hell, I hear you even got your pretty little wife helping take a slice more of the pie."

"She's just pitching in to help out here and there," said John. It was obvious to him that this conversation was headed in one direction. "Anyway," he lied, "it's good to have you back. We can sure use the extra hands."

"We?" said Jesse. "Who the fuck is we? Last time I checked, your last name wasn't Crosby, and it sure as shit ain't Lennox. There's always something a little off about you, John Steele. If that's your real name."

Jesse's words burrowed in, and John froze inside as they slowly pierced his guts and the past threatened to come spilling out. A familiar click jolted him back into the present.

"What do you want, Jesse?"

"What do I want?" said Jesse. "I want what's mine. And I want you and your bitch wife and that fuckin' redskin out of my sight. Buck's wore out. I'm guessing he's about done. And this little game you're playin' here's about to be over."

Zeus rose to his haunches as Jesse stepped toward the end of the workbench. The last glimmers of daylight coming through the partially open shed door caught just enough of the shiny-dull gunmetal in Jesse's right hand to confirm its presence.

John pointed to the bank of drawers underneath the middle section of the big workbench. "It's all safely locked up in there," he said. "Ledgers and records that show what's been going on with your father's business while he's been sick. Everything's in order, Helen made sure of it."

Jesse took another half step forward.

"Course she did," he said, "so those papers ain't worth shit far as I'm concerned. I seen the old man up at the hospital today. He wasn't too happy to see me, I guess. Said some things. But so did I. Him and his fuckin' lectures. Been takin' shit from him way too long, and the whole time he's whacked out?"

Jesse's words confused John. "What are you talking about?" he said. "What do you mean by that?"

"They think no one knows," said Jesse, "but I seen it since I was five years old. Some days the old man couldn't even get outta bed unless my mother stuck a needle between his fuckin' toes. Seems maybe all that dope's startin' to catch up to him now. Still think the old man's a straight shooter?"

"Doesn't change what I know," said John.

"Yeah?" said Jesse. "Well, here's what I know. The only things I want from Buck fuckin' Lennox are small and green and made of paper."

Jesse tugged on the top drawer handle, then tapped the scarred and stained work surface above it with the barrel of the pistol. "Unlock it."

"There's no money in there, Jesse," said John. He needed time. "You think Buck keeps cash sitting around? Somers pays out Friday night, we get paid Saturday, and the rest goes to the bank every Monday morning. Since forever. But you wouldn't know that, would you?"

John inched a half step closer to Jesse, catching a strong whiff of alcohol among the familiar oil and gasoline and tobacco smells of the shed.

"Fuck you!" said Jesse. "You think I'm gonna end up like my old man? All wore out at fifty? I rode the shitty end of a fuckin' saw for a while and that ain't for me!"

"So what's for you?" said John. "Stealing from your own father?"

John stood dead still as Jesse stepped forward.

"It ain't stealin', asshole," said Jesse. "I earned it. I went to the fuckin' jungle and I fought for it."

"That right?" said John quietly, contemptuously. "Except you didn't. Buck told me. You were a cook."

The pistol came up hard and fast, catching John on the left side of the head. The impact spun him onto the workbench, then he fell to the floor. In a split second, Zeus was airborne, clamping his jaws on Jesse's left arm like a bear trap, his seventy-five pound mass knocking his prey backward. Howling in pain, clearly terrified, Jesse brought the gun down hard.

From a hundred miles away, from somewhere below an ocean, John heard a dog yelp in pain, but it was the all too familiar deafening crack of a round leaving the barrel of a weapon in close proximity that propelled him back toward the surface.

Instincts and adrenaline kicking in, struggling to clear the roaring fog that had suddenly enveloped him like a shroud, he rolled onto his back. Battling through almost impenetrable darkness, he called out desperately, to alert anyone who might hear.

"Achtung! Eingehend! Sich verschanzen! Sich verschanzen!"

Through wide open but barely seeing eyes, John sensed as much as saw a gun barrel inches from his face. In the distance behind it, he could just make out a man standing over him, legs wide apart.

Darkness closing back in, lightning flashes going off behind his eyes, John struggled to turn his head enough to locate the source of the incessant animal whining coming from his right while he fumbled in his left jacket pocket. Through it all, he tried to make sense of words seemingly spoken into a long, thin tube.

"The fuck did you say?"

John barely felt the boot impact his ribs, but instinct curled him into a defensive ball as the fingers of his left hand closed around the screwdriver handle.

Seconds later, Jesse's voice was close, loud.

"I heard you, fucker! I heard you! Buck tried to spin some French Canadian, down east bullshit 'bout you, but there's enough old Krauts around here that I know fuckin' German when I hear it!"

Now, John thought.

Or never.

He swung his arm as hard as he could, burying the screwdriver tip more than two inches deep in Jesse's inner thigh.

He thought he heard the distant, piercing scream, imagined he saw an axe handle slow-motion bounce off the grimy concrete floor beside him, and almost certainly felt the dead weight of Jesse's limp body falling onto his. But somehow, through it all, he dreamed he heard the voice he lived for.

"Oh my God, John! Oh my God, I… Oh my God!"

John sensed himself moving, felt a throbbing, drumming, pulsing nothingness consuming him. He fought hard to transform his swirling confusion into calm words. And he fought even harder to get them out, as whispers into the last of the dying light.

"Ich liebe dich, Helen. Für immer."

I love you, Helen. Forever.

53

For more than two hours, Helen had been alternating between pacing the hallway beyond the pale green windowed wall and sitting and staring bleary-eyed at a rabbit-shaped blotch on the waiting room's linoleum floor. Mobile or stationary, Darlene had been squeezing Helen's hand like a warm vise for so long that it had almost lost feeling, but a sudden increase in pressure and a couple of shakes told her to look up. Agonizingly slow time stopped completely as a white-coated doctor made his way over to them.

"Mrs. Steele," said the doctor, "your husband's got a few stitches in his face and a pretty bad headache, but he's going to be okay."

The relief washed over her like a flood. That brought out another of Darlene's white handkerchiefs and generated an even tighter squeeze of Helen's hand.

"He's got a minor fracture in his left orbital bone and a concussion to go with it, so he's going to need lots of rest. With any head trauma like that there may be some residual effects, we just won't know for a while. He's also got quite a few scars in other places, the kind I've seen far too many times these past few years. So I'm guessing," he said as he smiled and gently squeezed Helen's forearm, "he's the kind of guy who probably won't be too worried about any new ones, if you aren't."

Helen smiled back at him through her tears.

"And you probably already know this," said the doctor, "but it's not the first skull fracture he's had. X-rays showed evidence of some long-healed, likely childhood injury and surgery. At any rate, he's a very lucky man."

"Thank you, Doctor," said Helen. "Thank you."

Helen wiped her eyes with Darlene's handkerchief.

"Any idea," said the doctor, "how it might have happened?"

"No idea," said Helen, "I...I just found him like that. On the floor in the workshop. Maybe he...maybe he fell, or something fell on him. I just don't know."

"Well, as I said," said the doctor, "he's a lucky man."

"Can I see him?"

The two women made their way through the doors and down a corridor, with Darlene gripping Helen's elbow tightly and more than filling the silence until they reached an echoing green stairwell. "I just can't imagine," said Darlene, "how you got that great big lunk into that pickup truck all by yourself, but the good Lord must have made you a whole lot stronger than you look."

Helen sniffled and grinned. "And I can't imagine," she said, "where all those handkerchiefs came from."

They paused at the third floor landing, and Darlene gave Helen a warm bear hug. "What's the odds?" she said. "Both our men end up in this place at the same time? I'm just so glad they're both gonna be fine. Didn't feel right to tell you before, but now that we know John's gonna be okay...well, Buck's coming home in a day or two. They said pneumonia and cigarettes don't mix, but this penicillin they're giving him is a downright miracle."

Helen smiled and squeezed Darlene and kissed her on the cheek, then she wiped a sleeve across her face and ran her hands through her hair. In the time it took her to cover the short distance to room 31, she tried to settle the anxiety and relief and exhaustion and nervous energy she felt. She added surprise to that list when she pushed open the door to discover that the room already held more than one occupant.

From close behind her, Darlene's sharp whisper immediately cut the silence.

"What on earth are you doing in here, mister?"

Looking like a ten year old who'd gotten caught with both hands in a cookie jar, Buck got up from a chair tucked between the bed and the window and grinned sheepishly.

"Well, sorry," he said, "but I heard this guy was staying at the same motel as me, so I figured I should swing by. Doc said it was okay. I, uh, didn't think to check with you."

White bandages covering almost his entire head, John Steele lay motionless on his back. On the verge of losing her battle to hold back all of the day's events, Helen took his hand.

"Buck Lennox," Darlene gently scolded. "You get your butt out of that chair! These two need a minute."

54

The police car parked in the Crosby and Lennox yard at 6:55 a.m. on a Saturday morning instantly set off alarm bells. Slowly, Paul backed his pickup out onto the road and told Albert to get himself into its driver's seat and keep the engine running.

High stepping through the scrub and pines along the north side of the shed, Paul got himself to a place where he could press an ear against the cold corrugated metal. From inside, he figured at least two, maybe three men's voices.

Carefully, he worked his way around to the big sliding doors and lay facedown on the muddy gravel. Through the two inch gap where the wind usually came howling in, the voices came trickling out.

"Right about there," said a man. "Kinda looked like maybe he was tryin' to bust into those drawers. That there's where I took him down. Fool shoulda known there ain't no money in there."

"You, uh, say you took him down?" said another voice.

"Yeah. He, uh...he come at me with an axe handle. Got me pretty good one time. And he stabbed me with a fuckin' screwdriver when I took that off of him. So I smacked him with it! Caught him good, too. Like Babe fuckin' Ruth swinging for the fences!"

Paul inched forward and edged his eye around the base of the door. Twenty feet away, Jesse Lennox was limping toward two cops.

"But here's the weird thing," said Jesse. "After he went down, he started babblin', talkin' some right fuckin' nonsense."

"What kind of nonsense?" said the shortest cop.

"First," said Jesse, "I couldn't tell, but then it kinda twigged. My old man said somethin' 'bout the guy livin' in Canada or Maine or some fuckin' place when he was a kid, but I'm thinkin' that's bullshit. Pretty goddamn sure that prick was babblin' German. He's gotta be a fucking Kraut."

One of the cops said something unintelligible to the other.

"Right, right!" said Jesse. "I hear they been looking for a couple of 'em got away. This guy claims his name's Steele. For all we know, could be Adolph fuckin' Hitler."

Paul had heard enough.

He shuffled backward over the wet ground, and at the corner of the shed, he pulled out his knife and ran in a fast crouch, first to the right front wheel of the police cruiser, then to the rusted car parked close by.

When he reached his truck a few seconds later, he yanked the driver's side door open so fast that Albert almost jumped out of his own skin.

"Slide over," said Paul, "we gotta move."

"Is it true?"

"What do you mean, Paul?"

Eyes puffy, face shining, Helen stood in the open doorway while Zeus wagged furiously behind her, clearly hoping for some of the familiar visitor's attention. She tried her hardest, put forward her best pretend Helen, but within seconds she knew in her heart that Paul wasn't seeing or hearing any of that, and she knew in her suddenly ice-chilled soul that the real Helen was dangerously close to the surface. She took a couple of steps backward as Paul stepped inside and closed the door behind him.

"Jesse Lennox told the cops he caught John trying to steal from Buck. I don't believe that, but… he said he hurt John bad." Paul stepped forward. "And he said John's not John."

Suddenly short of breath, light-headed, almost dizzy, and stunned by the actualization of the fears she'd held for so long, Helen couldn't keep the cold in her soul from seeping into her veins. She opened her mouth to talk, to say something, anything, but instead, she turned away from Paul's glare and retreated into the cabin, mind scrambling to find some way to make it all go away, and to stop her anxiety from bursting her chest wide open. In the five steps it took her to reach the kitchen counter, her brain played out infinite scenarios, but her heart told her it was over. Tears and panic rising, she turned to face Paul.

"He hurt John, yes," she said, "but…I can't explain right now, there's no time… I—"

Paul cut her off.

"Is it true, Helen?"

She swallowed hard and leaned back against the counter, willing herself to focus on a thin space between two floorboards, fighting the smothering blackness beginning to overwhelm her. Suddenly exhausted, she closed her eyes and breathed in a deep lungful of air. Then, finally, she surrendered, and allowed her words to wash away the facade.

"Oh, Paul," she said, voice breaking, "we didn't mean to—"

"Didn't mean to what?" said Paul, his voice accusing, almost sad.

"Didn't mean," she barely whispered, "to be anything but good."

Urgency clawing at her, afraid of hearing what might come next, she ran to the bedroom and dropped to one knee.

With clammy, trembling hands, she reached under the bed and dragged a heavy canvas duffel into the light. When she stood, Paul loomed in the doorway.

"Tell me."

Eyes closed, Helen took a breath and exhaled her next words.

"We're...we're not... Neither of us is who we say we are. We never meant to hurt anyone. It's just what we had to do to be able to live in peace. It all just kind of happened. I'm...I'm so sorry, Paul."

Motionless, Paul looked at Helen without expression, without offering her any hint at all about what he might be feeling or thinking. Suddenly, he reached down and took the heavy bag from her hands, lifting it as if it were empty. Breath caught in her chest, terrified at the enormity of all the half-truths and falsehoods that had culminated in this moment, Helen stood transfixed, eyes locked on Paul's as he spoke slowly, his soft, deep baritone heavy in the tiny room.

"My grandfather," he said, "told me a person can lie about lots of things, but they can't lie about what they are. Well, I've lied plenty. Told nuns'n priests what they wanted to hear to make the pain stop. Told police what they wanted to hear so they'd leave me and my family alone. Told government agents what they wanted to hear so they'd believe we respect them and their laws."

In four strides he reached the cabin's front door.

He turned to her.

"Maybe I don't know who you and John really are," he said. "But I know what you are."

Helen's eyes overflowed as she watched him open the cabin door and toss the bag into the back of her truck, then scoop up the limping but excited Zeus and gently place him beside it. She willed herself to gather up the blanket and grocery bag she'd set by the door another lifetime ago, then she forced herself to walk outside, into the real world.

As if in a dream, she got herself into the truck and unconsciously twisted the ignition key. As the engine sparked and rumbled itself to life, in the rearview mirror she saw Paul poke his head through his own truck's open driver's side window and saw Albert immediately slide over behind its wheel and back it out of the gravel driveway. Seconds later, mind a thousand places, thoughts racing, she jumped, startled and almost fearful, as Paul's big hand yanked the driver's door beside her wide open.

"It's okay," he said softly, decisively.

"You're in my country now."

For a second, the big man hesitated, held momentarily captive by the gallery of dour faces hung like grim warnings on the hospital corridor's green walls. But in that brief moment, he looked into their loveless eyes and saw them for what they really were: afraid that all of their cruelty and lies and hate would fall back on them.

And suddenly strong, suddenly invincible, Paul took the stairs three at a time.

The minutes were hours.

She'd chewed a nail and picked at it until her finger bled.

And she'd paced.

And hoped.

And prayed.

But the sight of a huge man helping a barefoot, blanket-wrapped, pajama-clad and bandaged figure stumble out of the trees and across the gravel parking lot toward her lifted her spirits like no church service ever could.

"Oh, God, Paul, is he okay?"

When she heard the reply, a wave of relief washed over her.

"When did this guy," John croaked, "get to be a doctor?"

"Oh my God, thank you, Paul! Thank you!"

She jerked the truck's passenger door open, and as the two familiar men drew close, Zeus jumped to his three good feet in the back of the vehicle, tail wagging furiously.

"It's okay, boy," she said, fingers in his fur, her breaking voice belying the intended calmness of her soothing words. "It's okay."

She ran around to the driver's side and watched Paul gently hoist his patient into the truck and arrange the blanket over him. Then he put a hand on John's shoulder.

"Helen told me," he said. "Everything. Don't matter to me one bit."

John struggled to turn his head. "Listen, Paul, I…"

"We all tell the world," said Paul, "what we need it to know. We all got secrets, 'cause that's what holds the whole damn thing together. I know your truth."

Eyes glistening, pulse racing, Helen pressed the backs of her fingers hard against her lips as John extended his right hand. Paul shook it, and he held onto it as he looked first into Helen's eyes, then John's. His next words carried a sad smile into her heart.

"Steele," Paul said, as he shook his head. "I'm never gonna look at a chainsaw the same way again."

John opened his mouth, as if he might be trying to say something, but the only sound Helen heard was the slamming of the truck door as Paul took a half step back.

"Now go, you two," he said, voice resonant through the open window, "and don't be sad. We're part of each other now. For me, and I hope for you, a real good part."

Right hand alternating between pressing hard on the blanketed leg to her right and trying to wipe away the teardrops that just wouldn't stop running down her cheeks, Helen glanced in the shuddering truck's rearview mirrors at least ten times before its wheels left the gravel and found the road.

"The fuck you doing here?"

Jesse Lennox had burst into the room, barely contained anger like a grenade with the pin pulled, noticeably limping, eyes wild and violent below his bandaged forehead, practically frantic.

Two cops trailed him a few seconds later.

The man on the bed looked up, calm and composed, as if he'd been expecting the incursion for some time. The big man sitting in the mustard yellow visitor's chair said nothing.

"He came to see how I was doing," said Buck. "Real question is, what're you doing here?"

"You know why I'm here," said Jesse. "Where's Steele?! That son of a bitch…"

Paul stood. "You okay, Jesse?" he said. "You look like something fell on you."

Jesse took a half step forward, but the tallest of the two cops clamped a hand on his shoulder and pulled him back.

"Mr. Lennox," said the shorter cop, directly to Buck, "I'm Officer Carlson. This is Officer Hughes. We have reason to believe that a man in your employ, goes by the name of Steele, may in fact be an escaped prisoner of war. A German. We also believe that he, uh, assaulted your son here, during the course of an attempted armed robbery at your place of business."

Buck stared at Jesse as the cop spoke. Jesse stared at the floor.

"You guys really expect me to believe," said Buck, "that someone with the keys to my shop—and who delivers envelopes full of cash to me every Friday night—broke in to rob the goddamn place?"

Jesse's jittery eyes flitted from the floor to the shorter cop, then back to the floor. His mouth remained shut.

"Look, Mr. Lennox," said the cop, "allegations have been made, and we have to follow up. We have to do our jobs. Now, we know Mister, uh, Steele was injured and was admitted here for overnight observation. His chart says the nurses checked in on him just about an hour or so ago, give or take, but now he appears to be miss—"

"Oh, come on!" Jesse barked. "The fucking guy's not here, and his bitch wife sure as hell ain't around either, so fucking figure it out for chrissakes! He's gone, what? An hour? Maybe you should be out there doin' your goddamn jobs instead of standin' here flappin' your fucking gums?"

The short cop loudly cleared his throat, eyes fixed on Buck.

"As I was about to say," he said, "we've got an APB out on the suspect, and there's only so many roads out of Kalispell. Course we're hoping you might be able to shed some light on him, given your, uh, relationship. When was the last time you saw Mister…?"

"Jesus!" Jesse barked. "Ask this fuckin' redskin! No secret him and the Kraut are thick as goddamn thieves. I bet this piece of shit's in on everything!"

Abruptly, Buck flipped his sheet and blanket back and got to his feet. He reached the window in a single step and leaned against its frame, his back to the room. For a moment, he stood tall, head up, but when his chin sank to his chest and a loud exhalation filled the room, his shoulders slumped, as if his lungs had shed something more than stale air.

"Well, Mr. Lennox," said the tall cop calmly, "anything at all you might be able to tell us?"

Beyond the window, the black-firred, pink-tinged mountains were beginning to merge with the darkening afternoon skies. "Sorry, boys," said Buck, his voice quietly loud as his breath fogged the glass. "I got no clue where they might be. I figure where they go and what they do's their own damn business, long as they aren't doing anyone any harm. So I got nothin' for you but this. John and Helen Steele have never been anything but good to me and Darlene. Almost like family, you might say."

Buck turned and looked at Paul.

"One more thing," he said. "My family includes this young man right here." His voice dropped a notch lower as his glistening eyes finally settled on his son. "So either you get yourself okay with that, or you get yourself gone. You understand me?"

"Fuck you, old man," Jesse spat back. "You choose a fuckin' Injun over me? You choose a fuckin' Kraut?"

"Oh, Jesse," said Buck. "I didn't choose. You did."

55

Through one blurry eye, John watched Helen maneuver the pickup truck to a stop a couple of hundred yards down a tree-tunneled dirt road. She killed the engine, and in the ensuing silence—but for the tick-tick-ticking of the hot exhaust pipe and the wind in the softly roaring forest—he allowed himself a small wave of relief. When Helen dropped her forehead to her hands on the top of the steering wheel, he reached out.

"It's going to be okay, Helen. I…"

Abruptly, she leaned against the seat back, eyelids squeezed tight. She dragged her right forearm across her trembling lips. "I know," she said, clearly trying to convince herself. "I know. We knew this day might come, and now we're living it. But we're living it together, right?"

When she turned to him and rested her hand on his, he squeezed it gently, and her squeeze back almost reassured him, too. A scratching sound behind them turned Helen's head, and she smiled through her tears at the sight of the big furry face looking in. Although it hurt a little, John couldn't help but smile, too.

"Yeah," he said, "the three of us."

Helen breathed out hard and turned to face straight ahead. She pressed her hands to her eyes, then dropped them into her lap and sat, unblinking, almost dead still for a long moment, her gentle breathing and the little thought indicator on her forehead, John noticed, her only detectable movements.

"Okay," she said finally, like she meant it. The force of the word almost startled him. "What if we…we just stay right here tonight and most of tomorrow, let you rest up a little more, then move on? There's lots of weeds poking up through the road, so it doesn't feel like anyone's been down here too often."

The heavy air in the truck suddenly felt clearer as she talked, and he could feel her energy level rising.

"If anyone's looking for us, they'll probably think we're hell bent on getting as far from the hospital as possible. So how about we do the opposite?" She turned to him and breathed out a convincingly decisive, almost optimistic breath. "What do you think?"

"What do I think?" said John. He smiled as he grimaced. "I think you might be the smartest officer I ever served under. You're definitely the most beautiful."

She smiled a smile that lit up the cab.

"I even brought food and blankets and some water this time," she said. "Not like our first date."

John squeezed his unbandaged eye shut, smiled, and nodded his head gently, but the pounding in his temple, the sharp twinge in his cheek, and the inadvertent groan that emerged from his lips reminded him, once again, not to do that kind of thing.

But he couldn't stop himself.

Pain be damned, he turned to look at her.

"I don't recall," he said, "wearing pajamas on that date, either."

She laughed a little and held out her hand. As he reached for it, something triggered a soft clunk on the floor at his feet.

Helen stretched down and rummaged around under the blanket. When she sat back up, she showed John the fruits of her search.

"You brought a knife from the hospital?"

About ten inches long, sheathed in tanned leather so timeworn it looked like cloth, a few red and black glass beads still clinging to its hide-wrapped handle, John recognized it instantly. Words suddenly caught in his throat, he took it from her and cradled it gently in his hands.

"You okay?" said Helen.

"Yeah," he said softly. "I'm okay."

"What is it?" she asked. "Where'd it come from?"

"It's Paul's."

"Maybe he dropped it by accident," she said. "When he helped you into the truck?"

John shifted his one-eyed gaze to the raindrops beginning to make their presence known on the windshield.

"No," he said. "The only way it's here with me is because he wants it to be."

"What do you mean?"

John looked down at the knife.

"He told me he made it when he was a kid, to honor someone he had a lot of respect for."

"On the way from the cabin to the hospital," Helen said softly, "Paul told me not to worry, that honor was on our side. I asked him what he meant, and he said something odd. 'The past cuts like a knife.' What could that mean?"

John smiled, and Helen smiled, and together they listened to the rain for a long moment.

The soft creak of the truck's driver's-side door jolted him back to the present. He turned to see Helen digging around in the truck bed for a few minutes while an insistent Zeus demanded her attention. Seconds later, the big dog apparently happy under his tarp, her arms full, she climbed back into the cab. She set a brown paper bag on the dash, then arranged the blanket over both of their laps.

Ever so carefully, she slid a little closer to him.

"This evening," she said, "I'll be serving delicious peanut butter and crackers accompanied by apple slices. When we get settled in some-place new, you can serve me schnitzel. Deal?"

He strained against the pain to reach up and touch her cheek.

"Best deal, ever."

56

"I figure we're somewhere right about here."

There wasn't a dot anywhere on the map even remotely close to Helen's chewed-to-the-quick fingernail, just a faint, pale green line leading essentially north.

"This is the road we turned off of," she said, her finger tracing the line to the spot where it met a thicker one about an inch or so south. "Right here it leads northwest, to Idaho. But you can see," she said, her finger traveling up and to the left, "there's a fork right here where we can go west or north. Whatever strikes us, I guess. I don't know why, but I'm thinking anyone looking would figure we'd head south. Like maybe California or somewhere. Maybe they'd think there's a whole lot more crowds to get lost in down that way. What do you think?"

He was sitting beside her on the truck's open tailgate, the map on his lap, one arm resting on a sleeping Zeus. Earlier, Helen had helped him change into work clothes and a jacket, and together they'd struggled to wrestle his socks and boots on. She'd buried his hospital pajamas in the forest.

"Well," said John, voice rough. "I think you're wonderful. I think you're smarter than you are wonderful. And I think you're driving, so I guess just wake me up when we get someplace. Long as I'm with you, I'm okay."

"Okay, Boris Karloff," she said, jumping down from the tailgate. "But maybe we should get this wrapper off you. They're looking for a mummy, remember?"

John watched her eyes and lips and the little dot on her forehead as she began to peel the gauze from around his head. Suddenly, he reached out and put his hands on her hips and pulled her close. The pounding behind his eyes was worth it.

"This is kind of how we met, remember?"

"Seems like a lifetime ago, doesn't it? Now hold still, you."

She unwound the rest of the bandage and dropped it in his lap. Then she gently caressed the four stitches in his black and purple and yellow cheek.

"Well, Mister Steele," she said, "you got a nasty looking cheek and a pretty solid three-day beard going, but you're still a movie star handsome devil. I told you, it's a good thing girls love scars, 'cause you've got plenty of 'em."

They'd waited until close to dusk before beginning to make their way back down the dirt road to the paved highway. More than two hours and almost sixty-five miles after getting underway, John opened his eyes to a sign of civilization—bright red neon letters that spelled out most of the word "vacancy."

"I'm all checked in. Room 11," said Helen. "Just a girl on her way from Helena to Bonner's Ferry to see her second favorite grandma."

"Are you scared?"

So tired he couldn't sleep, yet barely able to keep his eyes open, John felt as if he'd been hovering someplace between here and there for hours, maybe days. The sound of Helen's voice floated him back to warmth and softness. Gingerly, he pinched the bridge of his nose, then ran a hand through his hair. "No," he said, "but not *not* scared…"

"I am…" she whispered.

He stroked her hair.

"Just be here now," he said.

"I don't know how," she said, her voice catching. "I'm worried. About tomorrow. I…I want a lifetime of tomorrows with you."

Lost for words, he pulled her closer. Her warm hand on his chest, the scent of her hair, and the sound of her soft breathing almost surreal in their simple beauty, he stared into the dark, and for a few minutes, or a few hours, he allowed himself to think about the possibility of shared tomorrows. But all too soon, his thoughts—as they so often did in the twilight between the real world and the remembered one—took him nine thousand seven hundred kilometers to the east.

o o o

They'd all known the assault was coming.

As usual, the reconnaissance reports had trailed the rumor mill, and Bernhardt had already known that the Tommies had been massing men and equipment long before he'd been tasked with conducting a probe beyond the Devil's Gardens, the sweeping belts of more than three million mines that in theory, at least the generals said, would protect them from the British and the New Zealanders and the Indians and the Australians.

Under cover of darkness, traveling light, Bernhardt and his squad of five men had carefully worked their way almost seven kilometers beyond their barbed-wire perimeter. When the barrage had suddenly begun—a thousand Eighth Army guns firing in a continuous thunder to light up the night like day—they froze, caught between the muzzle flashes ahead of them and the impact points to their rear.

Wide-eyed and breathing hard, Hartmann—Bernhardt's young Unteroffizier—scrambled over to him. "Herr Leutnant!" he shouted, panic clearly rising in his voice. "Should we go back?"

"Calm down," said Bernhardt. "Map."

Hands shaking, Hartmann unfolded the paper against the ground, the staccato flashes of the allied guns almost eliminating the need for his flashlight. Swallowing his own fear, trying his best to project control in what he knew had become an uncontrollable scenario, Bernhardt scanned the map for landmarks, found one. They were exposed, caught on a relatively flat, hardscrabble plain of sand and rock that stretched approximately fifteen kilometers to the north and east. Just to the south, the Ruweisat Ridge, like a parade of headless sphinxes, rose from the desert floor.

Bernhardt stabbed the paper. "We're here," he said.

He stabbed it again. "We're going there."

Crouched, they ran, each of them no doubt hoping and some of them likely praying—as Bernhardt certainly was—that the deafening, blinding, ground-shaking barrage would continue long enough for them to reach their destination. He knew that as soon as the big guns began to go silent, the men and machines would appear.

Covering the distance in just under twenty-two minutes, they flopped into the sand and rocks behind a cluster of small boulders.

Sweaty, and breathless, but without a shred of actual fatigue, Bernhardt could see the barely suppressed terror in his young soldiers' faces as they white-knuckled their weapons and rubbernecked nervously, the thousands and thousands of tons of Allied artillery shells arcing through the skies overhead weighing on them like a coffin lid.

Fear, he thought, *is alchemy.*

"Breathe! And drink, but not too much!" shouted Bernhardt. "You're going to need everything you can get later!"

They were trapped, and Bernhardt knew it.

The rumors and a few previous reports had made it clear. To the east and north loomed the first wave of the inevitable Allied advance. If his patrol retreated, they'd run the risk of being killed by their own comrades dug into the shallow trenches arrayed along the minefield's edge, or being shredded by the British artillery shells now pounding that area into oblivion.

He gathered them in close.

"We have to wait!" he shouted. "Until the barrage slows! Then we'll know the actual attack will be about to begin! The only chance we've got is to move to the west as fast as we can ahead of the Tommies and try not to get killed by our own guys! We can flash the safe signal and hope they see us!"

He almost believed that plan might actually work.

"Intelligence says they'll come from over there!" He pointed to an area just northeast of the ridge. "Schafer! You and Becker get behind those rocks there and keep your eyes wide open, you understand?! Hartmann! You take Zimmermann about three hundred meters to the south! Keep within visual distance of Schafer and Becker! Grunhagen, you stay here. I'm going to take a look over the top of the ridge, and I might be coming back in a big hurry. If you see a crazy man running at you, don't fucking shoot him!"

Bernhardt took a small swig from his canteen, checked his watch, and picked up his rifle. Stooped low, bent at the waist, he threaded his way uphill between car-sized boulders until he reached a sort of crest almost eight minutes later.

Through his binoculars, he finally saw them.

In a narrow gully eerily illuminated by periodic artillery flashes, the predators sat idling, waiting. He counted fifty-two British tanks, personnel carriers, and self-propelled guns, and although he couldn't see them, he knew the infantry that would accompany those machines would also be there, likely hunkering in shallow trenches like animals nervously awaiting the signal to walk into the slaughterhouse.

He squeezed his eyelids shut and tried to focus on his breathing, fighting hard to keep the cold claw of fear from ripping his guts out. *What a stupid fucking thing*, he thought, *for any of us to be here, in this godforsaken place, on this godforsaken night.*

He waited.

When his watch ticked over to 0430, the beginning ended. The booms and flashes and ripping sounds of the overhead shells diminished slightly, and in the disorienting, intermittent brilliance, he watched as hundreds of men began to materialize from the sand and rocks, as if conjured from thin air. With fixed bayonets bobbing, they ran, bent over and awkward, essentially northwestward across the rough terrain. Behind them, the tank and armored car crews brought their steel coffins to full roaring life, and he watched as they moved one by one into a line astern formation before following the foot soldiers, presumably through a mine-free path.

Heart pounding against his sternum, Bernhardt quickly retraced his steps back down from the top of the ridge. As he approached the place he could have sworn he'd left Grunhagen, he flashed his torch— two short, one long, one short—and hoped like hell Grunhagen would recognize the signal. He got no signal in return. Heard no shots. No shouts. Nothing. Moments later, he reached the split boulder behind which he and Hartmann had originally sheltered. Just bootprints in the sand. He ran to the south, covering a couple hundred meters.

"Hartmann! Zimmermann! Where the fuck are you?!"

With rising desperation, he searched among the rocks, but found only a discarded canteen. Synapses struggling, instincts outweighed only by training and hard experience, he fought to control his panic, to think. Helpless, impotent, infinitesimally small beneath the billion star sky, he squatted behind a boulder and clenched his teeth.

The search for the others had taken too long. Within minutes, it began.

As Bernhardt knew all too well, there's nothing quite like the sound of a tank battle in the desert. With virtually nothing to baffle them, the sound waves carried forever. The roaring and creaking and grinding of vehicles, the crack of small arms fire, and the thunderous sounds of exploding mines and artillery shells and anti-tank rounds clanging through steel enveloped him. Inside that cacophony, he knew, were the screams and cries of the terrified, the confused, the wounded, and the dying.

There was nothing to do but wait. If the Brits came scurrying back in defeat, he'd know his next move. *If they don't,* he thought, *well…*

Almost imperceptibly, the horizon behind him began to glow a gentle orange, and the sky before him turned gray, as hundreds of grimy plumes merged into a shroud that floated up to obscure the waning stars. That phenomenon, he knew, temporarily marked the slaughter and disfigurement of hundreds—possibly thousands—of young men from all over the world whose callous superiors had plunged them headlong into a meat grinder.

Suddenly exhausted, Bernhardt lay back against a rock and closed his burning eyes. *Just for a moment,* he thought.

Jerked from his shallow slumber by a soft sound—too close to be anything but a threat—Bernhardt swung his rifle. The barrel smacked something hard, and the impact directed a single bullet skyward.

Adrenaline instantly burning away the fog of his fear and fatigue, he scrambled to his feet in time to see the frantically bobbing backside of a tiny goat disappearing around a pile of rocks.

He squinted at his watch, the intense glare of the morning sun sending sparks into his brain. Suddenly realizing the sheer stupidity of firing off a round, then standing bolt upright in a daylit combat area, he immediately dropped to a low crouch, his back hard against the shadowed side of his personal boulder, eyes scanning left and right, over and over, as he worked to regain his bearings. The remaining lukewarm metallic drops from his canteen helped him gather his wits, and again, he checked the time. He let ten more uneventful minutes pass, then chanced a quick look over the top of his stone ramparts. Below him, the now silent plain stretched out as far as he could see, toward the columns of dirty smoke clouding the shimmering north-western horizon. He dropped back into a crouch and took inventory of the things he knew.

It didn't take long.

He was alone, as far as he could tell. He had almost no water. And he was some distance to the southeast of what had clearly been a signif-icant battle, the outcome of which he had no way of knowing. His countrymen, he hoped, were still somewhere to the west. His enemies were most definitely to the north and east, but also now possibly to the northwest. If he stayed where he was, or went south, he would live, but without water, certainly not for long. If he went north or east, he might not live long enough for the desert to kill him. Wiping the sweat from his forehead, he said goodbye to his boulder.

Less than thirty minutes later, the carnage began to reveal itself.

Bodies and parts of bodies, tanks and parts of tanks, shattered artillery pieces and smashed and burning and smoking armored vehicles were strewn over an enormous area.

Maybe, he thought, *we were able to stop them right here?*

Ten minutes further revealed more northwestward vehicle trails, proving his hopeful theory wrong. Knowing he was now likely well inside the Devil's Gardens, he made sure to walk in the ruts left by tanks or armored cars whenever he could. Other than the flames and plumes of smoke still emanating from some of the scorched and bent wreckage, shimmering heat waves provided the only movement, his own labored breathing, the blood pumping through his veins, and his boots shuffling in the sand and rocks the only sounds.

How very strange, he thought, *to be the only life in an otherwise lifeless place.*

As he knew it would, the heat soon began to take its toll.

He fought hard to keep his mind from wandering, but a random thought from his childhood popped into his head. "Like walking," he whispered to no one, "on Jules Verne's moon."

A hundred or so meters ahead and to his right, the shattered hull of a British Crusader tank squatted like some dead thing in the sand. Bernhardt could easily read the signs of its demise: one of its tracks trailed out flat behind it, no doubt the result of a mine or a disabling anti-tank round. Its severed gun barrel lay some five meters to its rear, likely sent airborne by another anti-tank round. His first thought—*deathtrap*—was quickly pushed aside by a second, more urgent one. *Maybe there's water in there.*

He clambered onto the sweltering hulk and peered through a hatch into its pitch-dark bowels. The sun's brilliance made the vehicle's interior a sinister black cave, but Bernhardt's burning throat compelled him to set his rifle on its scorched deck and extend first one, then the other boot into the void. He lowered himself into a crouch once both feet contacted something solid. The intense stink of burnt fuel and rubber and spent ammunition and the almost sweet aroma of charred meat threatened to overwhelm his senses. Ignoring them, he closed his eyes, rubbed them with the heels of his hands, and waited for the afterimages to subside.

A soft groan from somewhere deep in the shadows triggered a loud, involuntary gasp and a physical recoil that immediately reminded Bernhardt that he was only wearing his forage cap, rather than a steel helmet.

"Jesus fucking Christ!" he shouted. "Is someone there?!"

A second guttural groan emanated from the almost impenetrable blackness below a glaring ten-centimeter hole near the front of the vehicle. Bernhardt craned his neck toward the sound, straining to make out its source as his eyes struggled to contend with the harsh contrast.

A man, or what had once been a man—likely a driver, Bernhardt guessed—had somehow survived the fiery blast that had evaporated or disintegrated his crewmates. Slumped against the tank's scorched side wall, the soldier's virtually unrecognizable charcoal and crimson torso was partially illuminated by the brilliant shaft of sunlight that shone through the hole left by the projectile that had no doubt ended the vehicle's life. The man's uniform had been mostly burned off, but a few shreds of what must once have been fabric had fused with his almost liquefied flesh. His lips and ears had essentially melted, and from what Bernhardt could see, his eyelids appeared to be seared shut.

"My God," Bernhardt whispered. "My God…"

Somehow, this horrendously damaged soldier had managed to endure what could only have been hours of agony. And now, Bernhardt thought, he was clinging desperately to whatever life was left in him.

He thought wrong.

"Kill…me…"

Despite the baking heat inside the steel oven, the animal sounds of the almost incomprehensible words—wheezed out past skeleton teeth—chilled Bernhardt to his core. This man had no business being alive, let alone being able to speak.

"Kill…me…"

The soldier's words birthed an unrecognizable panic in Bernhardt, different from any he'd ever felt before. Desperately sucking in air, he shrank back toward the open turret hatch, the azure blue sky calling for him to escape this black hell and get back to the yellow hell of the midday desert sun.

Leave the poor bastard, Bernhardt thought. *It won't be long. No one will ever know.*

And then he imagined, just for a second, what he himself might want from this man, should their roles be reversed.

Eyes squeezed shut, breath coming in short bursts, the images suddenly formed in Bernhardt's mind: old man Schroeder brandishing a pistol, standing wide-legged over the carcass of his ancient horse as a six year old Bernhardt sobbed uncontrollably in the middle of a wet cobblestoned street. His father had dragged him away by the scruff of his neck, as over and over he'd screamed the words that had been drilled into him on countless Sundays.

"Thou shalt not kill!"

That evening, his mother had sat on the edge of his bed, stroking his forehead and speaking in hushed tones in the dark, no doubt fearful of spoiling a rare moment of solitude with her son that had only been enabled by one of his father's bottles.

"Blessed are the merciful, for they shall receive mercy."

The words she'd used to excuse the old man's actions had confused Bernhardt ever since, and suddenly they blended with the gurgling, rasping English words that dragged him back into the broiling desert.

Here I am, he thought, *expected to kill men with whom I have no quarrel. Without mercy. For the Führer, and for God. In that order.*

He'd gunned down soldiers in combat, he was absolutely sure of it, though most of the time he'd sensed that he and almost everyone else involved in this idiotic battle for control of nothing was firing at mirages and shadows. But this was a world away from any of that.

A young man, maybe not so different from himself, lay an arm's length away from him, scorched and mangled and torn beyond all recognition. Whatever future he might once have hoped for had been incinerated, and all of his loves and hates and indifferences had been replaced by nothing but unimaginable pain and anguish.

The almost inaudible bubbling of the man's shallow breathing was suddenly overpowered by a tiny metallic click.

Bernhardt looked down at his shaking hand, its weirdly ice-cold fingers slick with sweat against the pistol's grip. When he looked up, deep blue eyes had somehow opened. Terrified, ashamed, he tried to look away from the man's tears, but he simply couldn't. This poor, poor creature, he knew, had already stopped seeing this world, and had instead begun looking desperately toward the next one.

Two conflicting thoughts battled for possession of Bernhardt's deeply confused soul as he cocked the Luger, held it to a spot just above the man's empty eyes, and curled his finger around its trigger.

Thou shalt not kill.

Blessed are the merciful, for they shall receive mercy.

Almost six and half hours later, under a vast and brightly starred but moonless desert sky, Bernhardt had managed to navigate his way between sporadic piles of unidentifiable debris and past the rust-brown hulks of knocked out tanks and shattered armored vehicles, and had threaded himself back through the wire.

He was enormously grateful to have achieved that miraculous feat without encountering another live human being.

Calculating his position to be somewhere between two hundred and five hundred metres out, he flashed the signal and waited.

Nothing.

Wrong place, he thought. *Or they're all dead. Or I'm dead.*

Rocks digging hard into his elbows and knees, he crawled forward for what he estimated to be another twenty-five meters, then flashed again.

Nothing.

He closed his eyes, cursed to himself for about the thousandth time, and wished like hell to be somewhere else. But when he looked again, nothing had changed. He was still lying on his belly in a lifeless black desert.

Still dead, he thought.

Thirty grinding meters further on, the rocky ground dropped out from beneath him and he slid face first into a shallow trench. Almost immediately, a volley of shots rang out, and he shouted into the choking dirt at the top of his lungs.

"Hold your fire, you fucking idiots! Didn't you see the fucking signal?"

Seconds later, no more than ten meters away, a torch clicked on, its dim beam hugging the ground before briefly rising up to blind him, then immediately clicking off. From somewhere behind its after-image, a disembodied voice whispered hoarsely.

"Who are you? Where the fuck did you come from?!"

Bernhardt could barely force the words past his moisture-less, grime-caked lips.

"Outside the wire. Reconnaissance patrol."

Another soft click produced another dim flashlight glow, closer this time. Bernhard watched it hover and weave crazily over the bottom of the trench as it made its herky-jerky way toward him, accompanied by the muffled jangle of ammunition belts and a canteen and assorted paraphernalia and the unmistakeable sound of boots shuffling over sand and desert rocks.

"Are you fucking crazy?"

With three fingers partially covering it, the dusty, cracked torch lens came up into Bernhardt's face for another brief moment, its glare leaving fresh ghosts in his retinas.

"Fuck, Lang!" said a familiar, hoarsely whispered voice. "Is that really you? We figured you were dead!"

"You mean I'm not?" Bernhardt croaked, as Major Himmelman's hand clapped him hard on the shoulder.

"Well, shit!" said Himmelman as a few more men scrambled up. "Twenty-four hours in the Devil's fucking Gardens. And still alive?! You're not Leutnant Lang anymore," he said. "You're Leutnant Gartner. You're the fucking gardener!"

57

The only black and white in the early morning gray, its headlights glaring off the rain-slicked road, John noticed the cruiser behind them about thirty seconds after they'd left the motel parking lot.

"Don't worry," he said, head low. "Let's just pull into that filling station and let him pass by."

Slowly, casually, Helen steered the truck up beside the pumps and shut off the ignition, halting the sweep of its wipers mid-windshield. For a few seconds, they sat like statues and watched as the black and white continued steadily down the road.

"Did that guy look over here?" said Helen.

"Hard to say," said John, "but I don't think so. But if he did, what could he see? Rain's coming down pretty hard, and it's barely light."

While the gas jockey topped them up, John hunkered down, his damaged face mostly under the blanket. A soaking wet Zeus watched warily from the back of the pickup. Helen asked the kid to check the oil, just to burn a little more time, and a minute or so after she'd paid him and he'd shuffled back inside, she turned the key and rolled the truck about twenty feet forward, toward the road. She paused there.

"That police car," she said, "made me jumpy. How about you hop out with Zeus, and I'll drive down the road to the edge of town. If the one bored cop in Libby, Montana is looking for a dark blue pickup with two people and a dog in it, he won't see one."

"I don't know," said John. "I don't like that detective novel stuff."

"It'll be okay," she said, confidence beginning to return. "Just wait here, and I'll come right back in a couple of minutes."

Mostly convinced, John stepped out of the truck and dropped the tailgate, then, his head still feeling as if were being squeezed by a giant hand, he helped the waterlogged furball down onto the oily concrete. From the darkest shadows they could find, tucked in beside the dull red Coke dispenser beneath the dripping southwest corner of the gas station awning, the two of them watched in silence as Helen drove away, one of them unable to shake the hollow feeling in his stomach. When the familiar headlights reappeared a few minutes later, both of them breathed sighs of relief. One of them wagged his tail in excitement.

"Okay," said Helen. "I didn't see anything or anyone. Seems to me not a soul's up and at 'em around here yet, so I'm guessing nobody saw me. Let's get out of here."

She drove through town at a crawl.

When they reached a sign marked Route 37, she pulled over, and together they made the snap decision. Northwest instead of north.

"Let's go see my second favorite grandma," Helen joked. About three minutes outside of town, a set of distant headlights suddenly appeared in the truck's mirrors.

Helen's eyes narrowed. "Is it him?"

John strained to turn his head.

"Hard to tell," said John. "He's way back there. But even if it is, he's probably just waiting for you to break the speed limit so he can squeeze some coffee money out of us. Look, if he pulls us over and asks hard questions, I'm going to tell him. I'll tell him I made you help me."

"No!" said Helen. "No way."

Not thirty seconds later, the flashing red from the cop car's cherry lit up the inside of the truck's cab. Helen's suddenly wide eyes jumped back and forth from the rearview mirror to the winding black road stretching out ahead. John only watched her for a second before he understood that a decision had been made. Helen looked over at him, jaw clenched. He'd seen that look before.

"I'm never giving you up," she said. "Ever."

The truck surged forward, its sudden acceleration sending Zeus slip-slamming into the tailgate. The vehicle picked up speed as the road narrowed to two lanes, nothing but solid black forest on their left and periodic glimpses of a ribbon of gunmetal water through the dense pines on their right.

"Let's give up, Helen," said John, right hand braced on the dash, struggling to swivel his gaze from the shiny road ahead to the almost black road behind them. "I won't let anything happen to you."

Seemingly alone for a moment, the pursuing lights temporarily out of sight, the truck surged again. At a sharp right bend in the road, Helen glanced in the rearview mirror, and that momentary distraction was all it took for the pickup's right front tire to veer onto the gently sloping gravel shoulder. Panicked, her reactions obviously supercharged by fear and adrenaline, she jerked the steering wheel a little too hard to try to get them back onto the blacktop and the tire dug in deep, spinning the truck around crazily until luck and the pressure of her foot stomping on the brake pedal finally skidded it to a stop.

Breathing hard but suddenly oblivious to any pain, John craned his head around to try to get himself oriented. A seemingly frozen Helen looked over at him open-mouthed, both hands gripping the steering wheel. Tongue hanging out, an obviously agitated and heavy-breathing face appeared at the back window. The engine still rumbled and the wipers still flapped furiously back and forth, almost able to keep the windshield rain-free.

"We're okay! We're okay!" John shouted, mind racing to formulate some kind of a plan. Any plan.

They were straddling the road, almost perpendicular to it. In the glare of their headlights he saw it, just off to the left, a narrow footpath leading into the trees, toward the river.

"There!" he yelled. "Kill the lights! Go!"

Reanimated, Helen simultaneously punched the headlight switch and stomped on the gas, crashing and scraping the vehicle through the gloom of the clawing, squealing brush for at least ten claustrophobic seconds until the narrow footpath widened to a gravel patch and the canopy of trees gave way to open air. At John's shout, she skidded them to a stop. Adrenaline masking his pain, he swiveled again.

"No cop," he said, "and we still have a dog. Let's go!"

Grabbing Helen's hand, he dragged her out through the passenger door into the dull gray light and the hammering downpour.

"Come on, boy," he called to Zeus. "You're okay!"

The big dog jumped over the side as if he'd always had only three good legs, and John reached into the back of the truck to snatch up the duffel. Then he grabbed Helen's shaking hand and pulled her to face him. Blinking away the raindrops, he looked hard into her eyes, and she looked back.

"I don't know if he saw us," he said, "but if he did, I don't think he can drive as far through the trees as we did, so we've probably got a few seconds."

He led her away from the truck, away from the road and the cop, toward another small path that seemed to lead in the direction of a low roaring sound.

"You hear it?" he said. "We're near the river. Rapids or falls. I saw a sign in town. I think maybe there's a footbridge here somewhere, so we get across and, I don't know, shake this guy, or cut the ropes."

"Now you're talking detective novel stuff!" said Helen.

"The best we've got right now," he said. "Can you run?"

"Better than you, mister."

When they were about forty yards into the seventy-five yard path that led toward the sound of fast-flowing water, lights swept across the trees and bushes around them. Filtered through the combined roar of the river and the falling rain and the air whooshing in his lungs and the blood pulsing through his body, John only thought he heard a faint shout. He heard the pistol shot that rang out loud and clear.

Helen stumbled and fell, and Zeus nipped at her playfully as John yanked her back to her feet and back into motion.

"Is that guy shooting at us?!" she shouted, the fear in her voice palpable. "Is he crazy?"

Another twenty yards on, Helen stumbled again, but this time, instead of pulling her to her feet, John dropped to a knee in the mud. He let go of the duffel bag and wiped the raindrops from her face with his scarred hand. And he spoke quietly, firmly.

"Don't be afraid," he said. "It's over. It's me they want."

Tears mingling with the rain, Helen's intense, pleading eyes bored into his.

"No!" she said. "I won't let them take you from me!" She glanced toward the roaring sound as she stood. "There's a bridge right there. We can make it!"

Now she dragged him forward. Again he couldn't be sure, but through the powerful roar of rushing water, he thought he heard a second shot ring out. Helen let go of his hand and gripped the bridge's wet rope. As she stepped onto its first wooden slat she turned to him, offering him a terrified but beautiful, brave, and hopeful smile in the middle of a brutally cold reality. He put his hand on her cheek, pulled her to him, and kissed her hard.

"It's okay!" he yelled. "You go! I'm right behind you! Promise!"

John's heart skipped a beat as Helen stepped forward and the narrow spiderweb structure wavered under her weight. He looked away for a moment, to search the silhouetted trees for their pursuer, to sling the duffel bag strap over his shoulder, and to bend to pick up Zeus. Then he stepped onto the slick wooden boards. He'd made it about a third of the way across the span—and Helen had almost reached its far side—when the sharp crack of a third shot echoed off the rocks. In terrifying slow motion, John saw Helen stumble and drop to one knee, then rise slightly and turn toward him, her hand at her throat.

Eyes wide, he saw her lips move as she tried to call out, but her silence was deafening, and when she reached for him, her fingers were dark and wet and trembling.

Before she'd tumbled through the ropes and vanished into the roiling torrent of white water some twenty feet below, she was already gone.

Horror and shock and anguish tearing at him like no pain he'd ever felt, John's knees buckled. He opened his mouth to scream, but heard nothing. He ran, frantic, his boots sliding on the boards. Gripping the rope railing, he raised his right foot to start the climb. Eyes not really seeing, ears not really hearing, his only thought was to find her, but the rain-diluted ribbons of blood beneath his left foot and the thunderous white rapids below the bridge told him in no uncertain terms that he never would.

Chest heaving, heart pounding, he squeezed his eyes shut against the shattering event they'd just witnessed, and a thousand images of what had been and what might have been appeared and vanished in a fleeting moment. He roared again, and this time he heard himself.

Rage gripped him.

He was more than halfway back across the bridge when he saw the cop reach the muddy patch at the end of the footpath. Through blurred eyes, he thought he saw the man's mouth move, but no sound could pierce the roar of the river or the thunder inside his own head. In half a dozen strides, his boots touched wet earth, no more than ten feet from the cop, who was stumbling backward, waving his pistol around as if he had no idea where to point it. Another shot rang out, loud this time, and John was on the man in seconds. With his left hand forcing the gun up and away, he brought his right knee up into the cop's groin, folding him forward and collapsing him facedown. John stomped hard on the man's wrist, and as the gun fell away, he immediately twisted the cop onto his back and brought his full weight down, both knees on the man's biceps. With his left hand, John grabbed a fistful of short red hair and shoved the cop's face sideways into a puddle of liquid mud and grit and pine needles. Again, he squeezed his eyes shut, desperate to be anyplace else, to feel anything else. When he opened them, Paul's knife was in his right hand, its hide-wrapped handle firm and true in his grip, its honed tip poised to thrust upward through the small indentation just below the cop's ear. Over and over, the terrified, choking man's mouth gaped open and closed, as he tried, John knew, to find a way to live.

"Why?!" John screamed. He pressed the sharp point of the blade into the soft flesh. "Why?!"

Whimpered, desperate words reached John's ears from far away. He turned the cop's face to the graying sky, and in that brief moment, the downpour washed clean a pimply and freckled and pale face. The cop, John realized, wasn't a man, he was just a kid, his watery green eyes wide with terror, his tremulous voice barely audible.

"I'm sorry! I…didn't mean…! I just…I just wanted to stop you!"

"You fired at us?!" John screamed. "For what?! For what?!"

"They said you were dangerous. That…you tried to kill a man… You ran, so I…I just… I'm sorry…!"

Virtually every last shred of John's energy suddenly left him, and his pounding head slumped toward his crushed heart. Suddenly, he couldn't tell his own tears from the kid's tears, couldn't distinguish any of them from the torrent of frigid raindrops carrying the dirt and pine needles from the kid's face to the soggy ground. From somewhere deep inside, from a long-buried memory burned into him by a place with no rain, he recognized the empty look in the cop's eyes.

The terror had left them, replaced by something worse.

Pulse pounding in his ears, hands shaking almost uncontrollably, John pulled the knife away from the cop's neck.

"None of this had to happen!" he cried, his voice breaking under unbearable weight. "She did nothing but love me, and she died because of it! Now I have to live with that!"

Barely able to muster the strength, John willed himself to his feet and stumbled through the mud toward the roaring river.

When his boots touched the wooden slats, he turned, and he shivered as his tears fell and the cold deluge washed over him and the muddy ground and the dazed young cop and the swaying trees and the bridge to nowhere, each drop carrying mute memories of everything it had ever touched into the violent current.

"I have to live with it!" he screamed.

And then, quieter, "And so do you."

58

Lantern light fading, embers down to their last, he drew the blanket tighter, a pointless exercise, he knew too well, since the shivering never had anything to do with the cold.

He glanced down at the book in his lap, but the words on its yellowed pages swam crazily. Breathing deeply, he blinked hard and fast to try to clear his vision—another pointless exercise. Exhausted, defeated, he tossed the worn volume aside and reached for the bottle, but from years of bitter experience, he already knew that the few drops of solace it still contained would never be enough.

It was decided, once again.

Head laid back, the musty odor of the broken down old couch almost overwhelming even against the damp stink of the moldering log shack and the foulness of his own being, streaming eyes squeezed tightly shut, he tried to focus on the sound of the black rain falling on the mossy roof, listening with the last shreds of his strength until its relentless thrumming merged with his own pounding heartbeat and the rhythmic breathing of the old dog at his feet.

Then, suddenly, mercifully, he was simply not there.

He was miles and years away.

Her beautiful face radiant in the snow-bright sunshine, she turned to him and laughed as she puffed at a loose strand of hair. In agonizing slow motion, her lips moved, and he knew she was calling out to him, and though he tried to answer—tried desperately to move to her, to hold her just one more time—he was paralyzed, his voice trapped deep inside, blocked by something bitter and hard and metallic.

In the brutally scarred vee of his right hand, its familiar weight had been comforting. But a moment or a lifetime later, its unforgiving steel rattled menacingly against his chattering teeth as his index finger tightened on the trigger.

He wanted this.

He wanted it because his guilt and his longing and his anguish and his love had become so intertwined that he could no longer tell one from the other.

For a brief second, he saw her perfect lips move again, and this time, ever so softly, her gut wrenching words reached him.

"Love me. Live for me."

So despite the unbearable pain, or perhaps even because of it, he opened his streaming eyes.

And once again, as he knew he always would, he did as she asked.

59

On a blazing hot afternoon in August, 1957, a tall, muscular man walked out of the dense forest just southeast of Cranbrook, British Columbia. Following a crumbling strip of road, he found his way to a deeply rutted dirt track that led westward into the towering trees. There, as his traveling companion waited patiently, he paused to check the name on the carved wooden sign against a wrinkled piece of paper pulled from his pocket. Squinting at the sun through the trunks and branches, he elected to inhale one more cigarette before heading toward a tumble-down cluster of buildings hidden in the shadows of the forest a few hundred yards in.

The faint sound of a transistor radio grew progressively louder as the man approached the open doors of a corrugated tin shed. From a tiny speaker somewhere deep inside the workshop of South Kootenay Logging, he heard a singer with a beautiful voice revealing to all the world that he was, in fact, a great pretender, adrift in a world of his own.

In the shade of a stand of massive hemlocks, the man dropped his duffel bag and bent to one knee to ruffle the gray-tinged fur on his ancient dog's head.

"Wait here, Zeus," he said. "I'll be right back."

Seconds later, the man stepped through the big doors, and two overall-clad figures standing at a workbench cluttered with tools and machine parts and nuts and bolts turned to him.

He moved forward and extended a heavily scarred right hand to the nearest of them.

"My name's Frank Gardner," he said. "I need a job."

60

He'd surfaced, sweaty, shivering, eyes wide. As always.

Instinctively, he searched the wall to the right of his bed and tried to focus on the space between the curtains and the windowsill—a technique developed over time to try to keep the past from following him into the present.

Mouth pasty and metallic, throat desert dry, he reached for a tepid, half full glass of water, then, knowing better than to try to fight another unwinnable fight, he struggled to his feet and shuffled to his bathroom sink to try to splash himself back to reality. After wrestling himself into some clothes, as he'd done a hundred, maybe a thousand times before, he stepped out onto his porch for a little air.

He was lighting up his second cigarette before the sound actually registered. Distant sirens, growing in numbers.

Something going on down in town.

Two minutes later, he was in his truck, mindlessly navigating the familiar short drive, and eventually guided by the increasing intensity of flashing lights bouncing off houses and trees.

When he got to where he hadn't known he was going, Frank knew exactly where he was.

In a pelting downpour one Saturday afternoon or another, he'd delivered Joseph Holliman here, insistent against the kid's protests, intent on saving him from a drenching walk home from the usual school drop-off spot.

The red fire engine lights flashing off the snow and the trees and the house and the barn and the helmeted men and every other thing they touched combined with the cloud-filtered moonlight to create a surreal, almost eerie scene of semi-coordinated chaos. Frank rolled past and parked near the end of the block, then surprised himself by half jogging back to a shadowed spot in the house's front yard.

He spotted a couple of firemen hauling a hose.

"Hey!" he shouted. "What's going on?! Everyone out?!"

Fully engaged in the task at hand, neither man turned his way. Another fireman hustled past without looking in his direction. Frank yelled after him. "Is everyone out?! Can you tell me if everyone's out?!"

Hearing no reply, anxiety rising, he looked toward the road to scan the small crowd of red-lit onlookers, but found no kids among the faces.

No Joseph.

The decision immediately made itself, and seconds later, he burst through Principal Lionel Holliman's front door.

Assuming the bedrooms were on the second floor, he took the darkened stairs two at a time. At the top, he turned to his left. Stepping through a partially open door that led him into a spartan room, he called out Joseph's name. Empty bed. Empty closet. Adrenaline temporarily providing him with a young man's physical capabilities, he dropped to his knees and peered under the bed. Finding nothing, he practically jumped up and hustled to the wide open door at the opposite end of the upstairs hallway. That room was disheveled, bedding on the wet floor, furniture tipped over as if a panic had gripped its occupant.

The upper floor was devoid of life.

He almost ran back down the stairs.

At the bottom he followed his instincts, looking every which way as he moved through the small living room and into the frigid kitchen at the back of the house. Exiting the already-open kitchen door, he found himself in the yard between the house and the barn.

To his left, a fireman exited the barn, shouting incomprehensible commands as he followed two others hauling a hose down its far side.

Frank ran across the yard. Just as he reached the edge of the glow from the hooded lightbulb over the partially open big doors, a sudden movement to the right caught his eye, maybe forty or fifty feet away, in the shadows at the back end of the outbuilding. Breath coming hard, he turned quickly, just in time to see a figure softly illuminated by flickering yellow-orange light.

"Hey!" Frank called out.

A tall, thin man with a coal black beard and stringy hair glanced in his direction, and for a moment, their eyes met. The man nodded almost imperceptibly, and Frank sensed a glimmer of recognition, but before he could make a mental connection or call out again, the man vanished into the stand of pine trees bordering the Holliman property. Unable to make sense of what he'd seen, Frank covered the remaining distance to the big barn doors in seconds.

He stepped inside.

"Joseph?! You in here?!"

Eyes wide in the gloom, he picked his way through the space, pupils struggling to adjust as weak rays from the rotating fire engine lights out on the road periodically swept over the rusted Chevy coupe and the handful of old farm implements crowding the barn's confines. On the back wall, he saw a workbench and vise and a few hand tools hanging from hooks on perforated panels.

He almost didn't see the black metal ladder.

Seconds later, he dragged himself through a rectangular opening onto the plywood floor of the almost pitch-black hayloft. Hands on his knees, gasping for breath, he sucked in the unmistakable, acrid smell of woodsmoke. Convinced he'd seen all there was to see, he made the decision to get the hell out of there.

And then he spotted it.

In the back wall at the far end of the loft there was a small door, no more, Frank guessed, than four feet high. Finding its black iron handle cool to the touch, he pulled it open. A soft ray of yellow-white electric light spilled across the hayloft floor.

Pulse quickening, Frank sucked in a deep, smoke-tinged breath and crouched to squeeze his bulk through the tiny opening.

A staircase so narrow he could barely negotiate it led up toward a hazy, exposed light bulb. At the top of the claustrophobic passage, he found himself in front of another small closed door. When he leaned close to put a hand against it, he heard the faint but unmistakable sound of muffled pleas. Panicked, he twisted the handle hard and shoved the door inward with his boot, immediately amplifying the whimpers and cries.

Fears racing, he bent low and struggled through the opening.

Directly in front of him, in the harsh glare of a naked lightbulb, someone was lying facedown across a small wooden table, head facing the far corner near the slope-ceilinged room's burlap-padded wall.

It only took a split second for Frank to realize it was a grown man, his pale, shirtless back pockmarked with a constellation of small, circular scars, long healed. The man's trembling left hand was manacled to a short chain bolted into the grimy wooden floor, his barefoot right leg restrained the same way. From an iron hook on one wall hung a heavy leather strap and two coiled, rubber-encased metal cables, one of which led to the corroded terminal of a black car battery that sat in a puddle of liquid and cigarette butts beneath the man's wet pajama trousers.

"Who's there?! Is someone there?!"

Even absent its usual condescending tone, Frank recognized the voice instantly. He stepped forward, into the narrow space between the table and the wall, and into Lionel Holliman's field of view.

The principal's sweat- and tear-streaked face was completely devoid of color, his wild, terrified eyes puffy and red-rimmed. "Mr. Gardner! Frank!" he cried. "Thank God you've come! Please, you've got to get me out of here! That horrible man…forced me here! He had a gun! He—"

Suddenly calm, almost relieved, Frank cut Holliman off.

"I don't have to do anything."

Holliman jerked wildly against his restraints, his untethered right hand clawing at the locked manacle biting into the raw red skin of his left wrist, the muscles in his back twitching as he tried to raise his scarred torso from the equally scarred and stained wooden tabletop.

"Please!" he shouted. "Please, Mr. Gardner! That boy's father, he thinks I had something to do with his…! You've just got to help me! Please…"

Frank stepped back, jaw clenched, breath coming in short bursts, his heart threatening to burst from his chest as the face of the bearded man with the stringy hair suddenly crystallized in his racing mind.

"Help you?" he said. "I saw the red rings on little Robbie Marsh's wrist. I saw them on your own goddamn son."

"I… Mr. Gardner! I…I'm a teacher! I teach them! As I was taught!"

When Frank breathed in hard, the heat and the fumes and the intensely dull, muffled roar came rushing back to engulf him. Suddenly, he reached down, grasped Holliman's untethered and flailing right arm at the wrist and twisted it hard, forcing the clammy hand against the sweat-glistening skin of his scarred back. Then, as if in a trance, Frank slid the knife from the leather sheath on his belt, placed its hide-wrapped handle in Holliman's upturned palm, and folded the principal's trembling fingers tight around it.

Instantly, inexplicably, Holliman's body went almost completely slack, leaving his voiceless mouth—gaping as if it belonged to a fish out of water—to provide the only movement in the tiny room.

Frank leaned down toward Holliman's upturned ear. When he finally spoke, his voice was low and measured and steady.

"Someone who thought my truth was worth saving gave me this. Now I'm giving it to you. If you think your pathetic truth's worth saving, you can use it. Or you can burn."

Frank released Holliman's wrist.

The confused principal immediately brought the knife into his field of view, eyes wide with terror, and for the briefest of moments, Frank watched him hold the trembling blade above his manacled left wrist. Then, abruptly, he turned and ducked through the low opening into the choking fumes and almost unbearable heat at the top of the narrow staircase and pulled the small door shut tightly behind him.

No more than sixty seconds later, Frank Gardner found himself out on the road, watching from the deep shadows behind the crowd of onlookers as the firemen did everything they could to try to prevent the roaring flames on the back side of the Holliman barn from taking it all the way to hell.

61

On the short drive home, the truck's hopelessly dim headlights had seemed almost unnecessary in the rising dawn, but in the sweep of the twin beams that illuminated the patchy snow at the end of his driveway and pierced the gloom of his front porch, there he was.

Knees up, head down on his crossed arms, a jacket around his hunched shoulders, he was sitting with his back against the wall. Frank closed the distance between his still-running truck and his porch as if he was eighteen again.

"Oh, Jesus H. Christ, kid!"

When their eyes met, Frank's bursting heart practically leaped into his mouth.

He didn't expect answers, but as he bent down and snatched up the shivering boy, he asked a relentless barrage of questions all the same. Then, no longer able to hold back the flood of relief streaming down his cheeks, he kicked opened his front door and carried Joseph Holliman safely inside.

62

As he'd figured they would sooner, rather than later, the cops finally made an appearance shortly after eight. After finding Joseph Holliman sound asleep under a blanket on Frank's old couch, Whitmore had come back out to the porch and immediately opened his notepad.

"Frank, did you have permission to bring that kid here?"

Frank puffed out a long white cloud. "Need to write that question down so you could remember it?"

"Come on, Frank," said Whitmore. "Just doing my goddamn job."

"I didn't bring him here," said Frank, sipping coffee. "He must have brought himself. So I don't know, what do you think?"

"I think you might have a problem."

"That right?"

"Yeah," said Whitmore. "You were seen, Frank. Couple of firemen mentioned you poking around. So I gotta ask. What were you doing at the Holliman house?"

"I dunno," said Frank, flicking a burnt match onto the slushy, wet gravel. "I guess maybe I'm the kind of guy who wants to find out what's going on when he smells trouble from his porch at four thirty in the goddamn morning."

Kusyk spoke up. "Listen, Frank," he said, "you see how this looks, right? I think we can understand you were just helping out by bringing the kid here, but—"

"Jesus Christ," said Frank. "I just told you. I didn't bring him here. But so what if I did, I'd be what? A criminal? Seems to me you guys are so busy looking for crime you can't see it when it's right under your goddamn noses. Or maybe you can, but you look the other way because you just don't give a shit."

Frank saw Whitmore glance over at Kusyk, thought he saw some unspoken message pass between them. Abruptly, Whitmore snapped his notebook shut and stuffed it into his breast pocket.

"Look, Frank," he said, "the kid's gotta come with us."

Frank said nothing. He just set his coffee mug on the porch railing and took another deep drag on his cigarette. Whitmore took a half step closer to Frank. Kusyk hung back.

"Listen," said Whitmore, voice low. "There's gonna have to be a formal inquiry into the fire. It's serious, Frank." He nodded toward Frank's front door. "And we all know someone who likes to play with matches, right?"

Frank glared at the cop. "Don't even start with that crap."

Whitmore turned before he got to Frank's front door. "Here's the deal, Frank. The firemen found a body when they were checking over what's left of the Holliman barn this morning."

"Well, that's too bad," said Frank, huffing smoke, gut suddenly ice cold.

"It was Lionel Holliman, Frank. We know the kid's been working here with you. And we know you and his father didn't see eye to eye. Seems everyone who was at the school last week knows it, too. Holliman called in that afternoon. Gave us the names of a few people he said witnessed you threatening him, people who'd corroborate his story.

I didn't put too much thought into it then, but some hard questions are gonna have to be answered now."

Again, Frank said nothing. He just stared at the back of Whitmore's head as the cop spun on his heel and let himself back into the house.

Kusyk spoke up.

"Look, Frank," he said, "the kid's, well, he's got no father now, and we've got no idea where the mother took off to. He can't stay at that house by himself, and we sure as hell can't leave him here. There's a place on the south side of town, where they take… It's called the Perryman Home. He's gonna have to go there until we can locate any relatives and see if they'll take him. If that doesn't turn out, well, he'll be in the hands of the provincial authorities. Sorry, but that's just the way it's gotta be."

"That's a shit sandwich," said Frank, "and you know it."

"Procedure, Frank," said Kusyk. "You know we've got to follow procedure."

"Yeah," said Frank, "you guys just love that bullshit."

Kusyk kicked a line of crusted snow on the shadowed porch step.

"Listen," he said, eyes on Frank's front door, "I…I shouldn't be telling you this, but let's just say I don't think anyone's going to want to get too deep here."

He stepped closer to Frank and dropped his voice even lower.

"Look Frank," he said, "Bob and I both saw Holliman's body. Where it was found. All I can say is…well, it seems to me that barn's gotta hold a whole lot of secrets. And my guess is a lot of people are gonna think it's best if they stay in there."

63

When the letter had arrived, Frank had been unsure, and of course Bill Haversham had done what lawyers got paid to do and cautioned him against it. But Frank hadn't been able to say no.

At exactly 8:30 a.m. sharp, she walked in and made an immediate beeline for his table, the only occupied spot in the place this early on a freezing cold Saturday morning. Frank simultaneously stubbed out his cigarette and levered himself to his feet as she smiled and extended a hand.

"Mr. Gardner?" she said. "I'm Janice Hamer."

Young and earnest and dressed more like a college student than he'd imagined a seventh grade teacher might be, on first impression she was the polar opposite of what Frank had assumed, and a stark contrast to anyone and everything he'd experienced relative to Joseph's school.

They sat for a minute and made the smallest of small talk, about the weather, and about the strangeness of the brand new year, and she ordered coffee, black. When the waitress brought her cup to the table, she complimented the young woman on the song she'd just selected on the diner's jukebox, somebody singing an upbeat song about never needing anybody else, in any way. And then she got serious.

"Thank you for agreeing to meet with me, Mr. Gardner," she said. "With the, ah…well, with the inquiry and all, I wasn't sure I should even ask."

"Please," said Frank. "It's Frank."

She smiled and nodded.

"Frank it is," she said. "And I'm Janice. I'm Joseph's teacher."

"Oh, don't worry," said Frank. "He's mentioned you more than once." He smiled at her wide-eyed, quizzical expression. "All good."

"Well, that's nice to hear, Mr. Gardner… Frank. Look, I'll…I'll get right to it. I don't think Joseph has ever been a particularly happy boy," she said. "I mean, I've only had him as a student since September. But with everything that's…with everything that's happened, and now him having to live at that Perryman Home and all, well, I'm worried."

The waitress swung by to top up their cups, and Janice Hamer proceeded to focus on meticulously soaking up each and every stray drop of coffee with a white paper napkin before she continued.

"It can't have been easy for him," she said, "being the principal's kid. I mean, if it hadn't been for his one good friend, I don't think he would have even shown up at school. I don't know if you're aware, but that family has just moved away, so now even that motivation is gone. I know Joseph is bright, deep down, but he's never really tried hard. When he's not turning in his homework assignments late, he's doing the bare minimum. I've tried to talk to him, but he just… Look, he's mentioned you, too. More than once."

"Oh, yeah?" said Frank.

"Don't worry," she said, smiling. "All good."

Frank smiled back.

"When I told him I was coming here today, to meet with you… he…well, let's just say he, uh, brightened a little."

"Oh, he did, did he?"

"Yes," she said. "And look, he knows you're not allowed to visit him while the investigation is ongoing. So he said to give you this."

Frank recognized the small, rubber band-wrapped notebook immediately.

"I don't know what's in it," she said. "I solemnly promised him I wouldn't look, and I always keep my promises. But he wants you to have it."

After she'd said her goodbyes, Frank had stayed put.

He'd flagged down the waitress for one more reheat, and sparked up one more cigarette while he'd contemplated the potential contents of the notebook on the table in front of him. When he'd reached for it, he'd found himself not nervous, exactly, but more... Well, he'd just not been able to put his calloused finger on it.

By the time he'd climbed into his truck almost three quarters of an hour later, he'd learned a few more things about Joseph Holliman. He'd also learned a few more things about himself, and—much to his surprise and relief—most all of them had been good.

Between a few of the notebook's cursive- and doodle-jammed pages, the kid had stuffed all sorts of what Frank could only guess might be things that had grabbed his attention: newspaper clippings about airplane crashes and archeology, slivers of magazine pages with pictures of exotic places and submarines and old people with deeply lined faces, and scraps of paper with what were clearly his own random, scribbled thoughts.

But two items in particular weighed on Frank as he maneuvered his pickup along the road that ran beside the river. Near the back of the book, between a couple of pages that had been left conspicuously blank, a bright yellow candy bar wrapper had been folded like a blanket around a small, black and white photograph.

The wrapper had immediately made Frank smile, but something about that image—two clearly happy young women captured, however momentarily, loving life—had shaken him.

It had reminded him of things he'd only briefly known, and he'd stared at it, lost for a time in a place so joyful it was almost unbearably sad, until the jarring sound of the waitress dropping his change onto the Formica called him home.

64

Down at Granger's, he'd grabbed some supplies—a steak, a carton of smokes, a case of beer. A few people had nodded. A cheerful "Thanks for shopping at Granger's today!" were the only actual words that had been directed his way.

He'd spotted it in the rack by the door on his way out, and had immediately spun around and deposited a quarter on the counter. And then he'd sat himself in his truck and read every single word of it.

Twice.

On the short drive from the store to his place, Frank had shed about a thousand pounds.

He set the grocery bag on the counter, and a minute or two later, provisions stowed, beer in hand, he flopped his bulk down in his chair, a sudden fatigue beginning to overtake him.

He lit a smoke and picked up the newspaper. For a few seconds, he stared at the familiar top half of the face visible above the fold. The dark slick of Brylcreemed hair. The horn rims. The ice cold eyes. Then he flipped the paper over to reveal the rest of the image: the thin-lipped smile, the tie like a razor sharp black dagger against a crisp white shirt, framed by a perfect black suit jacket.

With what felt like a herculean effort, he got himself to the edge of his seat and dragged the black metal fire screen aside. He grabbed the newspaper and pulled the front and back page signature away from the others, then crumpled the broadsheet and stuffed it down between two bars of the grimy, ash-covered grate. He spent a minute or two carefully building a little pyramid of kindling around the balled up paper, then took a match from the box in his shirt pocket and ran it sharply across the rough strike patch. Holding the flaring stick between his thumb and forefinger for a few seconds, he watched as it came to brilliant, energetic life before settling into its inexorable death burn.

Jesus, he thought. *Don't we all?*

When he touched the elongating flame to the folded edge of the newsprint, it caught almost instantly, flickering orange immediately beginning to transform the paper—and all of the lies printed on it—into ashes.

The official inquiry had lasted more than eleven weeks.

The endless hours that he and Haversham had spent in Whitmore's cramped, pea-green interview room had cost him a few bucks in legal fees, and more than a few sleepless nights. And now, it seemed, the countless official meetings, not only with him, but with firemen, and the coroner, and Joseph Holliman, and with many others who had and had not been present on the night in question—but whose opinions had most definitely mattered—had determined what the investigators had declared were "the facts of the case."

Today, the official story had been made public.

Electrical Failure Cause of Fatal Fire

The investigation into events surrounding the tragic December 19 death of respected educator, administrator, and community leader Lionel J. Holliman has been concluded. Sadly, Mr.

Holliman was overcome by fumes while attempting to battle the fire that consumed the historic barn at 92 Swanson Road. The cause of the unfortunate incident was determined to be an electrical malfunction.

Flopping into the threadbare comfort of his chair, Frank lit up another smoke and sipped his beer as the flames began to devour the bone-dry kindling with a vengeance. With an involuntary groan, he leaned forward and laid a couple of larger pieces of wood on top of the shrinking pyramid.

Instantly, the weight of the new fuel disintegrated the last of the blackened newsprint's ghostly remains, combining them with the ashes and chunks of charcoal already lining the bottom of the fireplace.

Then Frank laid his head back, closed his eyes, and quietly huffed out another lungful of smoke.

History, he thought, *is where facts go to become fiction.*

65

Sixty-three miles.

Might as well, Frank thought, *have been ten thousand.*

On the agreed-upon Thursday morning, he'd made the drive, the last five miles or so of the trip taking almost as long as the first fifty. Finally admitting to himself that he was lost, he'd stopped in at a gas station for directions, and the less than confidence-inspiring pump jockey had eventually pointed him south about two miles, toward a gravel road that he'd said would run toward the river. To Frank's surprise, the caved-in old barn had loomed from the trees right where the kid had said it would, and he'd made the turn and crunched to a stop on a gravel patch in front of a tarpaper-clad bungalow a few hundred yards or so after that.

Suddenly self-conscious, maybe even nervous, for a few seconds he debated leaving the bouquet of flowers right where it lay on his truck seat, but hell, he figured, he'd already spent the ninety-five cents.

The news hadn't been all good.

Haversham had spelled it out. He'd pursued the issue as far as he'd been able, but when all was said and done, Lionel Holliman's will had prevailed. The house and all of its contents had gone to the Anglican

Church of Canada. Only a paltry sum of cash had been left in trust for his one and only son.

But Frank's frustration had been soothed by Haversham's second announcement: that in just a couple of months, he'd managed to do what he'd warned Frank he might never be able to do.

"It's not Graffton," the lawyer had said as he'd handed Frank the small photograph. "It's Grasston. Basically due south of here, almost on the border. Kootenay River runs right down that way."

The door swung open almost before he'd finished knocking.

"Mr. Gardner?" she said. "I'm Marian Luke."

With a gracious smile framed by short gray-black hair, she took the flowers and laid them across her lap. As instructed, Frank shut the door and followed her as she rolled into her kitchen and immediately began to rummage in a low cupboard.

"Can I, uh, help you with something?"

She laughed. "Mister Gardner," she said, "I've been living life sitting down for more than seven years now, three of those all by myself. So yes, you can help. I assume you know how to make tea?"

At the tiny kitchen table, she held the black and white photograph in shaking hands, turning it over and over. When she finally looked up, cheeks glistening, Frank knew her eyes weren't seeing him.

"God, we were just kids, really. Not a care in the whole world. How quickly it all changed for Angela." She gripped the armrest of her wheelchair. "And I guess for me."

He'd only meant to stay for a few minutes, just enough time to help her put a face to the name she'd first learned of in the letter Haversham had sent. But the conversation had just flowed, and Frank had found himself immersed in the streams of words and laughter and tears that had poured out of her as if she'd kept them bottled up, just for him, and for far too long.

By the time Frank stooped to hug her goodbye—and had been thanked for about the hundredth time for everything he'd done for Joseph—promises had been made, and something Frank had known instinctively for virtually his entire life had once again been made abundantly clear.

Not all prisoners are locked up.

66

Haversham's Buick was already out front, and Frank rolled his truck up right behind it. Three minutes later, informed that Mrs. Molyneux was just finishing up a phone call and wouldn't be much longer, the two men sat in silence outside her office, Frank wondering why the hell a family of butterflies had decided to make its home in his stomach today, despite the fact that he'd been visiting this place at least three times a week for more than seven months.

When the door finally opened, a smiling, middle-aged woman invited them in.

"Hello again Mr. Gardner," she said with a nod. "And you must be Mr. Haversham? I'm Edna Molyneux. It's so nice to finally meet you in person. Won't you have a seat?"

They all settled in.

Edna Molyneux hoisted a pair of glasses to the bridge of her nose, freeing their tiny silver chains to swing gently back and forth as she peered over the top of half-moon lenses at one man, then the other.

"So," she said. "Mr. Haversham. I understand that you, ah, have some paperwork for me?"

Haversham nodded and smiled and unlatched the briefcase resting on his knees. He took out a manila folder, and from that, he withdrew two identical sets of documents, each with a tiny triangle of thin blue cardboard stapled at the top left corner of the crisp white papers to make them seem, Frank thought, extra official.

Haversham held on to one set, and slid the other across the desk. "I believe you'll find," he said, flipping to the second page, "everything's in order. Notarized permissions and various supporting documents from the boy's aunt and only surviving blood relative, Mrs. Marian R. Luke of Grasston, British Columbia, granting Mr. Frank Gardner here co-legal guardianship."

Mrs. Molyneux scanned the papers, then pushed a button on her black telephone, triggering a distant, muffled buzz. She spoke softly, but officially. Returning the handset to its cradle, she smiled. "Shouldn't be more than a minute or two," she said. "Apparently he's been dressed since about five o'clock this morning."

In spite of his best efforts, Frank just couldn't calm the creatures circling slowly in his stomach. Seconds later, a soft knock on the door jolted them into an absolute frenzy.

"Come in, please."

A young woman entered the small office. She paused just inside the door, and called into the hallway behind her. "It's okay," she said. "Your visitors are here."

A moment or two later, Joseph Holliman's eyes locked on Frank's, and a massive smile lit up his face. Tentative, Joseph stood stock still in the open doorway, so Frank got to his feet. "Not just here for a visit today, kid," he said. "You wanna get out of here?"

Joseph's eyes flicked from Frank, to Bill Haversham, then to Mrs. Molyneux, and then back to Frank.

"I don't just mean for today," said Frank. He nodded toward the documents on Mrs. Molyneux's desk. "Those papers there say you can walk out of here forever, right now. But only if you want to."

Mouth seemingly unable to form a sound, Joseph took two quick steps forward and threw his arms around Frank, and Frank's big paws came around to envelop him like a blanket.

"What do you say, kid?" said Frank. "Time to start a new chapter? 'Cause we got some place you gotta be."

Joseph could barely get the words out past his grin.

"Pitter-patter," he whispered, "let's get at 'er."

The wax-paper-wrapped bacon and tomato sandwiches and luke-warm Thermos-flavored coffee had gone down better than anything Frank had ever tasted, and the sun and the clouds and the trees and the mountains and the blacktop carrying them south were more beautiful than almost anything he'd ever seen.

"Gonna be a while," said Frank, "if you wanna close 'em. I know you were up early."

"You kidding?" said Joseph. "I've got to see everything today."

Just under an hour later, Frank pulled to a stop near the caved-in barn at the end of the now familiar driveway, the tiny, tarpaper-clad house he'd come to know so well laying like a sleeping dog beneath the trees at its far end. The engine sputtered itself to stillness.

"Go on kid," he said. "This is your walk to make."

Between the soft clunk of the truck's passenger door closing and its creaky reopening more than an hour later, the skies had grayed, and Frank had burned almost half a pack. Joseph's eyes pointed at the floor as he climbed in.

"You okay, big guy?" said Frank.

"Yeah," said Joseph. He slammed the door. "No. She cried a lot. So did I."

Frank stared into the trees beyond the rain-dotted windshield as Joseph wiped a forearm across his eyes, then under his nose.

"She said she doesn't know why she trusts you," said Joseph, "but she said she does. What'd you say to her?"

Frank smiled and shrugged.

"I don't know," he said. "Lots of things. Gotten to know her a bit, I guess, and maybe she's gotten to know me a little. And I must have passed the test with her friends. Anyway, we talked it through, every which way we could think of, and Marian thinks this is what's best right now. I know one thing for sure. She's all torn up inside about what happened, about the way it all went, but there was nothing they could do. The police couldn't do anything."

"My mom was here... the whole time," said Joseph, his voice choking, his eyes flooding. "She could've come and got me..."

"Look, your father..."

"I know," said Joseph. "Marian told me."

For a long minute, Frank let quiet fill the space between them.

"I know it's hard," said Frank, "but your mom did what she did for you. Marian, too. They both knew if they ever came near you, ever tried to contact you, and your father found out, he'd take it out on you. Same way he kept your mom away from Marian after your uncle got killed in the car accident. You gotta know how tough that must have been for them."

Frank reached over and put a big hand on Joseph's shoulder.

"Marian says your mom talked about you every day. Every single day, Joseph. But in the end, well, maybe she loved you too much. Your mom tried. She really, really tried. But she just couldn't hang on, away from you like that. She just couldn't help herself... I'm guessing Marian told you. The things your mom turned to...to try to take the pain away... well, they took her away. I'm just so sorry, kid."

Joseph stared at the tiny droplets on the side window as Frank turned the engine over, put the truck into gear, and steered them out onto the road.

At the tiny white church, they climbed out, and at first, Frank led the way through the rows, between the old stones and faded wooden markers. When they got close to the spot, tucked away in a corner in the shelter of a canopy of gently swaying hemlocks, Frank held back as Joseph went on alone.

When Joseph slumped to his knees in the rain-wet grass, Frank looked away, and let his watery gaze fall on the muted softness of the gray mountains beyond the gently flowing river.

67

Two hefty and—to Joseph—boring looking books sat on the desk in the shed. Frank read from a note as he tapped the topmost volume with his index finger.

"First, Miss Hamer says junior high school is serious school, so it's time to get serious about math. She says you know the adding and subtracting and multiplying and dividing stuff just fine. She wants you to work on percentages, like, what percentage of this shed do you think you built? And what percentage do you think I built? And you gotta be able to back that up with numbers." He held up the copy of *Practical Mathematics 8*. "She says it's all in here. Chapter 6."

Joseph made an exaggerated sour face.

"And let's see," said Frank. "You've got a science assignment, too. A one page report on what you're made of. She means really made of, scientifically speaking. And you'd better be able to explain it to me, because honestly"—he paused and smiled—"well, I may have forgotten a few details myself. That's all she's got for now."

Joseph grinned and nodded. "Okay."

"Okay," said Frank. "Look, I gotta head into town for a while. You get hungry or whatever, you help yourself to anything you need. Just one rule, and I know you already know it. You use something, you clean it and put it back where it came from."

Frank turned to go, but paused at the door. "Oh, I almost forgot," he said, "I got an assignment for you, too. You gotta write me a story. One a week."

"Come on!" said Joseph. "I don't know how to write stories."

Frank yelled over his shoulder as he walked away. "The hell you don't," he said. "I read your notebook, kid!"

The following Sunday evening, Joseph read Frank his single page composition—about a boy who'd prevented a terrible car accident by turning himself into a raven.

And then, to Joseph's stunned surprise, Frank read his own effort out loud, a story about a man who'd skied so fast that he'd somehow passed into a magical world of nothing but blue skies and sunshine and snowcapped mountains and a big dog and someone wonderful with whom to share it all.

And the man had lived there forever.

Happily ever after.

68

When Frank had first proposed that it was time for Joseph to learn how to drive, Joseph's immediate response had been "Hey, I'm only fourteen!" Frank's response—"Well, you're almost fifteen, which means you'll be fifty before you know it!"—hadn't made any sense to Joseph, but the kid had pretty much taken to it like a natural.

They'd waved goodbye to Marian, and with Frank pretending to be terrified, Joseph had managed to maneuver the truck about as far down the old logging road as it would allow. They'd trekked the rest of the way to the river on foot, carrying poles and creels and a cooler and folding lawn chairs and other assorted paraphernalia.

"Man," said Joseph, "you gotta haul a ton of stuff for this."

"Well, yeah," said Frank, "because you're leaving the weight of the world behind."

At the river's edge, they turned south, and near sparkling pools set just below some gentle rapids, they spent a couple of solid hours working hard at doing nothing.

When the sun dipped behind the mountains and the river began to flow into shadows, they built a small fire and settled in to enjoy the fruits of their so-called labor under a flawless sky.

"Y'ever see or smell or hear anything better than that?" said Frank. He leaned over to poke at the contents of the frying pan with a fork. Orange-red cutthroat sizzled among potatoes and onions, and the delicious aromas filled their already brimming senses. Frank shoveled a load onto a paper plate and passed it to Joseph before piling one high for himself, then he sighed like he meant it and slouched back into his aluminum lawn chair.

"You ever love anyone, Frank?"

The question seemed to come from nowhere, but by now Frank had learned that nothing Joseph Holliman ever asked had just popped into his head.

"What do you mean?" said Frank. "Girls at school starting to look a little different?"

"Come on," said Joseph, face turning slightly cutthroat color. "You know what I mean. You ever meet someone you couldn't live without?"

Frank conveyed a chunk of fish into his mouth, then wiped his lips on his sleeve.

"That's a question," he said, "anyone alive can't say yes to."

"Now what do you mean?"

"Well, most folks probably think they can't live without someone. But I figure that's just talk, 'cause from what I've seen, mostly, people just go on living. They're just not living the same."

They chewed in silence for a minute or two.

"I thought I couldn't live without my mom," said Joseph. Frank scooped another chunk of potato out of the pan, but said nothing.

"I think that's because we're molecules," said Joseph.

"Wow," Frank mumbled, drowning the hot potato burn with river-cooled beer. "Was that in that science textbook?"

Joseph smiled. "Not exactly," he said, "but, I mean…everything in the world's made of different combinations of the same stuff, right? So maybe I'm made of some molecules from my mom, and I miss her because those molecules want to be with the molecules they used to be with, until one day, they get used to being with new molecules. Maybe Auntie Marian has some of the same molecules my mom had, so I like being with her. Or maybe some molecules from my mom are in a fish or a deer or a tree out here somewhere. Maybe my molecules and your molecules used to know each other. Maybe they just keep on being, but as something else. That kind of makes sense, right?"

Frank looked into the fire. "You really thought this through, huh?"

"Yeah," said Joseph. "So…?"

"So what?" said Frank.

Joseph laughed. "So, are you going to answer my question?"

Frank fixed his gaze on the river for a long moment.

"Yeah," he said. "I had someone I thought I couldn't live without. For a long, long time, I…I didn't even want to…"

Joseph said nothing as Frank suddenly went dead quiet, his voice unable to escape his past. A good ten or fifteen seconds passed before the silence broke.

"Kinda funny," said Frank. "Your theory. She told me something like that once. She got it told to her by an old Indian lady who looked after her when she was a little kid. After her mom died. She said we're all rain."

"What's that mean?" said Joseph.

Frank leaned forward and tossed his paper plate into the fire. His eyes glistened as he watched it flare to yellow-orange and vanish into the embers.

"I think it means people been thinking about what you just said since way before anyone ever figured out what a molecule was."

69

On a dreary late November day, he'd spotted the cast iron Woodstock No. 5 monster in Weatherby's window and made him an offer.

Cleaned up, oiled up, new ribboned up, Frank had tucked the thirty-something pound machine—plus a stack of crisp white eight and a half by eleven paper, a musty copy of *The Wiese-Coover Kinesthetic Method of Learning Touch Typing*, and a few other assorted odds and ends—under their little tree while Joseph had been asleep.

He'd even managed to tie on the red satin bow he'd bought down at Granger's.

During a brilliantly sunny, snow-bright Christmas morning, the two of them had spent a couple of hours shredding wrapping paper, drinking coffee, eating pancakes and maple syrup and extra-crispy bacon, and tapping out black letters on white paper.

By midafternoon, they were spruced up and in Frank's truck. With a cardboard box full of beer, food, and poorly wrapped presents bouncing under a tarp in the back, they were on their way to Grasston.

"Three fingers and a thumb?" said Joseph. "You know that's not exactly what the book says to do."

"Well," Frank laughed through a cloud of white smoke, "I never had that book to tell me what to do when I learned to type, and I'm too goddamn old to unlearn what's wrong and learn what's right. You, on the other hand, are brand new to the game, so you got a chance."

Joseph smiled and watched the evergreens zoom past his window for a second or two. When he turned back toward Frank and spoke, his voice was low. "Thanks to you," he said, "I feel like I do."

Frank glanced over at Joseph and winked.

In his hands, Joseph held a paper thin, eight and a half by eleven inch gift.

"Think she'll like it?" said Joseph. "Now that it's all typed up and everything?"

"Kid," said Frank, "you coulda scratched that damn thing onto a piece of bark and it'd still be fantastic. I'm guessing a story about a couple of girls on a beach might just be one of the merriest goddamn Christmas presents Marian Luke ever got."

o o o

Over the next weeks and months, as Frank suggested, Joseph dutifully typed out pages from some of his favorite books. Accordingly, his Sunday night stories steadily acquired a more polished look to go with their increasingly polished tone, and Frank began to file each one in the typing paper's original green carton as soon as its author had finished his weekly narration. He'd just closed the lid on a tale about two typewriters—one that could talk and one that couldn't—amazed at what he'd just heard.

"You've got a voice, kid," he said. "Miss Hamer says so, too."

"Gee, you're kidding."

"No, smartass," said Frank. "As a storyteller. As a writer. You've got a voice that's your very own."

"Well, jeez, old man," said Joseph, "who else's would I have?"

Frank laughed so hard he practically coughed himself silly.

70

"Okay," said Joseph, "dishes are done enough. Time for something sweet."

At Joseph's request, Frank had made his version of schnitzel, and they'd devoured it with barely a word passing between them before jumping into their after-dinner wash and dry routine.

"Sweet?" said Frank. "You make a pie or something?"

As he sat himself opposite Frank, Joseph slid a small white envelope across the table. Frank read the return address on its torn back flap.

"New York, New York? What is it?"

"A city in the United States," deadpanned Joseph, to a smirk from Frank. "And that's an envelope. With a letter inside. Read it."

Frank extracted a piece of paper, unkinked it, and read its contents out loud.

"'Dear Mr. Holliman. Congratulations! I'm delighted to inform you that "Glove Story" has been awarded third place in the 1969 O. Henry Short Story Awards. We will be in touch soon regarding the particulars of the award itself. Again, my hearty congratulations on this significant accomplishment. Yours sincerely, Ernestine M. Rutherford, Editor in Chief.'"

Frank looked up, eyes wide, mouth open.

"It was Miss Hamer's idea," said Joseph, grin splitting his face, energy rising. "She thought the story was pretty good so she, uh, talked to my English teacher and he agreed. We sent it off, and I guess they liked it. Well, they liked it enough to give it third place, anyhow. Pretty sweet, huh?"

Frank grinned and nodded his head. "Wow, kid," he said. "I mean wow. I told you you had a voice." He looked back down at the letter as he reached over and squeezed Joseph's forearm. "I got a question, though," he said. "What's the 'B' stand for?"

"Huh?"

"The 'B.' It's addressed to Joseph B. Holliman."

"Oh, that," said Joseph. "A while back, I asked Marian how come I don't have a middle name. She said I did, but not officially, because my mom wanted it to be her maiden name, and my father wouldn't allow it. So that's my middle name now. Brant. Joseph Brant Holliman. What do you think?"

"I think," said Frank, "J. B. Holliman sounds exactly like the kinda name a famous author might have."

"Well," said Joseph, "that William Sidney Porter guy called himself O. Henry, and he did okay."

Frank laughed.

"Yeah," he said, "but you're gonna need a bigger chocolate bar."

71

"Marian says to eat it all. She says it'll put lead in my pencil."

The very day Joseph had gotten his actual driver's license, Frank had insisted he take the truck and go by himself. And almost every Saturday morning since—for a few months now—he'd made the trip to Grasston, mostly solo. This Sunday night, he'd returned with something so delicious Frank could hardly believe it.

"That's salmon?"

"Yeah," said Joseph, chewing. "Salmon candy. Marian's friend Charlene's cousin out west makes it."

"How's she doing, anyway?" said Frank. "Marian?"

"Okay, I think. You know her crazy friends are always around, and we all talk a lot. I even tried to make her schnitzel."

Frank laughed and tapped a cigarette out of its package.

"Best thing, though," said Joseph, "she tells me tons of stories. About my grandparents. And about when she and my mom were kids. Stuff like that. I like it, and I think it makes her happy."

Frank smiled and nodded, lit up, and flicked his burnt match out into the gravel. He coughed out the first puff a little.

"You really oughta cut back," said Joseph. "It was in the paper."

"Yeah, so I heard," said Frank. "Hey, listen, I, uh, I wanna talk to you about something. About school."

"What about it?"

"Well," said Frank, "about what's next, I guess. I saw Janice Hamer about a week ago, our regular coffee at the Town Dump. She says you're doing really well, and your report cards prove it. Well enough that she says you could think about the next step right now, if you wanted."

"What kind of next step?" said Joseph. "What's that mean?"

"She says it means you can graduate early. And get yourself to college," said Frank. "University."

Joseph took another bite of salmon candy and chewed it as he looked into the trees. "I… That costs money, Frank."

"Everything costs money," said Frank. "You think I worked all these years for nothing?"

Joseph smiled, dipped an eyebrow. "But that's your money," he said. "Plus I'd have to leave here, right? Leave you and Auntie Marian, and—"

"Well, yeah," said Frank. "But if you wanna go places in this world, sometimes you gotta, you know, go places."

"Not sure I want to leave."

"You sure you want to stay here?"

Joseph scanned the porch, and the gravel driveway, and the trees. He looked at his hands.

"It's what I know."

"Look," said Frank, "you don't strike me as someone who's gonna be satisfied with what he knows. You never seemed like the kind of kid who thinks the world only stretches as far as he can see. I saw a map you made once. In your notebook. Pretty sure it included London, Paris, New York. Mississippi. Couple of places that don't even exist, if memory serves."

"What," said Joseph, "Narnia?" He smiled a little sheepishly.

"Did I figure right?" said Frank. "Those were places you thought you might wanna go?"

"I was just being a kid," said Joseph.

"You're still a kid," said Frank, "but Janice Hamer thinks you're a kid that should be going places. I do, too."

They sat in silence for a few seconds.

"You ever been anywhere?" said Joseph.

Frank looked down at the cigarette between his fingers and rubbed the scar on his right hand with his left thumb. He took a deep drag, and when he exhaled, a tiny little truth slipped out.

"Yeah," he said, "I been a few places." He took another long pull, and let the smoke curl out slowly. "Sometimes I wish I never went, because I've dragged some of those goddamn places with me ever since. Looking back, though... I guess, well, all of 'em led me to people who changed my life for the better. And all of 'em led me here. If I hadn't gone to those places, I'd never have gotten to be me, right here. Right now. Y'understand?"

"Yeah," said Joseph. "No. I don't know."

They watched a couple of ravens touch down on a high limb before gliding away. Joseph's next words caught Frank off guard.

"I hear you sometimes."

Frank exhaled another cloud, and tried to look at Joseph without looking at him.

"At night sometimes," said Joseph, "when it's quiet. I hear you."

"That's just dreams talking," said Frank. "I get 'em sometimes."

"Yeah," said Joseph. "Me, too."

"I know you do," said Frank.

"But sometimes," said Joseph, "it sounds like you're not even speaking English."

Frank puffed out the last of his smoke, and without looking at Joseph, he ground the butt into the ashtray perched on the arm of his chair.

"Must be speaking Narnian," he said.

He pushed himself to his feet.

"Anyway," he said, "you think about it. Next steps. New places. It's your decision, but if you want to try, Miss Hamer says you're more than qualified. She said she'll help you write the letters and stuff, and I'll help you any way I can."

Joseph nodded and looked up.

"Okay," he said, "but you dodged my question. You never said where you've been."

Frank smiled and swallowed hard.

"One day," he said, "I'll tell you my stories. And that'll make me happy."

72

Janice Hamer could barely contain her excitement. "He's in, Frank!" she said. "He's been accepted. But more than that, they offered him a pretty good scholarship!"

She slid the letter across the table.

"University of Montana. Missoula. Not far, really. Closer than Vancouver. I've got friends down that way. My college roommate's in the English department, and she connected me with the right people. Honestly, with his grades I'm sure he would've gotten in, anyway, but his writing award just clinched it. I'm just so happy for him."

Frank scanned the typewritten words while he suppressed the cold feeling in his gut. "Wow," he said. "It's real now, huh?"

"It sure is," she said. "You think he'll actually go?"

"I can't say for sure," said Frank. "He's gotta come to that on his own, but he sure as hell gets all fired up about those guys going to the moon and whatnot. Maybe he's realized he does wanna get away from here. You know, change the future?"

The smile in her eyes dropped away as she nodded and looked down at her hands. "I wish I could change the past…"

Frank interrupted her. "Yeah," he said, "don't we all…"

"Please," she said, "let me finish."

She leaned forward, elbows on the table, and she glanced around before locking her eyes on his. "What happened that night," she said, her voice almost a whisper, "the night of the fire… Look, when I first arrived here, some of the other teachers, they…well, they made a few comments. About Principal Holliman. Of course I…I didn't know what to think, being new and all, and he was certainly strict with the children, but I never in a million years…"

She looked out the window before turning back to Frank, her eyes glistening and sad, her jaw set.

"Joseph told me," she said, "a few weeks ago. He told me a little… well, a little about his father. And that he never wants to talk about him again. So they were right, weren't they? Those teachers. They knew."

Frank tried not to let his eyes do the talking for his stomach.

"And I want you to know this," she said in a voice so low Frank could barely hear it. "The night of the fire. I was there, out front. I live a couple of blocks over, and I…well, I saw you come out of the Holliman barn, Frank."

She clasped her hands together and held them to her lips. Frank could see the pressure in her fingers and knuckles.

"And I don't know why," she said, "but not long after, the police asked me if I'd seen anyone go in or come out of there, and I…well, I lied. I told them I hadn't seen anything. I lied to the police, Frank, and I've prayed and prayed on it ever since."

Frank took a sip of coffee, his turn to look out the window. For a few seconds, he focused on a solitary raindrop on the glass, temporarily immune to gravity until it gave up its struggle and joined all of the other drops being dragged inexorably into the flow.

He turned to her.

"I…I don't know what to say."

"You don't have to say anything, Frank," she said. "As far as I'm concerned, whatever happened in that barn was God's plan."

Frank nodded, and they sat like that for a few moments, until a heavy spray of water spattered against the window and turned both of their heads. Frank drained the last of his coffee as a car rumbled past, windshield wipers in a frenzy.

"Look, Janice," he said. "I don't know how to make sense of the world like you do, because I just don't have what you have anymore. That...belief. Honestly, I wish I still did."

Frank's gaze shifted from his own hands to her eyes. He could tell she was keeping her thoughts to herself.

"I always figure..." he said. "Well, I figure we all make decisions that either help or hurt people. We get to decide how to use whatever power we have. So I'm grateful to you, for using your power to help Joseph. And me. We're both lucky to know you." He smiled. "I don't know much," he said, "but I guess maybe if I still believed in the things you believe, I'd chalk you up to being part of God's plan. I do know one thing for damn sure, though. I may end up in the hell you believe in, but I won't be seeing you there."

Janice Hamer smiled a tight-lipped smile, and she reached out and squeezed Frank's hand. He nodded, tucked the letter back into its envelope and stuffed it into his jacket pocket. Then he dropped a couple of bucks on the table, and they made their way to the door.

Outside, under the diner's dripping awning, Janice popped open a bright red umbrella. As she stepped out onto the shining sidewalk, she turned.

"Let me know what he says, Frank," she said. "That kid matters."

Frank smiled and nodded, then he watched through rain-wet eyes as she walked away.

73

The phone calls had been few and far between, but the letters had arrived regularly. Detailed and funny and written like short stories, they sometimes made Frank laugh out loud, and sometimes they made him feel empty, but mostly they made him feel proud.

The rusty piece of junk they'd picked up for him to drive down in had made it, a fact, Joseph had informed him, that Marian's boisterous and opinionated best friend, Charlene, had attributed solely to her passing what was left of her good luck to him. But, Marian had said, she'd really known it was because he and Frank had spent the entire summer tearing the engine down and figuring out how to put it back together with only a few parts left over when they were done.

Joseph had let on that he'd wished Frank had been able to go with them, but he'd said he'd understood why, and Frank had convinced himself that he believed him. He'd been massively relieved that Marian and Charlene had both made the trip to help get Joseph squared away, but he knew that his excuse—some story he'd concocted about an important meeting with Haversham—had been piss poor, at best.

The latest letter had arrived yesterday, and Frank had read it four times already.

Joseph had admitted that for the first week, he'd been nervous as hell, but that eventually he'd figured out where to go and what to do. In this letter, he said he'd actually started to feel okay about it all, especially, he said, when one of his English professors had held up a copy of a magazine article about the O. Henry awards in front of the whole class and announced that they had a celebrity writer in their midst. All those eyes looking at him with what appeared to be mostly admiration had sure been a first, he'd said. And so had not being afraid to look back.

"Says he'll be coming up home for the American Thanksgiving weekend."

Whitmore had wandered into the Dump, and much to Frank's surprise, he'd shot him a nod and made a beeline to his booth. Even more surprising, he'd asked about Joseph.

"Well, I'll be damned, Frank," said the cop. "Kid's doing all right, huh? Gotta say you're looking a little rougher around the edges than normal. You doing okay?"

"Yeah, I'm good," said Frank. "Good'n old."

The waitress called out, and Whitmore smiled as he stood. "Be seeing you around."

"Yeah…" said Frank. Whitmore interrupted him before he could get the rest out.

"I know, I know," said the cop. "Not if you see me first."

Frank shot Whitmore a nod and a wry smile as the cop grabbed two takeout coffees and headed for the door.

He lit another smoke. As he turned to watch Whitmore's car back away from the curb and head off down the street, he caught his reflection in the window.

Jesus, he thought. *That's how goddamn old you can get when you don't have anyone around you to keep you young.*

74

Energized, he'd made the run down to Grasston in what must have been record time.

Spruced up in his best work clothes, hair almost combed and smelling like soap, Frank stood at the back of the small crowd and watched as the battered old matte black and rust brown Ford finally pulled into the driveway. Its young driver jumped out and embraced his aunt first, and she fussed and fiddled with his hair, commenting on how handsome he looked in his college clothes.

"Handsome and groovy!" said Charlene, as she and Annie offered Joseph hugs and Ernie clapped him on the shoulder. When Joseph's eyes met Frank's, the kid's grin made itself spectacularly present.

At Marian's fancied-up dining table, the six of them plunged into their first American Thanksgiving like pros, the volume in the small room steadily increasing as Marian and Charlene and Annie prodded their guest of honor for details about his adventures down south.

"Getting used to it, I guess," he said. "I don't know. People look at me differently there."

"That's because no one looks like you," said Marian. "I bet the girls are just gaga!"

Joseph laughed. "I don't know about that," he said. "Girls down there like brains maybe more than they like looks."

Marian laughed right back. "Well," she said, "I've got news for you. It's the same right here, and you've got both of those things enough for two people."

"You're staying clear of those protest marches and all that stuff, right?" said Charlene.

Joseph smiled and nodded. "Yeah, basically. Well, sort of. But it's kind of everywhere. We got into a class discussion a couple of weeks ago, and a professor said something about fighting for freedom. When I asked him why American kids had to be forced against their will to fight for somebody else's freedom, the class got pretty fired up, and he got red in the face. I don't think he likes me."

"Long as you like yourself," said Charlene, "you're doing good."

They all chipped in after dinner, Joseph explaining to Frank and Marian for about the thousandth time—and to his aunt's friends for the fourth or fifth time—why it was better to wash than to dry, with Frank, as usual, arguing the exact opposite.

"I'll be coming home at Christmastime," said Joseph. "Well, you know what I mean."

"Yeah," said Frank, "I know what you mean. And don't you worry about that. You got two homes now, and this is the one you should be spending time in. Easy enough for me to meet you here."

"Yeah, I know," said Joseph, "but I…well, I kinda miss that shed, you know."

"Yeah, me, too," said Frank. "Just keep sending me those notes once in a while, huh? We're both pretty bad at phone calls."

Joseph smiled, and eyed Frank.

"You look like you need to eat a lot more salmon candy."

"Oh, yeah?" said Frank. "You just worry about you. Janice Hamer says to keep your nose in those damn books, and I agree with her."

"Don't worry," said Joseph. "And tell her I am. My favorite prof says head in the clouds, feet on the ground."

Frank smiled. "I think I might like that prof. That mean you got a plan?"

Joseph laughed. "Yeah," he said, "Sort of. My plan right now is to get a plan."

Frank clamped a hand on Joseph's shoulder, then he draped his dish towel over the oven handle. At the front door, he grabbed his jacket and they nodded their goodbyes.

In the chilled, shadowed cab of his pickup, Frank choked down a couple of white pills as the engine rumbled to life. In his rearview mirror he saw Joseph on the porch, silhouetted in the glare of a naked light bulb. The kid was still standing there like a statue when Frank made the turn off the gravel and onto the long road home.

75

Frank ripped the big brown envelope open as soon as he got into his truck. Five identical magazines slid out onto the bench seat. The note tucked into the topmost issue of *VOX*—dated February, 1971, and adorned with a strange painting of a horse galloping headlong toward an oncoming train—gave him the details.

> Hi,
> Thought you might want to see this. I didn't want to tell you ahead of time in case it didn't happen. It's a story I wrote about a fisherman who risks his life to rescue a trapped fish. It's fiction, so don't go thinking it's about anyone you might know.
> Joseph
> PS Yes, they paid me for this.

Frank flipped to page thirty-one. Then he did his best to hold the magazine steady in front of his suddenly blurry eyes.

That evening, he read the story one more time before carefully placing the stack of magazines under the little lamp on the desk beside the old typewriter.

He shuffled his chair forward, then caught himself unconsciously patting his chest for his smokes until he remembered he'd promised himself he'd leave his shirt pocket empty.

The rubbery roller sucked in the bright white piece of eight and a half by eleven with its familiar, satisfying buzz, and he placed the index finger of each hand on the round metal keys and hovered his right thumb above the space bar. Eyes closed, for a moment he almost thought he felt warmth radiating from the cold, mechanical thing, its physical memory enveloping him as the words he wanted began to form in his mind.

It's raining today, Joseph...

Twenty-two minutes and five failed attempts later, he dropped a single piece of paper into an empty green box, then he clicked off the desk lamp and waited patiently in the softly drumming silence for his eyes to adjust. Beyond the handful of rivulets on the glass, black cedars materialized, waving gently in the breeze, silhouettes barely visible against charcoal clouds.

He closed his eyes, and that helped him see more clearly: an old couch and a low table covered in books, and a big brown dog sleeping in front of a glowing fireplace. For a moment, he thought he heard the echoed strikes of typewriter keys and the gentle roll of distant thunder, and through it all, the most beautiful voice he'd ever heard, calling the name of someone he'd once been.

And he smiled as the tears fell.

76

Frank heard the faint ringing of the phone that almost never rang as soon as he opened his truck door.

Hoping whoever was on the other end might give up, he took his sweet time gathering up a couple of grocery bags before shuffling his way up onto his porch. It wasn't until he'd gotten to his door and the damned thing was still at it that the notion that it might be Joseph getting ready to hang up dawned on him. Suddenly anxious, he fumbled the paper bags onto the deck at his feet and burst in.

Not five minutes later, eggs and tin cans and beer and pork chops still on the porch, breathing a little too hard and coughing a little too much, he climbed back into his truck and got the hell out of there.

He made the sixty-three mile drive south without noticing it.

At the crowded house, he threaded his way through sad eyes and grim smiles and mumbled greetings to find Joseph in the kitchen, and they shared a fleeting moment before being submerged by all of the things that needed to be done.

Four hard days later, a substantial crowd had gathered in the small white church, to honor her, and to say goodbye. Charlene had insisted that Joseph say something, because, she'd said, Marian was just so goddamn proud of him and his words, and because that's exactly what she would have wanted.

From an otherwise empty pew near the back, Frank watched Joseph stand in front of the assembly. Alone with his thoughts, he'd been wrestling with the tiny but unmistakable feeling that he didn't belong there—that he really didn't belong anywhere—but when the kid began to speak, his words washed all of that away.

"For a brief, but huge part of my life," said Joseph, "she spoiled me. She told me stories about my own life that I never knew. She made me laugh, and cry, and think. She told me how badly she wanted to be there for me when…well, when she just couldn't be. And she told me about my mom. I loved her for all of that. I wish I could have done more for her, because she just had too much to bear, but I feel lucky. To have known her. To have been able to at least try to take care of her a little. And hopefully, to have given her a little joy. She didn't deserve any of what happened to her, but she held her head high through it all. Her life may have been hard, but it wasn't empty, because you all filled it up. She was a friend to some of you. Neighbor to others. She was an auntie to me. But she was way, way more than that. She was my connection to what's real, and to what's true, and to what I'm most proud of. I'll be forever grateful for that. And for her."

Afterward, back at the house, Frank watched Joseph shake hands with the men and hug the ladies who reached out to him, moving from person to person and making time for anyone and everyone who wanted to talk, because talking was the only thing they could do.

Only when the last of them had said goodnight and the dark driveway had all but emptied out did Joseph take time for himself, slumping in one of the old kitchen chairs out front.

"You did real good today," said Frank. "She'd be so goddamn proud. Your mom, too."

He put a hand on Joseph's shoulder, felt the strength leave it. Joseph smiled weakly and looked around, exhausted eyes moving over the tarpapered house and the rusted tools and assorted junk propped up against the garage.

"She had nothing, Frank. She lived a life of pain and suffering and frustration. Her own parents and her husband and her…her sister…" Joseph paused to collect himself. "Jesus, Frank. All of that, and sick and in a wheelchair. But she kept on going."

"She did," said Frank, "because not all of her life was sad. Like you said, she had happy times, and she had good people around her. Most important, in the last couple of years, she had you."

"That's not enough," said Joseph. "It's not even close."

Frank dragged a chair up beside Joseph and dropped into it with a heavy sigh.

"She was a good person," said Frank, "and she did her best."

"Doesn't someone like that deserve better?" said Joseph. "Don't they deserve a chance at a good life, or at least not a shitty one? This was all just bad luck, that's all. She couldn't change it."

Frank smiled and nodded, and he looked away as he suppressed a cough and swallowed its burn. They sat silent for a good long while.

"You got yourself a plan yet, kid?"

"Shit, I don't know," said Joseph. "I thought I did. Maybe I do. I remember you said someone told you that words can make someone good with the world. I thought about that a lot. I didn't know what that meant until I heard Marian's stories. I learned what other people's words did to her and to my mom, and, I guess, to me. And I learned what Marian's words did for me."

He glanced over at Frank.

"People tell me I'm starting to get pretty good with words now, and I'm starting to believe that. So I think I want to get really good with them. I wanna figure out how to use them to help people get good with the world. I want to use words to do things for people," he said, "not to them."

Frank nodded, and again he reached over and squeezed Joseph's arm. Without another word, they sat still, taking in the perfect sounds of the wind rustling the trees, and the hollow echoes of a dog barking somewhere far off. Frank took a deep breath and got to his feet. "Time for me to hit the road."

They walked to Frank's truck. Frank climbed in, yanked the door shut, and rolled down the window. "You've got a few weeks of school left," he said. "What are you thinking for the summer?"

Joseph glanced back at the ramshackle house.

"There's paperwork, I guess," he said, "but Charlene says Marian said she wanted me to have this place. I got some work with Marian's friend Billy if I want. Just odd jobs and cutting trees and that, but enough to make a little bread."

Hands on the top of the truck's driver's side door, Joseph toed at the gravel for a second or two before looking up. "So, listen," he said, "I was wondering…"

"Wondering what?" said Frank. "If you should be making dollars instead of bread?"

Joseph grinned.

"Wondering how you'd feel about another project. You know, like the old days. On weekends." Joseph stepped back. "I used to know someone who would sure as shit hate that."

Frank coaxed the engine to life and wrestled the truck into gear, then he stuck his left elbow and head out of the window, nodded, and winked.

"Groovy," he said. "I'll pick us up some new gloves."

Joseph grinned as Frank slowly pulled away.

"Hey, one more thing!" Joseph yelled. "You quit smoking?!"

In his side mirror, Frank saw Joseph laugh and roll his eyes at his predictable, growly response.

"Didn't even know I was on fire!"

77

Over the course of five and a half weekends, two brand new pairs of leather work gloves had been transformed into two well-worn pairs of leather work gloves. Broken down car and old junk gone, what passed for a lawn mowed regularly and looking almost green, they'd done what they could outside. Inside, they'd applied fresh paint, inserted a couple of new floorboards here and there, and swapped out a few light fixtures. On this particularly hot Sunday morning, they'd put the final touches on some gently used kitchen cabinet doors.

"Got a hell of a deal on these," said Frank. "Guy's got a nice pile of shiplap that might work for us, too. Never hurts to make someone an offer. Worst they can say is no, right?"

Joseph grinned. "Your natural tendencies come in handy, huh?"

"Tightwads," said Frank, "love tight budgets."

Joseph leaned back against the counter. "Speaking of budgets…" he said. "You know I'm going to pay you back. For my tuition and—"

Frank focused on screwing a metal handle securely into place as he interrupted. "I'm not paying your tuition," he said. "You are."

"Uh, I don't think so."

Frank tossed the screwdriver into a bucket and hauled himself to his feet. "You earned that money," he said. "You think Janice Hamer really asked you to figure out what percentage of the shed you built?"

"I thought I helped rebuild the shed to pay you back for almost burning the old one down."

"Come on," said Frank, "you worked enough to pay for that scrap heap about five times over."

Joseph looked at the floor. "Listen, I…I appreciate you letting me work with you. You know I wanted to do it, right? I mean I lived for that…and everything else that came with it."

Frank smiled. "Me too, kid," he said. "Me too."

With the last cabinet door secured, they called it a day, and made the trek to the river. They rigged their lines and got themselves squared away, but Frank's energy had gone elsewhere, and from the slouch in Joseph's shoulders, he figured Joseph was about as interested in catching fish as he was. *Sometimes,* Frank thought, *doing nothing feels like everything.* When Joseph's voice found its way into Frank's consciousness, it was as languid as the afternoon river.

"Heard some of this area might be underwater not too long from now."

"Say what?" said Frank. "What's that mean?"

"They're building a dam downriver. Near Libby, Montana."

A minuscule, malevolent something dug its claws into Frank's gut. "Jesus," he said, suddenly energized. "What happens to the people who live along the river?"

"Gotta go, I guess," said Joseph. "No choice, really. They say even north of the border it's gonna turn some parts of this little stream into a lake. Provincial government says people who live in those places gotta go someplace else. Same down south. People aren't happy about it, but what can they do? It's for the common good."

"Well," said Frank, "common good can be uncommonly bad for some people."

Hats pulled over their eyes, they went back to slouching in their lawn chairs for a while, with nothing but the sounds of summer between them, until a series of coughs broke the peace.

"Okay," said Joseph. "It's time."

Frank opened his eyes to see Joseph staring at him. "Time to go? It's early still. Fish are just getting themselves ready to be dinner."

"No," said Joseph. "Time for you to tell me what's going on. With you. With the cough."

Frank hunted around for some way to stall, wishing like hell he could light up a smoke to buy more time. "Oh, that?" he said. "Doc Ellis said I needed to put the smokes out for good."

Joseph looked at him sideways. "And?"

"And…" Frank breathed out hard as he felt the pressure building behind a dam of his own.

"Come on, Frank," said Joseph. "Cut the shit."

"I've had a few tests."

"Jesus Christ! And?!"

"And…I've learned a few new words…"

"Come on, Frank!" said Joseph. "Just fucking tell me."

"Okay, okay," said Frank, "I…I just didn't want to put any more weight on you than you already had, with school and Marian, and…"

"Jesus, Frank!"

Frank took a deep breath and got the words out fast, before he was able to swallow them again.

"It's got more syllables," he said, "than anything has a right to have, so they, uh, call it OGJ. It's a kind of…throat cancer. Diagnosed me four or five months ago. Been getting treatments every three weeks up at the hospital. Doc says the prognosis isn't totally bad."

Joseph launched himself from his chair and walked away, pausing near the water's edge about twenty yards upstream. Frank willed himself to his feet and made his way over the rocks and pebbles until his shadow met Joseph's.

"Look," he said, "don't worry, okay? I'm gonna be here awhile."

Head down, Frank watched Joseph's shadow turn towards his. He swore he could feel disappointed eyes boring holes into him.

"Yeah?" said Joseph. "You're goddamn right you're gonna be here. Right here. With me. I'm gonna quit school, and I'm gonna look after you until you're better. I'll tell Billy I need full time, but I'll need the odd day to drive you up to Cranbrook."

For a moment, Frank thought about looking at Joseph, but the water lapping the pebbled riverbank near their shadows seemed like a safer option. "Listen," he said. "I'm sorry for not telling you sooner. For making you ask. But the reason I didn't wanna tell you I have this damn thing is the same reason you don't want me to have it."

The shadow of Joseph's head turned away from him.

"I know you know what I mean," said Frank. "When you care about someone, you feel what they feel, too. All of the good and twice the bad." He summoned the courage to look at Joseph, but his eyes found only slumped shoulders. "Look," he said, "the future's not here yet, and I'm okay right now. It's just this stupid cough, and I'm on a sunny riverbank with you. I'm okay."

Joseph's voice came back low, and calm, and firm.

"I'm quitting school," he said. "You're coming to live with me. That's the end."

"Come on, kid," said Frank. He shook his head. "No way. You just got your fuse lit, and you're getting ready to go to the moon. There's no sense quitting all that to spend time with an old fart who's starting to burn out."

"Jesus Christ, Frank! Don't say shit like that! You think I can go back to Missoula knowing you're holed up alone in Cranbrook? Sick? That's just not happening!"

Frank took his time toeing a smooth, two inch diameter stone disc out of the sand.

"Tell you what," he said. "What if we compromise? What if I, uh, move down here for a while? Charlene's always around. And Ernie and Annie. There's plenty of things I can do at the house to keep me busy. I can make the drive up to Cranbrook when I need to, and you can get yourself back to school knowing I got people around me. What do you say? Common good?"

Joseph looked down, pushed out a few heavy breaths. "Okay," he said, "but you've gotta let people take care of you."

"I think I can give it a shot."

"Goddamn right you can, and it starts right now. I'm taking you home, I'm making dinner, and I'm washing and drying. And tomorrow I'm driving you up to your place to get what you need. You're just along for the ride, and to tell me every detail you know about this thing. And you can bet your ass I'll be checking in with everyone from now on to make sure you're doing exactly what you're told."

On the virtually silent walk back to the truck, Frank couldn't help but wonder how he hadn't noticed that Joseph had gotten about six inches taller.

78

"Rummy!"

"Damn it, Charlene. If you were any luckier you'd be the Queen of England."

"Bullshit, Frank. If she were any luckier, she'd be me."

They all roared at that one.

They'd begun to make Tuesday night gin rummy a habit, Charlene and Ernie and Annie turning their initial "Hey, we're inviting ourselves over to see Joseph's spruced up place" into a regular thing. Frank had needed instruction at first, but he'd caught on pretty quickly, and he'd found himself looking forward to the chips and dips and the beers and the good-natured competition and BS-ing that filled a few hours every week.

They counted up, then Charlene shuffled the deck.

"How's that kid doing down there among them Yanks anyway?"

"Last time I talked to him," said Frank, "he said he had something big cooking, but he'd wait to tell me in person. I'm guessing that either means he's met a girl, or he's running for president, or both. Anyway, he's coming up end of the month. How'd you all feel about coming over here for a do? I'll invite Billy and Frenchy, too. What do you say?"

His three guests nodded at each other.

"Pick a day," said Annie. "We can all bring something."

"Sounds good to me," said Charlene. "One thing, though, Frank. That boy ain't running for president. Pretty sure you gotta be an actual American for that."

"So it's gotta be the other thing, right?"

Charlene made a point of slapping the final card for Frank's next hand down with a bang, then leaned over and grinned into his face.

"That boy's so handsome and smart," she said, "he's probably met a whole bunch of girls."

Frank laughed. "I'll get a bigger table."

o o o

A roast turkey, a ham, salmon, venison schnitzel, and a dozen side dishes and desserts were within hours of making their way onto the makeshift plywood table Frank had cobbled together in Joseph's living room. Charlene and Annie had come early, hauling in a few folding chairs and laying their various plates and knives and forks on the paper tablecloths they'd Scotch-taped together.

"Make sure I get my steak knives back, Frank," said Charlene. "Took me about ten years to buy enough laundry soap to complete the damn set!"

Joseph's car rolled into the gravel driveway at around one.

From the shadows of the living room, Frank watched Joseph run around to take a pie from the hands of a striking young woman as she climbed out of the passenger side door. She was tall and slender and beautiful, like Joseph, with stunning black hair and eyes to match, and as the two of them began to walk toward the house, Frank instinctively but ineffectively ran a hand through his stubbly hair.

"Ain't gonna help," said Charlene, her grinning face suddenly looming right over Frank's shoulder. Frank laughed, once his feet re-contacted the floor.

"Thanks a lot," he said. "Goddamn good thing I took a shower last week, though, huh?"

Charlene flung the front door wide open and charged outside. "Welcome to your own house, kid!" she bellowed. She planted a big wet kiss on Joseph's cheek, then turned her attention to the young woman. "And welcome to you!" she said, crushing her in a bear hug. "I'm Charlene. Not exactly Joseph's auntie, but close as damn it is to swearing."

Over Charlene's shoulder, Joseph's eyes met Frank's, and they grinned at each other. When Charlene had released the smiling girl, Joseph stepped forward. "Everyone," he said, "this is Lizzie Perreault. We, uh, go to college together."

Before anyone else could say a word, Charlene's booming voice filled the air once again.

"Well," she said, "I'm not one to jump to conclusions, but you do more than just go to college together. You two go together!"

Frank smiled and extended his right hand, but to his surprise, Lizzie Perreault stepped right past it and hugged him.

"Mr. Gardner," she said, "I feel like I've known you forever."

"You know," said Charlene, "a lot of people say that after spending their first thirty seconds with him."

"Then you'd better call me Frank," said Frank, suddenly conscious that he was grinning like a fool.

Charlene took the pie from Joseph and walked toward the house. "You guys got an early start, huh?"

"I guess we kinda did," said Joseph, his right hand in Lizzie's left.

"Weren't excited to see this guy, were you?" said Charlene. "We see him all the time, and it's really not that great."

Joseph chuckled, Frank grinned some more, and Lizzie smiled.

In the kitchen, Charlene set the pie down, spun around, and leaned against the counter, arms crossed. "So?" she said. "Frank said you told him you had some big news."

Joseph grinned. "Well," he said, putting an arm around Lizzie's shoulders, "of course, Lizzie's the biggest news in my life, that's for sure, but yeah, I've got something else to spring on you. Tell you at dinner."

Some five and a half hours later, nine of them had successfully laid waste to a lovingly prepared mountain of deliciousness, and had ferried its ensuing wreckage to the kitchen, many hands making light work of the cleanup before returning to the boisterous hubbub of the big table.

Alone in the relative calm by the sink, Frank watched and listened as the conversation continued, Joseph sharing more stories about life at college, and gazing intensely at Lizzie as she talked about growing up in northern Montana but having relatives in Alberta, and how she'd met Joseph after he'd dropped a paper cup of coffee on her foot.

"I'm pretty sure," she said as she squeezed his hand, "he did that on purpose."

Frank smiled as he turned away from the babble and laughter to give the stove and countertop a final wipe. He'd flicked the overhead kitchen light off, and was headed back toward the noise when the realization hit him.

In the semidarkness he leaned against the kitchen door jamb.

The laughs and smiles and the aromas still hanging in the air, the overlapping voices and the soft sound of whoever it was on the record player wishing someone could read his mind: it all felt good. It felt good to be surrounded by people who looked out for each other, who lovingly ribbed each other, who were connected to each other because they just damn well wanted to be. It felt good to be in a loud, happy house that smelled like roast turkey and schnitzel and apple pie and love.

For a brief moment, his thoughts threatened to plunge him into what might have been, but Lizzie suddenly bounced into view, grabbed his hand, and pulled him toward the fray.

"Okay, Mr. Gardner," she said as she guided him back to his chair at the table. "Joseph's got an announcement to make."

Joseph stood as Frank sat, and he shot Lizzie a little smile as the room eventually settled into expectant semi-silence.

"Well," he said, "it looks like I'm going to be a published author. I wrote a book. A novel. It's coming out in the spring."

A burst of applause and cheers and shouted congratulations and a torrent of questions about the title and the plot and the characters followed, and it wasn't long before Lizzie held up the small camera she'd been snapping pics with all evening.

"Let's go, mister," she yelled at Joseph. "Over by the fireplace so you look like a bigshot author!"

Joseph grinned as he put a hand on Frank's shoulder. "Come on, Frank," he said. "You're as much a part of this as I am."

"How do you figure?"

Joseph grinned. "Because the book," he said, "is basically about a guy who thinks he's doing one thing, but he's really doing something completely different."

"On purpose?" Frank asked. "Or because he doesn't have a clue?"

Joseph laughed as he grabbed Frank's elbow and pulled him to his feet.

"Well," he said, "you're just gonna have to wait and see."

° ° °

The drugstore prints had arrived in Joseph's mailbox a few weeks later, just in time for Frank and the regular Tuesday night players to flip through them. They'd laughed and joked and rehashed the entire day, especially the part, Annie reminded them, where the whole damn horrible mess of them hadn't somehow scared Miss Lizzie Perreault away forever.

Charlene had already shuffled through the photographs once, but on her second go she paused, and held one image in particular outward to the group. Lizzie's flashbulb, Charlene declared, had captured the essence of the two people standing in front of the fireplace just about perfectly.

"One looks incredibly smart and handsome," she said, "and the other one looks like Frank."

When the round of laughs subsided, Charlene's voice got a whole lot softer, and she reached over and squeezed Frank's hand.

"That's two people," she almost whispered, "with life in their eyes, and love in their hearts."

79

"April showers bring May flowers? That's what these assholes think passes for news in this fuckin' town?"

Substantial bulk almost completely engulfing the red vinyl pad on the top of the chrome plated stool, elbows among the toast crumbs and coffee drips, the mildly perspiring man clutched a newspaper, bacon grease obscuring any text unlucky enough to find itself within reach of his fingers and thumbs. On the diner's tiny radio, a woman's voice asked some guy named Mr. Big Stuff the same question over and over and over.

Irritated, he shouted extra loud to make sure he was heard.

"Hey! One more hit here, darlin'!"

The young waitress took her sweet time covering the twenty or so feet. Expressionless, she topped up his cup, then tore a check from her pad, laid it on the pale green counter, and retreated. As the man refolded his newspaper, he let loose another mumbled oral discharge. "Goddamn peaceniks," he said to no one, and to everyone. "Nixon should just shoot 'em all."

A few seconds later, the man glanced at his check and dropped it onto the newspaper, then he lurched to his feet while simultaneously struggling to wedge a paw into a snug front pocket. Mission accomplished, he threw down a few damp dollar bills, then put both hands on the counter and leaned over to double check his math just one more time.

"Son. Of. A. Bitch."

It wasn't the short article about some college puke writer that had gotten his attention. It was the photograph that accompanied it that commanded another look.

Leaning down and squinting hard to bring the tiny caption below the image into focus, he read the words out loud. "'Author Joseph B. Holliman, a University of Montana student, poses with his friend Frank Gardner, apparently the inspiration for his newly published novel.'"

He snatched up the newspaper and held it right under his nose to be double goddamn sure the black litho dots that formed the image actually did combine to project a version of a face—and a scarred hand—he'd once known all too well.

"Frank fucking Gardner," he muttered.

"What's that, Smitty?" the young waitress called out to him from the relative safety of her spot beside the pie cabinet.

"Nothin' for you to worry about, honeycakes," he said.

Then he tucked the folded newspaper into an armpit and rumbled toward the door, his voice rising in volume as he jerked it open.

"But somebody," he said, "oughta be getting himself ready to have a bad fucking day!"

80

Whitmore slid into the booth and laid his hat down on the vinyl bench seat.

"How you doing, Frank?" he said. "Haven't been seeing much of you around here lately."

"Been staying down near the border," said Frank. He sipped his lukewarm coffee. "Got a little project down there. Coming up to the big smoke here for supplies and whatnot once in a while."

"Right, right," said Whitmore. "Listen, Frank, I, uh...stopped by your place earlier. I figured maybe you were in town. Took a chance I'd find you here."

"Lucky us," said Frank with a wry grin. "'Cause here we both are."

Whitmore smiled weakly and glanced out the window. "Look, Frank. I...I don't exactly know how to tell you this."

"How come," said Frank, "you didn't write it down?"

The cop turned back toward Frank, his downcast head shaking slowly from side to side. "No," he said. "I wish I didn't even have to think it."

"What's going on, Whitmore?"

"I gotta ask you to come with me, Frank."

A hundred thoughts and questions stampeded through Frank's head. He took a decidedly intentional sip, then carefully returned his coffee cup to its saucer. "Come with you?" he said. "You need me to help you pick out some curtains or something?"

"No, Frank," said Whitmore.

"Then what the hell are you talking about? Come with you…"

"We got a call," said Whitmore, "from, uh, from the FBI. Seems some guy down in Montana thinks you might be somebody else. Crazy, right? So I've got to ask you to come in. You know, get some paperwork squared away. Go through the motions. Set things straight."

Something scaly stretched its sharp-clawed legs in Frank's gut. "Well, yeah, that is pretty goddamned crazy," he said. "Only people I know in Montana are a couple of college students. Who the hell am I supposed to be? What motions? What kind of paperwork?"

"Look, Frank," said Whitmore, "it's a weird one, that's for sure, but it's really nothing to get worked up over. You just gotta show a few documents and that'll clear it all up. Birth certificate, passport, social insurance card. That kind of thing. Probably just a case of you looking like somebody else, right?" He grinned. "Poor bastard."

Frank smiled, but the thing in his gut had burrowed in and laid eggs, a prickly heat was rising under his collar, and his heart suddenly felt too big for his chest.

"Well, shit," he said, "that's a hell of a mistake for somebody to make. Who's saying all this stuff? And how the hell would they put something like that together?"

"Some guy saw your picture in a newspaper," said Whitmore. "In an article about that famous young college writer you been hanging around with. Guy says way back, he used to be some kind of military cop or something, and I guess somehow he got it in his head that you're a long lost fugitive. Apparently made a big stink about it."

Whitmore slapped a hand on the table.

"Tell you what," he said, "I'll follow you to your place, you grab your paperwork, and I'll drive you over to the detachment. We can get all this processed, and I'll get you home later this afternoon."

Frank had thought about it almost every day for a long, long time, but so many, many days had come and gone without it happening—and so much else had happened—that he'd almost put it out of his mind. But now, here it was, the long shadow finally falling on him on a warm and sunny mid-June morning.

"Not sure I'll be able to lay my hands on any of the documents you mentioned," he said. "I'm thinking some of that stuff might've got burned up in that shed fire, a few years back. Oh, and I, uh, I gotta get over to the hospital about eleven."

"The hospital?" said Whitmore. "Somebody sick, Frank?"

"Yeah…" Frank looked out the window. "Look, you…well, you might as well know, I guess. They've been pumping me full of chemicals for a while."

"Jesus, Frank…" Whitmore's voice trailed off to nothing, and the two men sat in silence for a time.

"How about I go get my next dose of poison," said Frank, "and I'll get myself over to your office tomorrow so you can do whatever needs to be done?"

"Okay, Frank," said Whitmore. "Sorry to make your day worse."

Frank forced a smile. "You know how it is," he said. "Sometimes the world hands you a big shit sandwich, and all you can do is take a big bite, chew it up, and choke it down."

"I'm afraid, Mr. Gardner, that until you can provide sufficient proof of your identity, we're going to have to, uh, detain you."

"Jesus," said Frank, "you're arresting me?"

"Well, no," said the man in the suit and tie, shuffling his papers, "not exactly."

Haversham spoke up.

"If Mr. Gardner is not under arrest, then what, exactly, is his status? I've known this gentleman for more than ten years, and have served as his counsel on numerous business and real estate transactions during that time. He's a solid member of this community, and since he's not been charged with any actual crime, I'd suggest that he simply be released until this matter can be cleared up. I'd also like to point out that Mr. Gardner is currently undergoing regular treatment for a quite serious form of cancer, so he's hardly a flight risk."

Whitmore had apologized more than once before he'd asked Frank a whole lot of odd questions that had been provided, he'd said, by people south of the border.

"Have you ever served in the armed forces of any country?"

"Do you recognize the places in these pictures?"

"Do you speak any other languages?"

"Have you ever been to Montana?"

When they'd finished the back and forth, the Crown attorney scratched his head, nodded at Whitmore and the other cop—some kid Frank didn't recognize—and closed his file. Then the three of them stood up and stepped out, leaving Frank and Haversham alone in the all too familiar room.

"Jesus," said Frank, "I was really hoping not to make this goddamn place a regular stop."

"Look," said Haversham, "don't be too concerned. It's really just a simple matter of us producing some form of official identification documents. Birth certificate or passport would do the trick. We'll just contact the appropriate government departments for replacements if you can't locate them."

"And what if I can't get those documents?" said Frank. "What if they've, I don't know, lost my records, and it all boils down to my word against some other old guy's word? How does that work?"

"Well," said Haversham, "I don't think that's very likely."

The attorney and the two cops reappeared a few seconds later, and Whitmore laid it out. "Okay, Frank," he said, "you're free to go home. But I mean your home. Basically, you've got to move back to your own place for the duration of this. Until we get your documents and clear this up. It's not exactly the kind of thing we've dealt with before, so we need to get it right."

"Get it right?" said Frank. "Get what right?"

The attorney interjected. "There are some serious complicating factors at play here, Mr. Gardner," he said. "Serious implications for the Dominion of Canada. It needs to be sure of the facts."

Frank snorted. "Implications for the Dominion of Canada? What about the Dominion of Frank Gardner?"

"Hey, you'll be closer to the hospital," said Whitmore.

"Well, sure," said Frank, nodding. "Exactly where I wanna be."

Whitmore put a hand on Frank's shoulder as they walked out of the room. He nodded at the new cop. "Constable Jensen here will drive you down to Grasston to collect whatever you need, and he'll help get you settled in your place when you get back here. Fair enough?"

"Nothing fair about it," said Frank with a sardonic grin, "but I know you're just doing your job."

Frank reached out a hand and Whitmore smiled as he shook it.

"You might," said Frank, "wanna write that down."

81

There was a cop car parked in front of the house.

The sight naturally set off alarm bells, so as she was prone to do, even without the kind of very goddamn good reason she had now, Charlene knocked and walked in at the same time.

"Hey, Frank!" she called out. "You join the Mounties or just steal one of their cars?!"

Even though she'd seen the official vehicle outside, she was still taken aback by the sight of a uniformed RCMP officer stepping out of Joseph's kitchen.

"Afternoon, ma'am."

"Afternoon to you, too," said Charlene. "What's going on here? Where's Frank?"

"Mr. Gardner?" said the young cop. "He's just packing up a few things. Through there."

Charlene followed the cop's nod—and the sound of a cough— down the short hallway. She stepped into the second bedroom to find Frank stuffing a checkered shirt into a canvas duffel.

"Got yourself a new friend?"

Frank's feet nearly left the floor.

"Jesus, Charlene," he said. "Didn't hear you come in."

"What the hell's going on, Frank? What's that cop doing here?"

"Oh," said Frank. "He's making sure I don't fly off to Hawaii."

"Uh, what?"

"He's here to keep an eye on me," said Frank, "and to take me back up to my place."

"What? Why? That still doesn't tell me what the hell's going on."

Frank zipped the bag. He decided to share some truth.

"Seems some guy down Joseph's way mistook me for somebody else, somebody who might be wanted or something. The FBI called the horse cops, and until they figure out what to do they wanna keep me close by. As if I'd be going someplace."

"Who the hell besides Joseph knows you down there?"

"The guy doesn't know me," said Frank. "He saw my picture in the paper. The one Lizzie took of Joseph and me after the big dinner. I guess they did a little article on him and his book and he gave 'em the picture."

"You mean to tell me," said Charlene, "there might be some poor bugger somewhere who looks like you?"

"Well, this much handsome," said Frank, "would sure be wasted on one man."

They walked out to the living room, and as they passed by the kitchen door, Frank called to the cop. At the front door, he turned to Charlene.

"Nice having a personal driver."

She furrowed her brow, gave him a serious smile, then wrapped him up in a big hug.

"We gonna be one short for next Tuesday night?"

Frank grinned. "School's out in a week," he said, "so Joseph'll be home. He can take my spot until they turn me loose. You'll let him know what's going on, right? I have a hard time getting through on the phone. Maybe ask him to call me at the house?"

"Sure thing, Frank."

Charlene squeezed Frank's hands and winked at the young cop as he grabbed Frank's bag and headed out to his car.

"Listen, Frank," said Charlene, still holding his hands, "before you go… Look, Marian and me, we always knew you were way more than you ever let on. And we figured that had to be a good thing."

Frank played that thought over and over in his mind for the entire drive back up to Cranbrook.

82

For the first time, Joseph had brought Lizzie up to Cranbrook with him, and they were touring "the scene of the original crime," as Frank had called it, to Joseph's mild chagrin. Wordlessly, she looked around the shed, ran her fingers over the desktop, and the old Woodstock typewriter, and the stack of magazines under the gooseneck lamp.

Turning to Joseph, she smiled, reached up and stroked his face, then dropped her hand to his heart.

"I feel this place, J.B."

They were on Frank's porch, the remains of Lizzie's apple pie still on the plates at their feet, her fast asleep beneath a blanket on the couch inside.

"She calls you J.B.," said Frank.

Joseph smiled. "Yeah," he said, "she does."

They sat in silence until Frank spoke up again.

"You're different with her," he said.

"Different good?" said Joseph.

Frank grinned. "Look," he said, "I'm old, and maybe I'm not that bright, but I'm not blind. She lights you up."

Joseph smiled. "You were right, you know."

"Not sure I ever heard you say that before," said Frank. "Right about what?"

"It wasn't up to me."

Frank smiled and nodded, and he stared at the weather-beaten decking. "Molecules?" he said, arching his eyebrows.

"Yeah," said Joseph, nodding. "Molecules."

They sat together in a long silence, and Frank found his thoughts drifting, pulled along by some invisible current that he'd never been able to understand. Joseph's voice jolted him back to the world, and he turned his head to look into an intense glare.

"You going to tell me, Frank?" said Joseph.

"Tell you what? About… the fire? About the goddamn cancer?"

"You know I never cared one iota about that first thing. And I already know about the second."

Frank swallowed hard. "So you mean the lawyer stuff?" he said. "The hearing coming up? Told you about that on the phone."

"No," said Joseph. "I mean about you. About Frank Gardner. It's just, well, this whole damn situation's been messing with me. Got me thinking things I guess I tried not to think about."

"Like what?" said Frank.

Joseph scratched his forehead. "Like how come I've only known Lizzie for a few months, but I already feel like I know more about her than I do about you."

Frank looked into the trees, black against the indigo sky, then dropped his gaze to his dirty boots.

"You know me."

Frank felt the stinging cut of that lie, because he knew it cut Joseph, too. Joseph smiled sadly and stood, and Frank watched the kid's big hands scoop up their plates and forks.

From the corner of his eye, Frank saw Joseph disappear into the house. When he reappeared a few moments later, he was carrying a blanket and a coffee mug.

"Here," said Joseph, "take this. Charlene says I gotta make you drink it. She says it might put some color back in what's left of your hair. Her grandmother's recipe."

Frank reached out, gripped the coffee mug handle, and nodded a thank you. He brought the steaming liquid up, close enough to inhale its tangy, earthy scent. It smelled, he thought, like dirt and pine cones. But it smelled real. And genuine. And true.

Eyes closed, he took a sip, surprised to find that, somehow, the stuff tasted nothing like its aroma. He felt its burn in his throat and his eyes watered behind their lids, but far below any of that, way down, deep inside his bones, in a place he'd thought he could ignore forever, he felt the numbing heaviness of a lifetime of deception.

Frank glanced up as he sensed a blanket settling over his knees, then gently shooed Joseph away as he attempted to tuck it tight against the night air.

A few seconds later Frank heard a match strike, and he blinked fast more than a few times, just, he told himself, to get used to the warm, diffused glow of the lantern.

Joseph sat, and Frank turned to look at him. But when Joseph's gaze met his, Frank's chest tightened, and he squeezed his liquid eyes shut again. Then Frank Gardner took a couple of deep, cool breaths, and found the strength to surrender.

"I was born a long, long way from here," he said, his voice gravelly and low. "And it's a hell of a story."

Hearing no reply, tentative, not quite afraid but something very, very close, unsure for the first time what he might see, Frank opened his eyes and looked at Joseph.

When he saw that warm smile, when he heard that deep and soft and caring voice, the massive weight he'd carried with him for so many years began to fall away. But the lump in his throat doubled in size when Joseph reached over and squeezed his shoulder.

"You ever meet anyone," said Joseph, "who loves a story more than me?"

83

The wood-paneled meeting room was undersized and overheated.

"Already feels like a prison cell in here," growled Frank.

Arrayed in an orderly fashion on its conference table top, the various files and stacks of papers and scribbled notes Haversham had produced from his briefcase seemed less than substantial, but they were all they had. Joseph and the lawyer were sipping coffee, with Frank only wishing he could.

"Now remember," said Haversham, "this isn't a trial. It's not even a preliminary hearing. It's a special session to try to establish process, I'm guessing as much for them as it is for us."

"So what's your prediction here?" said Joseph. "We've still got no official documents for Frank."

"Well, that's true," said Haversham, "but it's not really unusual for these government departments to take a significant amount of time to respond to inquiries or requests. We're already on our third round of correspondence with the passport office alone. It's only been a month or so."

Sitting in a wooden chair tipped back against the wall, Frank had taken almost five minutes to catch his breath.

"Jesus, Bill," he rasped, "they hold all these goddamn meetings up five flights of stairs?"

"I only counted two, Frank," said Haversham, "but you know I'm better with words than numbers."

Joseph had been pacing since they'd arrived. He finally came to rest with both hands on the far end of the table. "So what if we can't prove," he said, "that Frank's Frank?"

"Well," said Haversham, "we really don't have to worry about that today. And besides, that's highly unlikely. I'm sure it's just a matter of time…"

"But what if?" said Joseph. "What if there's some huge screwup and we can't get the paperwork? What then?"

"As I said, that's highly un—"

"But what if?"

"Then I suppose," said Haversham, "it wouldn't look too good. Look, you asked for my prediction for this process. I'm guessing that without some definitive proof that Frank is actually Frank, the US government will push for extradition based on this man Smithson's sworn affidavit. Now, the Canadian government may just deny that request unless it's provable that Frank is actually who this man has accused him of being. Of course, if proof of Frank's Canadian citizenship doesn't materialize, the Canadian government has hinted that it may charge Frank itself and keep him here. Charge him with what, exactly, they haven't actually said, because frankly, I don't think they really know."

"Jesus," said Frank. "Is everyone just making it up as they go?"

Haversham smiled.

"There's no precedent as far as I've been able to tell," said the lawyer. "Of course, we just need to prove you're you. Or the US needs to prove you're this other man. If neither identity is provable, then the Canadian government will be perched on the horns of a mighty sharp dilemma, I would think."

"Driver's license not good enough, huh?" said Joseph.

"Seems there are plenty of ways to acquire a driver's license," said Haversham. "The federal government recognizes the holes in the provincial systems."

"So, let's play this out," said Joseph. "No documents. Frank can't prove he's Frank. Some old guy in Missoula's saying Frank's really an escaped prisoner of war. How can the guy prove that? I know we've been over this a hundred times, but maybe we should review one more time?"

"Of course," said Haversham. "This is what we know. This man Smithson asserts that Frank's really a man named…Bernhardt Lang, born in…Chemnitz, Germany, captured in North Africa and brought to the United States as a prisoner of war in 1943."

Joseph shot Frank a quick glance as Haversham shuffled through a couple of files.

"Apparently this Lang fellow," said Haversham, "along with two others, escaped from a POW camp near Bridger Falls, Montana in late 1945. The man who made the accusation was a camp guard, and he asserts that Bernhardt Lang had a distinctive V-shaped scar on one of his hands. As does Frank."

"If scarred hands are suspicious," said Joseph, "every old logger in the world better have an alibi."

"Look," said Haversham, "I'm sure you're right, but you've got to admit that Frank at least fits the bill, age-wise and scar-wise."

"Sure, he fits the bill," said Joseph, "like a hundred other guys probably fit the bill."

"Beyond the accusation pertaining to identity," said Haversham, "the real issue for US authorities may be that a young woman went missing on or about the same day as the three prisoners. Coincidence, maybe, since she left a note saying she was heading to Florida, but she's never been accounted for. A vehicle registered to her father's company was found hidden in the trees outside the town of Libby, Montana, more than a year later, so it's possible this Lang fellow stole the vehicle. Possible, also, that he might have abducted the young woman, but the father told police he received a telephone call from her in the spring of 1946, and she apparently assured him she was okay. But that's where her trail goes cold."

Once again, Joseph's eyes met Frank's, then quickly looked away.

"Setting all that abduction stuff aside for a second," said Joseph, "some guy who was brought to the States against his will decided he wanted to stay there. So what?"

"So," said Haversham, "he's considered a criminal—unlawfully at large—possibly an unlawful resident of this country, the authorities now suspect. Of course there's the potential connection to the missing woman, but nothing about that has ever been proven."

"The guy was taken prisoner," said Joseph, "so how can he be an unlawful resident? I mean, he didn't ask to go to Montana. What were they gonna do with him when the war ended?"

"I presume he'd have been sent back to his place of origin," said Haversham. "Back to Germany."

"The other two guys, they both got recaptured, right"

"Correct," said Haversham. "Helmut Fischer was arrested in… let's see." He shuffled a few papers. "Eugene, Oregon, in November 1945. Anton Schlemmer was captured in Hamburg, New York, in January of '46."

"So what happened to them? Were they charged with anything criminal?"

"No. They were both deported."

"To where?"

Haversham glanced back at his notes. "Fischer to…Cologne. Schlemmer to Lübeck. West Germany."

"West Germany? Where was this Lang guy from?"

"Sorry?"

"Where's the town he was from? What part of Germany?"

Haversham looked back at his papers. "Chemnitz," he said. "But actually, it says here it's been renamed. Karl-Marx-Stadt. It's now part of East Germany."

"Renamed?"

"Yes."

Joseph furrowed his brow. "So the place this guy allegedly came from isn't even in the same country it was when he left? If they catch him now, what? Are they gonna send him to another foreign country?"

"Well," said Haversham, "you may have a point there, Joseph."

"And who captured him?" said Joseph. "I mean in the first place?"

"I believe it was originally British soldiers who took him prisoner," said Haversham. "Well, Commonwealth soldiers, at least."

"And they, what," said Joseph, "just gave him to the Americans? How does that work?"

"Well, yes," said Haversham. "I'd have to go back through the documents to be sure, but I believe he was, at some point, also under Canadian jurisdiction, disembarked at a port in New Jersey by a Royal Canadian Navy ship, I think. But what are you getting at?"

Joseph stepped to the window. For a few moments, he watched a young couple walk arm in arm through the park across the street.

"Man, I don't know," said Joseph. "What do you think this is really about? I mean really."

"Well," said Haversham, "it's about us proving that Frank is not this man Lang."

"I thought," said Joseph, "it was really about the US government proving he is. So someone can decide who owns him."

"Oh," said the lawyer, with a nod and a smile, "well actually, yes, technically."

"How the hell are they gonna do that?" said Joseph. "And even if they could, and Frank is this guy, what crime has he committed? Is it a crime to get captured in a war? A crime to get taken prisoner by one country, handed off to one or two more, and then be held by them against your will? Is it a crime to not want to be sent back to a country that was destroyed by the country that kept you locked up? Or to not want to be sent to a brand new country that was created by another former enemy country after you left it? What's the statute of limitations on any of this, since no one seems to know if any of it's really even a crime? I mean, does any of this make any sense to you, Mr. Haversham?"

"There's still the question of the missing woman."

"Sounds to me," said Joseph, "that connecting those dots would be a stretch after, what? Thirty years?"

Frank had been sitting silently as the conversation had unfolded. He suddenly leaned forward, put his elbows on his knees, and coughed loudly into his handkerchief. The two other men turned their attention to him.

"Wow," said Frank. "You been watching a lot of *Perry Mason* at that fancy college? He's buckin' for your job, Bill."

Frank forced himself to his feet and shuffled to the window. He put an arm around Joseph's shoulder.

"Look, kid," he said, "it's gonna be okay. None of this makes sense if you think too hard about it. We all wanna be free, and most of us believe we already are, but none of us really is. Somebody makes rules. And we're all supposed to live by 'em."

He squeezed Joseph's arm.

"For the common good, remember?"

"Nobody I know," said Joseph, "actually agreed to the rules they're supposed to live by. They just got born in some country that owns them. I mean, American kids who're lucky enough to go to college don't have to go kill and die in Vietnam? The hell is that? We need a better system. Better rules."

Frank smiled and nodded. "Yeah," he said, "I figured you'd say something like that."

Haversham glanced at his watch and began to gather up his documents as he interjected. "Well, gentlemen," he said, "that's a long philosophical discussion for another time. Right now, we're going to keep Frank Gardner as free as we can."

The hearing had taken a little less than an hour.

In an austere courtroom, empty but for the presence of those to whom the proceedings had directly pertained, Frank and Joseph had sat silently as Haversham had, in his words, "successfully sowed Joseph's well-considered seeds of confusion." Now, the three of them stood on the 11th Avenue sidewalk, the sun hot on their faces.

"So, what now?" said Joseph.

"Well," said Haversham, "you heard the magistrate. He basically implied that both governments were wasting his time and that they should come back when they have some serious evidence and case law to present. At any rate, proceedings have been put off until they do, or until a passport or birth certificate shows up. Both of those things could take a while, so for now, Frank, you're still Frank. Still free."

"I appreciate that thought, Bill," said Frank, "I really do, but I got something else that owns me now. Doc Ellis says they can try a few more things, but..."

"But what?" said Joseph.

"But it's gonna take me," said Frank. "Just a question of when."

"Well, you're gonna keep fighting, right?" said Joseph. "You just gotta do what the doctors say."

"Do I?"

"Well, yeah."

"Nah," said Frank, "I get to decide this one."

Frank smiled as he reached out to Haversham.

"Always meant to ask you," he said as Haversham shook his hand. "How did your parents know you were gonna grow up to become an overpriced lawyer when they named you Bill?"

The lawyer smiled. "Never heard that one before, Frank."

Frank smiled, his voice hoarse as he turned to Joseph.

"It's a beautiful day," he said. "What do you say we get the hell out of here and get back to pretending we're free?"

84

They'd brought him in, against his will.

"Just needed to catch my goddamn breath!"

"Oh, come on, Frank," said Joseph. "You scared the shit out of the cashier at Granger's. And Jesus, you know the nurses are just doing their jobs. They're not going to let me just take you home after that, so don't make any more trouble. They're going to check you out for a day and you'll be good to go."

"Unnecessary," Frank rasped. "And you know it."

"Look," said Joseph, "I never should've taken you to the grocery store in the first place."

Frank coughed and grinned.

"Yeah? Well, I asked you to, remember? I'm not in prison. Yet. And I'm sure as hell not dead. Yet."

"Well," said Joseph, "there's people trying to keep both things that way. Especially the second one. You just don't seem to be one of them."

Joseph put a big hand on Frank's shoulder.

"Look, the doctor says you're here 'til tomorrow morning. Lizzie and I have to run down to Grasston. Charlene's helping us get things set up for you. She said to tell you she always wanted to look after a giant old kid."

Frank grinned.

"We'll probably be back late," said Joseph, "so Mr. Haversham said he'd stop by later this afternoon to check on you."

Frank shot Joseph a wink. "Someone's gotta make sure the giant old kid doesn't make a run for it."

The nightmare was always the same.

Though he could never remember if it was the sounds of the torrential rain and the roaring river or the choking, metallic taste of the gun barrel that jolted him back into the light, this time, aching and weak and soaked in sweat, he'd surfaced to an unfamiliar face.

Slender and tall, red-gray hair cropped tight, a light stubble beard on his angular, freckled face, the man stood as Frank tried to focus.

"They said it'd be okay," said the man, "if I waited."

Frank worked to blink the sleep from his eyes and the fog of the past from his brain. He swallowed hard a few times and tried to clear his throat. "Do I know you?"

The man shook his head.

"Not really," he said quietly. He glanced at the folded newspaper clutched in his hands as he reclaimed his seat. "But, yeah."

Thirty-five minutes later, the man stood again. Tentatively, he reached out a hand, and Frank shook it.

"I'll never forgive myself," said the man, his voice barely above a whisper, "for what I did that day. And I couldn't never understand what you did, neither. Or more like what you didn't do. It's been a lot of years," he said, glassy green eyes riveted on Frank's, "a lot of long, long nights. And not one single day's gone by I didn't think about her. Or you."

The man nodded and walked to the door.

He paused to look back.

"Rest easy now, Mr. Gardner," he said. "And I thank you, but I want you to know that I never will."

Less than ten minutes later, a man walked into the Cranbrook RCMP detachment and asked to see the officer in charge of the Frank Gardner case. They ushered him into a small room, gave him a cup of bad coffee, and asked him to wait.

When the two Mounties walked in and introduced themselves, one of them pulled out a notebook and pen.

"I'm Staff Sergeant Whitmore," he said as he took a seat. "And this is Corporal Jensen. What can we do for you, sir?"

"My name's Ed Callahan," the man replied. "I'm a former member of the Libby, Montana, police department. I have some information that might be of interest to you."

85

"Hey, old man," he whispered down the hallway. "What'd you do? Sleep in?"

The muffled thumps and bumps became slow footsteps, and a few seconds later, Frank appeared in the kitchen, standard red and black lumberjack shirt underneath the wide suspenders that held up his perpetually dirty work pants.

They ate soft scrambled eggs, Frank struggling through. "I miss a lot of things," he whispered, "but coffee and cigarettes with breakfast gotta be at the top of the list."

Joseph washed. Frank insisted on drying.

"Got a call from Bill Haversham yesterday," said Joseph. "He says that Callahan guy's sworn affidavit pours a whole lot of cold water on the other guy's sworn affidavit. Plus he found out the other guy's got some serious credibility problems."

"Mmmm?" said Frank.

"Damn right," said Joseph. "Decorated former police officer's word against the word of a dishonorably discharged, convicted criminal. Bill's filed motions to get everything dropped just based on that. He thinks the Americans are gonna give up. He says they don't have any way to prove you're…well, seems they still don't really know what the charges would be anyway. But Canada's still fishing, now you're on their radar screen. I, ah…I don't see how we beat that, you know? Knowing what we…well, knowing what's real."

Frank smiled and tossed the final fork into a drawer.

"Real?" he croaked. "Older I get, the less I know what that word even means."

Joseph swirled the last of the soapy water from the sink and took the damp towel from Frank's hands. At the kitchen door, he switched off the light and watched Frank shuffle toward the living room before he took a quick detour in the opposite direction. Moments later, he was beside Frank, helping him get his jacket on.

"She says it's the weekend, we're crazy, and she's staying in bed all day."

"She's smart," Frank rasped. "We're not. Let's go."

They stepped through the front door and into the hushed, half-light world, the soft crunch of their boots on the gravel sharp and satisfying, the late September air smelling like air should—like pine trees and coolness and the dew covering almost every surface—the sky just beginning to bleed orange into indigo, hinting at the perfection to come. Joseph helped Frank into the truck before climbing in behind the wheel. He savored the reassuring thunk of its heavy doors, the low rumble of its engine, and its familiar squeaks and grinds, jarringly loud in the stillness as it rolled toward the road.

Poles and assorted gear in one hand, Joseph took Frank's elbow in the other. They walked slowly, at Frank's pace, Joseph making double damn sure of every step.

Near the water's edge, the two aluminum folding chairs sat right where they'd left them, ready and waiting. Joseph helped Frank lower himself into the familiar comfort, then draped a blanket over his lap.

By the time they'd rigged their lines, the rising sun had begun to warm their backs a little, and its glow had set the maples and alders around them aflame against the deep evergreens and brightening sky.

They didn't talk.

They just sat there.

Together.

Like they'd known each other forever.

When Frank's line went taut, arcing the tip of his fishing rod toward the cool, flowing water, the hoarsely whispered command was almost immediate.

"Pitter-patter," he growled. "Let's get at 'er!"

Grinning, Joseph got Frank to his feet and stood back as Frank slowly reeled the sleek three-pounder in. Frank managed to bend one knee to the sand and pebbles, then, as he'd done so many times before, he mumbled almost continuously as he cradled the suddenly placid creature and carefully extracted the hook.

"Who am I," he finally whispered, "to own you?"

As Frank lowered the cutthroat into the gently lapping water, the flickering sunlight glinted off its glistening, black-dappled, golden-red, and absolutely perfect form for the briefest of moments until, with a single powerful flick, it simply vanished into the river.

Silent grins saying everything that needed to be said, they settled themselves back into their chairs, and Joseph closed his eyes, just for a moment, to breathe, and to see everything more clearly.

Not thirty seconds later, he opened them, and he turned to his left to say something unimportant.

But Frank Gardner had drifted away.

86

Five weeks to the day after a surprisingly large crowd had laid Frank Gardner to rest in the shadow of a stand of sheltering hemlocks, Joseph and Lizzie had made the trip up from Missoula. They'd stopped in at the white church for a few moments, just to say hi, and they'd enjoyed a few cups of coffee and a lot of hugs with Charlene and Annie. And then they'd made the sixty-three mile drive north.

In Haversham's office, they made a little small talk, and of course they tried to talk about Frank, about the conspicuous absence of his larger-than-life presence, but it had immediately occurred to Joseph that both he and the lawyer had felt that just too damn much, and so the conversation had smoothly transitioned to the business at hand.

"He was a crusty guy," said Haversham, "but in Frank Gardner's case, crust rhymed with trust."

Joseph was simply unable to suppress his grin at the invisible irony of that statement.

"He worked hard," said Haversham, "and he always did what he said he'd do. People respected that. This is the cumulative result."

Joseph smiled. "Yeah," he said, "and a result of him wearing the same clothes every day for as long as I've known him."

The lawyer laughed. "No doubt a contributing factor. Anyway, other than a bequest made to the Perryman Home, he wanted you to have it. He said you'd know better than him how to put it to good use. Now, if you don't mind me asking, what's next for you two?"

"Get finished up at school in May," said Joseph, "then I don't know exactly." He squeezed Lizzie's hand. "Well," he said, "I take that back. One of us has got a solid plan. But I've…well, I've got some thoughts. I just need to think a little more."

"Take your time," said Haversham. "You've got your whole life ahead of you."

Joseph nodded, and smiled, and the words just popped out.

"Write your own story."

"Beg your pardon?" said Haversham.

"Write your own story. Just something Frank said to me a long time ago."

Joseph stood and reached out a hand to the lawyer. "Thanks, Mr. Haversham. For everything."

"It's Bill," said Haversham. "And if you ever want to talk, if you ever need anything, anything at all, you call me."

Five minutes later, Joseph dropped Lizzie off at the library, with a promise to be back soon. When he walked into the Town Dump ten minutes after that, the familiar man in the back booth gave him a nod, and he stood as Joseph approached.

"Thanks for coming," said Whitmore. He extended a hand. "I hear, uh, congratulations are in order?"

Joseph shook it, and slid into the booth.

"Thanks," he said. "Almost a college graduate, if that's what you mean."

"Well, yeah, that, too," said Whitmore. "But that book of yours. Might not mean much, coming from a dumb cop, but, man…"

Joseph smiled, and a waitress appeared. They sat in silence as she poured some coffee out for Joseph and topped up Whitmore's cup.

"Sorry I couldn't stick around after the service," said Whitmore. "Never knew Frank had so many friends."

Joseph smiled, and nodded as he sipped.

"I guess you know Frank and me…" said Whitmore. "Well, we, uh, we didn't always see eye to eye."

"That's an understatement."

"Yeah," said Whitmore with a grin. "Frank could be a little… bullheaded at times. Suppose I can be too. I guess I don't have to tell you that."

Joseph arched his eyebrows and shook his head. He focused his attention on his cup, the booth momentarily silent again.

"Listen," said Whitmore, "there's, uh…well, there's something I need to tell you." He cleared his throat. "I was dead wrong about you."

Joseph looked up and met Whitmore's eyes. He nodded once, and Whitmore nodded back. "Well, anyway," said Whitmore, "I'll be transferring out of here in a few weeks. Back to the east coast."

Abruptly, the cop flipped open the flap on the small leather case propped beside him on the bench seat. He reached in, withdrew an unmarked nine by twelve manila envelope, and slid it across the table. When he spoke his voice was low.

"I'm pretty sure Frank would've wanted you to have this."

Joseph opened the envelope flap and reached inside. His fingertips immediately recognized the time-worn, leather-wrapped handle, the sparse glass beads.

"I don't understand."

Whitmore was focused on something outside the window.

"Let's just say I, uh, found it," he said. "One night, a while back.

Maybe Frank lost it." He looked back to Joseph. "Or maybe he loaned it to someone."

As he stood to leave, the cop tossed a couple of dollar bills onto the table and grabbed his case and car keys. Then he settled his cap on his head, and turned to Joseph.

"You know what I don't understand?" he said. "I actually miss the bastard. Maybe I should write that down."

87

He bends to kiss her cheek and snug the quilt around her a little tighter, then, doing his very best to keep his movements tender and quiet, he watches, almost spellbound, as the closing door narrows the angular ray of hallway light that caresses her.

In the kitchen, he pulls on his boots and jacket before tiptoeing toward his new treasure.

Drawn to the soft sounds of rustling he knows will no doubt turn into something much more audible within minutes, in the night light glow he wraps and rewraps the blankets. Then he heads for the back patio door, softly shushing as he goes.

Outside, the day is breaking, but ever so gently.

Shiny slate flagstones lead him across the shadowed lawn and onto sand and pebbles, toward the million dawning grays of the trees and the river and the mountains and the clouds scudding low across the sky.

At the water's edge, eyes closed tightly, he pauses for a moment, just to breathe in the monochrome silence.

When the child suddenly wriggles energetically in the crook of his arm, he opens his eyes and, for about the hundred millionth time, he's awestruck and intimidated and inspired by the beauty of the life force pulsing so vibrantly against him.

He reaches down and adjusts the blanket.

Bill Haversham's handwritten note and thoughtful gift had arrived at Joseph's one room law office a week or so ago, congratulating him and Lizzie on the birth of their baby girl, and as always, encouraging Joseph to press on with his efforts "to seek fairness for those who so clearly and desperately deserve it."

In his PS, Bill had asked Joseph to swing by his office next time he was up that way, to "talk a little shop talk" and to relieve him, he'd said, "of one last, happy obligation." So yesterday, Joseph had hit the road early and made the long drive from Kalispell up to Cranbrook, naturally making a stop along the way.

"The guy's still telling me what to do," Haversham had said with a smile, "but I'm more than happy to be doing this for him. And yes, he was absolutely specific about its timing."

Per Haversham's detailed instructions, Joseph had walked the number-tagged key down the street and into the diminutive but fortress-like Bank of Montreal. From a shiny little safe deposit box in its fluorescent lit basement, he'd retrieved a single, crudely wrapped package. Back outside a few minutes later, sitting in his truck, for some reason—or maybe for many reasons—he'd elected not to tear off its inside-out grocery bag wrapping right there and then. Instead, he'd simply headed south. He'd glanced at the almost indecipherable blue ink scrawled on the brown kraft paper countless times as he'd made the three hour drive back home.

After supper, after things had finally quieted down, he'd sat with Lizzie under their warm kitchen table light, and she'd smiled at him and squeezed his hand, and he'd steeled himself enough to dare.

Although weirdly smaller now, there'd been no mistaking the shape and weight and feel of it. One look at its muted colors, one tiny whiff of its soft, dusty scent, and the years had fallen away, and Joseph had been twelve again, flooded in memories—good, and bad, and everything in between. For a moment or two he'd been swept away, carried along by his thoughts, as he'd imagined he might once have been carried along by the swirling currents of mighty Mississippi.

The words on the folded piece of eight and a half by eleven tucked inside the old yellowed paperback had almost drowned him, but as it had so many times before, Lizzie's warm and strong embrace had pulled him to safety.

The breeze along the riverbank rises slightly, so he turns to shelter the baby in the lee of his body. Then he pulls the folded white paper from his pocket, flips it open, and reads the typewritten words aloud, so she can hear.

"'It's raining today, Joseph, and that always gets me thinking. Someone I once knew told me that while we're alive, all we are is rain. I'm so fortunate, so incredibly goddamn lucky, to have spent even a tiny drop of my time between the clouds and the river with her. And with you.'"

The child begins to giggle and gurgle and squirm, and he smiles as he looks down at her, his tears mingling with the droplets of mist beginning to caress her precious and beautiful face.

Soft, and cool, and life-affirming.

Afterword

During the Second World War, more than 450,000 German and Italian prisoners of war (POWs) were held in some 700 camps scattered throughout the United States and Canada.

By the end of hostilities in 1945, POW employment across the US was estimated at more than 90%, and because of the availability of such inexpensive labor, tens of thousands of repatriations were delayed, many for a year or longer. The US also handed over German prisoners to France, which, despite being a signatory to the Geneva Conventions, used them as forced laborers.

And although the Soviets had never signed the conventions, the American government also transferred several hundred thousand German prisoners to them in May of 1945, as a "gesture of friendship." Some 6,000 of those men were subsequently imprisoned in the former Sachsenhausen concentration camp, which had become an NKVD (future KGB) "special camp."

After European newspapers reported that German POWs were being mistreated, Judge Robert H. Jackson, the chief US prosecutor in the Nuremberg trials, informed President Harry S. Truman that the allies themselves were, in fact, doing some of the very things for which Germans were being prosecuted.

More than 2,200 German POWs escaped from continental US-based camps during the war.

Seven were never accounted for.

Acknowledgments

This novel—as everything in my life—was a team effort, and my thanks go out to everyone who supported and contributed to it.

I'm enormously grateful for the time, patience, thoughts, encouragement, and love of my family: Candace, Quinn, Griffin, and Kendall. Huge thanks to my original English teacher—my mother Enid—and to my crazy-cool siblings, Paul, Ruth, and Andy.

To my writing partner, Dakota: oh, how I miss you, girl.

I most certainly owe debts of gratitude to commanding but kind editor Michelle Meade; to incredibly talented and relentlessly perfectionist graphic designer Pamela Kim Lee; to proofreadder Beth Attwood (that one's for you!); and to advisors Kimberly Hunt and Sara Stratton.

Finally, I want to send a few special shoutouts: to Neal McDonough, whose kind words helped fan the flames now burning so intensely; and to Ted Siebert and John Van Dyke, kindred spirits.

Peace out.

Made in the USA
Monee, IL
02 January 2025

75784150R00225